Photography: © John Mason

All of a Winter's Night

Also by Phil Rickman

THE MERRILY WATKINS SERIES

The Wine of Angels
Midwinter of the Spirit
A Crown of Lights
The Cure of Souls
The Lamp of the Wicked
The Prayer of the Night Shepherd
The Smile of a Ghost
The Remains of an Altar
The Fabric of Sin
To Dream of the Dead
The Secrets of Pain
The Magus of Hay
Friends of the Dusk

THE JOHN DEE PAPERS

The Bones of Avalon
The Heresy of Dr Dee

OTHER TITLES

Candlenight
Curfew
The Man in the Moss
December
The Chalice
Night After Night
The Cold Calling
Mean Spirit

OTHER TITLES

The House of Susan Lulham

Phil Rickman

All of a Winter's Night

CORVUS

Published in hardback in Great Britain in 2017 by Corvus,
an imprint of Atlantic Books Ltd.

Copyright © Phil Rickman, 2017

10 9 8 7 6 5 4 3 2

A CIP catalogue record for this book is available from the British Library.

Hardback ISBN: 978 1 78239 697 0
E-book ISBN: 978 1 78239 699 4

Printed and bound in Great Britain by Clays Ltd, St Ives plc

Corvus
An imprint of Atlantic Books Ltd
Ormond House
26–27 Boswell Street
London
WC1N 3JZ

www.corvus-books.co.uk

All of a Winter's Night

Part One

When I speak of darkness, I mean
the absence of knowledge

Anon, C14th

The Cloud of Unknowing

Ed. William Johnston (Doubleday, 1973)

1

The dead of Ledwardine

THERE WERE QUESTIONS you learned never to ask Jane. One of them was, *Won't it wait till morning?*

Awakened by the scrape of the bedroom door, Merrily sat up in bed, dizzied by the cold. The bedroom window was opaque. There had been several weeks of fog, November slipping out undercover, miserable, warmish and clammy.

'Mum…?'

A fan of weak light making an energy-efficient halo around the kid's head.

Kid. When you woke up and Jane was in the doorway, she was always a little girl again, the blue woolly dog called Ron under an arm and something in the darkness shaking her six-year-old sanity.

Mummy, you won't die, will you?

Well… not till I'm very old.

From all those years ago, Merrily remembered superstitiously touching the bed's wooden frame as little Jane came back for the specifics.

How old will *you be when you die?*

Next day, she'd said happily to Sean, *Mummy's going to die when she's a hundred and six.* And Sean had laughed. Sean who would die a few years later in the wreckage of his car on the motorway, aged thirty-three – same age as Jesus, although that was where the comparisons ended.

'OK, look…' Jane wavered in the doorway. 'I know you're out early in the morning and everything but if I don't tell you and then it turns out something bad's happened…'

Aged nineteen now. A woman. Dear God, how did that happen? Merrily pulled the duvet around her shoulders. There were still times when Jane wouldn't get a proper night's sleep if she didn't take a piece out of yours.

'It's the churchyard. Somebody's in there?'

'And…?'

Not exactly unusual to find people in the churchyard at night, even in winter. And on a Friday night – men walking home from the pub caught short. Just occasionally, some recently bereaved person who couldn't sleep, too British to weep publicly in daylight or be seen talking to the dead, in which case…

She scrabbled for the bedside lamp.

'Mum, *no*, don't put another light on, they might—'

'They?'

'I heard it, but I couldn't see much from my window, so I went down to the East Wing?'

Their name for the furthest bedroom, the only one that over-looked a corner of the churchyard. Unused for years; one of them would venture up there every couple of months to bring down the cobwebs.

'There seems to be a lamp. On the ground or a grave. Not moving anyway, except the light goes in and out, like someone's walking across it, but that might've been the fog. Managed to get the window open, and there was this kind of slapping. Like boots in mud. Suggesting a few of them.'

'What? Grave robbers?'

'I was thinking more like a bunch of kids holding a seance or something?'

Merrily sighed. It was not unknown. Also vandalism, grave-stones pushed over in a show of drunken strength.

'What's the time?'

'Not sure. Gone midnight. Like I say it could be nothing. Just thought you should know.'

Merrily was feeling for the old grey fleece she'd been wearing instead of a dressing gown, her eyes refocusing. She'd thought Jane was in her bathrobe, but now she saw it was the parka.

'Have you been *out*?'

'Not yet.'

'Well... don't.'

Merrily swinging her feet to her slippers on the rag rug, padding over to the wardrobe, reaching inside for her jeans as Jane came hesitantly to the point.

'I think it's near Aidan Lloyd's grave?'

'Oh.' Today's funeral – or maybe yesterday's by now. 'How near?'

'Very near.'

And she'd know. For Jane, it was a grave too far. Aidan Lloyd, killed in a road accident, was their nearest neighbour now, not far over the wall separating the apple trees in the vicarage garden from the apple trees in the churchyard. When they'd first moved here, there'd been more trees and bushes, even an area of mown grass, then new stones had come shouldering in. The dead of Ledwardine were crowding them. Jane didn't like that.

Merrily followed her down the passage, zipping up the night fleece, stuffing her vape stick into a torn pocket.

They left the passage light on and the door open to see their way into the East Wing with its bare boards and an old bed frame upended against a wall. Merrily pushed the window hard and it flew open with a bang into the cold, curdled night.

'Sorry,' Jane said. 'Should've told you I'd only wedged it. Can you...?'

'I'm not sure.'

Merrily put her head out of the window and the night wrapped itself coarsely, like a soaking lace curtain, around her face. Below her, the trees in the vicarage garden were wrestling in the fog with the churchyard trees over the wall.

And then, through the tangle, she did see it: a gaseous wisp swiftly smothered and then returning, as if from a distant lighthouse.

'OK,' she said. 'Yes.'

And yes, it probably was on or near the newest grave, just a patch of raised turfs awaiting a stone. She withdrew from the night, shut the window.

'What are you going to do?' Jane said.

'Guess I'd better check it out. If I'm not back—'

'Oh come on! Like I'm letting you go on your own?'

Jane against the feeble light, hands on hips, defiant.

Merrily shrugged.

'Yeah, all right, but we go quietly until we know what it is.'

'And then maybe even quieter.'

Too dark to see Jane's grin, but she heard it.

For days now, even weeks, Jane had been moody, not her normal self. Perhaps a gap year between school and further education wasn't always a good idea. Without some absorbing work-experience, it could be very flat.

Jane had never liked flat.

Down in the hall, Merrily stepped into her boots, unhooked her waxed jacket and pulled down a scarf.

She was thinking that going out there might not actually be wise. At one time you were expected to police your churchyard, but times had changed quite quickly; not so long since a vicar had been stabbed to death outside his own church. OK, not around here, but a warning had been sounded.

And fog complicated everything. Fog itself was aggressive.

Merrily unbolted the front door but didn't turn the key. Taking in nicotine, the e-cig glowing green, she exchanged glances with Jesus, still compassionately dangling his lantern in the framed print of Holman-Hunt's *Light of the World*, then turned to Jane.

'Don't suppose if we were to put a ladder up against the wall at the bottom of the garden...?'

'Too many trees.' Jane was locating the zipper on her parka. She looked up. 'Not that there will be soon if the graveyard goes on expanding. Couple of years' time we'll be burying people in our flower beds. Turning the shed into a mausoleum.'

'Unlikely. The diocese wouldn't devalue this place. When they get rid of me, they'll switch the vicarage to a little semi and flog this off to a nice big family from London. Anyway, you'll be at university soon.'

And might never come back here to live. Who knew? Merrily opened the front door, felt the air. Not at cold as the East Wing, but cold enough.

'I really didn't think that corner was part of the graveyard,' Jane said. 'How long have they had it?'

'Since before my time.'

'So it was just waiting there, getting mowed and weeded by Gomer, just waiting for somebody to die.'

'They're an odd family, flower. Wasn't what you could call a good funeral.'

Aidan Lloyd's service had been short and muted, not well attended for a farming family. The central aisle had separated the father from the mother and her husband. No conspicuous grief on either side, only a sense of impenetrable negativity which somehow seemed to go deeper than death.

'Got your phone?'

'So we can call 101 if necessary?' Jane patting a pocket of her parka. 'Then the cops take five minutes to answer and another five to put us through to Hereford? Where someone suggests we call back in the morning.'

'And it's switched on?'

'Yes!'

Jane jerking up her zip.

Merrily pulled on her gloves.

'Right, then.'

2

Cold air

IT WAS LONG after midnight when they agreed it was finished – the last track on *Toxica*, the Belladonna album that Lol was producing for Prof Levin's Thin River label. A complicated final mix, and they cracked it. But the whoopees were premature because Prof then got around to telling Lol the good news and bad news.

Although mostly bad, he said, and even the good wasn't all that good.

The sliding doors to the studio were shut, sealing them both in with a smell of coffee strong enough to burn your brain. Sunken bulbs in the false ceiling lit the beacon of Prof's domed skull. He set down a chipped earthenware mug in front of Lol, began to empty coffee into it. Lol held up his hands: *no more.*

Prof looked at him over his grandad glasses and kept on pouring, coffee splashes scalding Lol's fingers. He sat down, hands squeezed around his hot mug. Prof was a recovering alcoholic, caffeine his methadone.

'So I talked to the agency. It might go out for another month. But not, as I'd been led to think, abroad. Too British, Laurence. Too bleedin' British. Of course, they might decide to play it over something shot in rural Connecticut or somewhere, but...'

'Doubtful?'

'Doubtful.'

It always had sounded unlikely. One of those long, narrative commercials, promoting later-life mortgages. A micro-movie, and its soundtrack was Lol's song 'Camera Lies', with all its bucolic whimsy.

> *Remember this one, the day is dwindling*
> *Down in Powell's wood, collecting kindling.*

With peak-hour screening, Prof had said airily, the music on the ad would probably be making Lol a thousand a day for a while, paying off his mortgage before next summer. But that had been some weeks ago, before transmission. Perhaps, in the meantime, someone had played the song all the way to

> *Camera lies*
> *She might vaporize*
> *In cold air.*

Lol shut his eyes on the myriad LED lights sprinkled around the room like a meteor shower. Not like he hadn't always been dubious about this bittersweet ditty persuading mature couples to take out new mortgages.

'So what you're saying, Prof, is that the expected big earner has, um, vaporized in the commercial cold air of the—'

'It'll still make *some* money, Laurence. Still well worth having. Just no longer life-changing.'

'And the good news?'

Prof beamed.

'The good news, from what you tell me, is that you don't *want* your life to change. The dream cottage in the dream village with the dream woman, and I believe even the daughter isn't the nightmare she once was.'

'That's it?'

'Now you no longer have to agonize about swimming pools.'

Prof drank some scalding coffee, clearly glad he'd got that over.

'Thank you,' Lol said bleakly.

* * *

Thin River's farmhouse home in the Frome Valley was most of an hour's drive from Ledwardine, longer at night, and in darkness and fog… forget it. Thinking he could get back before dawn, Lol had edged down through the powdery air to what had seemed like the side of the lane, before realizing he was standing in the middle of it.

He walked back up the track. At least, in the fog, it was impossible to see the outline of the converted hop kiln where Merrily had gone to perform what had turned out to be an unhappy exorcism. According to Prof, the local people had wanted to demolish the kiln, like the council had with Fred West's house in Cromwell Street, Gloucester. But it was a listed building. A holiday let now.

Apart from the kiln, the Frome Valley was all good memories for Lol, especially Prof's granary, where he'd be spending the remaining hours of darkness, in the bed where he'd slept with Merrily on a hot and thundery summer's night. The first time, neither of them expecting it to happen. An intoxicating scent of cut hay in fields now suffocated by fog. Only days before, he'd written 'The Cure of Souls', a sour song about a man's perceived inability to win the love of a woman priest, his rival the ineffable Big Guy.

Tomorrow he'd have to tell her about the Camera Lies disaster, only weeks after proudly screening it in her bed on his laptop, those misty images of a not-quite-young couple strolling through an autumn wood and a village square with a church.

> *Here's a moment on the chancel stair*
> *The candles warm your face and light your hair*
> *Is this the edge of sacrilege?*
> *Do I care?*

He might've let the tears come if the fog hadn't parted to reveal Prof waiting for him outside the studio door. He was wearing his ancient navy-surplus duffel coat, the outside bulk-head lamp making his domed head glow like an old gas mantle.

'I've lit the paraffin stove for you, in the granary. The sheets felt a little damp to the touch so give them half an hour."

They walked across the yard towards the squat tower with the bleary light in a high window.

'This is still a *base*, Laurence. It's selling albums, selling downloads. Not the way it might've done fifteen, twenty years ago, but it's still a new foundation. To build on. And... I don't have another album for you to produce right now, but I can get you support gigs, in the spring.'

'Not the Mumfords.'

'*Not* the Mumfords. And don't knock support. So the sell-out audience doesn't know you, it matters not. You give them 'Camera Lies', and it all comes back to them. All those images, the expensive post-production...'

'From a TV commercial that's no longer running?'

'... the crackling leaves, the frost, the candlelight on the chancel stairs. Beautiful. Haunting. The only thing they'll have forgotten is that it was advertising a fucking bank, and where's the problem with that?'

'I can't do support in the spring,' Lol said. 'That's the problem.'

The stove put blue and pink flushes into the granary's interior walls of whitewashed rubble stone. It was a good stove, once you got used to the smell.

'What are you telling me?' Prof demanded. 'Early retirement, is that it? Vanishing into your own bucolic commercial?' On his feet now, finger pointing. 'Don't you *dare* give me that. You spend most of the summer doing chickenshit pubs and village halls with your friend, the farmer with the amplifier stacks in his barn, and you return, telling me you've finally overcome your agoraphobia—'

'It was never agoraphobia,' Lol said wearily. 'It isn't the same as not wanting to leave somewhere you've been happier than you thought possible, but you still—'

'A muddy bleeding field? It's not Glastonbury. It's going to be one of a hundred pissy little local festivals that might pull a few hundred punters if it doesn't rain. It'll do nothing for you. Take it from an old sound-engineer who still remembers ambition.'

'It's all they've ever asked from me.'

'Who?'

'The village,' Lol said. 'Well, Barry, at the Black Swan. His idea. He handles the commercial side, the catering. Me, I persuade good people to play for not a lot of money. So far, it's Moira Cairns, maybe Sproatly Smith and some others we're not ready to talk about.'

He stood at the bigger window, by day overlooking the Frome Valley where they grew hops for beer. An hour from Ledwardine which traditionally had produced apples for cider – the Village in the Orchard, home of the muddy field.

Prof sighed.

'And the vicar – still a street between you?'

'Close neighbours,' Lol said.

At night, he could look from his cottage windows across the street to the lights of the vicarage. Some nights, while Jane was away on her gap-year archaeological dig and he had a day off from touring, they would both look across from his bedroom, at no lights.

'She still doing that stuff like at Stock's kiln?' Prof said.

'With no encouragement at all from the new Bishop of Hereford.'

'They have a new one?'

'Craig Innes. Modernizer. Doesn't like spooky.'

'Pfft!' Prof said. 'Religion. All of it's spooky. Nature of the beast. Don't even ask me about Judaism.'

No way round this. Lol told Prof about Innes's links to a senior faction inside the C of E committed to wiping out what they considered to be medieval practices in the Church. All in the cause of survival in an increasingly secular age. A tougher job in Herefordshire, where the old ways died hard, but he was a determined bastard.

'If he drops her from deliverance – and he will, soon as he can justify it – she can hardly stay in the diocese. That's how she sees it anyway, and she might be right.'

Prof sat down on the side of the bed.

'If *she* goes… you would have to follow, yes?'

'I try to think it could be the best thing for both of us.'

Prof's chuckle was arid.

'Farewell to the place that gave you sanctuary when you were a lost boy? The place where you didn't realize you could ever be so happy? Oh yes, I can see the logic in that.'

Lol said nothing. He rubbed at the condensation on the glass. Nothing to see, and no sounds apart from the fizzing of the stove and a slow dripping from the eaves.

'So, essentially, Laurence, things are coming to a head, and you don't want to come back from some distant gig to find cases packed.' Prof's eyes were sad in the mauve light. 'Ah, the irony of it. A boy once disowned by his fundamentalist Christian parents for embracing the devil's music—'

'Prof, please, let's not—'

'—emerging from the darkest period in his life – this is pertinent – with an entirely understandable antipathy to organized religion, only to fall in love with a vicar? Don't tell me there isn't a part of you that secretly hopes this business with the Bishop will drive her out of the damn Church once and for all.'

Lol couldn't find the words to refute this. His hands were cold and wet from the condensation on the window, and he went to warm them at the paraffin stove. Prof stood up.

'You should've told me this earlier, you tosser, instead of going on about your chickenshit folk festival.'

'What's worst about this, Prof, is that they're never what you expect, the clergy. Especially now, with everything collapsing around them. Spirituality's the first casualty – especially at his level.'

'Knives out?'

'Croziers sharpened like hedging hooks.'

'I would like to suggest that you're probably exaggerating, but I fear you're not.' Prof felt a bedsheet. 'Not too damp. Listen, you need to decide if you want to marry this woman, you know that?'

'Known it for a long time.'

'Or work out what's important. And, who knows, hey, perhaps it's music. Perhaps you might even see that, one day. When it's too late.'

3

Trespass

VILLAGE FOG, RIVER fog, wasn't like the city fog she'd known as a kid, acrid with diesel fumes, but it wasn't like candyfloss either. You could get lost in your backyard on a night like this

She felt moisture like cold sweat on her cheeks. Her hands felt damp, as if the vapours had seeped inside her gloves. The year was too old to be autumnal, the lights of Christmas still unplugged. Just dark and damp enough to absorb sadness, so maybe a good month to be buried.

Merrily followed Jane out of the vicarage drive under trees bagged in fog.

Jane said, 'If this is nothing you're going to kill me in the morning, aren't you?'

'Flower, this *is* the morning.'

'Be something to tell the Legion at the Swan tomorrow, at least,' Jane said.

Merrily drew her woollen scarf over her lower face. Unless this involved illegal activity, she wouldn't be telling anybody. And you could say too much sometimes, to the clergy.

She'd brought the heavyweight Maglite torch they kept close to the front door. The beam wasn't brilliant but it was, as Frannie Bliss had said once, better than a baseball bat and less likely to come back on you in court if you wound up using it on somebody. She left it switched off. If they stayed close to the church wall they'd be OK.

'Mum, why don't you just call Lol?'

'Because he's not at home. His truck's not there. He's at Prof

Levin's. Probably decided to stay the night. I wouldn't like to drive in this. So let's just, you know, go in there very quietly, just to *see*. That's all. We do our best not to be seen, we don't speak, we *definitely* don't challenge anybody until we know what's happening.'

On the village square, the fake gaslamps had been switched off since midnight. The few buildings you could make out were vague and shapeless like museum exhibits under dust sheets.

'They say he did a lot of dope,' Jane whispered, 'did you hear that?'

'Who?'

'Aidan Lloyd?'

'Who told you that?'

'Heard it in the shop. You know how people are: if he'd been doing drugs he probably deserved to die. Especially being rich as well.'

'Yeah, OK, I heard whispers.'

Though obviously not something the family had wanted to discuss. She hadn't known the Lloyds, only seen their oilseed rape from afar. Aidan's father, Iestyn, was the man who'd painted Ledwardine yellow. In the process some old woodland had vanished, it was said. Old but not protected, so he'd got away with it.

She turned and found the church wall and held on to it until they reached the lychgate. To their right the tarmac path to the church, to the left the stony old path to the churchyard, the burial ground. The Lloyd family weren't churchgoers, except for other farmers' funerals.

'Someone said his old man found his stash after his death,' Jane said. 'He hadn't known. He would've gone ballistic.'

'You heard that in the shop, too?'

'Hairdresser's.'

No big deal these days, cannabis, even in the sticks, but could this partly explain the atmosphere at the funeral? Even worse after they wheeled the coffin out of the church. That pervading mood of restrained hostility, as the day had congealed around them in the churchyard. Aidan's mother had been half turned away from the open grave. Short hair, white, no hat. Her face compacted into what looked like permanent anger.

But the most persistent image of that funeral had been Iestyn Lloyd standing on the grave's edge, looking down – Merrily, bent to her open prayer book, the only person who would have heard what he'd whispered.

She was remembering the slightly wary attitude of Aidan's step brother when he'd arrived at the vicarage with an envelope containing some personal details for the service. Not all that personal, as it turned out. *He came through persistent childhood asthma attacks to emerge as a proficient and dedicated farmer.*

She'd tried for anecdotes, but the step brother didn't seem to understand what she was after. Warmth? Humanity? The sense of a valued life? Even trying to picture Aidan, she saw only the hollow eyes and the smudge of a half-grown beard from the photo in the *Hereford Times*.

'And then the woman from the gallery in Lucy's old shop,' Jane said, 'she apparently said he was out of his skull when he rode his quad bike out of the field gate. I'm bloody glad they're going.'

'The gallery people?'

Aware that Jane was talking to keep it casual, like this was routine.

'Always felt totally wrong, people like that in Lucy's shop.'

'Time to stop talking, I think, flower.'

Moving cautiously into the churchyard, finding the stony path thought to have been the end of an old coffin trail across the fields from outlying farms.

The churchyard was an alien place tonight, isolated in its own dimension, and all you could hear were heavy drips. Headstones were emerging from the fog like tree stumps in a marsh. Like a cartoon haunted graveyard. If there was one thing you learned from working in deliverance it was that the haunted graveyard was mainly for the cartoons but you still caught your breath when the first monolithic Victorian monument emerged like an industrial ghost from the fog.

Jane swung back, choking on a laugh, shrill relief overcoming caution before sliding back against a gravestone.

And then sinking, as if dissolving into the fog.

'Oh for—!'

'What've you—?'

Merrily went down next to her, a hand on Jane's arm.

'Mum, I can't get up.' Jane's voice splintered with shock and then penetrated by agony. 'Ankle. I've turned my bloody ankle on this... something grabbed my foot.'

'OK. Don't try to move, just...' She'd found it. She could feel the thorns through her gloves. Even dead brambles could snare a foot in the dark. 'Stay... just stay calm, while I...'

'Look... *look...*'

And, oh God, there it was in the middle distance, all the distance there was tonight. Like a pale, grounded moon, quick shadows passing across it like old windblown leaves. But there was no wind.

Jane inhaling sharply.

'You didn't believe me, did you?'

'I did believe you, I just...'

Neither of them moving now, dampness wrapping around them, about twenty paces, she was guessing, from where Aidan Lloyd lay amid a compression of noises: grunts, the weight of breathing.

A painful throb in Merrily's chest as she crouched next to Jane up against the stone. It should be anger. She was responsible for this place. She should stand on the lid of a stone tomb and turn on the Maglite, blast them.

'Jane...' Head down close. 'Phone?'

'I can't... get to my pocket.'

Merrily gripped the gravestone, watching the off-white light, going in and out as if it was signalling. It was like Jane had said,

18

shadows moving across it at irregular intervals. When the light broke through again, she saw shadows coalescing and heard a dull but solid and complex impact-noise before the shadows were breaking apart again. A slow blur of shifting humanity and not a word said.

'What are they *doing*?'

She was gripping Jane's arm, pulling her close, Jane's rapid breaths in her face. They were huddled tight to their grave which, she realized now, by the softness of rampant moss on the stone, was where Lucy Devenish lay, the old soul of the village, whose will had decreed that no growth should be removed from her stone.

Merrily pinched a loop of bramble between finger and thumb, pulling it steadily until she could fit the whole glove inside and wrench it away from Jane's foot.

'You're going to have to try and stand up, flower. Can you do that?'

'Not sure.'

'Try.'

Merrily wedged herself against Lucy's furry stone with its lines from Traherne: *No more shall clouds eclipse my treasures/ Nor viler shades obscure my highest pleasures.* Running the lines through her mind like a mantra, but Lucy couldn't help them now. At the end of a tunnel in the fog, the lamplight flared and then went out and stayed out, but the shifting sounds continued, and then there was a metallic chuckle.

Jane, incredibly, was trembling. Merrily switched on the torch, shading it with a gloved hand, though there was no need; its light was bleary, lukewarm, batteries so expensive now that you eked them out. The torch licked feebly at Lucy's stone like it didn't want to go any further.

Merrily froze. Really froze, as if her heart had stopped.

It was not a shiver. Nothing so pleasurable. It was like becoming aware that you were wearing a cold coat which was not yours and carried its history in every frigid fold.

In a moment of separation, she knew that another step would be trespass, and she was switching off the torch just as the fog shredded momentarily like rotting muslin, exposing the bony old apple trees and men like dark hawks under tall hats, moving like the figures on a Victorian automaton, closing sluggishly together and then parting to expose in grey light the suggestion of a face that she didn't want to believe was a face. Trespass. That urgent sense of being so close to trespass. The unquestionable need to flee.

4

No visible light

SHE'D AWOKEN THE kitchen woodstove, feeding it brittle twigs before pushing the Victorian sofa in from the scullery for Jane, helping her on to it, between plumped-up cushions. Jane scowling, the stove glass flaring yellow as the twigs caught.

'I *can* walk. I got back OK.'

She'd got back, but not OK. Hobbling together, arms around one another like the three-legged race at some old school sports-day.

Merrily added a little brandy to Jane's tea.

'I think you can stay there for a bit.'

'You going to call the cops?'

'I've not decided.'

They'd stumbled into the house, door banged, locked, bolts thrown. And all this meant nothing.

'If you're thinking of going back...' Jane lowering a foot to the floor. '... then we're both—' The foot had touched a stone flag. 'Oh *sh*—'

Bravado. It didn't need spelling out: Jane did not want to go back. Merrily helped her back on to the sofa then went across to the Welsh dresser and found some squat batteries in a top drawer. Dropped them one by one into the torch.

'Your hand's shaking,' Jane said.

Merrily tried the torch. Strong white light. She did up the poppers on her jacket.

'Mum, listen, I really hate to sound like... like your mother, or something. But you can't go back there on your own.'

'I'm not going all the way back. Just close enough to—'

'Call the bloody *cops*. When even *I'm* saying that…'

'I can't…' She couldn't say that she was only not going back to the churchyard because she was afraid. 'I can't even begin to think what I'd say to the police when I can't explain it to myself.'

Jane's eyes were clouded with uncertainty.

'We're not kids. We're not from some primitive society. We don't run away from things.'

'We couldn't run, could we?'

Merrily went down on her knees next to the stove, opening it up and feeding it a flaky, dry log.

'All my fault,' Jane said.

'Could've happened to either of us in those conditions. We did what you do when you're incapable of challenging anybody.'

'And that's all it was?'

No, of course it wasn't.

Ethel pattered in and jumped on the sofa next to Jane, who sat up, defiantly, hugging the cat.

'It's not a broken ankle, it's not even a proper sprain. Just give me a few more minutes…'

She reached her spare hand down to the twisted ankle, as if she was about to prove something, then stifled a sob, lay back, defeated, Ethel scrambling free.

Jane looked up, her smile a little crooked.

'Obvious why you won't call the police.'

Merrily stood up.

'Oh?'

'Because you can't have anything getting back to the Bishop. Anything he could use as evidence of your… precarious mental state.'

'Jane, that's—'

'He's turning your whole life into some narrow little path through a minefield. And in your job, you aren't even allowed to secretly hope he dies or something.'

22

'You'd be surprised.'

Jane tried to laugh, didn't get there.

'Can we at least talk about this? Like, what if… How did you know it was real?'

'Jane—'

'It didn't *look* real, did it? They did *not* look real. At the very least, it was like we'd walked into a play. Street theatre. Graveyard theatre. Or something that… wasn't there.'

'They were real. You know that or you wouldn't be suggesting I call the police.'

She didn't want to talk about this. Not now. Not the withdrawal of protection, the moment of isolation, the impossibility of prayer. It was not Jane's fault, it was *her* fault for not responding to the signals. For coming so close to *trespass*, her hand almost extended to grasp something… fibrous. She'd *been here before.*

She went to the kitchen window, stared at her own dull reflection, hair all over the place, eyes retracted into shadows. She didn't want to ask Jane what she'd seen. Or what she'd felt – especially that. But then the little voice was back, the *how old will you be when you die?* voice.

'Then why was I so frightened?'

'Because you were helpless.' She turned away from the window, went to kneel down by the Victoria sofa. 'And in pain.'

Jane looked down into clasped hands.

'I am… not like you.'

'No. Of course not.'

'Still a bit of a pagan.'

'It's your choice.'

'Because… because it's interesting. It's exciting. It brings the world alive for me – the fact that there are things *out there*, in nature, that we don't understand. It's bigger than the sad little politicians. Bigger than getting rich and having lots of clothes.'

'Maybe.'

'So why…' Jane looked up, tears in shocking dark, parallel lines down her cheeks. 'So why was I afraid? In my own village?'

Merrily sighed, gripping Jane's hand.

'If I knew that I'd sort it for you. Me and my mate, God. Look… it could be something stupid. Could be something we'll be laughing about. But equally…'

'You're avoiding the issue.'

'Yeah. Maybe I am. I'm sorry. It's my place, too.'

'If I could walk,' Jane said, 'I'd be up in the East Wing, now, and looking out of the window? Now we know what we've seen, it might just… I don't know.'

Why not? A small reprieve.

'OK.'

'Leave the torch, so I know you won't go sneaking out.'

'Oh, Jane…'

She put the torch on the dresser and went out through the hall to the stairs, leaving the lights off. As soon as she was in darkness, the images came back, jittering about to the fractured rhythm of their struggle home. The images were with her as she ran up the stairs, and down the landing, past closed door after closed door, then two steps down into the short landing with one door at its end.

She stumbled into the East Wing and leaned on the metal window frame until it scraped open with a thin screech and she was hanging out into the grey-green night, opening her eyes to shadows intermingling in the fog beyond the garden wall.

The pictures came up in her head again like some scratched old black and white movie: surreal light and shadow, men like predatory birds and the face that she hoped had not been a face.

She looked down.

Bare old apple trees, that was all.

No lamp. No visible light.

Nothing.

Dear God, maybe she could just wake up. She hung out there

in space, staring into the dense night, contempt for herself dampening the residual fear.

She should have asked Aidan Lloyd's father what he'd meant, standing on the graveside green baize in his long overcoat, looking down. That harsh whisper. The words she still didn't quite believe he'd said.

Devil took him.

The air thickening around Iestyn Lloyd, a narrow man with a grey moustache and a felt hat, the sun shrinking behind him until it looked like a blood blister.

Part Two

The sheer otherness of the display entranced him – it seemed to appear from the darkest, least conspicuous corners of English provincial life, and to be innately understood by the people who practised it.

Rob Young
Electric Eden (Faber, 2010)

5

No justice

FROM HIS OFFICE window, Bliss shared his breakfast with Sonia the seagull and watched the city manifesting out of the fog, nothing high-rise to hide the hills, the only visible towers attached to churches, still misty-pale.

Almost serene, like the council hadn't been *developing* Hereford, hadn't taken the cattle market out of town, replacing it with a concrete canyon accommodating chain stores and a cinema. A big cinema with drab grey walls like the Bastille, brutalizing the entrance to the city centre. Apparently, this was where the new police HQ would be, when they eventually left Gaol Street, somewhere behind the Bastille.

Somewhere Rich Ford, the uniformed inspector, would never work.

'Been thinking where we could move to, me and the wife, when I'm out of here,' Rich said. 'Little barn conversion maybe, over towards the Black Mountains, from where all you ever need see of the city is the distant fireworks on New Year's Eve.'

He'd be gone soon after new year. Couldn't come soon enough, he kept saying that.

'Actually, I hear parts of Eastern Europe are very desirable now,' Bliss said. 'Lovely scenery. Clean, unspoiled towns with terrific cathedrals. Friendly people. Very little crime.'

'Yes, very amusing, Francis.'

Bliss yawned.

'You said something about quad bikes?'

'Easy to move around, easy to dispose of. Always a ready market for quad bikes.'

'You know what, Rich?' Bliss said. 'I'm bored already.'

Seemed a couple of uniforms had found a selection of these farmers' toys in the back of a vehicle-repairer and dealer's premises out on the Rotherwas industrial estate. Jag's Motors, owned by one Wictor Jaglowski, about whom there'd been rumours. His brother, who had a half share in a Polish deli, was doing time for big-time ciggie-smuggling.

'It gets more interesting, Francis,' Rich said. 'Least, that's what my instincts are telling me. Actually, quad bikes come into the story again. Or one, anyway. Not that you'd get much for that, except from a scrapyard.'

Bliss stared at him, putting it together.

'This is the one on which the farm guy died?'

'That's why we went down the Rotherwas. The feller who ran into him worked for Jaglowski. Sort of.'

Bliss sat down behind his desk. 'Take me through it again, Rich.'

He always felt bad about it, but links with a death, even accidental, added a certain texture to a case.

A lot of new drivers on the roads of Herefordshire, and not all of them had a British licence. Including Lukas Babekis – and that probably wasn't his real name either.

Lukas was twenty years old and Lithuanian. He'd been people-smuggled, one of a bunch of Lithies secretly accommodated on a caravan site over towards the border with Worcestershire. All young lads, *working their passage*. Euphemism for slavery.

'He got lost while making a delivery for one of those cut-price couriers that employ freelance drivers with their own vehicles,' Rich said. 'Jaglowski was one of their operatives – fingers in more pies than the Pukka production line. He'd sub contracted Lukas, providing the van. Well, I say sub contracted...'

'He wasn't paying him.'

'I think he got free sarnies from Morrisons. Anyway... country lane, part of that network south of Leominster

connecting villages nobody ever goes to. Very few signposts.
So Lukas has lost his way in this maze of little lanes. No other
vehicles in the vicinity, no witnesses.'

'Remind me about the victim.'

'Farm bloke. Farmer's son. Coming out of field gate on his
quad bike. Off-white van comes whizzing round the corner,
smack. His face was mush.'

Bliss winced.

'Not much chance on a quad bike, have you?'

'One reason we don't like them on the Queen's highways.'

'I'm not entirely sure of the rules, Rich. Are they *ever* allowed
on a public road?'

'Only if taxed, insured and registered with the DVLA,
number plates front and rear. Mr Lloyd's vehicle met none of
these requirements. All right, he was only crossing from a field
on one side to a field on the other, probably done it thousands
of times. He bears a percentage of the blame. Or would if he
was still with us.'

'But?'

'Lukas was obviously travelling too fast for a single track
road he admitted he'd never been on before. Being as how he
was not long over from Lithuania. Admitted going too fast for
the conditions – two other deliveries and he was late. Kept
bursting into tears. Said it was all his fault and he never wanted
to drive again. Clearly unaware that unregistered, uninsured
quad bikes are not supposed to be on the road. The duty
solicitor, however, was.'

'Would've got him off, you reckon?'

'Not impossible, though *he* was obviously scared he might be
looking at a gaol sentence.'

'Vanished?'

'Probably back with his mum in Lithuania by now. Until
then, we didn't know he was an illegal. Jaglowski says he's
furious. But the boy had papers! Who can you trust these
days?'

31

'So Mr Jag, it was his van, right?'

'Jag has three or four, available for hire or his own contract work. We'd finished with the van that killed the farmer, and when he didn't show up to collect it, it seemed like a good excuse for an unscheduled visit. Jag was out, only a boy in charge. Opportunity for a little wander around in the back of the garage, where we clocked a variety of agricultural implements – three quads, collection of chainsaws, heavy duty hedge-trimmers, brush-cutters and the like.'

'Jag's fencing stolen kit.'

'Well, yeah, but I'm thinking more than that. You know how many farm thefts there've been in the county this year?'

'I know how many the bloody farmers *say* there've been.'

Big issue again this year. Another useful campaign for Countryside Defiance, the pro-hunting pressure group posing as a general rural-interests lobby.

'You know what I'm thinking, Francis? Wictor Jaglowski with his little fleet of vans?'

'Let me process it.' Bliss leaning his chair back against the window. Sonia had left the building. 'Fellers like this Lukas, out ostensibly on courier work, in plain vans, happening to get themselves lost...'

'I reckon Jag's sending blokes out into the sticks to have a discreet poke around, try a few shed doors, unlocked trucks, Land Rovers. Anything not padlocked to the wall goes into the back of the off-white van. And then he comes back for the Land Rovers.'

Bliss nodded. Made sense.

'Or even the odd sheep,' Rich said.

'Anything found in the back of the van after the fatality?'

'Nothing. But that doesn't mean he didn't get rid when he knew he was in trouble.'

'We know any more drivers going out in Jag's vans?'

'Shouldn't be too hard to find them. Think of the brownie points with the farmers.'

'We *never* get brownie points from farmers, Rich, nobody does. Still… thanks for this. I'll ask Ma'am if we can extend to an obbo. See how far up it goes. And then, if Jag's part of something more extensive, we can offload it on the NCA.'

Might be another layer of cop-bureaucracy, but the one good thing about the National Crime Agency was the way it saved you having to deal with foreign police and spend money on interpreters.

Rich nodded.

'Am I right in thinking you and the DCI are getting on better these days, Francis?'

'Well, you know, Rich…' Bliss carried on making a note on his pad. 'I find sleeping together a couple of nights a week makes for a much easier working relationship.'

Pause for laughter. They both knew that at least half of Gaol Street was convinced Annie was gay.

'Anyway,' Rich said, 'she en't gonner be around for much longer if her old man gets the big one next year.'

Bliss said nothing. Still hoping Charlie Howe would see the madness here and pull out of the contest for Police and Crime Commissioner. Or the government would have a rethink, scrap the commissioners and bring back the old police authorities which hadn't been up to much but at least there'd been a semblance of democracy.

'Somebody was saying,' Rich said, 'that his early manifesto's in today's *Hereford Times*.'

'*Already?*'

'He don't let the grass grow, Charlie. And he'll win. He always does. I've sent out for a copy.'

'He's bent, Rich. He was a bent copper, a bent councillor and the chances of him *not* being a bent police commissioner…'

Rich smiled down at his boots.

'Must've known four or five bent coppers in my time. I mean *real* bent, not just mavericks, real corrupt, free holidays at some old scrote's villa on the Costa-whatever. And you know one thing they all had in common, Francis? They were popular. In the job and out of it. Every bloody one of them.'

Bliss sighed.

'Jack the lad.'

'Whereas *Annie* Howe... dead straight. Painfully straight. In that way, at least.'

'And nobody likes her.'

'No justice, Francis,' Rich said.

6

Many of us

NOT QUITE TEN a.m., but it could have been dusk. It was faintly raining, but the village was still wearing the thinning fog like a dirty mac when Merrily came hurrying out of the churchyard, under the lychgate and on to the square.

Much relieved to spot the Animal, Lol's blue truck, at the end of the cobbles – no sign of it when she'd gone down to the churchyard – but there was no time to knock on his door or even run back to the vicarage to see Jane. The lanterns were on either side of the Swan's main door and there was Clive Wells at the top of the steps, at least half an hour early.

Languid Clive, old money and increasingly High Church – an incense swinger, in the face of what he saw as a corporate Canterbury cosying up to the secular society. Looking much the same as he had when they'd first met at Huw Owen's chapel in the Beacons to be initiated into the dark arts.

They hugged but then he held her at arm's length, peering at her, curious. Clearly, she didn't look so good, with the cursory make-up, hair a mess.

'Jane,' she said. 'Twisted an ankle. I've been... rushing around a bit.'

'Anything I can do?'

'No, no, she's...'

Much better, actually. Tentatively walking around the kitchen, saying, *I'm fine, go, go, check it out or you won't have time.*

Clive Wells followed her into the Swan, past the main bar to the polished oak door of the Jacobean lounge with a little sign on it that said tamely,

ANGLICAN ADVISORY GROUP

'You wimped out, then,' Clive said.

'Too right, I did.'

Officially they didn't even have a name. The Legion – that was someone's idea of a black joke. *My name is Legion – there are so many of us*, the demon tells Jesus through the possessed man in Mark, chapter 5. Merrily blaming herself for being dumb enough to ask if anyone knew the collective noun for a group of exorcists.

Not that there were *so* many of them around the Welsh border, which was why they'd extended the catchment area. It had been generally agreed that meeting twice a year was not a bad idea in these difficult times. Swap stories, discuss methods, slag off bishops. The first meeting had been up in Wrexham, this was the second.

Merrily and Clive went through into the long room with the dark oak panelling and wrought-iron hanging lights and a conference table with twenty chairs.

'Business brisk?' Merrily said.

'Strains credibility sometimes, I'm afraid. Or I'm entering my midlife crisis. Had a black-eyed kids situation a few weeks ago. People read about them in the tabloids and before you know it...'

Sometimes you thought you were losing touch with reality when it was just a question of allowing reality to expand, but black-eyed kids were outside the most flexible parameters. Merrily remembered the front-page splash Jane had spotted on Jim Prosser's newspaper rack. It had seemed less like evidence of a thinning of the veil between worlds as a narrowing of the gap between the *Daily Star* and the *Daily Sport*.

'First heard of, apparently, in the 1990s,' Clive said. 'Began in America. Combination of spectral dwarf and the traditional Roswell alien, with those large black eyes. People were claiming to have had encounters with what looked at first like ordinary children in hoodies. Except that witnesses spoke of feeling an inexplicable terror before even noticing that the kid's eyes were like chips of coal. Quite often, after an encounter, bad luck would befall the victim.'

'You had one in Gloucester?'

'Two. Knocking on doors. They'd have their backs to the door when the people answered the bells and then they'd turn around slowly. Bleeeargh!'

'They disappear, or just run off giggling?'

'In both cases, the householders were so horrified they just slammed their doors and didn't open them again.'

'What did you do?'

'Blessed the doorsteps, sprinkle of holy water. Far from satisfied that these weren't real kids who'd read the tabloids, but what *can* you do? Who else but us would do anything?'

How much earth did a coffin displace? The refitted turf on Aidan Lloyd's grave was substantially higher than the grass around it. It would sink eventually. Might be months before a memorial stone was in place. Jane moved carefully around the grave in the cold-steam air, and then as far as she could go on the other side before the burial area met the bare, bony, apple trees. Rain was gradually drowning the fog, but her mouth was dry, as she bent to examine the ground on the dark side of the grave, and...

... nothing. No obvious footprints on any side. It was like nothing had happened here since Gomer Parry had filled in the grave after the mourners had left.

This wasn't possible. Had Mum seen this? Jane straightened up unsteadily, flinging back the hood of her parka, tilting her head to let the rain sting her face. *Wake me up, for God's sake.* A blurring of her senses, like something was in the process of erasing last night, turfing over the memories.

She recalled being helped up to bed, her ankle splattered by

Mum with analgesic gel and bound up in a support bandage. Expecting nightmares, pathetically wishing Eirion were there with her. Eirion who, unsurprisingly, had stopped phoning. Maybe he knew something. Maybe somebody had told him about Sam.

No memory of dreaming at all. In the morning light, she'd edged slowly down the stairs to find Mum on the phone to Barry at the Swan, checking the arrangements for today. Examining Jane's ankle before swallowing tea and dashing out, dragging her coat and bag behind her. *Jane, look, I need to check the churchyard. I'll call you. Don't do anything, OK? Don't speak to anybody about what happened. Toaster's on.*

Jane had had honey and toast and rubbed more gel into her ankle, moving round and round the kitchen until she could walk with both feet. It was OK, more or less, just a question of taking your time. Mum had duly called from her mobile to say there was nothing to see in the churchyard. Really, nothing.

They had to have missed something.

Jane turned slowly at the sound of a cracking twig, drew a tight breath. There'd been nothing behind her but fog; now there was the huge, numinous imprint of the church emerging, with shimmering grandeur, from the thinning curtain. As if it was advancing on her. She felt momentarily afraid. Vulnerable. A sensation she didn't remember at all from being a kid. Not even when Dad was killed. Another aspect of becoming adult: learning to embrace fear because there was nowhere to run. No one to save you from yourself and your wrong decisions. Decisions made too fast because you thought you had to.

She'd bought some time, but it was running out. The gap year nearly half gone and nothing from it, this limbo state between school and college, supposedly a time to discover herself. A freedom that wasn't freedom at all. Ought to be applying to universities now, for next year, citing her work experience, her passion for archaeology. But why? *Why?* Archaeologists were ten a penny and nobody wanted to pay them.

She'd got talking to this supermarket manager in Hereford with a second in English Literature. Asked him if he couldn't get a job as a college teacher, and he'd said he'd rather be a supermarket manager.

The mossy shoulders of Lucy's stone felt warm under Jane's hands. Above the quote from Traherne, the stone said,

LUCY DEVENISH
of this village

No dates, as requested in Lucy's will – was that allowed?

As if she was not dead but still here, still functioning in some way. A witch in the oldest sense. *Talk to me, Lucy. You saw them. You know what they were.*

He was built like an old-fashioned wrestler, short and thick set, shaven-headed, overweight. He came creaking out of the leather-backed chair at the end of the conference table.

'At this point, I'd just like to ask, what do we think we're *doing*? Do we even know?'

There are so many of us. No more than a dozen, actually. Men and women from the coalface, some old mates, some new to the ministry, a couple whose names Merrily struggled to remember and this guy who she didn't know at all.

At first, she'd had him down as aggressively evangelical – the only one of them wearing a white dog collar at a jeans-and-trainers event – but maybe not. Accent too plummy. While the others were having coffee a short time ago, he'd bought himself a large glass of red wine.

'I'll be honest,' he said. 'I rather think I might be having a crisis.'

'Crisis of faith?' Clive Wells said.

'Certainly not that,' the wrestler said. 'Because I've realized that the deliverance ministry is *anti*-faith.'

Oh please...

Merrily was sitting next to Clive Wells who she'd persuaded to chair the gathering. Clive twitched a tired smile.

'Go on then, Paul. Explain.'

'Anti-faith,' the wrestler said, 'in that it has us hunting for evidence of the miraculous. For example, we deal with people who think their houses are haunted, and we – some of us – feel the need to become psychic investigators, as distinct from priests.'

Nick Cowan sat up. Nick the former social worker, now senior deliverance minister for Worcester, who had opened the morning session by making a thin case for the survival of exorcism at a time of dwindling congregations on the basis that people always came back to the Church when troubled by the unknown.

Merrily hadn't liked to mention the proliferation of paranormal-rescue groups with their digital recorders, magnetometers, resident mediums and baseball caps on back to front. Showing you digital pictures of your orbs, playing you EVP messages of your entity croaking through analogue radio static.

'Times change,' Nick Cowan said. 'People are more widely read on the paranormal and related issues. They've seen TV programmes, films, they expect more than a blessing and a pat on the head. They expect an explanation.'

'So we make one up for them?'

The wrestler leaned back behind folded arms, telling them how he'd been invited into deliverance by his bishop because of his experiences abroad with Oxfam and Amnesty International. This was around the time African kids were undergoing wholesale exorcism in parts of London, and there were hints of it in the Midlands.

'In areas of malnutrition and rudimentary schooling, evil spirits are very much part of the package. But even in Africa, I never encountered a child who seemed possessed by anything more than the earthly evils of deprivation, shortage of healthcare, poor schooling and parental apathy. Never encountered anything that I didn't believe couldn't be turned around through a combination of sympathy, prayer—'

'And foreign aid. Yes,' Clive Wells said. 'Paul, given that the policy generally adopted by Bishops for the appointment of exorcists would include, amongst its criteria, a level of scepticism—'

'Not about the nature of God, Clive, don't accuse me of that. I'm merely questioning the way we interpret people's ghost stories.'

'None of these issues are simple.'

'Or are we perhaps overcomplicating them? Which, I have to say, leads me to question the kind of clergy who allow themselves to be recruited for deliverance training.'

Merrily slid Clive Wells a note on the back of a menu. *This Paul – who is he?*

'So what would you do?' Nick Cowan said. 'What would you do if faced with a mother who's convinced her child is possessed by a satanic evil you don't really accept? Or, indeed, what *have* you done in that situation?'

The wrestler beamed savagely.

'Whatever it might be – delusion, psychosis or, indeed, alleged satanic evil – I throw the book at it. Certainly wouldn't waste my time *turning detective*. Just as I might not see it as my job to investigate the history of a so-called haunted house to try to give the alleged spirit an identity. Is the house built on the site of a pagan cemetery or something? Who cares? I don't want to get to know it, whatever it is, or find out what it's after, or why it might be *unquiet...* if it's some former resident who doesn't like the new decor. Because none of that can ever be proven and – in case anyone's forgotten – the Bible forbids us from having dealings with the dead. Does anyone want to take issue with me here? Anybody?'

He looked from face to face. Merrily thought his gaze lingered on hers, but maybe that was insecurity. Clive Wells was looking wary now.

'So what *do* you do, Paul?'

'I've told you. Leave it to the Holy Spirit. *We* don't exorcize, God does, at our request. As we have no means of understanding what's actually happening, we should regard it all as potentially evil – at least, in the sense that it could be opening doors to mental illness.'

'So you wouldn't follow the suggested procedure, beginning with, say, a house blessing?'

'I'd cut to the chase. Whatever I'm told has been experienced, be it a ball of light or a fragrant perfume, *it is an intrusion*. Or an *imagined* intrusion. I say a prayer, then tend to command whatever it is, in the name of Our Lord, to get the hell out.'

'Although you don't necessarily believe – yourself – in whatever it is you're supposed to be dealing with?'

'Clive' – the wrestler throwing out his arms – 'my personal reaction, as a human being, is irrelevant. I'm a tool of God. Equally, I'm suspicious of any deliverance minister who claims to use so-called psychic skills in his or her work. As you may know, Dom Robert Petitpierre, who edited the findings of the Bishop of Exeter's 1970s commission on exorcism, believed himself to be psychic but was determined to suppress it in his deliverance work. Not relevant. A distraction.'

'Let me get this right,' Nick Cowan said. 'You're suggesting the deliverance ministry is attracting people whose faith is weak. Who are looking for evidence of the paranormal to strengthen their belief in a supernatural deity?'

'Nicholas, I'm playing devil's advocate, if you like.'

Merrily poured herself a glass of water. Dissent was hardly unknown at a deliverance meeting. How many exorcists did it take to change a lightbulb before all the others blew?

Abbie Folley, a recent appointment from Merthyr, was playing with her bangles.

'And is that your problem, Paul? You don't know how much you're supposed to believe?'

'*My* problem...' Planting both hands flat on the table,

leaning forward. '… is that I'm unsure whether the sympathy and prayer I mentioned earlier should extend to appearing to share the convictions of the people I'm trying to help. All right, what's our most common form of apparent haunting? The so-called bereavement apparition. The comfort-projection following the death of a loved one. "Oh, yes, I saw him, vicar, clear as day, sitting in his favourite chair." Well, of course you did, Mrs Davies. Two sugars in mine, please.'

He laughed, looked up and down the conference table, face to face.

'Harmless, surely? Humour them.'

Merrily said carefully, 'In my experience, the bereavement apparition has its place in the cycle of grief.'

The wrestler grinned at her.

'Of course it does. "Oh, don't sit there, vicar, that's George's chair." But how do we *know*, Merrily? Is George imaginary or wishful thinking? Or, taking the negative viewpoint, is he a possibly harmful obsession? Or – if this was America, where so-called psychic intrusion tends to be considered demonic – something dark, malign and essentially alien. Something *not George*.'

'One of the problems we'd have to work out,' Merrily said. 'As best we could.'

'Why? How?'

'Consideration. Meditation. Prayer. Feel free to substitute your own word.'

He didn't do that. She became of aware of Abbie Folley looking at her, minimally shaking her head as the menu came back from Clive Wells.

Paul Crowden, Wolverhampton area. Seems to be a new member of the Lichfield deliverance panel. Former charity worker. Been there, done that. Ordained in middle-age. Making up for lost time. Bit of a PITA. (destroy this, please)

Paul Crowden said, 'Tell me, Merrily, do *you* feel it's part of your job to investigate the paranormal?'

'Well... not as an end in itself. But if background knowledge of something might help me confront a particular issue...'

'Is that what you think the Bible tells us to do? Investigate?'

Merrily felt herself frowning. She wondered what PITA meant.

'You mean the Bible which forbids us from having dealings with the dead? Thereby appearing to regard anything paranormal as potentially evil?'

'Some weeks ago,' Crowden said, 'an elderly woman approached a vicar in my diocese, telling him she was seeing, amongst other phenomena, the ghost of her dead cat. The vicar was fond of cats and asked my advice.'

'Oh hell, Paul,' Abbie Folley said. 'You didn't tell him to zap the poor bloody cat on the off chance it was demonic?'

Paul Crowden said nothing.

Merrily thought, *PITA*. Pain In The Arse?

'I have to decide quite soon,' Crowden said, 'whether to continue in deliverance or to tell my bishop that it's really not for me. That's why I'd like to know from all of you, with reference to the issues I've raised, how you approach this most problematic of ministries.'

Merrily looked up at a movement. Abbie Folley, in thigh-length crocheted sweater, black leggings, was pushing her chair back and standing up.

'Paul, I'm sure we all have a lot to say, and I can't wait to start, but all right, is it, if we have a toilet break first?'

'I'll come with you,' Merrily said.

Through the leaded windows, she could see the rain-shredded fog had become a translucent yellowy haze. Dispiriting. The fog had been better.

7

Cut sideways

THE SKY CLOSED in again and the sour, sporadic rain came back, but Jane was reluctant to leave and prowled amongst the graves. She saw where greasy grass had been trodden down in front of Lucy's stone – her own boots and Mum's, some evidence of their aborted visit.

She looked down towards Aidan Lloyd's grave, letting her breathing settle, blanking her mind, her gaze resting on the green plateau. Reliving the dark: those moments of pounding feet, intermittent glimmers of lamplight, the sense of…

… ritual?

A catch-all word in archaeology for anything which had no obvious explanation. A regular joke among the guys in Pembrokeshire, on her short-lived, gap-year, work-experience dig. *Well it's obviously not a settlement so it must be a ritual landscape.*

Archaeological in-joke. She heard their laughter, maybe always there like tinnitus whenever she thought about the Pembrokeshire dig. They could be so cliquey, those guys. Except, of course, for Sam who'd got her into bed.

Jane choked on residual fog and gave in to coughing. Those texts and emails, continuing to arrive, mostly offering her work jobs on other digs. If she'd said yes to one of them, she wouldn't now be out of work. Just booked into the same B & B as Dr Samantha Burnage. Same room, same bed.

Oh God, God, *God…*

She walked uselessly away to where entrails of fog were

hanging from holly and apple trees, two of them bending like old and skeletal birds over Aidan's grave. Thinking back, it was like the trees themselves had come alive in the dead of night, gnarled arthritic limbs acquiring new muscle in a crackling of bark.

Don't laugh. This was part of the Ledwardine *ritual land-scape...* where the medieval orchard might well have been following the perimeter of a prehistoric henge. The idea of one day proving it was still the main reason she'd decided to become an archaeologist.

Destiny.

The big irony was that it probably wouldn't get excavated unless plans for a supermarket went ahead on the eastern perimeter of Jane's henge, which meant the council would have to sanction a dig before the ancient site became a building site.

Wasn't life a bitch? Jane sank her fingers into the moss on Lucy's stone.

No more shall clouds eclipse my treasures
Nor viler shades obscure my highest pleasures

The patrician voice in her head was as clear as it had ever been. Clear as the memory of the day Lucy had cut an apple in half, sideways, to reveal the fibrous green pentagram within, an everyday mystery most people were never aware of because they never cut sideways.

The warm, mossy stone under her hands, Jane imagined Lucy coming down from wherever to stand next to her. The poncho, the wide-brimmed hat. *Looks like an old Red Indian scout, talks liked a headmistress*, Mum used to say. Did wise old Lucy have any kind of degree? Who knew? She'd just run a dark little shop called Ledwardine Lore, repository of rural mementoes and ancient wisdom, and kept an eye on the quiet kaleidoscope of village life.

'Janey?'

Agony from the ankle as she whirled around to a tiny spark-shower in the air briefly reflected in bottle glasses under an old, patched flat cap.

'Gomer…'

'You're crying, girl.'

He was snatching the roll-up from between his lips. She hadn't even heard him approaching.

'I… I just like twisted my ankle, Gomer. I'm OK. I was kind of resting it for a bit?'

He stared at her. She guessed he'd only come in here because he – or someone who'd told him – had spotted her alone and limping under the lychgate. You couldn't move in Ledwardine without somebody grassing you up.

'Sorry, Janey.' Squeezing out the red end of his roll-up. 'If I'd a knowed it was you, see, I'd've had the ole baccy stick goin'.'

Jane collapsed into a grin. She'd brought him back from Pembs an e-cig pack, in a bid to prolong his life. Embarrassed about it now.

'That was… intrusive of me, Gomer. Keep meaning to apologize.'

'No, no, girl, I'm gettin' on all right with 'im.' Gomer fishing out the e-cig to show he'd still got it. 'He d'work better'n I reckoned he would.'

'That's what Mum says.'

'It's the *rollin'* of 'em, I misses, see. Gives you time to think.'

The sun slid palely into view and then vanished like a coin into a slot machine. Jane nodded at Aidan Lloyd's turfed-over grave. In the absence of Lucy nobody knew more about the hidden side of Ledwardine than Gomer Parry.

'You come to check that out? Like make sure it's all… settling down?'

He looked at her like she was daft.

'Janie, I been diggin' graves since before your ma was born.'

'Sorry.'

'Earth'll take care of him.'

'Right.'

He looked at her, curious.

'You knowed this boy?'

'Did anybody? I mean, I saw him around.' She remembered this thin, quiet, vague-looking guy, dark eyes, dark jaw, sitting in the Swan, making a half of cider last a long time. 'Heard things about him.'

'Oh, aye, we all yeard things.'

'We didn't *know*, though, did we?'

'Village folks, you don't go around tellin' everybody your life story, they makes one up for you.' The brim of Gomer's cap dipped towards the grave. 'Less'n half as old as me and bloody gone already. What's that about?'

'I suppose it's about tobacco on its own helping you concentrate, but hash...'

'Oh aye?' Gomer looked up. 'That's what they reckons, is it?'

'They're like... his brain must've been fried when he drove out of a field into the path of a van. Could be he hadn't smoked anything at all that day, but hey...'

Gomer looked pensive.

'Couple years ago, we done some field drains for Iestyn Lloyd.'

'Did you get paid?'

The bigger the farm, the tighter the farmer, that was the general rule.

'And a borehole, too,' Gomer said. 'Boy come out with us. Walks round a bit, then he goes – bit hesitant, like – mabbe sink him yere?'

'The borehole?'

'And bugger me if he wasn't right.'

'He knew where you'd find a good water source? He was a dowser?'

'Didn't have no forked twig, mind. He just knowed.'

'It's just an aid, the twig, or the rods,' Jane said. 'They reckon if you're really good you don't need any of it. Blimey.'

'Feller once told me I could do it, but I never found the time, see.'

'Bet you could, Gomer.'

'Allus folks around can do it better, so best leave it to them. I recall the boy says could we not tell his ole feller.'

'Why?'

'Just din't want him to know he done it. Or mabbe as he *could* do it. Iestyn Lloyd, he got no time for that ole wallop. Modern farmer, see. Works hard, works his ground hard. He done well, mind. Hell of a big farm now.'

'Too big. And all that oilseed rape. I used to think it was pretty, but now it just looks alien. And all the pesticides he must be putting on the fields, killing all the bees.'

'He got focus, Janey. Goes quietly on. Buying up any fields as comes up for sale. Three times the size of what it was when he took it over, and that can't be more'n fifteen years back.'

'Oh. So the Lloyds are from Off? Hadn't realized that.'

'Well, not *Off* Off. Down south of the county. Kilpeck. You know Kilpeck? Inherited Churchwood Farm from his uncle, Eddie Lloyd. Not much more'n a holding, them days. Eddie, he just kept a few sheep, sold the rest off. Iestyn starts buyin' it back, bit by bit.'

They were right on the edge of the new grave now.

'Mum said it wasn't a very happy funeral. If you see what I mean.'

Well, he'd been there. The gravedigger was always discreetly waiting in the churchyard to fill in the hole as soon as the mourners were gone.

'Sarah Lloyd as was,' Gomer said. 'Boy's mother, her looked like thunder. See, you ask some folks, they'll say her went off with another feller, but that en't true. Her just went off. Went to live with her ole mam up in town. Six years, sure t'be, before her got wed again. But her'd done her bit. Give Iestyn a son. Farmer allus gotter have a son.'

Gomer said Sarah had been Iestyn's secretary and already had a baby from another relationship when he married her, Iestyn bringing up the boy as his own. Then Aidan came along, his future ordained before he could walk.

'No picnic being Iestyn's son, mind. Other boy come off best, his ma reckoned.'

Jane stopped walking. The sun was pushing damply against low cloud like a mint in a handkerchief.

'What was *happening* here, Gomer?'

He peered at her, clearly happy to help, but she wasn't sure what she was asking for. Anything that might explain something that had even frightened Mum; but there was no way she could talk about last night.

Gomer activated his e-cig.

'I had some nice dry soil set aside.'

'Sorry?'

'For the nearest and dearest to toss on the box. Nobody wanted it, see. Just get him bedded in.'

They were standing very close to the raised turf of the Lloyd grave. Through Jane's half-closed eyes, its image darkened and blurred into memories of shuffling, feathered figures, and she was aware of her own heart beating harder, its pounding becoming the lumpen thudding of feet around a lamp on the ground. Really wanted to tell him, but it should come, if at all, from Mum.

Where the lamp might have been, she saw Gomer bend slowly, his fingers moving over the grass. Like an osteopath, Jane thought, exploring someone's back.

'Gomer…' Moving forward, she felt a slithery sense of foreboding. 'You all right?'

'Sure t'be.' He came very slowly upright, rubbing soil from his hands. 'I better be off, then, Janey. I forgot, feller up at Bearswood needs a hestimate for a new soakaway.'

She walked back with him, out through the lychgate, and did not ask what was on his mind. Something he wasn't sure about so wasn't ready to tell her. It was like the Lloyd funeral had created a cloud of secrecy that fed on the fog which still hung around the square, mingling promiscuously with the applewood chimney-smoke.

As they walked down Church Street she saw Dean Wall shambling ahead of them towards Ledwardine's second pub, the Ox, no longer the loutish kid she'd been at school with. They'd all grown up.

Gomer's cap was tilting in Dean's direction.

'Got hisself in the *Hereford Times*, then.'

'Must've been relieved it was only a suspended sentence.'

'Wassat mean exac'ly, Janey?'

'Means if he gets caught dealing drugs again – or anything, really, he's straight in the slammer. Still…' Thoughtful, now. '… that doesn't mean he can't talk about it.'

Gomer gave her a sternish kind of look.

'You wanner be a bit careful, Janey. Dean Wall en't a boy n'more.'

8

Zapping the cat

IN THE ROSY light of the Ladies', Abbie Folley pushed her dripping hands into one of those air-blade driers.

'Dunno if it's just me, Merrily...'

'Mmm?'

'Is there something almost *sexual* about these devices?'

Merrily blinked.

'Probably *is* me.' Abbie was looking around at the dark-pink walls, the gilt-edged period basins fitted between pillars of sinewy old oak. 'Lovely, all this, though, isn't it? Tidy.'

'Barry's done a nice job.' Merrily examined her face in the mirror. 'Especially with the lighting. Takes ten years off your reflection.'

Abbie grinned, withdrawing her dried hands with all their rings: left hand rubies or similar, right hand emeralds or similar.

'He's Sass, this Barry, that right?'

'Was. Wouldn't kill a woman, though.'

'Love the eye patch.'

Abbie rolled a sleeve down over her fish tattoo which ran wrist to elbow. How old was she – twenty-eight, thirty? Merrily nodded at the hand-drier.

'Wash them again if you like.'

'No, no, have to ration it.' Abbie looked at her, dark-eyed and thoughtful. 'You all right?'

'I look ill?'

'Bit fragile, to be honest.'

'Tired. Didn't get much sleep last night, for one reason or another. No, not *that*. He was away. Working.'

'On tour?'

'Been producing an album for Belladonna. If you remember her.'

'Oh, now, *there's* attitude.' Abbie hunching into the mirror, applying cerise lipstick. 'You ever met her?'

'I'm afraid I have.'

'Ex*citin*'. What an exotic life you have in the New Cotswolds.'

She dropped the lipstick in her bag, and Merrily held open the door for her, but Abbie didn't move.

'Merrily…'

'Mmm?'

'Paul Crowden? You met him before?'

'Never.'

'Remind you of anyone, does he?'

Merrily let the door close, put her back against it.

'Actually, he does. In a way.'

Abbie dumped her bag on the wooden ledge between the basins.

'Thought he might, the bastard.'

Abbie Folley was part of a deliverance panel in an area still stalked by industrial demons. It might or might not have been true that she'd wound up at theological college as a small act of rebellion against her parents, good old Valleys commies. Going to call her Karl, they were, if she'd been a boy. Or so she said.

Abbie also said she didn't envy Merrily. None of them did.

Merrily glanced nervously at the door.

'Relax,' Abbie said. 'Men expect women to spend an hour in the lav. Tell me about your bishop.'

'How long have you got?'

'Or, better still, I'll tell you. Craig Innes, I was a curate in his parish. Temporary assistant junior curate for maybe two months before he left on his journey skyward. Fair play, he was nice enough to me, in his bluff, rugby-boy way.'

'This would be when he was down near Newport?'

Abbie nodding.

'He'd done a deliverance training course with Huw Owen, by then. I only realized later that was in a know-thine-enemy kind of way. What could I have said anyway? My first job, it was. Too timid in those days to paint my nails.'

Abbie turned on two taps, full gush.

'Saw this in a spy film. Merrily, look, you don't have to tell me or anything, all right? But the word is Craig's been sent in to sprinkle disinfectant around Hereford.'

'To get rid of the Hunter stains.'

'The hunk who hired you, right?'

'Mick Hunter. Scion of an influential ecclesiastical family with strong political connections. Classic candidate for the fast-track.'

'And was he *really*... you know?'

'Working the night shift? As Huw Owen would put it. *Did* put it, in fact. Well, you know, it wasn't that simple, really. Leave the theology out of it, and you might just be looking at an atheist and a sex addict. Hung out in dark alleyways in his youth, thus exposing himself to blackmail later.'

'Not good for a bishop, mind.'

'Hardly the first to abuse his position. They're appointed for their managerial skills, not their spirituality. Admittedly, it was more spectacular than most. But... they put the lid on it quickly enough by appointing Bernie Dunmore. A nice man but essentially a time-server. Bernie just picked up the crozier and carried on as if nothing had happened. But, yeah, even though it never quite came out, it embarrasses some people to this day. Hence Innes.'

She didn't look at Abbie, knew she was underplaying it. But Abbie had picked it up anyway. She turned off the taps, serious now.

'So Craig's specific mission, Merrily, is to get rid of anything that smells of Hunter.'

'And, yes, to some people in the general vicinity of Canterbury

I *stink* of Hunter. Christ, wrong words.' Throwing up both hands. 'No, I bloody *didn't* sleep with him, why does everybody—? All right, he probably wanted to, if only to make sure of me. Youngish woman given a significant job she was far from qualified for, by a famous lech in purple, how could it *not* have gone that way? That's more or less what Innes said in a discussion with the Archdeacon, secretly recorded by … a friend.'

'Look, I didn't mean to—'

'Huw Owen,' Merrily said. 'Huw confronted Innes and, I think, reminded him about one of his early successes. A woman who believed she was being haunted. Who he'd sent to a psychiatrist and who went on to take her own life.'

'Jenny Roberts.'

'You know.'

'Everybody down there knows about Jenny, but only people in the Job know about Craig Innes virtually telling her she was mentally ill.' Abbie pulled her bag over, drew out a packet of cigarettes. 'You want one?'

'I'm vaping now. But… No, all right, go on.' Accepting a cig. 'Got to be an extractor fan in here somewhere.'

'Well…' Abbie lit up. '… thank you so much for telling me all this, Merrily. I just didn't want to drop anybody in it without a good reason. Even Crowden, who probably has his problems.'

'I'm sure.'

'He won't remember me.' Abbie put away her lighter. 'We only met the once, very briefly. In my nervous, no make-up, sleeves-rolled-down days, this was. Craig had an old friend to stay for a weekend. Introduced as a man he played rugby with at college.'

'I had him down as a wrestler.'

'Scrum-half, I think. Put a bit of weight on since then.'

Merrily stared up at the sunken lights in the false ceiling.

'You were right. It… it could almost've been him talking in there. Innes. Keep it simple. Throw the good book at it or leave it to the shrinks.'

'Soulmates, Merrily. If that's the word. This is all about fitting the Church into the real world. Saving it from itself. First, lose your loonies – that's us.'

'And you learned about the mission to adjust Hereford history... how?'

'I think you'll find they all know out there.' Abbie waving her cig at the door. 'One or two had calls from Paul, asking about you. His first meeting of the Legion, first time in Ledwardine, didn't want to put his foot in it – that's what he was saying. It was clear he wanted to know what people thought about you. Did they like you? The way you worked.'

'*What?*'

Merrily watched her illicit smoke rising to the ceiling lights. She felt like a lab rat enclosed in glass. Maybe there was a CCTV pinhole camera fitted into the Tampax machine.

'Paul's not the subtlest of implements, is he?' Abbie said, 'so maybe Craig *wants* you to know.'

'He wants me to *quit*, Abbie. This confrontation between Innes and Huw Owen. I wasn't there, but Huw threw Jenny Roberts at him and as good as told him to get off my back. And then it got... Anyway, since then, no contact between Innes and me. Not that there was much before. He works through other people.'

'That'll make it worse,' Abbie said. 'He didn't like Huw to start off with.'

'Like Huw gives a toss.'

'Not the point, Merrily, you're in the middle. Never mind the Hunter legacy, the last thing he'll want is a good mate of Huw's in your position. I get it now.'

Merrily took a pull on the cigarette. Getting rid of a vicar, as they both knew, was not easy. Not without evidence of serious malpractice, robbing the parish, messing with the choir...

'And Crowden turning up here today as... what? Some kind of agent provocateur? Warn us *all* off?'

'I don't think it's about all of us,' Abbie said. 'Not yet,

anyway. He's made a start and when we go back in there, or maybe after lunch, he'll be going to work on you proper. Now... you're obviously knackered. Go back in there, you'll say the wrong things. He'll *make* you say the wrong things. He's a bully. You'll get home and realize what you should've said, only it'll be too late.'

'It's a private meeting.'

'If you think *that*...'

'He's not being very discreet, is he? If he's out there blatantly singing from the Innes hymn sheet and noting the reactions to feed back to his mate, he must know I'm going to put it together at some stage.'

'But if it adds to your paranoia and you leave under your own steam... *Result*.' Abbie caught cigarette ash in her left hand. 'Pat on the back for Craig. Job done. Now *go*.'

'What?'

'Bugger off. I'll tell them you were called away. Dying parishioner, I'll think of something.'

'Abbie, I'm supposed to be hosting the entire—'

'You probably know the back entrance better than I do.'

Abbie shouldered her bag, swung back the toilet door, exposing the short, deserted passage.

'Zapping the cat,' she said. 'How bloody heartless is that, Merrily?'

9

No mates

AT ONE TIME he would've been jeering, watching for boob-swing as she took off her parka. Never the subtlest kid on the school bus.

And never a mate. Not at all. Not since that night, a few years ago, which had looked like it was going to end in something close to rape. Which, given the company he was keeping at the time…

On his own, mind, Dean Wall had never been a threat. He looked wary, almost worried, when she pulled out a chair at his table in the Ox, with its brown paintwork, its varnish and its coloured bulbs. Ledwardine's number two pub, kept drab and utility; serious drinkers liked that.

'How're you, Jane? Get you one?'

If he'd noticed she was limping, he hadn't commented. He'd had the table to himself, between the bar and the broken jukebox where he'd usually be found at lunchtime. Since the last time she'd seen him, he'd shaved off his beard, which couldn't have taken long. He must be twenty, now, maybe twenty-one. A year ahead of her at school, but without the beard he looked like a big kid again.

'I'll get them.' She hung her parka on the back of the chair, nodded at his pint cider glass. 'Same again?'

'Er… yeah. All right. Ta, Jane.'

Now he *did* look worried. You had to laugh. The four months suspended was for possession with intent, but she really couldn't see him as a career criminal. With Dean, it would've been all about image. Proudly collecting his gear in a plastic carrier bag from a maisonette with a steel-reinforced front door on the Plascarreg estate in Hereford. Would never have occurred to him that he might actually get nicked for it. Not out here in the sticks.

He'd be walking on eggshells now, stepping over pavement cracks. Accepting he just wasn't destined to reach the same plateau as the Hereford club owner Rajab Ali Khan, whose expensive car had recently been stupidly vandalized by his younger brother, Jude Wall, while parked outside Ledwardine vicarage. Mr Khan, who would probably never have a criminal record or place an elegant shoe on the Plascarreg, believed he owed Mum for spiritual assistance – Jane happy to capitalize on this for as long as it lasted, Dean Wall being shit-scared of Mr Khan.

She came back from the bar, put down his cider and a half for herself.

'Just looking for a bit of information, Dean. In confidence.'

He didn't reply. Jane sat down and swallowed some cider: too dry, too rough, the kind that gave her heartburn. Never mind.

'Aidan Lloyd,' she said.

He didn't look at her.

'He's dead, Jane.'

'Yeah, well I know *that*.'

About all she did know, except that he'd had the ability to dowse water without implements, which was interesting. She put down her glass and leaned back.

'He get his dope from you, Dean?'

'Aw *shit*!'

Wall sat up hard, scraping his chair, spilling his cider.

About a dozen people in the bar, mostly men; none of them had been looking at Wall, but now they were. Jane smiled and then felt a little sad, remembering being in here with Colette Cassidy, years ago, both of them underage drinkers, wondering aloud if Dean Wall, aged about sixteen at the time, actually shagged sheep.

'Somebody tell you to ask me that, Jane?'

Wall's eyes had narrowed. She remembered thinking that night that if they were much further apart he'd actually look like a sheep. What patronizing little bitches they'd been.

'Nobody told me to ask you anything,' Jane said. 'Until ten minutes ago, I didn't know we'd be having this discussion.'

'Just I'm fed up of this, Jane. Like it's me who fuckin' killed him?'

'So he *did* get his—'

'No! The answer's no, all right? He din't get nothin' off me. Didn't hardly know him. Nobody did. All I knows about Lloyd is some migrant van driver flattened him on the back road. Buggers shouldn't be let in. None of 'em can drive for shit.'

'So where *did* Aidan get his weed?'

'*I* don't know, do I? Listen…' Wall leaning across the table. 'I wound up doin' the trade in the ole black and white villages for… just mates, it was, at first, and then it's mates of mates. And then it gets outer hand and some of the posh bastards from Off comes sniffin' round. The kind as likes a couple of spliffs after their dinner parties?'

Wow. Dealer to the gentry. No way he could convince her he hadn't been loving that at the time.

'I reckon that was where it all went to shit.' He stared into his cloudy cider. 'Previously, the stock I had in, you could pass it off as personal use. What I reckon is one of the rich bastards muster shopped me, 'cos suddenly the law's all over me. So now I'm layin' off, all right? Not worth going away for. Plus, everybody's killing theirselves with legal highs these days, anyway. You can't compete there.'

'Unless it's on health grounds, have you tried that?'

His eyes narrowed, as much as Dean's eyes ever could, and then he got it and smiled.

'You want the truth, Jane? After Lloyd got hisself killed, I was scared they was gonner be down on me again. Them bastards, if they want you for dealing and they can't prove it's you, they'll just plant some gear on you.'

'Why would they bother?'

''Cos Lloyd's ole man's a bloody big farmer and he en't exac'ly gonner be over the moon about this, is he?'

'No. Probably not.'

'He's gonner want a bloody scalp.'

'It's not the Wild West, Dean.'

'En't it?'

His eyes swivelling. Nobody was looking at them now, but Jane recognized a couple of blokes as farmers. A strange, marginal world, agriculture. Men with hundreds of acres around them who still could feel paranoid. Millionaires, on paper, with old patched jackets and no cash to spare. These guys drinking in the Ox because the beer was a couple of pence cheaper than the Swan's.

'So what is it with Aidan Lloyd?' Dean said.

'I thought you might know.'

Wall frowned.

'All one way with you, ennit, Jane? Don't tell nothin' to the peasants, they wouldn't get it.'

'That's not fair.'

'Should listen to yourself.'

Jane drank some cider. It was all an act, anyway. Truth was, even as a kid of fifteen she'd been a bit scared of Wall and his mates, what they might do, although you must never let them know that. Was it about *respect*? Was it still that primitive? Because kids *were* primitive; out here or on some city estate, territorial issues were the same. But then they weren't kids any more.

She sighed.

'So you weren't a mate of Aidan Lloyd?'

'Never give up, do you, girl?' He looked weary, suddenly.

'No, we wasn't mates. He was ten years older'n me. More. Allus the bloody same, ennit? Somebody gets splattered all over the road, and it's in the paper, everybody knew him, everybody was his mate. Listen, he hadn't *got* no mates. Not from yere. Even these blokes who come for his funeral and stayed all night we din't know 'em from—'

'Hang on.' Jane sat up. 'What blokes?'

Dean Wall said nothing. Jane didn't look at him, tried hard to dampen her excitement, keep it casual.

'We're talking about some blokes who went to the funeral but, like, didn't go home afterwards?'

'Are we?'

'Come *on*, Dean...' Damn, she couldn't hold it. '*What blokes?*'

'I still don't get what you're after, Jane.'

She sank back into her chair. Don't say any more.

Dean Wall thought for a few seconds, half smiling, then came slowly to his feet. Walked over to the bar where a fat guy they called Bing, son of the licensee, was playing some game on his tablet. Bing didn't look up.

'Same again, Dean?'

'Not yet. I needs a word.'

Dean looked over his shoulder. No sign of anybody else coming to the bar. Jane edged her chair a little closer, leaned forward to listen.

'Them fellers you had B & B the other night,' Dean said. 'Where'd they come from?'

'Who wants to know?'

Bing prising himself away from his tablet, a bit irritated. Dean put both arms on the sodden beermats on the bar, leaned in, lowering his voice.

'Police en't been in yet, then?'

Jane saw Bing shove his tablet under the bar.

'You on about?'

Leaning in towards Dean who shuffled further up the bar,

turning his big back to Jane so that she lost the conversation, which went on for several minutes until Dean eased back and pointed a finger.

'But you was nosy, Bing, right?'

'Gotter be a bit careful…'

'Still sounds like a bloody joke, mind.'

Couple of minutes later, Dean Wall came back to the table, didn't sit down. Picked up his cider, drained the glass, wiped his mouth and nodded at the door. Jane stood up and pulled her parka from the back of the chair.

Outside, it was raining harder. Jane dragged on her parka and Dean went back into the Ox's porch to light up a cig. An ordinary cig. He peered out through the smoke, grinning like a troll.

'You owes *me* now, Jane,' he said.

10

Wrongness

IT WAS LONGER and tortuous, but there was no other way of getting back to the vicarage without crossing the square and being seen from the Black Swan.

Hooded and anonymous in the downpour, she was going to ground in her own parish. Another intimation that this was the beginning of the end. So many omens now, and coming faster like the rain.

Down into Old Barn Lane, conical Cole Hill glowering through the weather as if in judgement. Cowardice. Was it? Probably. *He'll be going to work on you.* What could Crowden do, for heaven's sake? Priests argued, always had, always would. You followed your own spiritual path, listened to the silence. Or that was how it used to be. It also used to be concealed blades and whispers in darkened cloisters. Now you could be shafted in an email.

The rain came in harder, grim and grey, better than fog but only just, as she went the back way, past baby-pink new homes, the kind of flat-pack housing that seemed to go up overnight. Finally dropping down through three centuries into Church Street with its crooked cottages climbing organically from the river.

She crossed the street and walked up to the vicarage just around the corner, let herself in and went through to the kitchen. Nobody there except Ethel watching from her bed near the stove, deciding it wasn't worth getting up.

'Jane?' She walked back into the hall, called up the stairs. 'Jane!'

Evidently gone out. Too much to expect her to rest the ankle.

Merrily caught sight of her face in the hall mirror, wet hair stuck to her furrowed forehead, recoiled. *Bit fragile, to be honest.*

She spun away, went back outside and found herself across the road, where the cobbles of the square, with its few shops, gave way to the tarmac of Church Street and a small nameplate said *Lucy's Cottage.*

Lol had had it made after Jane had said there ought to be an official blue plaque. Merrily stood there at the window, saw him at the desk, backlit by the woodstove, the Boswell guitar across a knee. His lyric pad would be open on the desk with his iPhone in memo mode for the tunes. Lol had taken to working strict hours, like he had a proper job, and perhaps that was what it had become.

He spotted her. She found a smile, pushed back her hood and Lol sprang up – how many times had she done this: *Sanctuary, sanctuary* – and then he was standing in the open doorway in his old grey sweatshirt with the fading Roswell alien across the chest, peering at her over his glasses.

'So, um… what happened to the Legion?'

'Infiltrated,' Merrily said, 'by an emissary from the Witchfinder General.'

Feeling the sting of either rain or tears.

Jane let herself into the vicarage. Hung her parka next to Christ with his lantern, kicked off her boots, hurried up to her apartment in the attic.

There had to be images and they had to be better ones than the faintly comic pictures in her head. She stood at the window, looking down between the vicarage trees to the square, where the fog had been shredded by the rain, exposing a darkening sky, clouds low and leathery.

Behind her, the computer cheeped and groaned, while she went over it all again in her head: what Dean Wall had told her in the porch at the Ox. Something so far from what she'd expected that it really did, as he'd said, seem like a joke.

Dean – you could underestimate his ingenuity – getting some things out of Bing by telling him the police were interested. He hadn't got everything – no names, for a start – but it was enough for now. Essentially, she was faced with a whole tradition about which she knew next to nothing. A man-thing, surely. Like dominoes and darts. An archaic, uncool, plodding man-thing.

The computer settled and she sat down in front of the screen and went into Google Images, thinking it might take some time. But it didn't take long at all, although it was still crazy.

Lol made tea and listened. Built up the logs in the wood stove and listened. Watched the day darken and went on listening to Merrily, while picking up stray echoes of Prof Levin.

You don't want to come back from some distant gig to find cases packed.

It didn't even need a distant gig. You came back from one fog-related overnight in the granary at Knight's Frome to hear about the Bishop at work again, but that was only this morning.

As for last night…

He slammed the stove door.

'What were you *thinking*, going out there?'

He'd talked in depth to Huw Owen – just the two of them – only once. Merrily had told him how Huw had tried to talk her out of deliverance, telling her how, as a female exorcist, she'd become a target for *every psychotic grinder of the dark satanic mills that ever sacrificed a chicken.* Memorable. It had stuck with Lol, too, and he'd asked Huw about it. Huw had smiled. *I thought it sounded a bit bloody daft at the time, if I'm honest, lad. Like the script for one of them cheap TV ghost shows, where all the ghosts are demons and every house has a portal to hell. But I'm glad you've remembered it.*

'What else could I do?' Merrily said. 'I'm just sorry I let Jane go with me. But then, what would I have done to stop her?'

'Who were they?'

'I don't *know*.'

'Could they have known you'd seen them?'

'Don't think so.'

'Was it some kind of religious…?'

'You mean was it satanic? I don't know what that word means any more.'

She'd sat on the sofa and kicked off her shoes. She had on a cowl-neck sweater and jeans. What little make-up she was wearing had run and dried. She looked a mess. She looked heartbreakingly wonderful.

He said, 'You could've called me. I would've come back, you know that. Might've taken a while, but—'

'And you might've piled into the back of a long-distance lorry in blanket fog. And if you'd been there, too… I don't know. I don't know what would've happened. Maybe nothing good. In the end, nothing was damaged except Jane's ankle. And a night's sleep. And now I don't know where Jane's gone or if her ankle…'

'She seems OK. She's been past here twice.'

'Going where?'

'No idea. Would hardly be surprising if she'd been up to the churchyard, though, would it?'

'No.' Her eyes clenched shut. 'I *really* thought I knew this place. I thought we were all…'

Marry me, Lol thought, a persistent ache awakening. *Please marry me.*

'There are no havens any more,' Merrily said. 'Nowhere's safe. Everywhere gets infiltrated.'

'But there's nothing in the churchyard this morning. You did say you'd—'

'No. Nothing there. It might never've happened. It might – whatever it was – be all over.'

He sat down on the rug, opposite her.

'But not for you,' he said.

Knowing instinctively what she was thinking.

The word 'portal', Huw had said, *is much misused. In the American ghost shows, it's always in the basement, next to the washing machine or the chest freezer. In reality it's in here.* Tapping his head. *Or here.* His heart. *Or, if you want to get really technical, there.* His solar plexus. *Or it's a far bigger and still uncharted area... like, for instance, the women's ministry. We're all too shit scared of being accused of sexism to say it, but the women's priesthood's still new enough to be a magnet for mad bastards. Let's not say it but, bloody hell, we need to be aware of it.*

'You're wondering if things like this never happened before you came,' Lol said softly. 'And if they'd stop happening if you weren't here.'

'I don't know. What I do know is I keep running away. Last night I ran away from whatever was in the churchyard—'

'Yeah, but you had no—'

'And this morning, just now, I ran away from Paul Crowden. I should've gone back in. Taken him on.'

'I don't think so. Your mate from Merthyr was probably right. A trap? I mean, I wouldn't know about that, but it can't do any harm to make a few quiet enquiries before you get drawn in.'

'Oh, and yesterday, I buried a man I really knew nothing about. I mean, how...' Her eyes widening. 'How could I have done that? All the warnings you get in the deliverance ministry about the dangers of the perfunctory funeral. And I did that. I conducted a perfunctory funeral.'

'But it was what they wanted, no fuss. You were in their hands. They could've had him buried without a minister at all, if they'd wanted. Couldn't they?'

'Not in my churchyard.'

She smiled. He wanted to weep. Should they discuss marriage before or after he told her that the TV commercial for mature people's mortgages would not, after all, be securing their financial future?

'So you're making a definite connection with the funeral,' he said. 'With the Lloyds.'

'Not sure.'

'In the churchyard, apart from the shock and everything, you got a sense of…'

'Wrongness,' Merrily said. 'There was an overpowering sense of wrongness, which I've avoided talking about to Jane, because Jane's still attracted to paganism, and if that's what we saw…'

'Evil?'

'That's a much deeper word.'

Lol watched Merrily cupping her face in her hands, gazing into the stove. He felt helpless.

'Wrongness all down the line.' Her eyes seemed to lose focus. 'From a cold funeral to some clandestine ritual in the fog that I can't ask questions about because *A*, the family wouldn't want it, and *B*…'

'B is for Bishop,' Lol said.

He stood up and walked over to the window.

'That shouldn't stop me,' Merrily said. 'When the inevitable happens, I'll just be regretting all the significant things I didn't do in an effort to keep my job a little bit longer.'

Lol could see that the rain had thinned but the clouds hadn't gone anywhere. It was going to be a short day. In his head, Prof Levin said, *Don't tell me there isn't a part of you that secretly hopes this business with the Bishop will drive her out of the damn Church once and for all.*

'Jane,' he said.

'That's another problem.'

'No, I mean Jane's coming across the street. Barely limping at all.'

11

Crow-people

A LONG TIME since Merrily had seen Jane like this. A rare excite-ment. Face flushed under a tumble of hair. Burning up with something. A reminder of how, when you were nineteen, your whole life could accelerate past something in minutes, blowing off night-fears like exhaust.

'Not interrupting anything, am I?' Jane sinking into Lol's battered sofa, clearly not caring what she was interrupting. 'I just need... confirmation that I'm not losing my mind?'

A glance at Lol and then back at Merrily, who knew what she was asking.

'He knows about last night. All of it. Where've you been?'

'Been making myself useful for what seems like the first time in weeks. Talking to people you wouldn't think of approaching.' Jane took a long breath, let it go and stood up, moving across to the desk and Lol's laptop. 'Can I?'

'Just save what's on there first, would you, Jane?' Lol said. 'It's probably crap, but...'

Jane grinned briefly and nodded, saving the document and inserting a memory stick.

'Don't dismiss this till you see it properly. It's from the Net. Not exactly the Dark Net or anything. On the surface, this is all so innocent you'll probably laugh. Though *I'm* not laughing.'

Merrily saw she was actually quite angry.

'Jane, when you said you'd talked to people, you didn't *tell* anybody—?'

'No! Of course I didn't. Not a word. I just asked questions

70

about Aidan Lloyd. Who nobody seemed to know anything about until he got killed and then they were all over him. And his dope.'

'Quite.'

'What you're about to see isn't likely to get anyone too interested, either. It's not illegal, it's not irreligious – not that anybody would give a toss about that – and it's not—'

'Jane,' Merrily said. 'Just run it.'

Flashing a glance at Lol, who went to sit down on the sofa, hands clasped on his knees.

Jane stepped away from the desk.

'I need to give you the background first.'

The Ox. It was always the Ox. A scruffy pub with a far more interesting clientele, when you thought about it, than the more upmarket Black Swan, even though it only had two rooms available for overnight stays, three in an emergency.

Jane explained how they'd come in two Land Rovers. Seven or eight of them. They'd block-booked the Ox, paid up front. All male. Two of them had grey beards, a couple had local accents. Jane said Bing had thought he might've recognized one of them but he wasn't sure.

'*He* told you all this? Bing?'

'Kind of.'

If these strangers had gone to Aidan Lloyd's funeral, they hadn't turned up at the tea at the Black Swan, attended mainly by other farmers Merrily recognized.

'Back to the Ox afterwards?'

'Where they apparently spent the night drinking,' Jane said, 'though not excessively. They'd asked Bing for a key, saying they might want to go out later and walk it off.'

'How much later?'

'Put it this way, he watched them leave not long before midnight. Bing was a bit suspicious. Unusual for him, must've been something about them. He looked out of an upstairs window and saw them on the little car park at the back, unpacking what looked like a couple of those long cricket bags from the back of one of the Land Rovers. And then they took off their funeral gear and got changed behind the vehicles. Then they put on overcoats or whatever, to cover it all up, and just walked off. Over the river bridge and out of the street lights, and he didn't see them after that. Anyway, I went down there, and I'm guessing they took the footpath on the right, after the bridge.'

'Across the fields? Around what's left of the orchard?'

'Where they'd be able to pick up the old coffin path and follow it to the churchyard the back way. Bing didn't follow them, obviously, he wasn't *that* curious. I'm guessing, if he thought there was anything iffy he just didn't want to be involved. Landlords, I mean it's all about discretion if you want to keep your clientele. Also, some of them were big blokes, apparently.'

'Mmm.'

Merrily wondering what had led Jane to the Ox. Also trying to equate an all-male, post-funeral night out with the apparition in the fog.

'He wouldn't've found it that iffy, anyway.' Jane brought the laptop over to the coffee table by the wood stove. 'Must've seemed like a joke.'

She tapped the pressure pad and the YouTube video came up, in black and white.

No, it was in colour. It was just the central figures that weren't.

A dull day somewhere in middle England. The camera pulling back to expose a holiday-type crowd lining what looked like a town square, bunting strung between lamp-posts and trees displaying a first pale glimmer of spring greenery.

The black and white figures in the middle carried sticks. Otherwise, they were like Victorian beggars in greasy-looking bowler hats and jackets ripped into strips. Like clothing thrown away, Merrily thought, after being attacked with a Stanley knife by some embittered wife.

'It's called a rag jacket,' Lol said.

Merrily turned to him in surprise.

'Um, I *think*,' he said.

Their faces were blackened. They moved around like big spiders and then faced one another, the jackets suddenly spraying out like feathers. A smack of sticks as they closed in. Laughter. And then the music began.

'There were several clips to choose from,' Jane said when it was over. 'That was the clearest, but this is the one that brought the shivers on.'

In the second clip they were in silhouette against a sunrise. Raggedy crowlike things prancing on some hilltop, devilish.

'This is definitely the version that originates around here. I don't know how we've managed to avoid them.'

'We haven't,' Merrily said. 'It's just that the local ones I've seen are not like this. They're more... you know, white shirts and flowers in the hats?'

Thinking how, when she was a kid, in another part of the country, morris dancing, like the maypole, had been all about little girls and handkerchiefs and posies. Not that she'd ever participated; even then, when she was about nine, it had seemed silly and twee.

'This is Border morris,' Lol said as the crow-people flapped and spun. 'Not too many around these days. Couple up in Shropshire, but I think the only ones left in Herefordshire are down in Ledbury and Bromyard. And Leominster, of course.'

Merrily turned away from the screen to look at Lol. His expression was hard to read.

'How do you know all this?'

'Because, I...'

He looked slightly embarrassed now. Jane's mouth fell open.

'Oh Lol, you *didn't*!'

73

'Well, not for long. It was ages ago, before the band took off. We did a gig at a pub in the Cotswolds and there was morris dancing – Cotswold, obviously, rather than Border – and I... just kind of wound up getting in with the dancers. I was no good at it, but it was... fun. Then one of them was diagnosed with a cardiac problem and it all fell apart.'

Merrily said, 'So you're saying if *you'd* seen them last night, you'd've recognized...'

'I wouldn't like to say that.'

Jane froze the video.

'Mum, it was foggy, and it was totally unexpected, and all we were aware of was some kind of sluggish movement. You would not, even if you knew about this stuff, automatically think morris dancing.'

She started up the daytime dance again. A small band – accordion, guitar, fiddle – provided the slow, deliberate music. At one stage a song started up, about an old woman tossed up in a basket, nineteen times as high as the moon. No smiles, no element of playing to the crowd, no suggestion of friendship among the dancers. White men with black faces – could you even get away with that these days?

They met abruptly and sprang apart, leaving a *clack* in the air.

Not the *thock* of last night. Perhaps those sticks had been muffled.

If not the intent. You got the impression of a restrained savagery as the wind spread the coats out into streamers, like they'd been through a paper-shredder, and the bells rattled on their calves.

'I think it was the bells that gave it away to Bing,' Jane said. 'They took the bells, on these leather pads, out of one of the cricket bags. Then evidently decided not to wear them. Too noisy? We didn't hear them anyway.'

'And muffled the sticks. Some of this is not quaint,' Merrily said, 'not gentle, not picturesque. Quite... bleak.'

'And you're not laughing,' Jane said. 'You're not even picturing Lol in bells.'

One of the dancers split from the others, let out a feral roar. The crowd laughed nervously.

'Aggression,' Merrily said. 'Testosterone.'

She did not feel good about this. The apparent explanation was far from enlightening. It should have made her embarrassed about the very real fear she'd felt last night, but watching the ragged figures on the screen doing their wintry dance only brought it back, and it was still very real.

'What does it mean? Anybody?'

In the stove, a log collapsed into orange-white ash.

'A new grave?' Jane said. 'On a *new grave*?'

'Yes.'

Aidan Lloyd not twelve hours buried and some men had come out of the night, along the coffin path, to dance on his grave.

12

Having a laugh

IT WASN'T A crime. She didn't see how it could be a crime. And yet...

On Lol's laptop a different bunch of Border morris men were dancing on a hill against a deep grey sky. The music – accordion, concertina, drum – was slow and seismic, like rock strata shifting. A suggestion of entirely unexpected menace, like Santa Claus coming down the chimney with a machete.

Jane scowled and stood up. Lol took over her place at the laptop and lost the sinister dance.

'What you mean is,' Jane said, 'it isn't against the law to dance on a grave.'

'It isn't even trespass, flower, it's just weird and sick. Practical application of an old cliché.' Merrily looked at Lol. 'Was it Elvis Costello, that song where he didn't quite say it was about Margaret Thatcher?'

'I think Costello was just offering to tread the dirt down,' Lol said. 'Whether he ever did is anybody's guess. Probably not.'

'Could it be a breach of the peace? A hate crime?'

'Might just be an expression of extreme, if perverse, joy,' Jane said. 'Somebody's delighted that Aidan Lloyd's gone.'

'You sense any joy last night, flower?'

Jane just walked over to the window and glared into the fading light over the vicarage across the road. Merrily saw her reflection in the glass, and it was like looking into a hazy mirror. Only twenty years between them. In another twenty they'd be at opposite ends of middle-age. She was feeling achingly tired now.

'Breach of the peace.' Lol looking up from the laptop. '"Where harm is done or is likely to be done to a person or their property in their presence, or they're in fear of being harmed through assault, affray, riot or other disturbance." Doesn't mention the dead.'

'I'm prepared to say I was afraid of being harmed,' Jane said. 'I could say it was why we buggered off.'

'And did nothing,' Merrily said.

'Just because we haven't done anything yet...' Jane spinning back into the room. 'We do have to. You know that.'

'What if it was just a few blokes...'

The words slipped lamely away. Jane waited, expressionless.

'... having a laugh?' Merrily said. 'Blokes having a laugh. Or they did it for a bet.'

'That's what you really think, is it, Mum?'

'I just ask the question. It's not that silly. Or at least not much sillier than the whole—'

'It's bloody *not* silly. Were you there last night, or what?'

'They were drunk.'

'No! They'd been drinking, but not to excess, according to Bing, and he should know. And no spontaneity about this, no conspicuous... merriment. They'd come with the serious intention of doing what they did. All carefully planned. Even the route. The coffin path.' Jane turned to Lol. 'Am I wrong? Is there any other way of looking at this?'

'The question is, were these real morris dancers?' Lol said. 'Where from? You really want to ring up Leominster Morris and ask if they have a tradition of grave-dancing?'

'It did not feel good, Lol. Mum knows that. In all kinds of ways. Unhealthy. Although when...' Jane not quite meeting Merrily's eyes. '... when I said *we* had to do something, I didn't necessarily mean you.'

'Oh, right,' Merrily said. 'Thank you. That's me off the hook, then.'

'Jesus wept...'

77

'Well, what *could* we do? Jane, we're the only witnesses and we didn't accost them. Our word against eight of them? Even if we found out who they were, it'd just be raking up something that's going to distress relatives. You just have to accept that sometimes there are things that are never going to be entirely—'

The phone chimed in her bag on the floor and she brought it out.

It was Abbie Folley. Merrily covered the phone.

'Sorry, I think I need to take this.'

Lol let her into the kitchen and closed the door behind her.

Abbie said the Legion meeting had lasted no more than an hour after lunch. Clive Wells, already out on a limb with his Anglo-Catholicism, had fielded Crowden's question about the wisdom of referring to their group, even ironically, as the Legion. Not the funniest of jokes, Clive had said wearily, but it was a way of discouraging higher clergy. The Legion was a low-key, entirely unofficial gathering for the workers at the coalface. An opportunity to unload. Extra-mural. Off the record.

'Anybody ask where I'd gone?'

'I told them you weren't looking at all well and I'd persuaded you to go home. Lot of truth in that. Bit worried now, mind, that I said the wrong things. Don't want you thinking I'm some kind of conspiracy theorist. Although, fair play, I am, obviously. Couldn't grow up in my family without thinking they were watching you round the bloody clock.'

'They?'

'The Tory government, in my dad's case. Overreacting – would've taken half the spooks in Whitehall to keep tabs on all the red-hot Marxists in our valley. I don't want to overreact, but he was the first to leave. After you didn't come back.'

'Look… don't worry about me. I'll find out somehow what Crowden's doing, and if I'm the only one in the firing line I can either slip quietly away or I can sit tight and wait for it either to blow over or… blow up. There's nothing I can actually—'

Do. Nothing I can do. Just like she'd said to Jane. She felt a sudden contempt for herself. Yes, the deliverance ministry was about keeping your head down, wasn't a licensed role in any diocese, was as important or as negligible as any individual bishop saw fit to make it, but...

'It's *not just you.*' Abbie's voice growing almost shrill. 'You're not getting the sense of an attack on the whole ethos? What I'm saying, Merrily, is it looks like they're using you as a warning for all of us on where not to go. Like, all the times you've worked with the police. All right, never exactly been all over the papers, but it's pretty well-known. I'm thinking Crowden's repeated use of the term *psychic investigator*...'

'Yeah, well, I'm not psychic, never claimed to be, but it's like Nick Cowan said, we might be dealing with frightened people but they're not gullible any more.'

'What we're *dealing* with,' Abbie said, 'is the nearest most people get to... I'm not going to call it God... ineffable, he is. Make of him what you want. Call him a metaphor for the positive. *We're* never going to bloody well know, not in this life. Best we can hope for is a sense of something at work. But most of what we actually get is a sense of... you know?'

'Lesser phenomena.'

'Lesser phenomena... listen, that in itself... that can be bloody blinding when it happens to you. My mother? Did I *tell* you about my mam? What really got me into this madness?'

'Because they were atheists?'

'My dad's talking to me again now. My mam never did. At least... not while she was alive.'

'I'm sorry, I didn't know.'

'Angina. Complications. Sixty-two.'

'I'm sorry.'

'Sorry. That's what I heard *her* say. *I'm sorry, sugar.* Always used to call me sugar, my mam. The night she died – went in her sleep in hospital, she did, none of us knew till next morning – but that night she's standing by my pillow, in my flat. *I'm sorry, sugar*. My mam, this is, who didn't believe in God or his angels. In a white dress. And I wasn't dreaming and I hadn't been drinking. So when Crowden's talking about bereavement apparitions and patronizing old ladies for their *comfort-projections*, that really pisses me off, you know?'

'Right.'

'We're the only ones inside this bloody great asylum we still call the Church… the only ones helping people make sense of that kind of experience. Assure them they're not loopy. End of the day, we might be crap, but officially we're all there is. And they want to get rid of us? Don't you bloody dare slip quietly away into that good night.'

Merrily smiled. It was exactly what she wanted to do. Jane, too, probably, but they needed to get something to eat first. And, oh God, it was Sunday tomorrow and she had a sermon to finish.

'I'm not going anywhere,' she said.

It was colder now. Lol opened up the stove to a red bed, Jane carefully kneeling down and handing him small logs from the back of the inglenook.

'She's in denial, you know. Don't know if it's because she doesn't want to attract attention from the Bishop or just doesn't want to worry me, but there was something happening last night that was not good, and it wasn't a joke.' Jane looked around. 'Lucy would know. You ever feel her looking over your shoulder?'

Lol said nothing, thinking that Lucy, when she was alive, hadn't always been easy to share a village with, never mind a house.

'Maybe Mum should give the Church the elbow and move in here. Now you're making serious money.'

'Yes, well that—'

'The Church is going to destroy her. Nasty. Always was, and especially now it's threatened with extinction. The level of nastiness inside an organization dedicated to spirituality... I mean, *you* know that.'

Lol closed the stove, stood up.

'Not your problem. You're going to university. You're going to be a leading archaeologist with a mystical aura, presenting ancient history programmes on the box.'

'Huh. If I learned anything in Pembrokeshire it was that, with so little money in archaeology nowadays, competition for TV jobs is cut-throat. And you have to write crap academic books that nobody wants just to look credible?'

Lol saw the old sadness forming around her. It didn't take much. He glanced at the kitchen door, checking it was closed, bringing his voice down to a murmur.

'You, uh, heard from, uh, Sam?'

Jane shook her head, hard, probably regretting she'd taken him into her confidence about the drunken night in Pembrokeshire, the sharing of a bed.

'Eirion?'

'Not recently.' She brushed flecks of bark from her sweater. 'Who am I kidding? It's well over. Eirion will have another girlfriend by now. He deserves another girlfriend. Somebody normal. Anyway...' Jane arranged herself on the rug, one of the hearth cushions under her ankle. '... did *you* know Aidan Lloyd?'

'Not at all.'

'That's the thing, see. We don't know anything about him. We don't know anybody with a reason to hate him. Except these guys who came especially to tread the dirt down. I am *not* letting this fade away. If Mum won't go after them, I might as well. Nothing better to do.'

'No more digs?'

'Probably are. If I texted Sam, she'd come up with something, but what's she going to be thinking? She's a nice woman, I don't want to lead her on.'

'No, I can... I can see the problem.'

'Meanwhile… I don't want to drop Mum into it, but these bastards are just… they're not getting away with it.'

The room was dim, but he thought he saw Jane's hand shake. She gripped the wrist with the other hand. Whatever had happened last night had genuinely frightened her, in her own village, and Jane would resent that.

'It's my responsibility. I heard them. Saw them. Got Mum out of bed.'

'Oh, Jane…'

'It's not like either of you can stop me, is it?'

'Yeah, well, I think we realize that, but—'

'But you could help. I mean you, not Mum. You could find them, couldn't you? You're booking people for the folk-fest. You might want some morris dancers.'

Oh God…

'We probably would, yeah.'

'You could talk to people. Ask around. They have to be from somewhere.'

'And what would we do when we'd found them?'

'Let's just find them,' Jane said.

'I think you should sleep on it. You're both knackered.'

Jane squirmed sideways to take the pressure off her ankle.

'And like what if they come back, Lol? What if they come back tonight?'

13

Best year

ANNIE HOWE'S DAY off tomorrow, so Bliss had driven over to her flat in Malvern, bringing a copy of the *Hereford Times*. She wouldn't have seen it; if she had she'd have called him on the mobile.

'I knew it was coming,' Annie said. 'He just didn't tell me when. He tells me very little now. For obvious reasons.'

They spread the paper across the breakfast bar, under the window with its vast view of the lights of what Bliss thought was the Severn Valley but had never bothered to ask.

Charlie's manifesto was page 3 lead.

EX-POLICE CHIEF'S PLEDGE
ON COUNTRY CRIME

A high-powered police task-force could be out targeting farm thieves if an ex-Hereford CID chief is elected next year as Police and Crime Commissioner for West Mercia.

'Rural areas have been poorly served by the police for decades,' says former Det. Chief Supt. Charles Howe, who launched his election campaign this week. 'I'll be working hard to restore traditional policing reinforced by modern crime-fighting technology.'

'The old twat,' Bliss said.

'He'll do well in Hereford,' Annie said, 'if only because hardly anybody votes for the Police Commissioners. So if, say, Countryside Defiance calls on all its members to make a special effort...'

'We know for a fact he's got them in his pocket?'

'We know they think they have him in theirs,' Annie said. 'Which is what my father *likes* these people to think. I had it from the leader of the council, who... well, you know where *he* stands.'

Bliss twisted uncomfortably on his high pine stool. He'd studied the other contenders. There was an Asian guy who'd probably pull a fair bit of support in the east of the region, but it was clear none of the buggers had Charlie's charisma, or his local knowledge. Or his ability to lie through a compassionate smile.

Annie finished reading then folded the paper very tightly.

'Francis, this can't be done. He's virtually talking about bringing back village policemen with... with SUVs and mountain bikes. Where's the money coming from?'

'Probably also telling Countryside Defiance he'll be gerrin the shotgun licence extended to include assault rifles. It's what he does, Annie. He bullshits.'

Still only weeks since he'd been invited into Charlie's house in Leominster to be shown a sequence of pictures of Annie, in trench coat and hat, walking from her car to his semi in Marden in the evening light. A final shot of them embracing in the living room, taken through his wide front window, with a long lens from across the road by some retired cop who'd worked for Charlie in the 1980s. *Sheer disbelief when I first saw these.* Charlie's expression blending horror and triumph. *Won't need to tell you how very disappointed I was in Anne.* Pause. *Love, is it?*

A rare sneer from Charlie, the subtext all too clear: time for Bliss to forget everything he knew about the old bastard's past, his only hope of preserving him and Annie. Annie who, for as long as any kind of relationship with Bliss survived, was *only nominally* Charlie's daughter.

He'd actually said that. A question of priorities.

Love. What did Charlie love? He loved power, and he'd tell you he loved Hereford. Which was part of the same illusion. Hereford was out on the edge of England, small and separate enough for a man to feel in charge... as head of CID, then senior councillor. As Police and Crime Commissioner he'd be close to untouchable.

Realistically, how would this end? *Where* would it end? Bliss had wondered about trying for a move across the border to Dyfed-Powys. Acquired a couple of contacts over there during the Hay operation last summer. He wasn't Welsh, but he *was* from Liverpool. Almost there.

And Annie? Where could Annie go? Gwent? West Midlands? It would be feasible to sustain a relationship with that geography, but not easy. Without a move, Annie's next big step up would be Head of West Mercia CID. Not remotely possible with Charlie as PCC, even if she hadn't known about his twisted history.

She'd be invited by Headquarters to move on, and she'd accept that. Annie, see... Annie was dead straight. *Because* of Charlie. Also clipped and cold and distant, while Charlie was cheerful, expansive, everybody's best mate. Annie was scared of having mates. Bliss didn't know any other copper who even liked her. She was the ice maiden.

For him too, until a particular winter's night when circumstance had fitted them together like parts of a machine. Working one another. Interlocking. He remembered worsening floods all over the county. And the seepage of high-level corruption. The night that had ended with the nailing of a senior planning officer dealing drugs, and glimpses of a corrupt quango involving Charlie as a county councillor.

And still that lavish public smile had come through undimmed.

Bliss looked across the breakfast bar at Charlie's daughter, still in her work clothes: blue suit, white blouse – more of a uniform than the uniforms wore – and no make-up. Angular and almost plain, you might think if you hadn't been privileged to watch the surface ice shiver and fragment like a sudden emergence of the aurora borealis in a hard winter sky.

It was very weird, this. She was nothing at all like squashy-lipped Kirsty, the estranged Mrs Bliss, the kind of woman he'd found irresistible since he was about thirteen. No, he couldn't begin to explain it.

He shuffled on the stool.

'Annie, I just… there's probably been better times to say this, but I never have. Just realized it's coming up to a year now, since…. you know?'

'Christmas,' Annie said.

'Yeh. And the New Year. And it's… been the best year, you know? Best year of my whole life.'

He stood up, embarrassed, went to look out of the kitchen window. He felt secure up here, a few miles out of the county, out of the division. Back home – if home it was any more – on nights when he was alone he'd often awaken dry-throated with dread. How *would* it end, if Charlie was elected, or if he wasn't? Not well either way. Bliss and Annie would either be finished or punished.

First of all – no way this wouldn't happen, if it hadn't already – Charlie would see that it was leaked to Kirsty who, with the advice of her old man and his lawyer, would work out how to capitalize on it.

Bliss watched the lights of what might have been the Severn Plain and saw them blur. He heard the squeak of Annie's stool as she came to her feet behind him.

'Don't say *anything*,' he said.

14

Initiation

It was a sub-culture, Prof Levin had said to Lol. Buried deep in English soil. You thought it was dead and gave it a poke and a bearded man rose up with a heavy stick and beat you around the head.

Long years ago this was, the first time he'd actually met Prof. Just a kid in a folk band they'd named Hazey Jane, after a song by Nick Drake who'd already been dead for years when they'd fallen ecstatically upon his albums. Poor Nick, destined to be twenty-six for ever.

The pages of the scrapbook were dry and browning. It hadn't been a very expensive scrapbook; a few years later, in another era, it would've been a file on a computer which would've crashed long ago, taking the memories with it.

Lol found the picture: him in a borrowed rag jacket of many colours and a daft straw hat with a ribbon. Looking suitably embarrassed outside a big pub on the edge of the Cotswolds that might've been called the Golden Ball. Hazey Jane had been booked to play there that night, supporting a bigger band, now so long gone that he couldn't remember their name, only that Prof Levin had been there to record them live. They'd all heard of Prof Levin and hoped he'd notice them and want to produce their music and make them almost-stars. So they'd come early, in time to take in the morris dancing in the afternoon on the pub forecourt.

Those of them who'd wanted to.

'Spare us.' Karl Windling, their bass player stomping off

to the bar to get into the real ale. 'Can't abide them fucking squeeze boxes.'

But Lol remembered being mildly fascinated, watching the morris men. Never seen the real thing before, performed by grizzled blokes to a rolling rhythm from a band with an accordion, a fiddle and a side drum, under a syrupy August sun. It had seemed very ancient, like a stone circle.

It would have been to avoid having to match Karl, pint for pint, that he'd slipped outside. The more you drank the better you thought your playing was. A common delusion.

It had been a humid afternoon. He remembered it occurring to him, sitting on the steps, that the dancers were not dancing to the music, the musicians were playing to the dance. Which seemed so strange that he'd waited for a drinks break and gone to ask one of them. Odd, him doing that; he'd been so shy. He remembered getting into a discussion with a bunch of them, then the great Prof Levin coming across, peering over his glasses.

'Only one way to find out, son.'

'I can't play the accordion. Or the fiddle.'

'Not what I meant.'

Then someone was putting the daft hat on his head. They were taking the piss, but he didn't mind too much. It was good to be outside.

'Just follow me, mate, do what I do.'

Bulky bloke with a ginger beard and an earring you could use to hang a curtain.

The music cranking up again, slow and crunchy as an old cement mixer.

'... now turn side-on...'

'... up with the foot, now...'

'... and again...'

'I can't do it. I've got no coordination.'

'Nah, nah, you're thinking about it too much. It's not about your mind. You gotta bypass all that, let your body do the business.'

'Like sex.' A voice from the doorway. Karl Windling, with a new pint. 'He can't get that together either.'

He supposed it had *all* been about getting away from Karl – the reason he'd kept going back to the Golden Ball, driving up to seventy miles in his little van. If one of the side hadn't turned up, they'd let Lol in, even though he was crap. They were very patient with him.

The night his body got the message it felt almost as if he'd left it. As if his awareness had become detached from the arms and the legs, the hands and the head that were operating like slow, primitive clockwork. He'd never forgotten that. Moments of initiation.

But then it was winter and by the next spring, Arthur, the leader, had been fitted with a pacemaker, there was new management at the Golden Ball – disco and karaoke – and the side had broken up and he never saw those guys again.

The morris had been good to Prof Levin. Still making money from an album he'd produced nearly twenty years ago from some crackly vintage recordings of a Herefordshire village concertina player who'd accompanied dancers. Prof using contemporary instrumentalists to add muscle to the music.

'Collector's item now,' he told Lol on the phone. 'I may reissue it again next year. On vinyl. With an album of old photos.'

'Nice.'

'Never goes away, Laurence. An obsession for quite a few people – the essence of what it means to be English. Reasserting itself in the face of all this Scottish and Welsh cultural pride. A lot of that's as much bollocks as the bleedin' awful bagpipes, but I've always been happy to go along with it all, long as it didn't get political.'

'What's at the heart of it, Prof? I never did work it out. Does it come out of pagan ritual?'

He was at his desk in the window, with the lamp on, the phone tucked under his chin, the scrapbook closed. He'd run over to Ledwardine Livres before they closed and Gus had unearthed a pocket-size second-hand copy of *The Morris Book* by Cecil Sharp and Herbert MacIlwaine, a reprint of the 1912 original.

'Let's not complicate things,' Prof said. 'Some of them ramble on about drawing their energy from the earth, some just like to get rat-arsed on real ale. I never thought too hard about it. The earliest mention of it's about the fifteenth century, and it was a courtly dance, then, probably imported. But that don't mean it didn't merge with some existing tribal thing.'

Lol had pencilled a heading, <u>BORDER MORRIS</u>, on a fresh page of his lyric pad. Until the traditional folk revival in the 1970s, the black-faced men in rag jackets seemed to have disappeared from the Welsh border for a good few decades.

'Discredited, perhaps,' Prof said. 'It was never pretty, Border morris. No fluttering handkerchiefs and flowery hats. Not for genteel ladies to watch while sipping tea and eating cucumber sandwiches. Not that it was cucumber sandwich weather when they were doing it. Usually done in winter.'

'I didn't know that.'

'Nothing sinister. The dancers were usually farm labourers trying to raise some cash at a time of year when there wasn't much farm work around. Tour the villages, dance for the people, throw down the hat. Also explains the black faces. Didn't want to get clocked by their employers.'

'You think that's all there is to it?'

'Generates its own myth, Laurence. Short days, dark nights, black faces, undertakers' hats. And the drink and the violence in the dance itself. Some of them play up to it to this day. Essentially, less refined, shall we say, than other forms of the morris. A courtly dance it is not.'

'Where did they do it?'

'Anywhere they didn't get banned. Market squares, pub yards. Border morris usually demands more room for flailing around.'

'Churches?'

'Not sure. Processional folk-dances were performed during religious festivals when the dancers would lead villagers to church.'

'What about churchyards?'

'This is what you're planning at your chickenshit festival? To use church premises?'

'Would they have danced among the graves?'

'That might've been pushing it. The Church was boss in those days. Morris was lucky to survive at all. Graveyards? Who knows where they wound up if they were pissed enough? They were bleedin' hooligans. Maybe that's why it came back in the seventies – an air of the anti-establishment about it, Border morris. These days it's mainly January wassails and other pseudo-pagan events which no longer raise eyebrows.'

'What about funerals?'

'What?'

'Would they dance at funerals? Or afterwards?'

Silence in the phone except for the sound of strong coffee percolating.

'If it's a member of the side who's being planted they might dance in his honour, the way some professions form an arch for a coffin to pass under. I wouldn't know. Where you going with this?'

'I'll tell you sometime.'

He didn't think Prof knew that he'd kept going back to the Golden Ball.

'Be careful of distractions, Laurence. Too late in your career. Stick to what you know.'

About half-eleven when Lol put the phone down. He was tired, hadn't slept too well last night in Prof's granary, half dressed under damp bedclothes.

He switched off the lamp so he could see through the window to the vicarage.

No lights.

He looked past the open door into the hall, where Lucy Devenish used to hang her ponchos on the newel post at the bottom of the stairs. The winter poncho and the summer poncho in which she'd died.

His fleece coat was on the newel post now. He went into the hall and took it down, found his woolly hat in one of the side pockets, woollen gloves in the other. He really didn't want to do this, but he didn't really have a choice.

… like what if they come back, Lol?

At least there was no fog and no rain as he slipped out of the front door, closing it very gently behind him.

There was nobody about. Saturday nights at the Black Swan would become more animated in the run-up to Christmas, but not yet. Lol stepped down to the pavement, moving into the silent square, past the fake gaslamps, extinguished now, and the shiny beetle-backs of parked cars.

Under the lychgate, into the churchyard.

Just to make sure.

15

Space to settle

WITHIN FIVE MINUTES, he was edging into the church porch, stowing himself into one of the side benches. Hadn't given much thought to what he'd do if they did come back. Knowing that it was only if he *didn't* come out here tonight that it would turn out tomorrow that they had.

That was the way these things went. Doing the hard thing was almost an insurance. It would not be pleasant this time of night, this time of year, and he wouldn't be telling Merrily or Jane tomorrow that he'd done it, but how could he not? Who else was there?

He didn't want there to be anyone else.

Out beyond the Gothic entrance, a half-moon was up, indifferent as the frosted bulb in a fridge. It paled the coffin path, leading down past the worn, honest old graves to the ornate goth tombs from Victorian times. Past Lucy's mossy stone to where he thought he'd seen a glimmering.

God.

He'd have to go down there if only to be sure it wasn't the reflection of the moon from some marble tomb. When his breathing was steady, he stood up.

He had a small flashlight in his pocket and left it there. Slipped out of the porch and down the wet grass verge beside the path, pausing to stroke the moss on Lucy's modest headstone, for courage. Imagining her stomping ahead of him, elbows making batwings in the poncho, as he slid into the shade of a mock-Celtic obelisk from the age of flamboyant death.

The air was sharp with the smell of earth. Maybe it always was here, but you only noticed it at night, when smells were always stronger.

It wasn't like last night, when he'd stood in the middle of the lane at Knight's Frome and hadn't known it. Tonight the air was clear and he could see the half-moon snagged in a spidery apple tree at the end of the churchyard where you could climb over a stile and follow the coffin path into the fields. Also, a brighter light, earthbound, partly covered and split vertically by the T-handle of a spade.

The spade was sunk into the turf of what – oh Christ – could only be Aidan Lloyd's grave.

Lol went still, smelling rich earth and smoke.

There were no sounds of dancing, no sounds at all until the footfall behind him.

Merrily rolled over in bed. The cold had numbed her hands, disconcerting because, on the edge of real winter, she'd had a dream of the sticky end of summer. There had been ripening apples and the threatening bass rumble of men in a semicircle, *auld ciderrrrr…*

Sitting up in the darkness, rubbing her hands together to get the blood flowing, and something tumbled to the floor.

Ella Mary Leather's *The Folklore of Herefordshire*. It explained the dream. As sometimes happened when you were overtired, she'd got to bed and been unable to sleep and started looking up Mrs Leather's references to morris dancing, for some reason expecting the dance to be connected with the old harvest rites. But Mrs Leather, writing in the years before World War I, had said she could find only one morris side, in the north of the county. She'd watched them dance at Christmas in 1909. They had staves and blackened faces.

She picked up the book, set it down on her bedside table next to the phone and lay back, bundled in the duvet, in a place where priests had lain for centuries, eyes wide open to the same blotchy dark. Early nights never worked. They disrupted your sleep rhythm and you woke up worried.

Ought to have phoned Huw Owen who had apparently educated Paul Crowden in deliverance, who knew as much about the Innes agenda as she did, if not more, who had taken the Bishop on, in a direct, artless fashion that could lead only to cold war. He'd done that for her. He'd done enough. Maybe she shouldn't phone him after all.

How many ghosts do you find in the Bible? Craig Innes from that iPhone recording, talking to Siân, the Archdeacon. *Surely the message... is that we should disregard the probably – mythological byways – which distract from our focus on God.*

Innes trying to justify on theological grounds his crisp, new, modern fundamentalism, a stripped-back approach that allowed the Church to avoid the noises in the night. How could they have sent Innes to Hereford, the diocese on the border?

When she closed her eyes again, she heard the clash of sticks, the grunts and the springing apart, the clumping bass, the pounding of feet on impacted soil, the treading down of the dirt.

All right... yes... tomorrow...

Tomorrow, between Holy Communion and Morning Worship, she'd go to Aidan Lloyd's grave and *do something*. A blessing. Holy water. Something to top up an inadequate burial service.

She fell asleep devising something suitable from the *mythological byways*, and awoke again, what must have been only minutes later, from another foetid ciderhouse dream, the chanting men looking down at their boots, and then one looking up, and this time it had been Iestyn Lloyd, whispering *Devil took him, devil took him, devil took him.*

Something about him that was outside of time. He was all over those old brown postcards of rural life in the nineteenth century. An archetype. Indestructible, like baler-twine.

Lol sank back against Lucy's stone.

'Nobody else here is there?'

'Only the dead'uns,' Gomer Parry said.

Lol's flashlight brought up a dull glow in Gomer's glasses, their lenses speckled with flakes of something that looked like dried blood. He was in his overalls. A canvas holdall lay near his feet. He lugged it, rattling, towards the lamp on the raised turf.

'See this, boy? En't never happened to me before.'

He hadn't asked what Lol was doing here after midnight. It didn't seem to matter to him. He bent and slid his fingers into the ground, easing out a turf about a foot square.

'Looked like a proper job, but it weren't. No, no, shine him down there, that's it. You gotter have him so you can't see the joins, right? One o' the first things you learns. No gaps, no bumps. And you gives him space to settle. You knows exackly how much he's gonner need. Precision, see.'

'Gomer—'

'It's like I tole young Janey, I wouldn't normally come back next day. Let the earth do what he do. Then, bugger me, if I din't look down and see what I seen. Bloody *hell*.'

'What's wrong with it?'

'You can't *see*? It's a bloody tragedy, boy! Well, I hadda come back, obviously, but not when folks could watch. Don't look good messin' with a grave. Specially when you knows you done him perfect, and now he bloody en't. After all these years, you gets to know what your own work looks like. And this, Lol, boy, *this en't my work no more.*'

He picked up the spade, moonlight glinting off old, worn steel, then he was prising out a second turf.

'Take a few o' these off, and you can see how it was all put back in a hurry. Course you'd need a full hexumation to be sure, and there'd be red tape, but now *you're* yere—'

'Hex…?' Lol taking a startled step back. 'What exactly are you saying, Gomer?'

Gomer let the turf slide from the spade.

96

'Nights is gettin' real cold. Ole ground hardenin' up. Figured this might be the last chance I was gonner get.' He sniffed. 'Hadda know, see. One way or the other. Hadda know. And now I do. Some bugger's had him out, Lol, sure t'be. This boy been dug up.'

16

Turn her head away

THE MOON HAD been swallowed by night cloud. Gomer lifted up the metal battery lamp to reveal what was now a rectangle of red, abraded ground. He prodded it with a boot.

'See how loose the ole soil is? Put back real quick. They thinks if they puts the turfs on top reg'lar nobody gonner notice.'

'You're saying he's... not down there?'

'En't sayin' that, no.' Gomer sniffed. 'What I'm sayin' is, the box been took out. And... you watch this.'

He lowered the lamp to the edge of the grave tump, shifted some surface soil with the spade, then kept going, steadily until a stab of the spade sent it down vertically, very fast, and he stumbled and let go, jumping back.

'See? That's what happens when you shovels it in fast. You year that? No mistakin' it, boy, when you hits a coffin. Done it a few times when you got what you think's a virgin plot and there's some other bugger down there.'

Lol was confused.

'So the coffin's still there. He— Aidan Lloyd's still down there, right?'

'No, boy... the *box* is still down there. That don't mean he's in it, do it? Box en't down as deep as he oughter be, not by two, three feet. Sure sign he got put back too fast and likely at an angle. Amateur job.'

'I believe you, Gomer.' Lol didn't like this – come on, who would? 'It's just I don't think you can—'

'You're a witness, Lol, boy. I needs a witness.'

'Gomer—'

'If that en't proof… En't no way a coffin's gonner float up through two or three feet of bloody soil.'

'No… listen…' Lol picked up the spade. 'It isn't evidence of anything except you digging up a grave at night, and that's… that's against the law.'

'It's my bloody grave!'

Gomer snatching the spade back, glaring at him through the torchlight, sparks of electricity in his glasses. Oh God, this was personal now, but…

'Sorry…' Lol backed off. 'It isn't your grave, Gomer. Not any more. Not now it's… occupied. It's theirs, the Lloyd family. Listen, you… you have to put all the soil back and the sods and we have to get out of here. We'll go back in the warm, make a pot of tea and talk about this.'

'Woulder took more'n one feller to do it, mind.'

'Do what?'

'Haul him outer the ground. Even with ropes around him both ends, that en't a one-man job.'

'The coffin?'

'*Unless*,' Gomer said, 'unless all they needed to do was… open him up, kind o' thing.'

'Nobody would want to do that.'

… would they?

'Now then.' Gomer leaned on the spade. 'I remember yearin', not that long back, about a hincident like this down the Forest o' Dean. Woman got dug up for her rings or summat. Some relation who got left out o' the will, figured he was entitled. Some folks, they gets obsessive about what they's owed.'

Lol thought it was unlikely Aidan Lloyd was blinged up. He watched Gomer arranging the uplifted squares into two neat piles, like carpet samples, so he'd know exactly how they fitted when he put them back. Didn't look like he planned to do this anytime soon. Lol felt exposed among the bare trees and eroded stones with the church steeple behind them, a rigid, admonishing finger.

Gomer straightened up, bringing out his ciggy tin.

'Now then, boy, what if it's empty?'

'The grave?'

'The box. What if the boy got took out o' the box?'

'That's not something we're ever going to—'

'We could find out.'

'I don't think so.'

'En't more'n a couple o' feet down. Take no more'n about five minutes to have him out, the ole box.'

God, no. Lol backed off, hands up. *Please.*

'Don't even *contemplate* it, Gomer. You've broken enough laws already.'

'You don't have to stay, Lol, boy. All I'm askin' is you keeps quiet about it. Suppose they decides to put another in yere... mabbe Iestyn, when he goes? And there's the boy halfway up. What they gonner say? That bloody ole Parry... botched job. No way, boy. *No bloody way.*'

It had been a mistake thinking this was personal. It wasn't, it was professional, and that went much deeper – the dissing of Gomer Parry Plant Hire, working the border for decades with big diggers and a reputation for solid workmanship. Plant Hire was the business now, but gravedigging was the bedrock and Gomer took a serious pride in doing by himself what he'd keep doing till they had to lift him off the mini-JCB and into a box of his own.

The half-moon shone down like a lopsided grin.

'I seen that funeral,' Gomer said. 'I seen them folks round this grave, faces like rock. Next day I seen Janey walkin' down yere, and her couldn't hardly walk at all and her still hadda come. Didn't make no sense. And then I seen what these buggers done. And that wouldn't be nobody in this village, 'cos they all knows me, and they'd know as I'd know. And they'd all know what that d'mean.'

Lol sighed.

'And then you turns up. I en't asked you what you're doin' out yere middle o' the night, Lol, boy, and mabbe it en't none o' my business. But what all this says is that summat really and truly *en't right*. You tellin' me I'm wrong?'

Lol spun at sudden footsteps on the path.

'You're not wrong, Gomer,' Jane said.

Lol's fists tightened. How bad could this get?

What was she supposed to have done? Turn her head away from the window, go back to bed and try to forget about something that might never go away, as long as they lived here, that would go on creeping like ivy over the wall between the garden and the grave?

'Oh, and I'm walking a lot better now, by the way,' Jane said.

Hadn't hurt too much when she put on her boots. Letting herself out of the back door this time. Bringing the long black Maglite. You could really hurt somebody with that, especially if you saw him first, and she was far from ashamed of wanting to.

But not Lol. Not Gomer, placidly rolling a ciggy.

'You got the vicar with you, Janey?'

'The vicar's asleep. I checked. Anyway, this is nothing to do with Mum. This is just me unable to keep from looking through windows.'

The moonlight was sharpening the barbs on the wire that separated Aidan Lloyd's grave from the field. Jane frowned. Never used to be barbed wire there.

She looked at Lol, doubtless here because he was trying, as usual, to do the right thing. But sometimes what seemed like the wrong thing was actually the right thing.

'How long have you been here, Jane?'

'You mean how much have I heard? I'm guessing most of it.'

Lol seemed to sag.

'Just behind that mouldy pile with the Celtic cross,' Jane said. 'Mum and me were here last night, and we saw… well, not much, to be honest. But now we know, don't we? And, like, all I can say...' Squeezing the Maglite with both mittened hands. '... is as long as I don't have to watch, just *do it*. We don't want to keep coming back here night after night.'

Gomer put his ciggy back into the tin. Jane thought she saw Lol closing his eyes. She turned away.

'Yeah, we all know it's against the law. But Gomer knows what he's doing. And I... could do the lookout thing.'

Lol looked down at his trainers. They'd be sodden. His feet were freezing. He spread his hands.

'All right. I'll help Gomer. But you should...'

'I'm not leaving, Lol, I'm just not looking.'

Jane watched Gomer's soil-reddened fingers picking up the spade, a dreadful excitement growing. Whatever had happened last night, it was clear the old guy was about to make it very real. His big, sudden grin was close to demonic.

He pointed at the lamp.

'Hold that, boy.'

'No.' Lol was stepping forward, a hand out. 'You've done enough for one night. I'll dig.'

Gomer looked at the gloved hand.

'Nobody woulder thought twice about it, my day. Even the coppers'd turn a blind eye if they knowed you.'

'I can imagine. Now just...'

Gomer hesitated then shrugged and handed over the spade, its blade worn to a lethal edge by decades of digging. Jane thought he could probably shave with that spade. He bent to his workbag and brought out a roll of something bound up with a rubber band, which turned out to be a green plastic groundsheet. Gomer spread it out on the edge of the grave, weighting opposite corners with a hammer and a trowel, then he and Lol were both up on the tump, taking off the rest of the turf. You could see how loose the soil was underneath. She'd often wondered if Gomer would one day uncover some massive megalith, physical evidence of the Ledwardine henge, but that was for another night.

Jane huddled in her parka, fists clenched in pockets, the bitter soil an acrid taste in her throat. No megalith down there, only Aidan Lloyd in his coffin…

… or not.

'Take it slowly, boy,' Gomer said.

Before long, Lol had a steady rhythm going with the spade, she could see his breath and an earthmound accumulating on the groundsheet. She could feel him trying not to think about what he was doing. In the past he'd enjoyed helping Gomer, being a labourer, but this—

This was actually awful. Jane backed slowly away, the enormity of what they were doing washing over her like freezing water.

The lookout thing. She spun away and switched on the Maglite, shone it back along the path then amongst the graves. She started thinking about last night, about being sprawled, helpless, with a twisted ankle a very short distance from a bunch of men and an open grave and an exposed body in a shroud of fog.

Lol's spade clinked on what was probably a stone, but in Jane's head it was bone, and she winced, pulling her beanie down over her ears. All too soon Lol was knee-deep in the grave. Sooner or later Mum would have to learn about this. Or would she? It would depend on what they found.

She switched off the torch. It was no good; she had to force herself to face this. She drew a long breath.

As she turned back towards the open grave, there was a scraping sound and Lol came out of the hole very fast, saying he hadn't thought it would be so close to the surface. His voice unsteady as he leaned over the spade. Under the moon, he and Gomer both looked wavery and indistinct like characters from some black and white gothic movie.

Jane didn't move. She couldn't see the coffin. Hoped not to and was ashamed.

'Look at that,' Gomer said. 'Looks like they din't put no screws back. Clear the top off and the ole lid, he'll just slide off kinder thing.'

Lol didn't move. Waxy silence. No owls, no rustles in the undergrowth, no sounds from the village or the church. Jane looked warily up into the tangle of trees screening the side wall of the vicarage.

Somebody should stop them.

Lol was saying, 'Jane, why don't you go and wait by… with Lucy. Your mum would—'

'Listen,' she said before she could change her mind. 'I've got my phone here, if you want me to try for some… pictures.'

What? What had she *said*?

'Like, I'm thinking for Mum? For Mum to see, if necessary. If there's nothing in there…'

Seeing something through a lens, surely that separated you from it. And she'd probably seen worse. Wasn't as if Aidan Lloyd was someone she'd known personally. She thought of the worst experiences of her life, involving Colette Cassidy and Cornel the banker, then pushed away the images. They didn't make her feel any more prepared.

'Uh… thanks, Jane, but I don't think so.' Lol stepped back down into the grave, she heard his feet on wood. 'Don't want anything incriminating on your phone, do you?'

She listened to the scraping as Lol cleared the top of the coffin with the tip of the spade.

'That should do, boy,' Gomer said.

Jane turned away as both of them bent into the grave. Would Gomer have tried to do this on his own if Lol hadn't arrived? Probably.

'No hurry, boy. He'll come off. Right, now, if you hops out…'

Hugging herself for warmth, she watched Lol hauling himself gratefully from the grave. He'd be so hating this. If Mum was here, once she'd got over hissing at them to stop, she might be mumbling a prayer in their defence. *Was* there a prayer for the disturbance of the dead? Oh God, Lol was leaning back now to accept the coffin lid with both hands, ducking under it, his shoulders against the loose mound of excavated earth.

Jane heard herself asking if he was there. Aidan. In the coffin. Lol answered her from the top of the pile of excavated earth, hugging the coffin lid to his chest.

'Something is.' He turned to Gomer. 'Isn't that enough?'

'We come this far, boy. Might as well...'

He was right. What if it was just bricks in there or something?

The moon had gone again. They'd need some light.

The lamp was still on the grass between Jane and the opening, out of reach for both of them. She picked it up and took it to the edge of the hole.

'There you go...'

Remembering how he'd died. Instantly. Hit by a van. *Splattered all over the road*, Dean Wall had said. So there'd have been a post-mortem. She'd seen autopsy pictures in some magazine. Organs taken out, chest sewn up, skin all ruched like the edge of a meat pie. She was aware of the harshness of her breath as Lol asked her to just pass him the lamp and turn away.

Jane held the lamp high over the open grave and the open coffin. She waited for a sickening waft of putrefaction, but there was only this faint chemical smell that made her think of vinegar and, in her ears, a faint half-musical rattle, like loose bones.

'Jane, please.'

Lol's earth-streaked face in the lamplight.

But she was already leaning in, lowering the lamp. Holding the light and her breath, when she looked down, as she knew she must, into the coffin's interior, pale blue quilting, Lol going,

'Jane, *no*—'

Too late.

Part Three

They killed farming… by putting cabs on tractors.

John Lewis-Stempel,
Meadowland (Doubleday, 2014)

17

A dot on the map

BETWEEN THE EUCHARIST and the morning service, Merrily took her e-cig into the churchyard and went to stand, shivering in her surplice, by Lucy's grave.

No more shall clouds...

No clouds today. Winter – real winter – had come slicing in overnight, clean and severe. The last apple had fallen from the nearest tree to the vicarage but the blackbirds had got to it before the frost.

Come out without her cape again. Never mind, a few cold minutes never harmed anyone. She'd assembled a prayer to resanctify the spot, disperse any feelings of ill-will. She went over it in her head, fingers on the furry shoulders of Lucy's stone.

A wiry man in jeans and a fleece jacket walked past along the track, murmuring a mild good morning, and she returned it automatically, smiling vaguely, the way you did while thinking, *Who the hell's this?* because vicars were supposed to know everybody. And then she did know. Just that last time he'd been in a dark suit and tie, solemn, reticent.

She watched him walking all the way down to the bottom of the churchyard and stopping by the reconstituted mound of green turf. She'd only met him once, and the results of that meeting hadn't been too satisfactory.

With just under half an hour before she needed to get back to the church, she walked over.

'I'm afraid I didn't do a proper job.'

He turned to her, half smiling.

'In what respect?'

He had a steady gaze under short, fox-red hair. Her own age, maybe a little younger and more than a head taller. His name was Liam Hurst. He'd been sent to the vicarage with some details about the life of Aidan Lloyd, his half-brother. Details that were all too brief, printed on one side of a sheet of A4 and folded into an envelope.

'When you come away from a funeral feeling you haven't really made anyone feel better…'

'What?'

'You only get one chance to do that. Should've known more about him. Just because someone doesn't go to church…'

'That's daft.' Trace of a local accent, though not much of one. 'The way the population of villages changes and fluctuates these days, you could spend all your time working out who's who. Besides, if you didn't know too much about him… well, don't you think that might've been the intention?'

'I wondered.'

'My mother and Iestyn, they both just wanted it over. Only thing they've agreed about in years. Iestyn, he—' He turned away from the grave, as if exasperated. 'He's asked me to fix up a monumental mason, get a stone made. Nothing too ostentatious, so I was just… weighing up the location without too many people around.'

'I'm sorry if I—'

'Mrs Watkins, I didn't mean *you*. It's your churchyard. As for the funeral, that was never going to be a touching celebration of a full life well lived, was it?'

'There's still quite a lot to say about a life cut short.'

'Yes.' He sighed. 'I expect there is.'

'I did ask around, but nobody seemed to know Aidan all that well. So I was left with a good farmer and where he went to school. And the asthma.'

'It went away, the asthma. To Iestyn's relief. Mine, too, in a purely selfish sense, I have to say. If Aidan had been incapacitated into adulthood, I might've been set up as Iestyn's successor.'

'With the farm?'

Liam Hurst put on a shudder. He was staring over her towards the church, its sandstone steeple hard against the flawless sky.

'It's all going, as they say round here, to shit. Farming's a twenty-four/seven job, at a time when working hours are decreasing, leisure time expanding. Young people don't want it any more. Girls used to want to marry a farmer for the money and the big house. Now the money isn't what it was and the house is cold and drab with no prospect of decent Wi-Fi.'

'It'll come. Some places round here had a long wait for electricity.'

'Nobody wants to wait any more, Mrs Watkins. Farms get inherited and then sold as quickly as possible to city winners looking for barn conversions and pony paddocks. Or some of them think, what else can I do with a field that doesn't involve drenching sheep or milking cows? Holiday caravan site?'

Merrily thought about the village's other big landowner, Ward Savitch, who let out his fields for events, like next year's Ledwardine Folk Festival. Nobody was innocent. She thought of all the years of absentee landlords picking up grants, an annual income for doing nothing. But then she remembered when the payments had been made for numbers of livestock, and her grandad had been furious at the way his neighbours' fields were overstocked.

'No going back,' Liam Hurst said. 'I see it all from the outside now, and that's the best place to be.'

'So you're not involved in farming,' Merrily said. 'I just automatically assumed...'

'Oh, I'm *involved* in it, sure. And involved with farmers. Deal with them on a day-to-day business. Not the same thing as being one, though, fortunately.' He smiled, ruefully. 'DEFRA. Department of Agriculture. I'm a civil servant, with holidays and guaranteed pension. One of my functions is to inspect farms to make sure that what farmers put on their claim forms for various grants and payments has not been, shall we say, augmented.'

'That must make you popular in these parts.'

'An old chap once opened the door to me with his twelve-bore held meaningfully under an arm. Truth is, I sympathize. They're up against it. Livestock and dairy prices sometimes make it seem unsustainable. The suicide rate amongst farmers is not exactly going down. But I expect you know that.'

'I do.'

He looked down at Aidan's grave.

'If this had been Iestyn, I might've thought he'd deliberately driven himself into the path of that vehicle. At one time, anyway. When he was down on his luck.'

'Not down any more, surely? Must be a few hundred acres here.'

'Over a thousand.'

'Gosh.'

'Each of those acres to be individually worried about. It's a trap, Mrs Watkins. Bigger the farm, the tighter the trap. It's a big farm, but still only a dot on the map.'

He turned to look out over the stile at the end of the church-yard to where the coffin path had long since vanished into the frosted fields.

'Cattle, sheep, pigs, potatoes, fruit... maize. Oilseed rape. Diversification. It's a juggling act, but he's good at that, always has been. Only now it comes without the status or the local respect of the old days. Most of the country squires are long gone. It's all spreadsheets now – strategy, or you go under. Iestyn – give him his due – was one of the first to appreciate that when he was a farm manager and hired my mother to process the spreadsheets.'

'He inherited this... from an uncle, is that right?'

'Almost right. His uncle had left it to *his* son, who'd let it

112

go… to shit, as they say. Iestyn bought him out. So there *was* a family link to Ledwardine. A tradition to renew. Not that Iestyn would've seen it that way. He simply employed his skills to make it productive again. Buying more ground on all sides.'

'And one of the last available bits of the churchyard for his family grave.'

'Last bits?'

'We're virtually full. If you don't already have a grave to go into, you're now more or less limited to an urn space.' She nodded to the broken wall at the end of the churchyard. 'Unless whoever winds up owning that feels moved to donate some of it to the parish.'

'Iestyn,' he said.

'Sorry?'

'Iestyn bought that field a couple of months ago when the Rudge farm was finally broken up. You didn't know?'

'No. Blimey… Last I heard the family were still haggling over it, with Ward Savitch in the background, waving his wallet.'

'My stepfather tends not to advertise these things. This would've been the last dozen or so acres separating his ground from the village. I suspect he bid over the odds for it. May've belonged to his uncle's family years and years ago, I don't really know.'

She stared across the field, with its copse of bare trees and a single galvanized gate at the far end. So Iestyn Lloyd now owned what remained of the coffin trail. She didn't think even Gomer knew about this.

'Don't misunderstand me,' Liam Hurst said. 'I don't think Iestyn's sentimental enough to've bought it because it runs right up to the grave plot he'd acquired. Not consciously, anyway. Although if you look on the map, you'll see the farm-land narrowing as it approaches the village. Like an arrow. On the map, this field puts a point on the arrow.'

'The whole…' She hugged in her surplice against a sudden icy breeze. 'The whole farm pointing directly to the grave?'

'Ironic, isn't it? In a macabre kind of way. Not that Iestyn would notice. No time for superstition.'

'So what… what will happen to it, when Iestyn…?'

'Ah, the big question. The son's gone. Who'll have it now?' He shook his head. 'My mother fears he's looking at me. I do so hope not, because I'll have to say no. I'll help him all I can, as I always have, but, as I say, I've seen too many decent men destroyed trying to hold a farm together at the expense of a normal life. If he ever asks me, I'll advise him to sell while it's still profitable.'

'All this?'

He shrugged.

'You wouldn't feel tempted…?'

'Do I *sound* like I'd feel tempted? No way. I like my freedom and my holidays. Time to see the bigger world. A farmer gets himself stitched tight into the land and before he knows it he's become…' Scrunching his elbows into the sides of his chest. '… all tightened up inside.'

'Oh.'

She took a step back from the grave and all its sombre symbolism. Liam sank his hands into the pockets of his fleece, looking more weathered and farm-fit than you'd ever expect of a government official. He smiled.

'It'll sort itself out one way or another. Farmers are pragmatists. Mrs Watkins, I see your problem, but Iestyn will think you did your job. His grief is private grief. He sees no need to involve anyone else. Certainly not the wider community. Let them mutter.'

'Mutter?'

She registered a slightly strained patience on his narrow face.

'Personal use, you don't even get a police caution any more. He was a young chap. When people talk of industrial quantities, it's probably an exaggeration.'

'Erm…' Merrily folding her arms for warmth. Too late for the blessing now, but this was just as important. 'Can you tell me about him?'

He smiled, shrugged.

'I didn't know him that well. Seven years apart, you tend not to mix in the same circles. As a boy he was always quiet, inhibited by his asthma. Didn't want to ride or hunt. I was – to be honest – a little afraid for him when it became clear he was expected to take over the farm. So much on his shoulders and his father watching him like a hawk. Because Iestyn didn't really know him either. They *worked* together – isn't that what a farmer's son was born for? He was raised by my mother until the asthma was gone and then she left Iestyn, with his approval and me away at university. I've somehow been the go-between ever since. Get on quite well with Iestyn. All you need is to be able to *work* with him.'

'Did Iestyn really not know? About the cannabis?'

'Good God no.' Liam reared back theatrically. 'He'd've gone ballistic. His own father having lost his own farm because of drink, leaving the family near destitute.' He paused. 'Are you beginning to see what made Iestyn into the kind of man he's become?'

'But he knows now.'

'Hence the quiet funeral.'

'Erm… were there people in the village who didn't like Aidan… either because of the cannabis or anything else?'

He peered at her.

'Why do you ask?'

'I—' Her brain was scrabbling for something convincing when she became aware of voices behind her in the churchyard. A small congregation assembling. 'Oh, hell— Sorry. I should be in church. What I… I was going to mention him during the service. Something I often do after a funeral.'

Liam Hurst nodded. Then he smiled – a small, sympathetic smile.

'I rather think I've said too much already. But I suspect you can put two and two together from that. And draw a line under it.'

Merrily nodded. She wondered if he'd come here this morning – or been sent here – to make sure that line had been firmly drawn.

'Mmm,' she said. 'Thank you.'

'And just be a bit careful what you say in your sermon. That is… if you want Iestyn to spare a part of his field to extend the churchyard.'

'Right.'

'Joking,' he said.

18

Lucky day

A PALE MOVEMENT in the top of the window dragged Jane's gaze to the end of the garden where the vicarage apple trees tangled with the churchyard trees.

The butterfly-white thing could only be the vicar in her surplice.

Watching from the single window in the cold East Wing, Jane was struck, as frequently happened, by the utter strangeness of Mum as a priest – the anglican shaman, leaving early to celebrate Holy Communion.

Celebrate. Did that ever really happen or did you just get better at fooling yourself that it didn't all end in a muddied coffin in wet cold earth that even the moles avoided?

The vicar vanished and Jane looked down to where two blackbirds were manoeuvring a rotting apple under a bush, ripping bits away as they hopped around it in their...

... rag jackets.

She stepped sharply back from the window. The blue sky mocked her.

She'd slept, eventually. How had she slept? Had Lol managed to sleep? She imagined him scrubbing and scrubbing at his hands, his clothes, his trainers, at some point catching sight of himself in a mirror with streaks of grave dirt like red abrasions from his cheeks to his jawline. As soon as she was up she'd phoned him from her mobile but he couldn't talk, having been summoned to a festival meeting at the Swan, with Barry. Said he'd call her as soon as he could.

And they would talk about something Jane had seen for no more than two or three seconds before he'd gripped her wrist and the lamp had been taken away and there was only the half-moon, the smell of embalming fluid and that... metallic chuckle.

Did she really hear that? Would she keep on hearing it, the giggling herald of a repulsive memory that would live at the back of her mind for ever and would occasionally spring out in the night?

Jane went downstairs, gave Ethel a second breakfast. Hadn't made herself anything. Unable to face food. She'd managed a cup of weak black tea, despite smelling in the steaming pot the thin, astringent odour of what she now knew to be formaldehyde.

Oh, Christ, she had to get some air.

And there was something she had to do. She pulled down a cheerful scarlet scarf and her red beanie, dropped the phone into a pocket of her parka and let herself out of the back door. It was coming up to half past ten. Mum wouldn't be back from work for at least a couple of hours. Long enough to decide what – if anything – to tell her, but she really mustn't find this.

Jane moved carefully, still mindful of her ankle, down the frosty garden towards the gnarly old apple trees.

It would have landed just about... here? She bent and scrabbled in the grass and found its shaft amongst a scattering of rotten windfalls that the blackbirds hadn't got to yet. The blade shone. Gomer had given it a clean first, as you'd expect. She picked it up and hid it behind the shed.

It had been her idea that he should toss his spade over the vicarage wall rather than be seen carrying it through the dark streets. In Ledwardine, whatever the time, there was always someone awake.

Behind Barry, parched applewood was blazing fragrantly in the inglenook. A mild autumn had meant a healthy woodpile, fires all day in the Black Swan now the cold weather had come. Nothing brought in Sunday custom better than a log fire with a scent that settled over the village.

'The gallery couple,' Barry said. 'Ledwardine Fine Arts?'

'It's closing, isn't it?'

Lol looking up from his coffee. He'd thought they were supposed to be discussing the folk festival line-up, his failure to find another name as big as Moira Cairns willing to play for peanuts.

'They were in for dinner last night and we got talking. Amazing how many intelligent people swallow all that crap about Herefordshire being the New Cotswolds. They see a lovely old black and white village in summer and it entirely escapes them that the *old* Cotswolds are an hour from London while we're not within commuting distance of anywhere halfway affluent. Most people round here, if they want a picture on their wall they frame a page of last year's calendar.'

'So they couldn't sell paintings and now they can't sell the gallery?'

'Not as business premises, and it's too small to be any good for much else.'

'Not really been much of a business since it was Lucy's shop.'

'The Devenish curse, you think?'

'Just never seemed quite right, did it? Rural knick-knacks and apple mementoes, then she dies and it's posh, minimalist art at non-Hereford prices.'

'Anyway,' Barry said, 'they don't like to say they're strapped for cash, but they've been putting it around, quietly, that it's available for rent. Cheap enough for me to think I might just go for it as a retail outlet for specialist ciders. Then I had a better idea.'

'Tanning salon?'

Barry adjusted his eye patch.

'You all right, Laurence? You seem a bit out of it.'

'I'm fine.'

He could probably tell Barry everything that had happened last night, without risk. Digging up a corpse would get barely a blink from a former SAS man. But perhaps not.

'Go on,' he said. 'Tell me.'

'What I was thinking, we're gonna need a festival office.'

'Are we?'

'To take bookings and that. It was gonna be here, at the Swan, but then I'd have to lose a room. Whereas if we rented that shop... nice little mews off the high street that nobody can resist peering into. Music playing softly.'

'We could afford it?'

'We could sell related stuff, as well. I'm thinking albums by the artists on the bill. Books. CDs and DVDs. Your albums, even. Festival-linked tourist tat. *And* specialist cider.'

'Well, that...'

'I've talked to Savitch, looks like he might chuck some money in. Get it up and running early next year. What's to lose? Whaddaya think?'

Lol was remembering his own early days in the village, when he used to mind the shop for Lucy Devenish. It had been well overcrowded, full of apple pottery, books of apple recipes and apple folklore and a sign that said something like, *Lovely to look at, delightful to hold, but if you break it... don't worry it's my own bloody fault for running a business in such a grotty little hovel.*

Lucy. What a loss.

'It's not a bad idea, Barry. Of course you'd need staff.'

'We would. Might get volunteers for a while, but that's not really satisfactory.' Barry leaned back into a pale sunbeam, hands behind his head. 'What about young Jane?'

'To run it?'

'Gap year's not going as well as expected, what I heard. Girl seems at a bit of a loose end. I may be wrong here, but she doesn't look too happy.'

'It's, uh, that time of transition. Between two worlds. The

one where your future's always decided for you so you can rebel against it. And the other one, where you'll only have yourself to blame.'

Remembering Jane coming into Ledwardine Lore when he was looking after the shop for Lucy one spring afternoon. Back when he and Jane had never seen one another before and he'd never met her mother. Lol at his most neurotic, trying to avoid Karl Windling, the old Hazey Jane bass player who'd nearly destroyed him and then had the nerve to come back, years later, with plans to reform the band. Jane taking over from Lol in the shop so that he could creep upstairs and hide, like a mouse.

His time of transition. One of several. Sometimes he felt he was stuck in transition, never getting anything quite right. Like last night, when he should've come down from that earthmound, grabbed the lamp from her, guided her away. He'd replayed that scene so many times in the past few hours: how a thinking Lol Robinson might have prevented Jane from seeing what she'd seen and was unlikely ever to forget.

'You *really* all right, Lol?'

'Yeah, it's just...'

He should have gone back to the churchyard at first light, if only to check they hadn't left any evidence of what they'd done. He didn't *think* they had. His last memory of the church-yard was Gomer gathering together the tools holding down the groundsheet and then taking it to the stile before shaking off the flakes of soil and clay.

'You don't think it's a good idea?' Barry said. 'She'd get paid, naturally. Not hugely.'

'I think it's a brilliant idea.'

'But...?'

'No, it's brilliant, Barry. Really. Magic.'

Jane crossed the street, having to wait for a break in the traffic. That didn't happen often on a Sunday in winter. The sunshine had brought visitors into Ledwardine, a few early

Christmas shoppers, even. The antique-stroke-junk shop and the bookshop, Ledwardine Livres, had started opening on Sundays and the Swan did good lunches, not too expensive. It was even rumoured that a few seasonal visitors actually went to church.

Weird.

What was also slightly weird was that you could go for weeks without encountering Dean Wall, and then he was suddenly in your face all the time. She was barely halfway across Church Street, heading towards Lucy's Cottage to see if Lol was back, when he was hailing her from the corner. He was wearing a felt hat with a band around it, like a fedora.

'Your lucky day, Jane.'

'Well, it *might*'ve been.'

'You don't appreciate me. Listen. The gay-boys stayed at the Ox? You still interested?'

'Who said they were gay?'

'Little bells round their legs? You kiddin'?'

She jerked back the shudder.

'You have a very simplistic mind, Wall.'

'S'pose I could tell you name of the feller booked the rooms.'

'Yeah?' Jane trying not to look too interested. 'How'd you get that out of him?'

'Bing? Done him a few favours. And now I can do you one, Jane.'

'But then I'd owe you, right?'

'Then you'd owe me big time, girlie.'

Jane sighed.

'And what do you reckon would make us even?'

He thought about it for a few seconds, puffing out his big lips, his breath steaming.

'No chance of a shag, I s'pose?'

Jane instinctively tightened her scarf, letting the silence drift for a while before coming down to his level.

'Dean, if I said I'd rather bite off my own nipples…'

The worst of it was he actually looked disappointed. You could swear the light went out of his eyes.

'You don't help yourself, Jane.'

'*What?*'

He turned and began to walk away, but slowly. For the first time, Jane felt soiled enough to threaten him. She let him get fifteen or twenty paces away before calling after him.

'How about I try and put a word in for you with Raji Khan?'

A couple of shoppers turned round. Wall came shuffling to a stop. She walked slowly up behind him.

'I mean a good word. As opposed to a bad word.'

He stood there with his head sunk between his shoulders.

'I still don't get your connection with him.'

He didn't turn round. He'd asked her about this before and evidently hadn't believed the answer, involving, as it did, Mum.

'Being an alleged drug dealer doesn't prevent someone having a spiritual side. It's often quite compatible, I'm told.'

'Oh, you think you're smart, Jane, but you're so full of shit.'

'Anyway, he might be looking for, I dunno, a doorman for one of his clubs sometime? You'd have to wear a tie, of course. You got a tie?'

'Fuck off,' Dean Wall said. Then, 'His name's Gareth Brewer. From Kilpeck.'

'How's that spelt? The guy's name, not Kilpeck.'

He swung round.

'How much you *want?*'

'It's OK, I'll work it out.'

She saw Lol coming across the square, past Big Jim Prosser's Eight Till Late, looking casually from side to side. A guy in search of a home. Sometimes, in Ledwardine, he looked like he'd found it. Not today, though. She thought if she could see auras his would be deep mauve flecked with black.

Wall said, 'What are you into, Jane?'

She coughed; her throat was parched.

'For the first time, Dean, I can say with confidence that even you really don't want to know. OK?'

She'd seen that Lol was wearing suede boots and wondered if he'd burned last night's trainers.

19

Wild West

EXCEPT LATER, IN the photos, Bliss never saw his face. By the time he was pulling the Honda onto the forecourt, they had the lad all bagged up and ready to go. But probably a nice-looking feller, Karen Dowell said, before he was shot twice in the head from close up.

Karen had briefed him on the phone with her customary attention to unnecessary detail. Before he was out of the car he could almost smell it in his head, the engine grease and the blood.

The garage was where he'd thought it might be, at the rural end of the industrial estate, not far from Rotherwas Chapel and the council tip. Half the forecourt had already been taped off in front of a gaping entrance framed in stained concrete. Police screens across it now. Seven or eight second-hand cars parked outside, none of them priced over five K. But the purple and white sign over the entrance was new.

JAG'S MOTORS.

DC Vaynor came round one of the screens, clambering between the police vehicles like some kind of stick insect.

'Inspector Ford sends his regards, boss. He dropped by, before his Sunday morning pint.'

'How very thoughtful of him.' And how bloody prescient. Bliss leaning on his arms over his driver's door, peering up at Vaynor, who was close to seven feet tall and young enough to be still growing. 'First off... handgun – that confirmed?'

'Definitely. When did that last happen in Hereford?'

'Before my time, anyway. In fact it probably involved a retired colonel and a service revolver.'

'Far as we can tell...' Vaynor bent his back and lowered his voice. '... it's two headshots, fairly close range, one from behind. One probably done after he was down, just to make sure.'

'Which also kind of rules out suicide. And we know it's him, yeh? Wictor Justyn Jaglowski.'

Vaynor nodded.

'His girlfriend found him. She's English, so we didn't have to wait for a terp. She'd gone out looking for Jag when he didn't come back from mass. Ended up here. Doors unlocked but no lights on.'

'The garage wasn't open?'

'It's Sunday. Good Catholic.'

'Like me ma,' Bliss said. 'Mr Jag. Worra shame we didn't have a chance to run an obbo on him. Due to start tomorrow, as it happened. Terry Stagg was organizing it. He'd be miffed. 'Where's the girlfriend?'

'Her dad picked her up. Wasn't in any state to drive. We know where to find her, anyway.'

Bliss could see some action inside, more lights going on. Saw no reason to interrupt Karen. A good look round, an itemizing of everything, could prove productive, and it didn't need an audience. Best to keep it all low-key. It would blow up big time tomorrow.

'He was fencing stuff?' Vaynor said.

'As I'm sure Inspector Ford confirmed for you. Could've been obtaining items to order. Mainly of an agricultural nature. But was he treading on someone else's ground, that's the point? Doesn't take them long, these fellers, to mark out their territory. City's divided up in no time. Still... at least we've gorra good idea of time of death without pestering the doc.'

'His girlfriend have any idea why he might've come to the garage?'

'She says they didn't talk much about his business.'

126

'So we can take it he had a special reason to come in,' Bliss said. 'To meet somebody, maybe.'

'Who then shot him?'

'Anybody actually hear any shots?'

'It's Sunday. Not many people around to hear anything. As you see, we haven't drawn much of a crowd.'

Bliss turned and saw a couple of teenage lads across the road, one of them taking pictures on his phone. Nothing you could do about that. Vaynor pointed into the middle distance, where the estate crumbled away into scrub.

'Open fields, there. I expect there's some rough shooting on a Sunday, legit or otherwise. Couple of bangs wouldn't cause much of a stir. There's a petrol station a few hundred metres down the road, we're talking to them. That's the nearest CCTV, I'm afraid.'

Bliss sighed.

'The new gangland. Organized theft, people-smuggling, slavery – he was linked to the lot.'

He wrinkled his nose. It didn't scare him, but it didn't give him a buzz either. Migrant crime could be a drag, too reliant on the National Register of Public Service Interpreters. Dial-a-Terp. You could wait hours for the buggers to arrive, taking a big chunk out of your allotted twenty-four.

'Thing about gangland,' Vaynor said, 'is after a while, in the big cities, it gets sort of tolerated, doesn't it? On account of most of the time they're just taking out each other.'

'So many vacancies for gang bosses they're taking on kids with no proper qualifications,' Bliss said. 'It's a disgrace.'

Remembering the last time he went up north to see his mam, having a pint with an old mate, now a super with the major incident posse. Telling Bliss the Merseyside gangs were all little kids now. He'd said he felt like a headteacher who'd had his cane swapped by the Home Office for a handbook on child psychology.

At least these were grown-ups. Jaglowski was about twenty-eight. A veteran.

They watched him being brought out, all packed up like a futon from Furniture Village, Karen Dowell in a Durex suit following. Always been good with bodies, Karen, possibly down to an impaired sense of smell.

The meat-wagon doors clunked.

'You know what, Darth?' Bliss said. 'I realize the council's doing its best, but the way I see it, Hereford's not big enough yet for gang warfare. We don't stamp on it, we're gonna look stupid and ineffectual very quickly.'

'I suppose.'

'Besides,' Bliss said, 'it offends me, these scallies and their handguns. I realize this *is* England's Wild friggin' West, but Mother of God...'

'Charlie Howe as sheriff?'

'Sorry, son?'

'They elected sheriffs. In the Wild West.'

Bliss considered this.

'You're a big lad, Darth,' he said eventually, 'but not too big to get bounced back into friggin' uniform.'

Vaynor grinned. They waited for Karen to come over, unzipping her Durex suit, looking almost dismayed.

'Could be more complicated than we thought, boss. We've made a discovery in the inspection pit that puts a whole new slant on it. Four of them.'

'Four what?'

'Lovely little automatic pistols. All shiny and well greased. The business.'

20

Grave goods

JANE WAS DRAPING her parka over the back of Lol's sofa, pulling her phone out of one of the pockets, as if she was here for the long haul. Then flinging herself into the sofa and looking at him like he was crazy.

'Let things settle? Are you serious?'

Lucy's parlour was bathed in blue light, always stronger and brighter in winter with no leaves on the trees. Jane's anger was vivid.

'All I meant,' Lol said, 'was now we know what happened—'

'We do? Really?'

'What happened,' Lol said softly, 'is that we committed a serious crime. The kind of *distasteful* crime for which people usually get the book thrown at them. Maybe several books.'

Vaguely remembering some travellers stealing a child's body some years ago. Also members of an animal rights group jailed after unearthing the remains of a woman connected with a farm supplying guinea pigs for medical research. Custodial sentences in both cases.

'Gomer and me, anyway,' he said.

'*And* me.' Jane sat up hard. 'Come on! Accessory, at least. Worse – I told you to do it and, to compound it, I've just hidden Gomer's spade. So like… me, too.'

Defiant, glassy tears in her eyes.

'You just got into bad company,' Lol said. 'They'll understand.'

He sat down on the rug in front of the inglenook, realizing

she was hyper, watching her coming down, pushing fingers through her hair then shaking her head.

'Can we… can we go back to what happened? I mean before the… what we did. Exhumation. Is that the right word?'

'I don't think it is,' Lol said. 'An exhumation's legal.'

He hadn't slept well. No surprise there. Nor were the dreams. He'd been up early, doing some nervous checking. Once a body or even ashes had been buried in consecrated ground, you couldn't touch them without permission from the Church. And the Church rarely gave permission without a struggle, Christian burial still regarded as final.

'If relatives want to move a body to another grave or another cemetery, for some quite legitimate reason, they have to make a formal application to the diocese. Which, as far as I can see, means the Bishop. A very good reason to sit tight and say nothing to your mum. Much as I hate that.'

'She'd feel responsible. For the churchyard. And for us.'

'That's what I thought.'

'What about Gomer?'

'Gomer won't breathe a word. He's satisfied. He's proved his suspicions were not misguided. That he hasn't lost it and Aidan Lloyd's now properly buried.'

It had taken another half-hour digging out the grave to its original depth, lowering the coffin on ropes. A further hour replacing the earth, refitting the turf like carpet tiles.

'He apologized to me.' Jane smiled. 'Not something a little girl should see.'

'*Are* you OK?'

'Wasn't my all-time favourite Saturday night. But I suppose you need to learn to catch what life throws at you, and like…'

'Run with it?'

Perhaps she was right. They'd come too far to stop running with it.

But Jane had baggage to unload first and nowhere else to unload it.

'When I looked, I was convinced at first that his... his chest and his abdomen had been cut into strips. By the pathologist. Maybe that was what they did.'

'I really wouldn't know.'

'Like, a rag jacket wasn't going to be the first thing to come into my head when I'd never even heard of one till just a few hours earlier. What about the rest? Did he really have the rest of it on?'

'Yes. His body was dressed as a morris dancer. More or less. The bells weren't strapped to his legs, they were just laid on top. We pushed them down the sides of the coffin where they would've been if he'd been wearing them.'

'There was a stick.'

'I think it had rolled to one side when we opened the coffin. So I put it on his chest between his hands.'

'I can't believe you did that. I think I'd've just made sure he was in there and slammed the lid back on.'

'Maybe I didn't want to look like... not a real man... in front of Gomer. It had gone too far, anyway. We had to go through with it. And my hands were as cold as... as his, by then. Even with gloves on I couldn't feel anything. And I'm thinking... the guys who did this, they were all a bit drunk, weren't they? Not drunk enough to mess it up, but enough to see it through without going to pieces.'

'We were thinking they'd come to dance on his grave,' Jane said. 'But in fact they were *opening* the grave... so they could dress him as a morris dancer?'

It was as if the surrealism of this had only just occurred to her, as if she'd been so dislocated by the horror of what they'd done that the black humour in what they'd found had drifted past her.

'I can't imagine his family having him buried as a morris man,' Lol said, 'so we have to assume that someone thought he should be.'

'But like... nobody would *know*... at least not until archae-ologists in about a thousand years' time discover these bizarre

grave goods and it all just gets filed under the heading of...
Ritual.'

Jane's eyes found Lol's.

Ritual.

He asked her if Aidan Lloyd had been a dancer. She didn't know.

'But all of *them* in dancing kit,' she said. 'They dressed up in morris dancing kit to dig him out of his grave and put him into costume?'

'We have to assume that's what they did, yeah. I... hung out with these Cotswold morris men for... well, for not very long, but long enough to know that they were... not exactly a race apart, but they'd definitely developed a different mindset from most of us.'

She looked at him, curious, but he wasn't sure he could explain it. Knew he'd experienced it briefly – that moment beyond failure and fatigue when the body took charge. Or something took charge of the body. All the years when he hadn't thought about this, but it hadn't gone away. Whatever it was.

'OK, suppose what we were looking at is connected to some *Border* morris tradition that's never really been recorded. That isn't talked about.'

'We can find out, can't we?' Jane was on the edge of the sofa. 'This happened just a couple of days ago. This is fresh. And we have a name.'

'Tell me again.'

'Gareth Brewer. And a place. We have a place.'

'You been there much?'

'Kilpeck? Me and... and Eirion went there once. To check out the church. All these mysterious old carvings projecting from under the eaves. It's unique. Like a medieval picture-book in stone. We didn't stop long, it was raining hard and we... anyway, we didn't stop. Always meant to go back. Never have.'

'It's not a huge village, shouldn't be too hard to find him.'

'It wasn't.' Jane held up her phone. 'Seems to be only one Brewer in Kilpeck.'

'Oh, Jane—'

'H. G. Brewer,' Jane said. 'Farrier. Which of us is going to ring him?'

'We need to think about this.'

'No. You can spend too much time thinking. Lol, we can *sort* this.' She had her hands clasped in front of her and they were vibrating with energy and impatience. 'We know what they did. All they have to tell us is why.'

'They don't have to tell us anything.'

'We can lean on them. We know what they did.'

'But we can't tell anybody how we know.'

'We can get over that, you know we can. What if me and Mum saw everything?'

'No. God. I definitely wouldn't tell anybody that. We don't know who they are, and we don't know how important it is to them to keep a lid on it.' Coffin lid; he felt the weight of it between his hands, the wood slick with damp earth. 'This is the country, Jane. Different rules have always applied. You know that.'

They were both silent for some seconds. The light in the window was blue and cold and empty. Then Jane said,

'It was like... I don't know how to explain this, but last night, it was like my whole life coming down to this... this journey into death. Deadness. The grave. Finality. The reality of it. It was like being exposed to the greatest mystery, the reality behind the big taboo that we hide away in the earth and then turn away from and realizing why we turn away. And Mum out there – out there now – trying to tell people that it doesn't end down there in the soil and the clay and the shit. Do you really believe she's doing anything but—?'

'Positive.' He could hear his own desperation. 'She's doing something positive.'

'But is it a lie? Is she perpetuating total crap to make a handful of people feel better about where they're going, so when they come out of the church and walk past the graves they can feel something other than like, at least it's not me down there?'

She was staring into the red gases in the wood stove, the crematorium for logs, the alternative.

'And here's me, Lol... Here's me about to commit most of my life to unearthing more death. Getting all excited about ancient corpses and... oooh, are we looking at ritual here?' Her eyes were dry now, coming back to look into his. 'What about the face?'

'The face?'

'*His* face?'

'Yes.'

He was hoping she hadn't seen the face.

'Border morris is black-face,' Jane said.

'Mmm.'

For black-face you needed a face.

'He was wearing some kind of mask,' Jane said.

'Yes, he was.'

Because the coffin had been at an angle, the mask had slipped. As he and Gomer had seen when they'd taken off the lid.

This morning, he'd put Aidan Lloyd into the Net. Newspaper reports avoided these details, but Aidan had been hit by a van coming round a bend. He'd been on an open quad bike, probably not wearing a helmet. What they'd seen in the lamplight had been the results of the crash and also the post-mortem. And, finally, presumably, the attempts by the undertakers to make what was left of his face look less hideous.

They'd failed.

'Holes for the eyes,' Jane said. 'In the mask.'

Except that underneath there hadn't been any eyes.

'Which was wood,' Jane said. 'Wildwood. Twigs and leaves. Holly leaves. All stuck together.'

'And yew, I think. And mistletoe. In a wooden frame. It was a proper mask. It would have been tied at the back if it had been worn by a living person.'

'Is there a morris side in Kilpeck?'

'I've never heard of one,' Lol said. 'Leominster, the Silurian side down in Ledbury, the Bedlams up in Shropshire, the Foxwood in Hay. Kilpeck, no.'

Jane leaned forward over clasped hands.

'We could go and see him, Lol. Gareth Brewer. Both of us.'

'Just interrupt him at his forge to quiz him about digging up a grave?'

'Don't go cold on this now.' She pulled a tangle of hair out of her eyes. 'Sorry. I can hardly blame you.'

'All right, I'll call him.'

'When?'

'Today.'

'And you'll tell me what he says?'

'Of course I'll tell you.'

Jane stood up.

'Better go. I said I'd make some lunch. I'm sorry, Lol. It's just that…' She'd got her phone and was fiddling with it. 'This came.' She put the phone down on the sofa. 'See what you think.'

Lol went to pick up the phone; Jane raised a hand.

'No hurry. Give it me back next time you see me.'

'Jane, is there—?'

'I'd just rather not be there if it rings, OK?'

21

Latchkey kid

WHAT MERRILY NORMALLY did on the Sunday after a funeral was to invite prayers for the family.

It usually helped if the family was there to hear the first one.

Even a fragment of the family.

The stained-glass ripe apple glowed unseasonally in the window on her right, as, during the second hymn, she looked down from the lectern at the elderly regulars and the families – two couples who'd dragged their kids away from the Xboxes and taken away their phones in the hope that the seed of something worthwhile might take root during a period of being bored out of their skulls. She looked at James Bull-Davies, hands behind his back, who came because generations of his squirely ancestors had come on the Sabbath to occupy that same front pew.

About twenty-five people altogether – normal for a sunny winter Sunday when there was coffee afterwards.

And not one of them called Lloyd, unless...

Just one person she didn't know. A black-haired young woman dressed for the weather in a bulky black woollen coat, who had arrived ten minutes after the start of the service. Sometimes you'd get visitors or second-homers who never went to a church near their first homes, but they were nearly always couples.

This woman just sat there, not far from the doors, didn't sing or respond to prayers, remained blank-faced through the parish notices, and then slipped away – *bugger* – towards the end of the final hymn.

Merrily slipped away, too, pulling off her surplice, while Jim and Brenda Prosser from the Eight Till Late were serving the tea and coffee from the vestry. She left the surplice screwed up on a bench in the porch and went out into the churchyard in her cassock, cutting across the grass, looking from side to side.

Ah...

She'd reached Lucy's stone, its moss limelit by the cold sun, when she saw that the woman was standing by the small tump that was Aidan's grave, looking out across Iestyn's field.

Merrily stepped off the coffin path.

'Erm... I don't normally chase people like this, but... are you a relation of Aidan's?'

The woman turned. Early thirties. A lean, concave face, grey eyes, the black hair below her shoulders.

'Just someone who decided she ought to know him... a lot better than she thought she did.' A glance back towards the apple trees. 'Did they *tell* you to play it down? At the funeral?'

'Were you there?'

'In the church. For a while. Stayed at the back. Didn't attend the burial. Or the tea.'

'That was the general feeling, was it? That it was played down?'

'I don't know. I didn't talk to anyone.'

'I'm not too happy with the way I conducted that funeral. And I'm not blaming anyone else. Should've been more... curious. That is, I *was* curious, but I didn't know the family and I get worried about treading on people's—'

'I suppose they told you he was stoned most of the time,' the woman said.

'I'm sorry?'

'And that when the accident happened he was probably doped to the eyeballs, didn't know he'd even come out of the field.'

137

'Who said that?'

'While the tea was taking place, I went into the bar instead. You only had to keep your ears open.'

'Look, I'm sorry, I don't know your...'

'Rachel. There's no reason you should know me. I'm the woman who wasn't sleeping with him.'

Merrily said nothing.

'In the strictest sense. If I had, I might've known more about him. The significant things you learn when you spend the whole night with someone and wake up with them. You know? And I never saw him roll a spliff.'

'Listen,' Merrily said, 'my vicarage is just over that wall. Give me fifteen minutes to wind things up at the church, put some stuff away—'

'No...' She looked uncertain suddenly. 'I'd rather not do that.'

'Rachel, I've been told about the cannabis, for what that's worth, but nobody's mentioned you, or any woman, in connection with Aidan Lloyd. No reason they would, but...'

'He never stayed the night, you see. I used to think he must have had a wife somewhere. Wife and kids. I didn't really care.' Rachel frowned. 'No, that's wrong. Of course I cared. I just cared more when I found out he *didn't* have a wife. If he didn't have a wife, then why did he never stay the night?'

'Where did you meet him? Do you mind if I ask?'

'In a pub. After a talk, in Hereford, about the theory of universal consciousness. Wasn't very interesting, as it turned out. Amazing how some people can turn universal consciousness into something not very interesting, but there you go. I was with some friends and we went to a pub afterwards and he was there, and I remembered he'd been at the talk, so...'

'What was he like?'

'Ah, well...' Rachel very nearly smiled. '... that's it, you see. Do I really know what he was like? That's the whole point, isn't it? He was a quiet, sweet guy, hard to have a row with

138

him, he didn't argue. And he... was different to any man I'd ever met – and I've met one or two – and I still don't quite know why.'

'What do you do?'

'I'm a doctor. GP.'

'Oh.'

'I was quite surprised to discover he was a farmer, which was a bit pompous and patronizing of me, but there you go, I don't know much about farmers. I only see them when they're ill, and not many. I'm in a city practice.'

'What did you hope to find by coming here today?'

Something, definitely.

'Only I'm a stranger,' Merrily said, 'and you're telling me all this private stuff.'

'I Googled you.' Rachel smiled at last. Kind of. 'You're the woman who investigates hauntings and things. I didn't know the Church did that. But you believe in all that stuff, obviously.'

'Some of it. And, as a doctor, you...'

'I'm not saying I don't. I just wasn't sure whether I wanted to talk to someone like you. Still not sure, really.'

'It's usually nurses who tell me the stories.'

'In hospitals. Yes. We hear them, sometimes. Mine, however... all right, mine happened at home.'

'Oh?'

'What if I was to tell you Aidan came... came in last night?'

'Then I'd ask you again if you wanted to come over to the vicarage,' Merrily said softly. 'Or across the square to the Swan. Or anywhere.'

The Kilpeck number was scrawled sideways on the lyric pad, next to some phrases for a new song, a winter song. The pad was next to the phone. Lol was sitting there, touching nothing.

But then, if he didn't make the call, Jane would only do it, and Jane was not always subtle and, in her present state of mind, might say anything.

Should've told her mother weeks ago about Samantha Burnage. He could understand why she hadn't at the time, and now the time had passed and telling her wouldn't be so easy.

Sam. How it had all arisen out of gratitude.

Sam: the woman who'd taken her side against some of the archaeologists in Pembrokeshire who'd sneered at Jane's passion for folklore and earth-mysteries. Sometimes, Jane seemed to be living on parallel levels, the so-called real world and a numinous place where everything was interlaced, conditioned by the past.

Suppose I kind of worshipped Sam, like when you have a crush on your teacher.

Inevitable that an attachment would form, Jane on her own amongst qualified professionals, thinking she had only one friend. At the end of the dig, they'd got drunk together and Jane had woken up in Sam's bed, not entirely sure what, if anything, had happened in it. Back home, she'd actually approached Gus Staines, the friendly half of the gay couple running Ledwardine Livres, to find out if she might be a closet lesbian – like just so she *knew*. Gus, after quizzing her about the sex of her teddy bear, hadn't thought so.

Lol picked up Jane's phone and reread the email she'd left for him.

See what you think.

Hi Jane
How are you?
Listen, I have good news. A university
archaeology dept. with sudden money
to spare is looking for a project. Doesn't
happen too often any more.
I'm thinking of proposing your henge.
Wanna talk about it? In depth?

I can probably come over quite soon.
much love,
Sam.

In depth, huh?

She's, you know, a nice woman, Jane had said once. *I'm convinced she really does share my values. You'd like her.*

All right, then. What the hell.

He picked up the phone.

She'd cleared up at the church, made her apologies for disappearing so suddenly, collecting a reproving glance from Uncle Ted, senior churchwarden. She rang Jane, explained she could be late, why didn't Jane just get herself some lunch. A familiar scenario. She could've sworn Jane seemed almost glad.

When she made it to the Swan, the bar was crowded; she wasn't sure that Rachel would have waited. But there she was behind either a tomato juice or a Bloody Mary, at the most discreet table for two, under a small, milky mullioned window. She hadn't taken off the big black coat.

Merrily sat down. Too conspicuous in the cassock but it was Sunday.

'Often part of the parting process,' she said. 'But I expect you know that.'

'A stressful time,' Rachel said. 'I've had patients who... anyway.'

Shook her head dismissively.

'Huw,' Merrily said, 'the guy who advises me, has taken to calling them the Latchkey Kids.'

'Let themselves in?'

'Someone you know very well who lets him or herself in. For a while. More properly, the Bereavement Apparition.'

'I think I prefer latchkey kid. It certainly makes you question your— not your sanity, but your state of mind. I felt the need to talk about it with someone who wouldn't give me the psychobabble. Just wasn't sure I wanted it to be a vicar. I had a patient who was a woman vicar, and I certainly wouldn't have told her. A touch too mumsy. I suppose I watched how you took that service and came to the conclusion that you probably couldn't easily do happy-clappy.'

'Not happy enough. Would you like something to eat?'

'No thank you. I won't stay long. I was... against my will, becoming serious about Aidan. Never the intention. A farmer? Me?'

There was the sense of them being in a hollow in the crowded bar, the chat and laughter shifted back.

'I'm very sorry,' Merrily said. 'It was a truly awful thing to happen. I'm afraid I didn't know him. We just... it's a big village, growing all the time, and our paths didn't cross. I wished they had.'

'He didn't spend much time here, did he? He went to work on his father's farm. He *went to work*. Had what amounted to a bedsit there – live-in accommodation rather than a home. He told me all this, but never talked much about this village. Only about the one where he grew up. He did take me there once.'

'Just to get this right, you and he were...'

'An item? You'd say that, yes.' She looked into the mottled blue light of the mullion window. 'You'd have to say that now.'

Merrily didn't ask.

'It was an unusual arrangement,' Rachel said, 'but with my job I suppose it suited me. For a while. At first I thought I must be *using* him, you know?'

'How long?'

'Nearly a year. His death... I haven't really had anyone to talk to about it. Or him. Nobody knew about him. My parents live down in Berkshire. They didn't know about him. My partners at work, they didn't know about him. Mainly because *I* didn't know about him. Most men, they can't tell you enough about themselves, can they?'

'You didn't talk much?'

'We talked a lot, eventually. But not about personal issues – or at least I didn't think they were personal. Now I think perhaps they were. Issues verging on philosophy. I'd see him twice a week, three times lately. He was a quiet man, shy, but you became aware of… I can only describe it as an underlying energy. I don't really mean physical, although he was stronger than he looked.'

'You're talking about an inner…?'

'Oh, *powerfully* inner. A lot going on inside him, and I don't mean emotional turmoil, he was usually very calm. I'm not sure *what* I mean, but that was… that was what I saw, when I awoke this morning.'

'*This* morning?'

'It was strange. Because we'd never spent a night together, I never awoke with that empty-bed feeling. So what I saw – it was him, and… Oh God, I saw the energy of him. It filled the room.'

'You *saw* it…'

'Vividly. I saw him, very briefly, but the energy didn't go away for some minutes. The longest minutes of my life. Or perhaps it was only seconds. If someone came into the clinic and told me that, I'd have to write them a prescription.'

'And that was the first time…?'

'No. The first time was in the night. After the funeral.'

'Oh.'

Rachel looked down into her drink then pushed it away.

'Not good. I thought that was me. I'd done a lot of crying that night.'

'Did you feel anything at the grave, just now?'

'Nothing at all. It's not his place, is it?'

'Graves seldom are. This morning – were you frightened?'

'No. Not while it was happening. Afterwards I was frightened. But that's normal, isn't it? You're frightened something's wrong with you.'

143

'You said this was not his place. What *is* his place, Rachel?'

'Kilpeck,' Rachel said. 'Oh God, yes. If he talked with any enthusiasm about anywhere, it was Kilpeck.'

22

Confessional

A WOMAN ANSWERED.

'He's at work, I'm afraid.'

'I'm sorry. Didn't think he'd be working on a Sunday.'

'He doesn't usually. If you want to make an appointment—'

'It's not about horses,' Lol said. 'Or shoes or...'

'Who is this?'

'Um... my name's Robinson. I'm helping organize a folk festival for next summer. At Ledwardine. I'd heard Mr Brewer was connected with a morris dancing side.'

Pause.

'Who told you that?'

Quite sharp.

'Just a friend. Someone who knew we were looking to book some morris dancers.'

'Where did you say you were from?'

Wary now. Her accent was not local. South of England somewhere.

'Ledwardine. That's—'

'I know where it is.' Said very quickly. Suspicion here and perhaps something more complicated. 'Why do you need to talk to my husband about this?'

'I'm sorry, you mean he *isn't* connected with the morris?'

'Look. I'll give him your message, but he probably isn't going to be able to help you.'

'If I've got this wrong I'll just—'

He could hear children in the background, insistent.

'The Kilpeck Morris,' she said, 'are not available for book-ings. Didn't you know that? Rhian, leave that *alone.*'

'Ever?'

'I'll give him your message, OK?'

He had a sense of the telephone line between them stretched tight. At least he had an admission that there was a morris side here. But fully booked? For ever?

'Are you in the side as well?'

'I'm a woman.'

'All male. Sorry, didn't know that. Would it be possible to talk to your husband anyway? Would there be a time that might be convenient?'

'Look,' she said, 'you're probably trying to talk to the wrong person. If you leave me your number I'll pass it on to him. If he doesn't ring you back, I expect you can find somebody else. No! I said you could have *one.*'

'I'm sorry,' Lol said. 'You're busy. If he's the wrong person, who *should* I be talking to?'

There was a long pause.

'Do you know Sir Lionel?'

'Sir Lionel who?'

'No, I'm sorry, it's nothing to do with me,' the woman said. 'I'll pass on your message.'

Then she hung up.

By the time Jane returned, Lol had already Googled *Sir Lionel, Kilpeck Morris.* Not an overwhelming response, and no mention of a Kilpeck morris side. The nearest connection was

Reopening of forgotten Kilpeck footpath supported by Sir Lionel Darvill.

from a local parish website, relating how a long-disused right of way had been reopened, despite objections by farmers and landowners, after Sir Lionel Darvill had given permission for access to his Maryfields Estate, offering to install gates and stiles.

'Never heard of him,' Jane said.

She'd come without a coat and was down by the stove. Winter was coming at them like a slow train; its last carriage would have frozen windows.

'Me neither,' Lol said. 'This county's full of obscure titled people. We should ask Gomer. Gomer knows everybody.'

'This guy is in charge of the Kilpeck Morris side?'

'That's the inference. What's really odd is that if you Google Kilpeck Morris you get nothing at all.'

'I bet I could find something.'

'Please do.'

He hadn't expected her back so soon, hadn't had much time to think about the email on her phone. Few situations he liked less than when Jane had told him something he was forbidden to share with her mother – this occasional reluctance going back, he guessed, to the days when she'd seen herself as a committed pagan who couldn't trust Christians, only fellow weirdos, alive or dead.

'Your phone's on the desk,' he said.

'Thank you.'

'This Sam… she's continued to text you, send emails?'

'Yes. '

'But this is the first…'

'The first suggestion that she might come here, yeah.'

This looked clever. The possibility of the orchard that had once surrounded Ledwardine marking the perimeter of a Neolithic henge was central to Jane's perceived future. The big secret that she sometimes seemed convinced the village itself had confided to her.

'You told Sam all about the henge?'

'More or less. The buried stones in Coleman's Meadow, the idea about Church Street following the course of a processional avenue leading up from the river…'

147

'And the council?'

Herefordshire Council's long-term plans to expand the village, which meant that Jane's henge, if it existed, could wind up underneath executive housing and a supermarket.

'And our esteemed councillor, Lyndon Pierce, and his undisclosed links with the big business guys who'd benefit from the development. Yeah, all that.'

Lol winced.

'I know, I know. I was pissed. You know what it's like when you can't stop talking. Anyway, all archaeologists know most of their work is going to be investigating ground that *somebody* wants to build on. Thing is, a university-sponsored dig might be the best thing that could happen. Like, if it was found to be of serious historical importance we might be looking at protected status. Something to fight for, anyway.'

'Um...' This was awkward. 'Are you thinking that if Sam still has... a bit of a thing for you, then the possibility of a henge – might be of, um, secondary importance?'

'Worse than that. If it *is* a henge, it'll be *their* henge, won't it? The university's. I know that's selfish...'

'But you'd be involved, surely?'

'Involved?' Jane stared up at him, unblinking. 'You're not getting this, are you?'

'You mean if Sam was in charge, the extent of your involvement might depend on you and Sam being on the same side? As it were.'

'She's a nice woman. I don't think for one minute she—'

'It's more how you'd feel, right? Getting her here under false pretences?'

'All mixed up, Lol.'

'Jane, it's not yet one day since we did... what we did.'

Perhaps this was a good time to tell her about Barry's idea that she might run the festival shop. Although nothing had been signed, and if it all fell through...

'I'm assuming you haven't told your mum about Sam yet.'

'Correct.'

'You going to?'

'Not till I get to the stage where I can laugh about it.' Jane wandered over to the desk in the window. 'Maybe in ten years. Meanwhile, what do I do about this?'

Picking up the phone as if it was an explosive device from which the fuse needed to be extracted.

'You could tell her that… I dunno, maybe that it might not be a good time to alert certain people that there's interest in the site. Apologize for sounding secretive, but say things might be a lot clearer in a few weeks. Something like that?'

'You think?'

'Buy some time. Things can happen. Just don't think about it. Go to the meditation tonight, empty it all out.'

'You going?'

'Probably.'

'Maybe I won't. I've had enough of the church and the churchyard. Maybe I'll go deep into the Net and find out about the Kilpeck Morris, now we know it exists.'

'Just don't contact anybody… yet.'

'I quite like the idea of taking on an aristocrat.' Jane was looking out of the window. 'Some retired MP who got knighted for doing bugger all. Keeping his head down somewhere quiet so everybody'll forget about him and his sexual history in the last millennium. Oh—'

'What?'

'There's Mum coming back from work. Shivering in her cassock. I should go home, stoke up the stove, put the kettle on.'

'I'm wondering now if we ought to tell her,' Lol said. 'It might be more harmful that she doesn't know. Don't know what to do, really. Life's suddenly…'

'A bitch.'

When she'd gone, he sat gazing out of the window across the street to where leafless trees offered scant shielding to the black and white timbers of the vicarage. Its chimney stacks were already smoky silhouettes, the sky rusting fast. The paper with the Kilpeck number on it had turned pink in the sunset. In a couple of hours, Merrily would be off to the church to lead the Sunday evening meditation, very much her favourite service. He'd go too, because there were no hymns, no psalms, and she didn't wear the dog collar. She would be the Merrily of 'Camera Lies'.

A shadow moved on the edge of his vision. He stood up quickly and kicked shut the door to the hall and the newel post. Picked up the Boswell from its stand, found the basic chords for the song he was working. A regretful song about the winter solstice. As yet, it had only two short lines.

> *The old year turns on a rusting hinge*
> *Kids in the city on a drinking binge*

He struck the strings and the chord jarred, out of tune. He'd tuned it this morning. The Boswell didn't normally do this.

As for the mental image of Lucy Devenish raising a gnarled warning finger, that was... mental.

23

Inhale the darkness

ELECTRIC LIGHTS DOWN, candles lit though not for long.

Merrily took her seat in the well at the top of the nave, below the chancel. She was in a long black skirt, cashmere sweater. Small pectoral cross. Usual Sunday night attire. Sunday night was not about ministering. Guiding, perhaps, and then fading back in the shadows.

Introduction.

'We've got used to having Christmas as a beacon.' Conversational. 'The light at the heart of the winter.'

It had started last week, nothing too intense. An awareness of the time of year, the shortening days. Approaching the season governed by night. A mild meditation last Sunday to prepare the ground.

'OK, the trees are bare, the bad weather's started, but Christmas is coming – good food, office parties, family gatherings, an excuse to drink more, a new Bond movie on TV. The hell with winter.'

Over forty people here tonight, which wasn't bad at all. A lower age group than the regular services, even Communion. The assembly reduced to cut-outs now. Some of them would have seen the stack of slim paperbacks in the window of the village bookshop and twigged, but there would still be an element of uncertainty.

'But let's pretend, for a while, that Christmas isn't going to happen. No cribs, no coloured lights.'

A church was never entirely dark, but tonight was about promoting shadows. She came slowly to her feet, rustle of the skirt.

'In fact let's do more than pretend. Let's cancel it.'

She blew out the first candle. A segment of nave disappeared.

'Christmas. Not going to happen.'

Blew out the second candle. The thin rising smell of molten wax and blackened wick.

'Open ourselves up to the cold...'

The heating was on, but that wasn't the kind of cold she meant. Nearly all the faces had disappeared from the semicircle of rearranged pews and chairs. The stained-glass windows had turned to mud and then reanimated themselves in a grey and spectral way.

'... and the emptiness. The nothingness.'

She breathed on the third candle and tried not to think about Aidan Lloyd.

You had to keep returning to the dark.

She had a discreet battery-powered reading light, a narrow bar that she could shield with a hand so that it lit only the page, not her. Reducing her to a soft voice coming out of nowhere, intoning the words of the anonymous medieval mystic – who knew, it *might* have been a woman – laying out a pathway for the soul in search of light, but stressing that it could only begin in the dark, with the feeling of nothing, the knowing of nothing.

Very appropriate to the time of year. She'd thought about it last year but hadn't gone ahead, the motivation hadn't been there. Then Gus Staines at Ledwardine Livres had landed on a job lot of *The Cloud of Unknowing*, this luminous guide to contemplation, originally written, anonymously, in Middle English. No harm, surely, in supporting your local bookshop.

The nature of God entirely obscured by the cloud of unknowing. A wintry thought. No pleasure in this in the early stages. A loneliness there, even isolation. But you had to keep returning to the dark, until you felt at home there; only then could the yearning emerge. Perhaps, by then, assisted.

The church door creaked. She heard Lol padding in.

Couldn't see him at all, but she registered it was Lol. She always did. He sometimes claimed he only came as a voyeur, to watch her gliding around in black. She smiled invisibly. Not possible tonight, even if he'd had good eyesight.

She passed on the message from the fourteenth century that the state of contemplation could not be achieved through either knowledge or the use of imagination. Essentially, expect nothing. It was the basis of all real meditation. What all the best gurus told you. She didn't tell them that.

Sometimes, outside the church afterwards, someone would grab her excitedly, to talk about a flash of enlightenment or the fleeting sensation of separation from the physical. But that was only the crack of light under the door.

The crack of light – it could be amazing when that happened, although mystics and theologians would tell you it wasn't really significant in the great scheme of things. If you were religious, it might convince you that you were on the true path. If you were a committed atheist, it would simply be a useful lesson about the efficacy of brain chemicals.

The church door opened again. Not sure who this was, but too heavy-footed to be Jane. Hoping to God she had this right, she invited the unseen assembly in the nave to inhale the darkness.

Breathing in the bitter aroma of burnt wick and cooling wax. The real challenge would come next Sunday when she'd have to approach the spiritual power of love without sounding trite.

She didn't think that Rachel would be here. Dr Rachel Peel, who had declined any of the uncertain, counselling-based help usually offered to recipients of a bereavement visitation. If she was anywhere tonight, perhaps she'd be at Kilpeck Church, if it was Kilpeck's turn to have a Sunday evening service.

It ended, as usual, in five minutes of silent meditation. When it was over, she didn't relight any candles, found her way instead to the switches beside the rood screen and activated the highest ambient lights.

And thus – jolted hard back into the wooden screen, a hand to her mouth – was able to identify the person who had been last in and was now first out.

Outside, it was so cold now that you could almost see the frost crystals forming in the air, but they walked back slowly along the edge of the cobbles, Lol telling her about Jane bringing him the name of Gareth Brewer, finding his phone number. And why, in the end, he'd called it.

'Oh God, they're going to make the connection,' Merrily said. 'You do realize that?'

'I think Brewer's wife already has.'

He'd hesitantly taken her hand, something he still did outside in Ledwardine only in the hours of darkness.

'Lol, even if she doesn't know exactly why they came to Ledwardine, when she tells her husband she's had a call from someone here, *he* will know. And then what?'

'She knows something,' Lol said. 'Would've been better if I could've talked to him directly.'

'And put it to him that he was dancing on a grave?'

His hand tightened around hers, as if in spasm.

'This is Jane, isn't it?' Merrily said. 'She got the number, I don't like to think how, and she said that if you didn't call him, she would?'

Always a dilemma for Lol, how to handle Jane. Whether he realized this or not, his central discomfort had always related to coming across in any way paternal.

'It was my decision,' he said. 'But you're right, they're going to be wondering what we know. I need to get hold of this Lionel Darvill. *Sir* Lionel. When we find out who he is.'

'Maybe I'll sound out the local priest. Kilpeck's part of a cluster run from Ewyas Harold, where the rector's newish so might not know too much. I'm going in to see Sophie tomorrow, I'll check her out.'

'It's best,' Lol said, 'if you aren't involved.'

'Yeah, well, I'm getting tired of hiding.'

Screwing up her eyes to examine a small group of people crossing the square towards the entrance of the Swan. None of them looked like Paul Crowden, the wrestler. Merrily felt numb. It *had* been Crowden in church, hadn't it?

Lol said, 'Come back with me. Things I have to tell you.'

'I'd love to, but I've hardly seen Jane today, and she… doesn't seem too happy.'

'She isn't. But she agrees it's best you hear it from me.'

'*Hear—?*'

'Just come back. Please.'

The wobbly lights of the Black Swan, those warm leaded squares, glimmered from across the cobbles, and applewood fires perfumed the air. She thought suddenly, irrationally, or maybe not, *I'm going to lose all this.*

24

Big farming

JANE FOUND THAT Lol had been right. There was nothing online about the Kilpeck Morris and very little about Sir Lionel Darvill.

However...

What he *should* have done was followed the family name. Jane – grimly driven tonight – did some serious following on the laptop up in her apartment with Ethel sleeping on her bed and the old blow-heater death-rattling behind her. Whoever these guys were, she was coming for them.

The Darvills of Kilpeck.

You didn't have to be particularly famous to get a Wikipedia entry and there was quite a lot on the Darvills. The name had been spelled a few different ways over the centuries, notably *De Ville*, as in Cruella, for quite a while until it found its current form in the nineteenth century.

Well, of course, Jane knew that the British aristocracy had grown out of thieving and backhanders, favours to the Crown getting repaid. What changed?

The Darvills claimed their ancestors had come over with William the Conqueror or maybe a little later. These posh bastards were always lying about their roots. Whether this particular branch was descended from the original Norman family was open to conjecture, but they were certainly baronets, which gave them a title they could pass on but no seat in the House of Lords. Seemed like win-win to Jane.

She had to wade through two world wars and a lot of politics before finding something shining dully out of the dirt.

It was the word *mysticism*.

The key period began with Peter Darvill, who had inherited the title in the late 1960s along with a big farmhouse, rather than a mansion, called Maryfields, in the middle of a substantial estate just outside Kilpeck. Peter had become an active farmer, running the expanding estate for nearly ten years, very profitably, until he died, suddenly, the way a lot of active farmers died.

You didn't have to live in the sticks for very long to learn that, even today, a high proportion of accidental deaths on farms were down to tractor accidents. Peter Darvill had had this huge, expensive beast, a pedigree shirehorse of a tractor, a power symbol. He'd climbed down from the cab when it was on a hillside and gone round the back, apparently to check on something, somehow failing to immobilize it, and the great tractor had come rolling inexorably back, on its enormous tyres, over Sir Peter.

He was divorced, no kids, so the title went to his younger brother, Henry, which was where it got interesting. This was because Henry had no particular interest in agriculture, according to Wikipedia, while being fascinated by stuff that Jane could well understand people getting into: basically, human potential. Not how much money he could make but what he could *be*. What any of us could be.

Henry Darvill was a mystic with intent.

Jane – and his destiny, as it turned out – found him at an establishment called the College for Perpetual Learning, which he'd helped finance with much of his inheritance as second son when Peter had landed the farm.

The college had been founded in a small mansion near Pershore in neighbouring Worcestershire, to continue the work of the late George Ivanovich Gurdjieff.

OK, she was sure she'd heard the name, but nobody could be expected to know *every* eastern-European-bordering-on-Russian spiritual teacher.

Back to Google.

She liked the look of him at once: bald head, big black curly moustache and eyes that nailed you to the wall even in old black and white photos. Gurdjieff, dead since 1949, had spent years guru-chasing in North Africa and the East, before coming west between the world wars, settling in France, collecting a bunch of wealthy and cultured followers whom he'd tasked with menial work like toilet cleaning in the cause of attaining higher consciousness. He called it the Fourth Way because it was achievable in the course of an ordinary life. Gurdjieff's premise: you're all asleep, you need to learn how to awaken fully or you're stuffed in the afterlife. But don't think it's going to be easy.

Whether Henry Darvill ever fully awoke was debatable because he had to give up his studies at the College for Perpetual Learning to become *Sir* Henry.

After which the Maryfields estate would never be the same again.

Merrily was huddled into a corner of Lol's sofa, one sleeve of the cashmere sweater pushed up, he guessed, to hide a new hole, one hand gripping the other as if it might come away. Her shoes were off, her hair was loose. She looked younger, but not necessarily in a good way. As if she was throwing off all resemblance to an adult in control.

He'd turned the hard chair away from the desk to face her. The stove was burning low.

'I'm not going all self-pitying and using words like *betrayed*,' Merrily said, not looking at him, 'but I did think I could trust you. Of all people.'

'What could I *do*?' Lol's eyes shutting in anguish. 'He'd already started. I tried to talk him out of it. If I hadn't helped him he might've been there all night. I *like* Gomer.'

'We *all* like Gomer. Jesus Christ, we *love* Gomer...'

'He just had to know he was right. At his time of life, these things are important.'

'Lol, it's not what you did, abhorrent though it was. It's the fact that you conspired—'

'*Conspired?* Fucking *hell...*'

'Decided to hide it from me. You dug up the grave of a man in my churchyard and you thought it would *not* be good to tell me in case it offended my... Christian sensibilities?'

'What *would* you have done... if you'd known?'

'I don't know. Something. I don't *know*. It changes everything, doesn't it? This really *is* a crime. And you...'

'Yeah, I'm guilty, too. Just as guilty as whoever did it the first time.'

'And Jane—'

'Jane had no part in it.'

'Except to incite you to go ahead. While I... slept.'

Lol sat staring between his knees to the stone flags.

'We were wrong. *I* was wrong. I should've told you this morning. Should've been waiting for you outside the church door...'

'We can't go to the police now, can we? We can't even go to the police we *know*. We're in the middle of it now. We're part of it.'

'*You* aren't—'

'Don't you— You promise me *now* that you will never again—'

'Merrily, please—'

She looked about to cry. Put both hands over her face, and stifled it. Sat upright on the edge of the sofa.

'I'm sorry. You were there only because of us. Because of something Jane said. If you hadn't been there, Jane would still have turned up. Then God knows what would've happened. Jane and Gomer. A lethal cocktail. I'm sorry. It's time for me to do something. And don't... don't ask me what.'

The first thing Henry Darvill did when he took over Maryfields was get rid of the big tractor that killed his older brother.

Probably not realizing at the time how symbolic this would be. It would, according to Wikipedia, condition his whole future approach to farming.

Big tractor: big agriculture.

Bad.

Well, yeah, big agriculture *was* bad. Jane thought of old woodland getting chainsawed into oblivion, hedgerows ripped up, ancient field-systems lost for ever, wildlife habitats destroyed. She'd read that over a hundred species of wildlife were facing extinction in the UK because of pesticides sterilizing the countryside. Manure replaced by chemicals. You saw these massive crop-spraying machines too wide for the border lanes, all shiny metal discs and poisonous tubes coiled together. Meeting one was like facing some horror-comic alien invasion. Even before it had pushed you into the ditch, you hated it.

So the death of his brother had brought about this Damascene conversion in Henry Darvill. OK, maybe not Damascene – Wikipedia said it had happened over a period of two or three years; you couldn't immediately become an organic farmer, you had to ease the land back into the old ways. And you had to be prepared to lose money.

So, at first, profits sank, and Sir Henry didn't seem get along with some of his neighbours for reasons that were not clear but probably included stuff like reopening the old footpath between Maryfields and Kilpeck Church.

But Henry, in comparative penury, was on a high. At last he could live with himself as a big landowner with a title.

Though not with his farm manager. Jane read that the second big thing Henry did, which took much longer than getting rid of the tractor, was to dispense with the services of the very efficient, very professional guy who had made a lot of money for his brother Peter on the basis that Big Farming was the only kind that worked.

There were no details of this on Wikipedia, and it probably didn't matter, but Jane never liked to give up until she had everything the Net had to reveal. Besides, she hadn't yet found anything about Sir Lionel who, presumably, was Sir Henry's successor.

She found the crunch line eventually on a dense site dealing with industrial tribunals involving farm workers. It seemed the Maryfields farm manager's unfair dismissal case had been abandoned after he was bought off, at considerable expense.

Enough, it was suggested, to enable the farm manager to acquire a farm of his own on the edge of a village about twenty miles away.

Holy shit.

Jane stood up, images of oilseed rape soaking into her thoughts like yellow vomit.

Part Four

Above all, the performers must be infected with the true spirit of the dance. The Morris is something more than a severe, cold, unemotional dance, even if it cannot justly be called a merry, exuberant one...

The dancer must have complete control over his limbs and attain a balance and supple poise of body... after prolonged practice, the coordinated movements of arms, body and feet have become automatic. In the early stages the beginner is advised not to be afraid of erring on the side of force and strength.

Sharpe and MacIlwaine
The Morris Book (1912)

25

Looking at dead police

GAOL STREET, MONDAY morning. Bliss turning away from his office window, sitting down behind his laptop on the desk, bringing up another piccy of the garage man's upper half, lying in black grease and showing off the hole in the shaven side of his head.

'And now we know exactly what did that,' he said to Annie. 'It's this.'

He brought up another pic of a little automatic pistol with a brown handle, and turned the lappie to face her across the desk.

'Makarov 9-mil. Apparently a Russian old faithful from Soviet days.'

Annie studied it. She was in her dark blue business suit, white shirt, her white-blonde hair tied back. In half an hour she'd be chairing morning assembly in the Major Incident Room. There was already a buzz around Gaol Street, excitement not shared by Bliss. If he'd been sentimental about gun crime he'd be back Up North by now.

Annie looked up.

'Many of these getting imported? Do we know?'

'Of late, yeh. Less fashionable in Russia since the last cold war ended, so bargains to be had. Doesn't mean the Russian mafia, they're all over Eastern Europe. There's a Russian video on YouTube of some fat twat loading one and firing it. I say fat twat, because his gut's all you ever see.'

YouTube and Google. It had come to this. Not too long ago, you'd have to wait for some boffin in ballistics to serve up the background and it might take an hour or so; now it was a couple of clicks away. They were still waiting for the PM.

Annie opened her primeval spiral-bound notebook.

'Let me get this absolutely right, Francis, before we go in there. Jaglowski was shot with one of his own guns.'

'Not necessarily, but it's a working theory.'

Karen's team had found them wrapped in oily cloth in a strongbox at the bottom of the inspection pit under the ramp in Jag's garage. Also five boxes of bullets that looked like little Duracell batteries with rounded ends.

'The bullets that did for Jag were not your ordinary nine mil. Makarov ammo was made significantly bigger so they'd be incompatible with Western pistols in case there was a war and some got nicked by the enemy. Paranoid bastards, the Soviets.'

'But he wasn't killed by one of the pistols found in the garage.'

'None of them had been fired.'

Slim Fiddler, the chief SOCO, had told him all this. Bit of a ballistics expert, Slim. Been a hobby of his for years. Surprising what you didn't know about your colleagues.

'Fiddler was in a gun club, Annie. Used to go target shooting at an army range. Gorra Walther PPK of his own. Like James Bond?'

'Not at home, I hope.'

'Kept at the club, under lock and key. Obviously, we don't know where Jaglowski got these, but I expect they're all over Birmingham.'

'The point is he was dealing guns from Hereford.'

She looked faintly outraged. Annie had been born here. Now Hereford – on her watch – was becoming a city housing heavy-duty villains. As if a virulent infection had got in under cover of the fog and soon there'd be kids shooting kids in alleyways and across the spare land beyond the Plascarreg.

'Until his death,' Bliss said, 'all we knew about this man was that he was a small-time criminal fencing stolen farm machinery. If we'd known about that two or three weeks ago, had him under obbo – assuming we could afford that – we could be looking at a serious result by now.'

'We could also be looking at dead police,' Annie said soberly.

He didn't say anything. He'd never liked guns, never even wanted an airgun when he was growing up in a part of Merseyside that still had fields. Never done firearms training, felt nervous standing next to some bugger with body armour and a stubby machine gun, even if they were on the same side. Still…

'Don't like to talk about poetic justice, Annie, but if the only man trading in Russian handguns in Hereford is the first victim of one of them… No evidence of these weapons circulating in the city. Norra whisper. You wouldn't hold up a Tesco Express with one, would you? Chances are he picked them up for peanuts, couldn't bring himself to say no.'

'Do we know how many Makarovs were originally in that strongbox? Was it open?'

'No, all locked up. They found the key on his keyring – not very professional of him. Annie, listen… it's *one feller*. Not like there's been an eruption of gun crime. Jag was a general dealer operating behind a second-hand car business. Maybe this was a first time for him, and the fact that he let himself get shot is an indication of his inexperience.'

'Why didn't whoever it was take the rest of the guns?'

'Maybe somebody was making an example out of him. Gerrin a bit too ambitious. Lorra work to do here, Annie.'

'Yes, well, I've asked for expert advice. Someone's coming over from Hindlip.'

'You think that's really necessary?'

'*They* do. When I'm specifically invited to request assistance I tend to comply. One final thing. His girlfriend, the person who found him…'

Bliss smiled. Last chance saloon: could it have been a simple domestic?

'Don't think we didn't consider it. I got Karen to talk to

her. She's a local girl, Danielle James, twenty-two. Danni. Nice middle-class family. Dad's a dentist. She met Jaglowski at a club. She thought he had… *style.*'

Bliss found a picture of Jaglowski, alive. Black hair, shaven at the sides, long and implausibly wavy on top. Wide moustache. Annie was unimpressed.

'Looks like a Hollywood pirate. She lived with him?'

'Quite a nice rented flat in that new block down the bottom of Bridge Street. Not cheap. Been with him about three months. He was evidently doing all right for somebody who'd been here less than a couple of years.'

'She knew what he was into?'

'We reckon she knew he was into *something*. Part of his appeal, Karen thinks. Danni was all over the place last night, lorra squealing. But then, when Karen talked to her again this morning at her parents' place, it was all very different. Karen thought she was quite excited. Boyfriend getting gunned down? How often does that happen?'

'You're kidding.'

'I blame computer games. They don't know where reality begins. Anyway, she gave us her DNA, prints, good as gold. Let us search the flat. She could be cleverer than she seems, but Karen thinks not. We're gonna bring her in this morning for a proper job. She might be the best we'll get. In English anyway.'

'Out there,' Annie said, 'there's a handgun. Probably with somebody's hand around it. And he – or she – has done it once.'

'Done it more than once, you ask me.'

Annie looked quite unsteady. Not like somebody who'd be going upstairs in about twenty minutes to conduct the orchestra; this was someone who was afraid the concert season was only just beginning. He came round the desk, eyeing the closed door. Annie squirmed away.

'For God's sake…'

'It's only a career,' Bliss said.

Or two. Maybe two. They'd slept last night at his house in

Marden, in the flatlands beyond the city. Not quite so careful any more – what was the point now that Charlie knew? – and yet they'd still done the usual working-morning bit, him leaving alone by the front door, her departing more discreetly by the back door ten minutes later. Making their separate arrivals at Gaol Street.

'I was quite enjoying the fog,' Annie said. 'Not being able to see things coming.'

Closing up her big black bag with the spiral-bound notebook inside.

'It'll all work out,' Bliss said. 'Lorra decent Poles in this city don't like the way fellers like Jag are gerrin them a bad name. Somebody'll get fingered before long. And if it links up to regional organized crime, like Vaynor says, they might start taking each other out for a while, till it settles down.'

Not exactly the best line to take. Various situations had settled down nicely when her old man had been head of CID, and they all knew why that was.

'On the other hand,' Bliss said, 'Jag might just've been storing them for somebody who didn't think he was reliable.'

She didn't look at him. Some of the cold edge had gone from Annie and, for reasons he didn't care to contemplate, he'd grown quite fond of that.

26

Nothing set in stone

MERRILY STOOD AT the top of the stairs and listened. It was crazy, but every time she came up here now, she felt like a fugitive, as if there was a warrant out for her and hands would grab her as soon as she went in.

She waited for about half a minute, letting her heartbeat slow. It had been routine for so long. Monday: traditionally a parish priest's day off; for Merrily, the day she came into the Hereford Cathedral gatehouse office, Sophie's Deliverance tower, always parking in the Bishop's Palace yard.

Not any more. She'd dropped Jane off in town to do some shopping. Left the Freelander on the public car park down by the swimming pool and walked up to the tucked-away Cathedral under an unpromising bronze sky. An air of impermanence – builders and roadworks, charity shops, a city without focus. County-border signs carried the annoying slogan *HERE* YOU CAN. Can *what*? It just needed a cartoon of the council leader with a finger pointing at his head, going *duh*.

'Mr Unsworth rang, from Lang/Copper, to say the demolition of Susan Lulham's house would be going ahead next week, so if you were available to perform, ah…'

'A blessing for the site?'

'I think that's the idea.'

'Could you tell him I'd be happy to do it before or after. Or both.'

'I think he knows that. He just wanted to confirm the date. They're looking at next Tuesday.'

There was a general consensus that the house should be gone before Christmas. It was overshadowing the estate and becoming the wrong kind of tourist attraction. A group of well-off neighbours had bought it between them, for demolition. The site would be landscaped, trees planted to create an amenity area.

'According to Mr Unsworth, people keep driving up there and turning round,' Sophie said. 'Some of them hanging out of the windows taking photos on their phones.'

Merrily winced.

'How do these things spread?'

'Social media, I imagine.'

'Mmm. In which case… could you tell Mr Unsworth I'll call him nearer the time, but it might be best if we had the neighbours – those who want to be involved – gathered on the site just before first light. So as not to attract attention.'

Sophie nodded, sinking behind her desk to make a note. Merrily collapsed into her old chair, her back to the window overlooking Broad Street. Wondering how to approach what needed approaching.

Sophie said she'd never heard of Paul Crowden.

'Although I'm afraid the Bishop tells me less and less. Everything on a need-to-know basis. Dictates his letters over the phone or I go over to his office in the Palace. Mostly, however, I deal with Ben Adams. As…' Sophie frowned. '… does the Bishop.'

Canon Ben, the Bishop's clerical secretary. One of a coterie of canons, usually the Dean, too, who would support Innes whatever he proposed, while the archdeacon, Siân Callaghan-Clarke, sat uneasily on the communion rail.

Not easy for Sophie, lay secretary and confidante to Hereford bishops for more than twenty years. The role of lay secretary had been effectively diminished because Innes no longer trusted her. For which Merrily felt entirely responsible.

'I could ask Ben about Crowden,' Sophie said.

'*No*. Please don't. Don't chance it. Don't give Innes anything he can use. I worry about coming in here now, in case he thinks we're conspiring.'

Sophie rose, white hair spinning out of its loose bun.

'Don't you *dare* start limiting your visits. Essentially, nothing's changed. The Bishop has no solid reason to believe that you know anything about his determination to downgrade deliverance. And you weren't even here when Huw Owen... challenged him.'

'But if he's still insisting that all requests for deliverance are run past him...'

'Requests for exorcism, major, minor or peripheral, have always passed through the Bishop's office. Which meant me. Bishop Dunmore had no dealings with any of it unless it was brought specifically to his attention.'

'But not any more.'

'Nothing's been set in stone.' Sophie looking defiant. 'You're sure it *was* this man last night?'

'Pretty sure. The fact that he came in after the lights had been switched off and left as soon as they went back on.'

'You had the lights out?'

'I was using the opening of *The Cloud of Unknowing* for the meditation. The sense of the soul starting its search for enlightenment in total darkness. If he wanted to make something out of *that*...'

Sophie sighed.

'For what it's worth, I do remember, some months ago, when Bernard Dunmore was still Bishop, someone writing to him to complain about the suspension of evensong in Ledwardine. Replaced by something described as too experimental for a village. More suited to an urban area with a wider range of worship.'

'Who said that?'

'I can't tell you. I only learned about it because Bernard dictated a reply in which he said – more or less – that he found it rather patronizing to suggest that a Ledwardine congregation was unsophisticated. A second, less rational letter expressed the fear that the use of eastern practices—'

'*What?*'

'—might open up the congregation to undesirable influences. I didn't tell you about these, Merrily, because all bishops receive this kind of mail. Anyway, meditation is being used increasingly in churches. Probably also using non-Biblical texts as a basis.'

'These complaints – Innes would have access to that kind of history?'

'It's possible.'

Merrily smiled.

'Just after Crowden came in – although I didn't know it was him at the time – I invited everyone to *inhale the darkness*. What's that sound like as supporting evidence against someone suspected of intimacy with the allegedly satanic Bishop Hunter?'

'Far too clumsy.'

'Actually, I'm not sure it is.'

Paul's not the subtlest of implements, is he? Abbie Folley had said. But then Huw Owen hadn't been subtle either in the way he'd got Innes, temporarily at least, off her back. Only four of them knew what had happened on an autumn morning in the gatehouse office. Huw and Sophie were watertight and Innes surely would not talk about it, for reasons of face-saving, although it struck her now that he might think she and Huw would *not* be discreet, that what had happened might be a running joke.

'Can't go on like this, Sophie.'

'No. I suppose you can't.'

'Should I ask for a meeting with Innes? Have it out with him?'

'Not the way you're feeling now. I'll see what I can discover.'

'Thank you, but don't, you know, break cover. Don't let him think there's collusion.'

'Merrily, he *knows* there's collusion.' Sophie slipped back into her chair. 'Is there anything else I can help you with?'

'Bit of background, perhaps. Kilpeck. Part of the Ewyas Harold group?'

'Along with Dore Abbey and a few neighbouring parishes.'

'And the minister there is Julie...?'

'Duxbury. Arrived just over six months ago from South Gloucestershire, where she and her husband were both priests. Sadly, he died suddenly and she wanted a new start. Not quite new, as it turns out. They had a holiday cottage near Ewyas Harold and when the parishes became vacant some sort of deal was struck with the diocese to have it as the rectory.'

Sophie turned away to fill the kettle. She wouldn't directly ask why Merrily wanted to know about the priest in charge of Kilpeck, though she would expect to be told, eventually. This really wasn't the time for the full story.

'A man I buried last week – Aidan Lloyd – was born in Kilpeck.'

'The accident victim?'

'A friend of his came to church yesterday. Bereavement apparition. I've not been asked to do anything about it, so it doesn't need to go on the database. I just want to keep an eye on it. Maybe find out a bit about Aidan Lloyd's life before Ledwardine.'

'Mrs Duxbury's only been there since the spring. Although, if what I'm told is accurate, I'm sure she'd be eager to help. She's... enthusiastic. A people person. Worked in social services in the London area. Then, briefly, a Labour councillor.'

'Perhaps I'll call her before I leave. If she's in.'

Sophie peered over her chained glasses.

'The person you talked to – is *she* from Kilpeck?'

'No, no, she's here in Hereford. She's an educated professional woman, and she's very cool, very balanced. But I think… however you want to look at this, I think she's dealing with what you might call a powerful presence in her life.'

'Might this involve psychiatric input?'

'If it did, she'd know exactly how to get it.' Merrily picked up the phone. 'Have you got Julie Duxbury's number there?'

27

Being friendly

KAREN DOWELL HAD brought coffee and chocolate bickies into the interview room. Not quite Starbucks. Bit of cosy and a bit of edge, putting out conflicting messages.

Nice Karen, to start off with. Big sister Karen.

'Danni, we've talked to you about the last time you saw Wictor' – Danni James shuddered – 'alive,' Karen said. 'Now I'd like to go back a bit.'

'Jag,' Danni said. 'He liked to be called Jag.'

Bliss and Vaynor were watching on the telly up in CID. Maybe Danni had guessed they were there; everybody must've seen a reality TV cop show. If only they knew how often the system broke down.

Danni, dark hair, small but pulpy lips, was wearing a short purple leather jacket to match the gemstone in her nose. She seemed well up for the experience, taking in what few features the interview room possessed, eyeing the recording equipment.

'Don't worry, I'm not recording this,' Karen said. 'Just trying to establish some background.'

'I wasn't worried.'

Danni had a querulous little-girl voice. She'd probably still have it when she was an old woman, Bliss thought, as Karen asked her how she'd got involved with Jaglowski.

Deliberate use of the word *involved*, provoking the first small sign of alarm.

'My dad said if I needed a lawyer—'

'I'd tell you if you needed a lawyer, Danni. I have to.'

Karen in a dark grey woollen top with a pink silk scarf, poshed-up for the murder room. She got Danni talking about her few months with Jag. The weekend in Paris they'd had, staying at his mate's apartment. He seemed to have mates all over Europe. Karen tried for an address for the Paris flat, but Danni was hazy on street names.

'I was just, like, shopping in the daytime, and then we went to some clubs at night? He talked to people in French. I think it was better than his English.'

Cosmopolitan playboy? Bliss thought of the concrete garage on the Rotherwas, the array of bangers on the forecourt.

'—wasn't working for him or anything,' Danni was saying. 'He had an accountant and a woman in the office for all that. As well as the two mechanics.'

Danni was like *between jobs*. She'd been a receptionist at the Green Dragon; not clear why she'd left.

'Danni,' Karen said very softly, 'I should tell you that we've found evidence which, if Jag was still alive, could have put him in prison for several years. Do you know what I'm talking about?'

There was to be no mention of the Makarovs in the inspection pit unless Danni revealed some knowledge of them.

She was shaking her head, rapidly.

'No. No, really, I don't know anything about whatever it is. He never talked about his business.'

'What did you think his business was, then?'

'Cars? He was getting me a top-of-the-range Cooper.'

'Nothing exactly top-of-the-range on his forecourt,' Bliss said to Vaynor.

'What about his friends?' Karen said. 'Did you meet his friends?'

'Some of them. They were OK. Nice. Fun. Some of them.'

'Men? Women?'

'Both. Mainly men.'

'You recall any names?'

'Yeah. I think. One of them runs a bar in town. Thomas? That's spelt in Polish. Probably with Zs everywhere.'

'Were they all Polish, his friends?'

'Dunno, they always spoke English in front of me. I don't really know a Polish accent from whatever, but they were always really, you know, polite. Like, you could tell it was hard for some of them, speaking English, but they did their best when I was there.'

'Just like I'm sure they all will when *we* talk to them,' Bliss said.

He watched Karen bringing out a fresh pad and a pen, sliding them to the middle of the table.

'Danni, I'm going to ask you to write down for me as many names as you can remember.'

'They're all Polish!'

'Write it down phonetically. How they sounded. We'll work it out. But we'll leave that for now. What about his brother? Lech.'

'Well he's away.'

'He's in prison, Danni.'

'Yeah.'

'Do you know why he's in prison?'

'Cigarette smuggling, that's all. It was like a really stiff sentence? Especially when all he was doing was trying to help some friends.'

'Mother of God,' Bliss murmured. 'There were friggin' vanloads.'

'Close, were they, Lech and Jag?'

'I suppose.'

'Danni, did Wictor… Jag ever give the impression he might have enemies?'

'Not really. I only ever met his mates. He had good locks on the front door. Well, you've seen— But he had a lot of valuable kit in there – home cinema? But like he wasn't always looking over his shoulder and stuff. He kept saying what a great place to live Hereford was, and how he was going to buy a house in the country? He loved it here. He was having a good time. We went out a lot.'

'He had lots of money?'

'Yeah, he was… generous, obviously. He always carried cash. He wasn't into cards.'

Bliss smiled.

'And he always went to church?' Karen said.

'He went to mass. Kept going on about thanking God for looking after him.' Danni's mouth shrank. 'Yeah, right. Straight out of church to thank God, and then down the garage and gets himself—'

Her head went theatrically down into her hands on the tabletop. Bliss had listened to the recording of Danni's 999 call, from her mobile after she'd run outside the garage. *Yeah, my boyfriend… he's really badly hurt… his head's all… all blood? You've got to send somebody, it's horrible, he won't move…*

Karen found her a tissue, said, 'Do you know which church?'

Bliss nodded. The priest might be helpful.

'I'm not *too* sure,' Danni said, but I think—'

Then the picture went off. Sometimes Karen could fix it, but mostly not. Bliss turned to Vaynor, who was shaking his head slowly.

'Not going to be an easy one, this, boss. Whoever did it could be out of the country by now.'

'Or just in a different city. Might've come here specially to do the job. Lorra fellers up for it in Birmingham… Cardiff… Gloucester, even. You think she's telling us everything she knows?'

'They never do, do they? But I don't think she's covering for anybody. She was just having a good time with a bloke throwing his money about and not thinking too hard about where it came from.'

Bliss thought about it.

'Might be worth you having a word with the parents. If she

spent last night back in her old home being fed hot soup, something might've come out that Mum and Dad might feel better if we knew about.'

'We've spoken briefly. They're, you know, liberal-minded people. They met Jaglowski once or twice. Her mother said he was charming and her dad didn't want to be suspicious or disapproving, but I reckon he's having a re-evaluation now. You want me to visit his surgery?'

'Yeah, nab him in his lunch hour. We don't want Danni around. Or the mother if she found Jag charming.'

'Maybe he was. Snapping up a girl like Danni. Good-time girl, along for the ride. A lot to be said for it.' Vaynor was with a woman he'd known when they were at Oxford together. 'So I'm told.'

Bliss had been set up to do a short interview for Midlands Today with Amanda Patel who he got on with most of the time. Seasoned veteran now, Mandy, compared to the kids from the other networks. They walked out into the car park, where Bliss spotted ITV and Sky unloading their kit. *Gun-crime terror grips peaceful country town.*

'Might be easy to overreact on this one, Mandy. While a shooting in Hereford not involving a twelve-bore is comparatively rare... and we can't actually say there's *no* danger to the public... it's probably no more than an underworld disagreement.'

'Have you *got* an underworld in Hereford?'

'You'd be surprised. I'm just saying I wouldn't get over-excited about the idea of a dangerous armed felon on the loose.'

Mandy nodded. They walked down into the public car park opposite the red-brick magistrates' court.

'Frannie, what about this connection with the farmer who was killed?'

'Is there one?'

Bliss gazing out over the car park, keeping his voice loose.

'Didn't Jaglowski own the van that killed that guy on a country lane? Driven by a guy who came into the country through the people-smuggling trade and did a spell as a slave to pay for it?'

Bliss didn't look at her.

'Where'd you get that, Mandy?'

'Is it important?'

'Might be.'

If this interesting if possibly irrelevant connection was in the public domain, the chances were that it had seeped out of Gaol Street.

'I don't *have* to reveal my sources,' Mandy said, 'but, seeing it's you, think of a well-known local councillor running for high office in law enforcement.'

'And what exactly did he say about it?'

'Nothing. He just told me. Being friendly.'

'Yeah, that's how he is,' Bliss said, tightening up. 'Friendly.'

28

Severe stomach wound

MERRILY WAS THINKING that nowhere in Hereford had more of a sense of the living medieval than All Saints Church since they put a restaurant inside, reactivating the church as something noisy, vibrant, relevant and still a church. Wouldn't work in Ledwardine but here at the bottom of Broad Street, the one-time heart of the city, it was right. And full.

Jane had won £25 on a scratchcard this morning and insisted on paying for lunch. They went upstairs to the gallery, overlooking the top of the nave and the chancel and almost directly underneath the little wooden man flashing his medieval parts.

'Nobody seems to spot him.' Jane nodding towards the other diners. 'He's got to be miffed. A seven hundred year hard-on and nobody notices? Does he have a name?'

'Male exhibitionist,' Merrily said. 'Prosaic but accurate.'

'I meant like Sheela-na-gig?'

'Not that I know of. Although he does have a similar level of disproportion in his bits.'

'*Bits?* If he was real he wouldn't be able to stand up.' Jane sat down, spreading her few packages. 'Why did they do this in medieval churches? Think about it. All the porn – churches.'

'We're talking Kilpeck, right?'

'We certainly are.'

Jane had been across to the city library, consulting a whole pile of local books in the search for Kilpeck and the history of Herefordshire morris dancing and finding no obvious connection. So she'd settled on the church, Kilpeck's one claim to international fame because of its perfectly preserved collection of Norman Romanesque stone carvings, its unique medieval frieze. Also its Sheela-na-gig. The female exhibitionist.

Jane flicked a glance at the corner of the ceiling.

'Thought to have had one like him as well at one time. Story is, there was this Victorian lady who may have owned the church and threw a wobbly when she realized what he had in his hand.'

'That would figure.'

'Had him removed, along with a few other carvings.' Jane smiled, slightly eerily. 'You'll've noticed how I very carefully said "removed" rather than "pulled off".'

'Didn't, actually, flower, but thank you. How come she spared the Sheela-na-gig?'

Remembering the Sheela from a visit some years ago. Notorious worldwide for her vacant, slightly orgasmic leer and something resembling the entrance to a railway tunnel between her little legs.

'I think someone told the woman she was actually a bloke with a severe stomach wound from the war,' Jane said. 'Something like that. So naive, these Victorians.'

This frivolity, you could understand it. A determination not to dwell on what she'd seen in the churchyard. Not in public, anyway. Jane could be genuinely impressive sometimes.

The waitress brought up their veggie lasagnes. Jane waited till she'd gone.

'So you phoned the vicar of Kilpeck?'

'Rector of Ewyas Harold. Including Kilpeck. Yes, she does know Sir Lionel Darvill.'

'Tweeds? Rides with the hunt?'

'Certainly landed gentry. Baronet. Never quite sure what that means, except that he inherited the title. Norman name. Quite a few families of Norman descent along that part of the border.'

'It's a classic Norman parish church.'

'Darvill seems to feel a certain responsibility for it,' Merrily said. 'He's a significant patron. Not what you'd expect, though, according to Julie Duxbury. More old hippy than country squire. Though not old enough to have been an actual hippy.'

'What's that make him?'

'Makes him a hippy's son. Henry Darvill's values – the old good-life ethos – got channelled into something significant. Eventually became one of the biggest organic farmers in the area. Though not without casualties.'

Jane's knife and fork froze over her plate.

'Iestyn Lloyd.'

'Iestyn was appointed farm manager by Sir Lionel's uncle, Peter – must be over thirty years ago. He came from a farming family with land spreading into Wales, but they'd had to sell up, and Peter gave Iestyn a job running his estate. I mean, really running it. As if it was his own. Made Uncle Peter a lot of money.'

'Not exactly organic, though.'

'Practically industrial.' Merrily looked down at her vegetarian alternative. 'Much like he is now, maybe more so. Battery chickens, huge pig sheds, clearance of fields for arable crops.'

'Pesticides?'

'Obviously. Hugely profitable, anyway. Henry Darvill, fresh from his studies into higher-consciousness, was appalled.'

'Fires Iestyn…'

'Not immediately. Henry does seem to have recognized Iestyn's business skills. Didn't want to lose that. He was an idealist not a farmer, so he tried to convert Iestyn to organic. Well… *that* wasn't going to happen. You can't just turn a hard-nosed businessman into a green-earth philanthropist. They rubbed along painfully for a while, but in the end, yes, Henry invited Iestyn to accept a substantial pay-off. Iestyn exploded and went down the industrial tribunal route. The eyes of the agricultural world were suddenly focused on Kilpeck, and Henry… according to Julie, Henry couldn't face that.'

'Bought him off? That's what I read.'

'For an undisclosed amount, far more than he'd imagined. Had to sell land.'

'And that was how Ledwardine got Iestyn Lloyd?'

'Well... he already had a share in Churchwood Farm – inherited, with his cousin, from an uncle. What he collected from Henry Darvill was enough to buy his cousin out. Rest is history. But... I didn't know about the resulting feud between the Lloyds and the Darvills. You might argue that Iestyn's better off now than when he was just a highly paid employee, but I don't think that's how he sees it. Unquenchable hatred – that's Julie's phrase. Wars have started over less.'

Merrily ate slowly, thinking about it. She'd had the impression Julie Duxbury was still holding a lot back. Maybe just reluctant to discuss it on the phone. She put down her fork.

'According to Julie, Maryfields nearly went under. Iestyn wouldn't have gone out of his way *not* to leave things in a mess. Also, he was well respected locally and seems to have put the knife in for Henry, whose only mates were other organic farmers, mostly out of county. Establishing an organic farm takes time. Getting rid of the chemicals, attracting the nutrients back into the soil. He got there eventually, but it finished him. Wrecked his marriage, his health. Broke his spirit.'

'Bugger...'

'Killed him in the end. He was on medication for depression, died quite suddenly. But... his legacy survives. As does the tradition of morris dancing he began in Kilpeck.'

Jane's eyes widened.

'Hey, you got there!'

'If MI5 employed parish priests, flower...'

'So the Kilpeck Morris doesn't go way back?'

'Sir Henry Darvill formed a morris side with local men, most of them working on his farm. His son continues it. They still perform at certain times around the immediate area. And it goes deeper than entertainment, whatever that means. That's all I know.'

Jane sugared her tea.

'So now we have a serious link between the Darvills of Kilpeck and the Lloyds of Ledwardine. And a reason for...'

She looked around. There were people, too close. But, yes, they now had a reason for one family to despoil the grave of the heir to the other's fortune. Dancing on the grave – you could just about explain that, on a drunken, boorish level, but the rest of it...

'Sir Lionel Darvill.' Jane lowering her voice. 'Would he have been there on the night?'

'He clearly wasn't. The idea of Darvill being involved in this is appealing – if that word could be applied to this situation – except for one thing. He doesn't dance any more. He's in a wheelchair. Paralysed from the waist down.'

'Oh.'

'Nothing's simple, flower.'

'What happened to him?'

'He had a fall. Broke his back. They're clearly not a lucky family, the Darvills.'

'What are you going to do now?'

'Going over to see her. Julie Duxbury.'

'When?'

'We'll work something out. She seemed quite glad I'd rung.'

'What was your excuse for ringing? You didn't tell her...?'

'Course not. But I did say it was a deliverance issue, so she wouldn't expect me to say too much about it. Though I may have to when we actually meet. All I said was that I was chasing a ghost. I gave her the name, Aidan Lloyd.'

'You mention Lol and the festival?'

'No chance, even if he was interested. Julie says she made the mistake of confusing the Kilpeck Morris with public entertainment, innocently inviting them to perform at a parish fete last summer. A serious social gaffe. They didn't *do* village fetes.'

'That's what Darvill told her?'

'She says she went red, apologized and backed off. When

186

you're in a new parish, you tend to pussyfoot for quite a while. Always worried about inadvertently tossing a brick into a quiet pool.'

Jane sat up.

'Fuck *that*.'

Clapping a hand over her mouth as heads turned.

'Sorry, sorry, sorry… but I hate quiet pools.'

'Jane…' Merrily muttering, embarrassed, into her plate. 'Could be this will turn out to be something… rather less dark than it seems.'

'You reckon?' Jane said. 'You taking bets?'

Merrily glanced up at the little wooden flasher in the corner. You could almost hear him sniggering.

29

Safe ground

TUESDAY MORNING. A white sky. Powdery overnight snow in the cracks between the cobbles on the square, and Lol was at his desk in the window, messing with his wintry song, changing a few words.

The old year turns...

No, *hangs* was better. There might be a need for *turn* later in the song, and hanging suggested uncertainty. *Hanging*, yes...

The old year's hanging on a rusting hinge
Kids in the city on a drinking binge
And I can hear some ancient engine grinding

Maybe *grinding* wasn't right. Would depend on what the ancient engine was actually for. He didn't know, but the word *engine* insisted on being there. *Hinge, binge, engine* – closer to an anagram than a rhyme, as if it had formed out of the other words. It had been in his head when he awoke, along with the rhythm, the heavy clockwork, insistent, thumping, and when he'd rolled out of bed his leg muscles had been aching, as if he'd been walking all night.

He found his head was in his arms on the desktop.

What was the point? He needed to make some money again; 'Camera Lies' was no longer going to pay off his mortgage on Lucy's Cottage. But very few people were making money in this business any more. Kids were no longer obsessed with music, and what music they needed they could get free. The day of the Big Stereo was over. The vinyl revival was a comparatively small, elitist fad. There were no longer songs that everybody knew, with words embedded in the *zeitgeist.*

As for Merrily... He'd become aware of stories in the papers that at one time would have had no personal significance for him. One had said the Church of England would be moribund long before the end of the twenty-first century. Victim of the forces of economics and entropy. Part of a long-expired England where one son would join the army, the other would remain to run the farm and the third, the loser, would go into the Church.

hinge, binge, engine... who was likely to give a shit?

Lol sat up. It was a job and the only one he had. And it might need an extra chord change to accommodate *engine.* He was fumbling the Boswell on to his right knee when the phone rang.

'Hello.'

Never gave the number any more, not sure why.

'Robinson?'

'Um...'

'Darvill. Kilpeck.'

Shit. Lol stood up, kicking the chair back, stretching the phone wire to lay the Boswell on the sofa. Hadn't been expecting this. Half expecting something, but not this.

'You phoned Mrs Brewer.'

'Yes.'

'And she told you about me.'

'She mentioned you.'

An oil delivery tanker had stopped right outside, the driver leaning down to talk to Brenda from the Eight Till Late, probably asking directions to somewhere. The engine noise meant Lol had to strain to hear.

'—like most of these Nick Drake tributists, you don't sound an *awful* lot like him, do you? On your albums.'

189

Lol sat down at the desk, cupping the phone. Sir Lionel Darvill had listened to his albums?

'I was in a band that took its name from one of his songs. We were young and we'd discovered him. It was just a mark of respect.'

'My old man was at school with Drake,' Darvill said. 'Marlborough.'

'Oh?'

It figured. Nick Drake had come from a wealthy family.

'Used to enjoy telling me,' Darvill said, 'how they once shared a spliff in the shadow of one of those enormous prehistoric stones at Avebury.'

'Those were the days,' Lol said.

Trying to fit an image to the voice. It had a roll. You'd hear some aristocrat or a minor member of the royal family who'd dragged his cut-glass vowels through Estuary mud; Darvill's accent had been dipped in cider. Lol couldn't picture him in a wheelchair.

'Don't know if that's true or not,' Darvill said. 'Or it might've been some years later.'

'Unfortunately, Nick Drake didn't have too many years later.'

'I gather he went on to make more liberal use of cannabis. Which they say might account for his subsequent mental imbalance.'

'I don't know.'

'Some people, it comes without herbal assistance. You'd *certainly* know about that.'

Lol felt a prickle of sweat on his forehead; Darvill went breezing on.

'Brewer tells me you were asking his wife about the Kilpeck Morris. For some local fete.'

'Folk festival.'

'And she told you the Kilpeck Morris didn't do other people's events.'

'I hadn't realized that.'

'But you wouldn't let it go.'

'I just... I have to report back to the festival committee.'

There was no festival committee, only Barry.

'Don't know what you've *heard*, Robinson, but you probably need to forget it, don't you think?'

Lol didn't reply. You might forget what you'd heard, you never forgot what you'd seen. On a cold night. In a grave.

'Forget you ever heard of the Kilpeck Morris, hey? That'd be a start. Message getting through to you? The KM... en't public property.'

Lol gripped the edge of the desk; in his mind it was a coffin lid, slick with cold clay.

'The morris side I was once with... briefly... that was *all* about being public.'

'Which morris side?'

'It was Cotswold. You wouldn't know it. But I kind of interpreted it as being about spreading energy. About life, as distinct from—'

'Robinson. Listen to me.'

It went quiet. The oil tanker had moved on.

'You don't *really* want to get on the wrong fucking side of me,' Darvill said. 'Do you?'

Clunk.

He found Merrily alone in the vicarage kitchen, wearing an apron and an oven glove to push the emptied ash-tray back into the woodstove.

'It was actually a threat?'

'They don't usually stoop to threats, these guys, do they? However—'

'*These* guys?' She tossed the block into the stove and spun round. 'Lol, he's just... *another bloke.*'

Her apron rising like a tutu in a shower of wood ash.

'He said his dad was at school with Nick Drake,' Lol said. 'Marlborough College.'

'So?'

'He also seemed to know I'd done a stretch in a loony bin.'

'He Googled you.'

'Plus, he's from *here* – like his ancestors for eight or nine centuries – and I'm from Off. Therefore, it would be very much in my interests to let this go. It was a threat. Trust me, I'm a failed psychotherapist.'

'Like we agreed, it was a mistake to ring Mrs Brewer. Because Jane was pushing you to do something, and you find it hard to say no to Jane – I'm not *blaming* you for that, she was always a manipulative kid.'

'Where is she?'

'Food shopping at Jim Prosser's. We have the special privilege of filling a trolley and wheeling it across the road, on the basis that a vicar will always bring it back. How little he knows about the clergy. Listen… Darvill… he's in a wheelchair. Disabled people feel vulnerable. In a showdown they tend to fire first. Wouldn't you?'

'It wasn't a showdown. Didn't get that far. I'm not the showdown type. You know that.'

Merrily closed the stove door, brushed ash from her oven glove.

'I'm going to see Julie Duxbury this afternoon.'

'Perhaps you could ask her why they have a private morris side.'

'That doesn't make sense, does it?'

'It's always had its secretive aspects. Black faces, all that. But no, it doesn't make a lot of sense.' He felt suddenly helpless. 'What would happen if we just let it lie? It's the Sticks, weird things happen.'

Merrily frowned.

'Jane isn't going to let it lie. She's feeling displaced. No control over her own life. People doing things under her nose for their own reasons in a place she thinks she knows. If not owns. No, look, suddenly, I'm in a safer position than either of you. I haven't actually committed an imprisonable offence.'

'You vicars are so smug.'

She gave him the sardonic smile.

'I told Julie I was looking for Aidan Lloyd. Chasing a ghost, I said, in my mysterious exorcist voice. She came back about twenty minutes ago. Mrs Watkins, she said, I think I've found your ghost. And I said, What does that mean, exactly? And she said, I'm not going to dress this up, I think we need your advice. Some very peculiar things have been happening.'

Merrily let the smile go, but there was a change in her, a bit of electricity, an indication to Lol of just how much she needed what she called the Night Job. How reduced, as a person, she'd be if it were taken away.

30

Shopped

LATE MORNING, THEY brought Danni James back into the inter-
view room. No coffee this time, no bickies. This time Bliss sent
Vaynor in with Karen Dowell. The break had come through
Darth's visit to Danni's dad's dental surgery.

Karen had a clipboard with printouts that were nothing to
do with the case. She sat leafing through them for a minute or
so before nodding to herself and then looking across the table,
not smiling.

'Lech Jaglowski, Danni. Jag's brother. You met him... how
many times would you say?'

Danni moistened her lips.

'Dunno. Few times.'

'Lech and Wictor – Jag. You suggested they were mates. You
actually said they were close.'

Danni didn't reply. Bliss sat alone in front of the monitor,
watching Darth Vaynor putting on his nasty face.

Vaynor said, 'Only our information suggests otherwise. Or
at least that Lech and Jag's relationship was going through a
rough patch.'

'They didn't always see eye to eye,' Danni said. 'Brothers...
you know?'

'They had arguments?'

'Well, yeah. Sometimes.'

'What about?'

'I don't know. When they got going at each other, ranting,
they'd go off into Polish.'

Vaynor looked up. Bliss had heard he was taking Polish lessons. Probably have it cracked in a couple of months.

Karen Dowell said, 'Did you get any sense at all of what they might've been arguing about?'

'I kept out of it.'

'When was the last row?' Karen said. 'How close, would you say, to when Lech was arrested?'

'I dunno, few days?'

'How many days?'

'I can't... one, two... I'm not sure.'

'The last time they met, when you were there... was there a row?'

'Maybe.'

'How would you describe their relationship around the time Lech was arrested?'

'I dunno.'

'I think you do, Danni,' Karen said.

Danni's dad, the dentist, had told Vaynor he remembered her coming home to get away from the endless rows between Wictor and his brother. Lech arriving drunk, banging on the door in the middle of the night, disturbing Danni's beauty sleep. Two days after Danni had gone back home, Jag himself had turned up at their house with flowers and perfume and touching apologies that Danni's mother had found disarming in an old-fashioned way. How many of her English boyfriends would've done that?

Karen smiled at last.

'How did you get on with Lech?'

'All right.'

'Ever meet him when Jag wasn't there?'

'Who's been telling you this stuff?'

'He ever come round to the apartment when Jag was at work?'

Danni was messing with a ring on her left hand, turning it round and round.

'Nothing happened, all right?'

'It's not an offence. Danni.'

'Nothing *happened.*'

'But did Jag think something *might* have happened?' Vaynor said. 'This could be important, Danni, so you might want to think before you answer.'

'Why? *Why's* it important? Lech didn't shoot Jag, did he? He was in prison.'

Vaynor steepled his fingers.

'And what did Jag have to say about that? About Lech being in prison.'

There was none of the excitement of when you'd physically pulled somebody for a killing. Wasn't the same when the suspect was already doing nine months.

'What Danni says Jag said was this,' Bliss told Annie later, in her office. 'He said he felt quite relieved that Lech was off the streets as, back in Krakow, a rape charge against him had been dropped through lack of evidence. Jag said Lech had always been attracted to girls who said no.'

'That true?'

'We're trying to check, but probably not. It does start to look as if Jag arranged for his brother to be grassed up for the cigs. Terry Stagg's going back to the original sources, see if we can establish a link with Jag.'

'And this is because he thought Lech and Danni were...?'

'Danni claimed he'd told her to lock the doors when he was at work and if Lech showed up pretend she wasn't in. She also says Lech wanted to give up his shop and join Jag in the garage business, but Jag didn't want that.'

'If Jag got Lech nicked, did Lech know that?'

Annie tapping her teeth with the end of a pen.

'Well, this is it,' Bliss said. 'Jag would've done it through a third party, but, yeh, it's very likely Lech would know. And had a lorra time to dwell on it.'

What was going to take some work – and a few costly interpreters – was proving that it was Lech who'd arranged to have
Jag killed. Was it through a contact in Hereford? Was it somebody he encountered in prison?

'Does Lech inherit the garage now?'

Bliss smiled.

'Apparently not. The garage was rented, as was the apartment. Jag's estate, whatever that amounts to, goes to his mam
and dad in Krakow.'

'What about the pistols?'

'Yeh. What *about* the pistols?'

'If Jaglowski was shot with one of his own guns, we might
assume Lech knew he was dealing in firearms.'

Bliss shook his head, wearied by the weight of implications.
They were still waiting for the intelligent fellers at FIB to come
up with Jag's historic form, if any.

'I'm not saying this won't take for ever, Annie, or that we
can do it on our own. There's still a killer out there, but it might
well be a professional and he might be in Brum, or London or
anywhere in Europe.'

'Who's going to talk to Lech?'

He thought he'd send Darth. Lad had been on a roll lately.
Annie nodded, went across to the window to look at the dull
lights of Hereford. No high-rise, no neon. Maybe it seemed a
bit more like home now that the Jag killing was looking closer
to a domestic.

'At least it gets Charlie off our backs,' Bliss said. 'Didn't tell
you, did I? He's been passing tips to the media. Told Mandy
Patel about Jag owning the van driven by the Lithuanian lad
who knocked that farmer off his quaddie.'

'Where did Charlie get that?'

'Wondered that meself. Talked to Rich Ford about it and,
like he says, we never actually sat on that information but we
didn't put it out either. Charlie, however…'

'Still has friends in Gaol Street,' Annie said. 'Probably more than we know. But why would he talk to the media about that? Unless it's simply to show he's still in the loop.'

'Gorra be part of his campaign. No suggestion he told anybody about our suspicion that Jag was involved in farm thefts, though. Mandy thought he was just scaremongering about foreign drivers with no proper insurance bombing round the lanes in white vans.'

Annie sat down at her desk.

'Anything I don't understand about Charlie makes me feel insecure.'

'You mean there were things you *did* understand about Charlie?'

'Saw his girlfriend in town this lunchtime,' Annie said.

'Sasha?'

'She used to be all over me at one time, if I bumped into her. Like we'd grown up together.'

'Not now?'

'Cut me dead. Stared right through me.'

'Oh well,' Bliss said. 'That's at least one positive development.'

Annie didn't laugh. She was Charlie's daughter – though only nominally now, Charlie had said. Cruel feller, behind all that compassion.

31

An oven

THE SENSE OF *border* was pervasive here, hard country stalking soft under the darkening frown of the Black Mountains. Merrily drove down from Hereford on the Abergavenny road – long, straight runs beloved of boy-racers – before turning left into the little, sunken lanes in already-fading daylight.

Open fields, then sporadic housing, mainly modern, bungalows with cars in drives but nobody about.

Habitation but not an obvious community. A place, rather than a village, a loose knot of lanes, porch doors closed against the teeth of winter, a few chimneys pumping smoke from newly lit stoves and open fires. No landmarks, no obvious guardian hills before the threatening heights in the west. Kilpeck was haphazard, featureless, and the church wasn't in the centre. There *was* no obvious centre, and the tallest structure was a stocky electrical pylon enclosed by housing.

The sun's red eye, half shut, was squinting through a tangle of bare trees. She switched on the car lights. The Freelander crawled around a corner by a pub, and there was a village green with an oak tree. Then a parking area, a farmhouse, and Kilpeck ended with the famous church, as if it had been kicked out, put aside.

Hadn't always been like this, Julie Duxbury said.

She was pointing to the field to the right of the rounded apse.

'*That* was the village, once. All round there and back across the lane where that barn is and also behind the church.'

Nothing but fields now, and the occasional farmhouse, all the way to the low hills to the east and the north. They were quite alone under the amber sky.

'The Black Death,' Julie said. 'That's what they say. The old village never came back after the plague. But they seem to say that about so many places in this area.'

Her thick white hair was brushed back and tucked into the collar of her outsize bomber jacket. She was in her fifties, big-boned, brisk and fit-looking. Her red Renault Clio was the only other vehicle on the parking area which faded into greenery, and then there were meaningful mounds.

'So the slightly... disorganized community behind me,' Merrily said, 'that was...'

'Farmland, I suppose, when *this* was Kilpeck and the church was in the middle and the castle' – Julie followed an arm towards the mounds to the west – 'was its defence. And the reason for everything.'

Merrily saw a summit of jagged stone, partly concealed by the green ramparts.

'It's odd,' Julie said. 'There aren't many medieval castles in this area, so you'd expect even a sparse ruin to be a tourist attraction, but it just isn't. It used to overshadow the church, but now the church – metaphorically speaking – overshadows everything.'

'It's so small. I'm sure I've been before, but I just don't remember it as quite so small.'

It sat on a low mound like a half-bun. It had no steeple, no proper tower, nothing to take on heaven. It rose in three sandstone stages from the rounded apse to a little bell-mount merging into the blackening trees behind.

'We'll come back to it, if you don't mind. I see you're wearing boots – good.' Julie smiled – generous mouth – and strode off across the parking area. She wore tight black leggings. 'Before it goes dark, I want to show you where something happened. I don't imagine, having lived here for years and your job and everything, that it'll surprise *you*, but it scared the hell out of me.'

Merrily followed her up into the churchyard past an ancient yew, woody entrails exposed. Approaching the bell-tower side of the church, she glimpsed an arched doorway, voluptuously sculpted.

'Later,' Julie said. 'It gets dark very quickly now.' This was a different woman to the one she'd spoken to on the phone, hesitant and guarded no more. 'I probably wasn't particularly forthcoming yesterday. Have to admit I've always been a little wary of deliverance.'

'Never much liked that word either,' Merrily said. 'Makes me think of rednecks in the Everglades. Was it the Everglades? Long time since I saw the film.'

'There were banjos, I think. A man on a cliff or something exchanging plink-plonk notes with someone else, somewhere, and then it got faster and faster.'

'That was the bit I liked.'

Past a few graves and into a footpath pointing to the setting sun, a wooden gate appeared. Beyond it, the hint of a path rapidly became steep, the grass slick underfoot. Julie warning her to take care as the gutted shell of a stone tower rose before them, sooty-black against the fading winter sun, and Merrily realized she'd been climbing up earthen ramparts.

'That's the castle keep – what's left of it. Well battered in conflicts with the Welsh, but still in use in the sixteenth century, during the Civil War. Not much after that. Still, we're lucky to have a ruin.'

'It's on Darvill land?'

'No, this is the Whitfield estate, though I'm sure Sir Lionel feels a sort of spiritual possession.'

Beyond the castle mound, there was a vast view west, across fields that shone like tarnished brass, towards the Black Mountains and Wales. This was England, but Wales was everywhere. Not many centuries ago, all these fields would have been in Wales, the village as well.

'Right, then...' Julie stood on a shelf of ground below the

tower. 'There comes a point, Merrily, where one feels out of one's depth. Situations escalate.'

'Oh, they do.'

'Thought it was fog at first, we've had so much of that lately. But fog doesn't stink of petrol. Not here, anyway. It was actually quite a fine night for the time of year. Rather cold but reasonably clear, although no visible moon.'

'This was...?'

'Last Thursday. No, actually Friday, it would've been after midnight. I should've been in bed, but I had some letters to write – still do that, for friends, rather than emails – so when I had the phone call I was able to react quite quickly. One of those calls you don't forget in a hurry. The sound was smothered, as if something had been put over the phone to disguise the voice. "Is that the priest? Something you want to know about. Man on fire near your church." If I'd heard chinking glasses and general merriment, I might've thought twice about coming out here, but nothing like that. *I* didn't know who it was, probably never will... Ah, here we are, just here...'

Merrily bent to where the grass was scorched, blackened and grey with damped-down ashes.

'I parked where the car is now,' Julie said, 'and smelled it at once, and then you could see the smoke in the air. When I looked over towards the other field gate – that one, back there, there was Sir Lionel Darvill in his wheelchair – he has this sort of all-terrain chair with thick wheels and a motor.'

'He was there when you arrived?'

'I don't think so. His truck certainly wasn't there when I was parking, although it was when we went back down. They must've followed me in – Gareth Brewer was with him, and he came over. "Nothing for you here, rector, the church is quite safe." As if he wanted me out – or Darvill did. But I wasn't going anywhere till I found out what had been happening. And then I saw it. Oh my God.'

Julie looked back towards the castle ruins.

'A great glowing crucifix – that's what it looked like. A man with flames bursting out of his... of his head, for heaven's sake. Strands of flame coming out of it, like a Catherine wheel, and the face was just... raging with gassy flame.'

'Bloody hell, Julie.'

'Then I saw it was probably just a ball of cloth with a turnip or something inside it. A dummy. Like a scarecrow with a crosspiece to hang the jacket on. Burning through. An effigy? I tripped over the remains of a top hat.'

'Oh.'

'Evidently set on fire in the shelter of the tower to get it going. Darvill's shouting at me. "Julie! It's all right, Julie. Some silly buggers. All over, no harm done." Just kids, he said when I went over to him. Kids getting bored in the period between Guy Fawkes' Night and Christmas. No need for the fire brigade, he and Gareth would keep an eye on things. I don't think he *means* to be patronizing. But I found out later that he'd had a phone call, too. And I wasn't going anywhere, having heard the bells by then. The post was burned through and it collapsed in a shower of sparks, and the bells began to sound. Very eerie.'

'There's a hole here.'

Merrily had slipped a hand down into the paste of ash.

'That's where it was sunk into the ground.'

'Where were the bells?'

'Bound to the lower part of the post. Attached to this sort of leather pad. Little round bells. A cluster. I saw them afterwards.'

'A morris dancer's bells?'

'Correct. I just... wanted you to see this, to show I wasn't making it all up.'

'You told anyone else?'

'No, I haven't. No one was hurt. I thought at first it was a joke. We can go back now. Steady... it's harder going down.'

Because of the treacherous ground, they took a different route back, down a shallower slope, and out through a metal-barred gate to the car park. If this was summer, the sun would have been warm on their backs. Merrily was putting some-thing together like arranging a hand of playing cards, the dark cards, clubs and spades predominating. She looked up at Julie Duxbury.

'So let me get this right. Somebody had dressed a scarecrow frame in morris kit, sunk it into the ground and set it alight. Somebody who evidently wanted Sir Lionel Darvill to see it – unless, of course, he did it himself. Or had it done?'

'Oh no. It was too dark to see his face, but I imagine it as white with rage. I… felt his fury. His helplessness. He's a cour-ageous man, rolling through the mud in his off-road wheelchair, but he must be horribly aware of his limitations.'

'You think he knew who was behind it?'

'Oh, yes, he knew.'

'Would he have been looking in the direction of Ledwardine perhaps?'

'I think he would.'

'And the person who alerted him – could that've been the same person who rang you? What was the voice like?'

'I'm not sure. I thought at first it must be a local accent, and then I thought it was non-UK. It *was* an accent. I couldn't think why they'd rung me rather than the police, except that it would no doubt take the police for ever to get here even if they knew where to find us.'

'So what happened in the end?'

'Darvill invited me round for coffee next day. He has a woman to look after him – an American woman who's his physiotherapist and… whatever else. Several businesses work out of Maryfields, quite a little community down there. Because he didn't have an alternative after what I'd seen, he explained some of the history of the Darvills and this Iestyn Lloyd. And it… didn't sound at all healthy. I'd been told some of the history by various people but I didn't realize it was still… active. Quite venomously active.'

'What did you do?'

'I listened. I asked if I could help. He laughed rather sourly – as if, what could a priest do, a *woman* priest who couldn't even drum up a respectable congregation across half a dozen churches? I didn't say anything. But I knew I couldn't sit by and do nothing.'

They stood in front of Kilpeck Church at the heart of a disappeared village. It had looked so small and modest to Merrily when she'd arrived, but now she couldn't stop looking at it. It was as if it had been built to be hidden until sunset which, at this time of year, was a short-lived show but dramatic, more blinding than summer because of the leafless trees. Although the sun had nearly gone it looked as if it had gone into the church, turning it a deeper red, solar energy firing the stone from within. Like an oven.

'It glows,' Merrily said.

'Yes. Though it's a cold glow sometimes. According to the experts, this is *the* best example of a Norman church in all England – Romanesque, built in the classical style but with Celtic and Saxon, even Viking twists. Doesn't matter much to me. I don't want to preach to people who've only come to admire the building. Or the ones who come because they think it hides mystical secrets. They had a bunch of dowsers here – water diviners who now profess to detect former buildings and old stones and… energies.'

Julie scowled. Merrily could see the Norman doorway now, a big statement, hugely ornate archway, richly carved tympanum, stone figures in shadows. There were still areas of Britain where the magnificent was unobtrusive, almost subdued. Julie Duxbury stood with her hands on her hips and stared at the church with what seemed like resentment.

'I don't like being responsible for an enigma. And I don't like people who communicate in symbolism.'

'Did Darvill explain the significance of the top hat, the bells?'

'Only as an insult to his beloved morris. And the man who'd worn them.'

'This was on the eve of the funeral of Aidan Lloyd.'

'Yes.'

'And he...'

'Danced with the Kilpeck Morris.'

'Aidan Lloyd?'

'So I believe.'

'Hang on. I mean... still?'

'Until his death. The inference is that his father, Iestyn Lloyd, didn't know his son was doing this – coming here to dance. After his death, someone found his top hat, bells, jacket... and brought them back and... made a spectacle of their contempt.'

'Blimey. This... is a moment of revelation.'

Explained everything that happened in the churchyard at Ledwardine... to a degree.

'One thing, Julie. How could Iestyn Lloyd not have known his son was dancing with the Kilpeck Morris? I realise they don't exactly travel around, but presumably they are seen.'

'I'll let someone else explain that.'

'And this burning effigy... I can understand them wanting Darvill to see it, but why you?'

'I'm assuming that was someone who saw it and simply wanted me to know. I've certainly been taking it as a sign that I – as parish priest – need to do something about this. A long-standing feud – an active feud – creates a dreadful atmosphere of threat, tension, fear, affecting all kinds of people. It's not often that a priest is presented with such a clear opportunity to try and bring... healing, I suppose. Don't you think?'

'*I* think... you need to be a bit careful until you know more about it. Also, there's something else I can't quite grasp. How long did it take you to get here, after the phone call?'

'Less than half an hour, I'd guess. Twenty minutes?'

'It's just... if they soaked the effigy in petrol and set it alight and it was still blazing furiously when you arrived... after all that time you'd expect it to be just smouldering, surely?'

'Dear God.' Julie had unzipped her jacket, slipping a hand

inside to finger her dog collar glowing in the last light like a cyclist's armband. 'I didn't think. What does that mean?'

'Might mean you were phoned before the effigy was set alight, don't you think?'

'But that—'

'Suggests you were phoned by the man with the matches. It *was* a man, wasn't it?'

'Oh yes.'

'When did Sir Lionel get *his* call?'

'He said about midnight. Then he phoned Gareth Brewer, to meet him. Poor Gareth.'

Merrily flicked her a sideways glance.

'Why?'

'I'll let his wife explain. It's why I asked you to come over.' Julie rezipped her jacket over the dog collar. 'A duelling banjos situation, if I can put it like that. She's waiting for us, I hope.' She turned back to the church. 'In there.'

32

First brick

MRS BREWER WASN'T a particularly religious person; she just
wanted her kids to grow up with a sense of right and wrong,
Julie said. Until the secular society came up with something
that simple, that basic, she'd be pointing them at the Church.
Julie couldn't complain – this was what had brought her, a
committed socialist and once a committed secularist, into the
job.

'How do you get round the Old Testament?' Merrily asked
outside the legendary south door. 'Plagues of locusts, God
behaving like Herod on steroids.'

'I'm selective, Merrily. Aren't we all?'

'And you've known Mrs Brewer for some time?'

'Since we first bought the house. She used to ride past. Our
lane becomes a bridleway. This was before she had children.'

'Anything else I need to know?'

'Quite honestly, I think you'll find she's so disturbed by
what's been happening that she'll be ready to meet you more
than halfway.'

Framed by stones that looked as if they might hold all the
answers to all the questions, the oak door had great lyre-shaped
hinges and a metal ring. This door promised access to something significant. As Julie turned the ring, Merrily looked up
into a face with bulbous eyes and a great fish-mouth, luxu-
riant swirling foliage curling out of both sides. The doorway
had given pride of place to the Green Man. A character too
complex, Jane had once said, to be a Christian symbol.

Inside, it was all less awesome. Whitewashed walls and two Norman arches. Signs of Victorian modernization, but nothing too disruptive, nothing too grandiose. Little halogen lights made a nest at the bottom of the short nave, but the rest was in shadow.

'This is Mrs Brewer,' Julie said. 'Lara.'

'Who, I'm afraid, was rude to your... friend?' Mrs Brewer said.

Like she needed to get that out of the way. She was a tall, black woman, early to mid thirties, wearing jeans, a thick jumper and a quilted body warmer, a pink woollen hat over her tight curls. The three of them stood looking at each other next to the font, a huge hollowed mushroom on pillars.

'This is probably a mistake,' Julie said. 'We thought we'd come here because it would be quiet. Lara's mother's at home with the children, so we couldn't really meet there. But – one tends to forget – there's no proper heating in this church and it gets very cold after dark.'

'You live far away?' Merrily asked Mrs Brewer.

'Walking distance. A bungalow.'

She looked nervous. Julie led them under the first arch and soft lights came on in the chancel. Small, blue-cushioned pews faced one another and there was a matching chair, probably Victorian. Julie offered it to Merrily.

'I'm going to leave most of this to you. I've explained to Lara what you do – what I *think* you do – and why I've asked you to come, but I'm still a little uncertain. If you hadn't approached me I wouldn't be asking for your help now. Things... converge.'

'It's become rather surreal very rapidly,' Lara Brewer said. 'Can we just talk about it, before we take it any further? I'm feeling a little disloyal.'

'To whom?'

'My husband. I wanted him to get an appointment with a doctor. Even phone my dad – he's a psychiatrist.'

'Locally?'

Mrs Brewer shook her head.

'Back in London now. And then I get a call, out of the blue

from Ledwardine, which seemed to kick-start something. Then Julie appeared, and it all seemed too coincidental. And now an exorcist? From Ledwardine? Somewhere I've never been to,' Lara Brewer said. 'And never even had particular cause to think about until—'

Merrily took a breath.

'Until your husband spent a night there last week?'

First brick dropping into the quiet pool. Julie's head turned.

'For a funeral, yes,' Lara said. 'They went to Ledwardine for Aidan's funeral. The Kilpeck Morris.'

'For the funeral itself?'

'Don't you know? I thought you were the minister there.'

The words coming faster, as if Lara was chasing the ripples on the pool.

'I can't say for certain that Gareth and his friends were there,' Merrily said, 'because I don't know what they look like, and we weren't introduced. But I've been told they spent the night at a pub in the village. The Ox.'

'Well that— It was supposed to be a kind of wake. I realize wakes are meant to take place before a funeral, but— Oh God, look, *I* don't know. I've just accepted these traditions. Gareth said it was about saying a proper goodbye. Which usually means having a lot to drink. After which you don't drive home.'

'I didn't know, until just now,' Merrily said, 'that Aidan had been a dancer with the Kilpeck Morris. Would've been something to mention at the funeral, but I wasn't told. His family didn't tell me.'

'His family didn't know. Or weren't supposed to. Or at least his father wasn't, for pretty obvious reasons.'

'But Aidan and your husband…'

'Danced together for years. They're like a close family, the KM. In that way, Aidan had never left, and Gareth always said he belonged here. A primitive tribal thing, men dancing together. Like football… only different.'

'But the Kilpeck Morris,' Merrily said, 'that's not the same as all the others, is it? All those benign, village green dancers. Kilpeck doesn't do fetes and festivals.'

'Only religious ones. Festivals.'

There was a faint rustling from behind and Merrily turned her head, but there was nothing. The nave was less than half the size of Ledwardine's, though there was a small gallery reached by steps.

'When Lol enquired about the possibility of the Kilpeck Morris performing at the Ledwardine Festival, you referred him to Sir Lionel Darvill.'

'Yes.' Sound of Lara trying for a laugh that wouldn't come. 'Look, where I grew up, in Kent, if they kept something like this private, it'd be because it was a cover for sex games or something. Here, it's... a cover for itself.'

'This might sounds like a daft question, but I mean, if it isn't for public entertainment... if they don't play at fetes and festivals, what's it about?'

'It's about *itself*. Lionel's father had studied morris – its origins, what it meant. He developed new dances, which he insisted were actually old dances. I don't, to be quite honest, think Gareth could explain it himself. He's a part of it because of Sir Lionel.'

'Sorry, you'll have to explain that.'

'They're all tied, in some way, to the Darvill estate. A couple work directly for Lionel – one's his shepherd, one's a cheese-maker – ewe's cheese from the Darvill flock. Another makes cider from the Darvill orchards. And Gareth... he's the farrier, self-employed but his forge is on the estate. It's a prestigious work address. And Lionel knows lots of people, from miles around, who have need of a good farrier. He has friends all over the place, other organic farmers, people who cut hay with scythes and plough with big horses that need shoeing.'

'Sounds almost feudal,' Merrily said.

'It's *entirely* feudal. Except that Lionel doesn't take a share of their income. The rent for the forge is peppercorn. What he takes is their time and their commitment. Another thing... the Kilpeck of the Kilpeck Morris is not the rambling village you've just driven through, it's the one you can't see any more. Behind the church.'

'They do perform in public here, though.'

'Oh yes.'

'You see, I can't understand how Iestyn couldn't've found out his son was in the side. Even with his face blacked up.'

'Ah... he also wore a mask. He was the Man of Leaves. It's a rule of Border morris that they're not seen to put on or take off their—'

'Perhaps...' Julie leaned up alongside Lara on the pew, as if bored by morris talk. 'Perhaps you should tell Merrily what happened after Gareth returned from Ledwardine.'

'It's stress,' Lara said. 'I've been thinking about it and it's just stress.'

'When I suggested that, you didn't think so.'

'He's taken on too much work. He didn't want to... although he was upset about Aidan's death, he didn't really want to go to the wake. He was very tired that day. And he doesn't drink much. It all came down on him that night.'

'That's not quite how you put it before.' Julie sounding quite irritated. 'When I arrived at your house.'

'You caught me at a bad time.'

'Washing the bedding, yes. You were conspicuously upset.'

'It was the... Oh God...'

'The smell,' Julie said. 'I know. You said you were washing them a second time. The sheet, the duvet cover...'

Insistent now, stern. You could tell why Julie had been given these venerable parishes in the last days of Bernie Dunmore. Lara's voice came out wearied.

'Yeah, OK, I thought I could still smell it. Imagination. Paranoia. Julie, I never said he was possessed by evil or anything. I don't even believe in all that. I'm sorry, Mrs Watkins, I think Julie may have misunderstood.'

'Lara…' Julie was furious now. 'You're backing away from it.'

'Exorcism? Well, yeah, maybe I am. I'm not sure I even believe in God in the old sense. I mean, Christian principles, that's different. Being kind to people. Morality. But all this demonic possession—'

'All I do,' Merrily said, 'most of the time, is try and help people whose lives have been disrupted by something they can't easily explain. No black bag.'

'My parents were churchgoers, still are. All that worries me is the blurring of boundaries between what's good and what's— As for Gareth… I don't really know what he believes. Doesn't talk about it. If I'm making him sound like some taciturn yokel, he isn't. He just doesn't like to talk about what he doesn't fully understand.'

Merrily said, 'Do you know what they did on the night of the funeral?'

'Got drunk?'

'And when the pub closed? Do you know where they went when the pub closed?'

A silence. Lara swallowed.

'All I know is what happened after he came home.'

'Thank you,' Julie said firmly. 'Let's talk about that.'

If you learned one thing from funerals, it was that under the shadows left by death people behaved irrationally. Especially in the countryside where problems were shouldered rather than shared.

'What time was that?' Merrily asked. 'When he came home.'

'Not sure. When I came down next morning he was in the kitchen, drinking coffee. He said he had an early appointment at a trekking centre over in Wales. I asked him if he was fit to drive, he said he was fine. Didn't see him again until he came home that night, saying he was very tired. He went to bed early. When I went up, around eleven p.m., he was asleep, so it must've been about half past one in the morning when I awoke to hear him— I still don't know how to—'

'You don't have to interpret it,' Julie said, almost harshly. 'Just describe it.'

'I— I just know that he gave the impression of being somewhere else. Somewhere he didn't want to be. And he was terrified. It was dark, the bedroom curtains were drawn, I couldn't see anything, but he evidently could. It was— Oh this is ridiculous, how can I—?'

'Go *on*.'

'It was like he'd come from somewhere. And something had come back with him. And it was cold. Do you know what I mean? The cold we can feel now, that's just... cold. You know you can wear a coat to keep it out. This was... you could wear your thickest coat and a load of scarves and you wouldn't keep it out because it's already inside. Under your skin. Around your bones. Do you know what I'm saying?'

'I think so,' Merrily said.

'He was convulsing. I felt his body go rigid, as if he was having a fit? I switched on the light. His face was... I mean, he wasn't actually asleep but he wasn't awake either. I started shaking him. I must've been shouting because the children came rushing in. One's four, one's six. He was sitting up by then. I told them Daddy had been having a nightmare, and he was coughing and nodding.'

'A nightmare,' Merrily said.

'He went off to work the next day and came home looking a lot older than thirty-six. I persuaded him to go to bed early again. Took a while for me to get to sleep because I knew he was awake. Not moving, but you always know when they're feigning sleep, the breathing's different. I awoke around three a.m. and he wasn't there. Found him in the kitchen, drinking coffee, staring into space.'

'Afraid to go to sleep, you think?'

'He has this very physical, tiring job. Travels long distances in a van with a portable forge in the back. What if he falls asleep at the wheel? What if he isn't concentrating while he's working and some enormous stallion kicks his head in?'

A white tissue came up. Lara blew her nose.

'The next day was Sunday. He went to church. He goes occasionally. I mean, there isn't a service every week, anyway, Julie has so many parishes to look after.'

'He was sitting alone, in the gallery,' Julie said. 'I didn't think anything of it. People want different things out of a service, as you know. Some like to be sociable, some like to be alone with God or just their thoughts.'

'Or to get away from their thoughts,' Merrily said.

'He didn't want much lunch,' Lara said, 'and then he said he wanted some fresh air. I said me and the kids would go with him, but he said he had some jobs to do at the forge. I think he actually went to Maryfields to talk to Lionel. He… came back from Maryfields still looking like a ghost. Ate a meal he probably didn't even taste and then fell asleep in front of the TV, and I woke him up in time to make another attempt at going to bed. I was only sleeping in fits, as you can imagine. I just— It doesn't seem real. If Julie hadn't arrived when she did I'd probably be living with it for another week before attempting to do… I don't know what I'd do.'

'What happened?'

'He went to sleep. I lay awake. Waiting for it. About half one, I felt a pull on the duvet. His body had gone rigid. Put on the light, started to shake him. Didn't know whether I was doing the right thing. He started to breathe through his mouth, in great gulps, as if he'd been underwater, no air, you know? And the cold. And the smell…'

'Which you thought was in the sheets…'

'It was the kind of smell that comes up sometimes when you sink a spade into wet earth. Humus or something. Soil and a faint smell of… decay. Greasy, rotting. Seemed to fill the bedroom.'

'I don't suppose there's any chance at all that he'll talk to me?'

'Talk?' Julie Duxbury said. 'Needs more than that, doesn't it?'

Merrily was aware of nodding, an inescapable commitment, iron manacles closing with a dull clang.

'Maybe.'

33

Nice suit

VAYNOR WAS ON the phone from his car outside Hewell Prison in north Worcestershire. Bliss had been there a couple of times: Gothic mansion with red-brick extensions, often condemned as grossly overcrowded, famous for multiple suicides and a murder. Mixed bunch in there, from the newly remanded to the well-convicted, and Vaynor had expected problems.

Not the case, however. He'd got there before dark for his interview with Lech Jaglowski and he hadn't been kept waiting.

'Never what you expect, is it, boss?' he told Bliss on the phone.

'Darth...' Bliss leaning his office chair back against the window sill. '... I gave up expecting things long ago.'

'Good English, Lech,' Vaynor said. 'Well educated.'

'PhD, is he? You'd gerron with him, then.'

'Well, I did. It's easy to understand why they come here. Apart from the wage levels, they relate to us, the Poles.'

'Since World War Two.'

Vaynor hadn't taken a terp, which could've been dicey if Lech was being interviewed more formally, with a view to a charge. Defence counsel were notoriously good at proving clients didn't have the vocabulary to understand what they were being accused of, never mind cough to it.

But this was just a chat. Darth and Lech had talked for just short of a couple of hours in a private room. Before he left, they'd shaken hands. At one stage, he told Bliss, Lech had wept.

'You can call me a softy, boss,' Vaynor said, 'but I'd stake my pension on him not having done it.'

Bliss was unimpressed. At Vaynor's age, retirement was so far into the future you'd stake your pension on the Green Party winning a majority on Hereford Council if the odds were right.

'Due to being banged up at the time,' Bliss said, 'yeh, but—'

'Or got anybody else to do it for him. Not, frankly, that you could've blamed him. They let me talk to a couple of screws, and Lech doesn't appear to have formed any particular friendships inside.'

'Not even with the baccy barons? If they have them any more.'

'Spends most of his time reading to improve his command of English. The cigarette smuggling – he tells me that got well out of hand because of some mates of Jag who he didn't like to offend. He knew what he was doing, he was just afraid not to.'

'Heard that before, too.'

'Jag, undoubtedly, was a villain. The parents, back in Poland, according to Lech they could never see it. They thought Wictor, through no fault of his own, had got into bad company in Krakow, and he'd come to England to make a new start, clean up his act. Wrong, wrong, wrong, Lech says. He'd come to England to rob people.'

'My old ma thinks I have a nice job with the NatWest bank. But then, I suppose...'

'Lech, however... I asked him about the rape allegation. He said, You talk to police in Krakow, you find they never heard of me. Only Wictor. They knew Wictor all too well.'

'Go on, then,' Bliss said. 'Bugger up the rest of me day.'

It was true that Lech liked Danni. A lot. Knew Jag had been lying to her.

Jag had filled Danni up with all this crap about loving Herefordshire and wanting to spend the rest of his life here, but that wasn't true. 'Economic migrant' didn't come close to describing Jag. The garage was rented, so was the flat. No ties. Everything short-term. Including Danni. Lech, well meaning, had tried to get this over to her. Danni had told Jag. Hence the discord.

'Does he think Jag had him grassed up for the cigs to get him off his back?'

'That's open to dispute. It was an anonymous tip-off. I'm inclined to think – and this is a bit of a gobsmacker, boss, so let me just tell you what he said.'

Lech blamed himself. His own weakness. His naivety. He'd come to England with Jag, not realizing what that might involve. He had some money which he used to set up a Polish shop in which Jag was not involved. But friends of Jag had come after him for favours. It was difficult. More dangerous to refuse.

He'd told Vaynor he'd loved his brother but hadn't admired him – yes, his English was good enough for subtleties. When he came out, in just a few weeks' time, he was going back to Poland. He'd already offloaded the shop.

'He's scared,' Vaynor said. 'He says he never wanted to work with Jag at the garage, didn't like some of the guys Jag was doing business with. The caravan park down by Bromyard? People-trafficking. Slavery?'

The caravan park had been temporary accommodation for a string of Lithuanians who, having put the last of their new Euros into the hands of individuals assuring them they had guaranteed jobs waiting for them in Hereford, had ended up in forced labour, unpaid except for basic meals. Part of a much bigger operation, according to Lech.

'And Jag's role in that was what?' Bliss asked.

'He'd find work for some of the illegals. Apparently straight work in return for IDs put together in Birmingham. Quickly turning into criminal work. In which context, I'm thinking of the van-man who ran into the farmer. Can't remember his name.'

'Lukas Babekis. Who Rich Ford reckoned was sent out into the sticks to nick stuff for Jag.'

'There you go. Some of these people are very poor. Take anything they're offered.'

'You actually ask him if he'd had Jag killed?'

'I said a few people were saying that. That was when he started getting emotional. "Why these people want hang me?" All this.'

'Who does *he* think killed Jag, then?'

'He doesn't know. He was kind of fatalistic about it. Like he'd felt it coming. The final confirmation that he needs to go home.'

'Could've gone home anytime, surely?'

'That's what I said. He said he couldn't go home because Jag wouldn't let him. Jag was making his life intolerable.'

'Did he realize this sounded like a valid motive for removing his brother?'

'Has DS Stagg come up with a name for whoever fingered Lech for the cigs?'

'What's that gorra—?'

'If it emerged that it was Lech himself who alerted us to the cigs in his basement, which obviously it won't, I wouldn't keel over with shock. He wasn't telling me everything, but I'd guess farm theft and allied crime was the tip of the iceberg. He was storing the cigs for Jag, that's where he wanted it to end.'

'You're saying Lech would rather put himself inside with a criminal record than get dragged into it? Come *on*…'

'He got *extremely* worried when I asked him if Jag traded in firearms. "No, no, never, never." Though earlier he'd said his brother prided himself on being able to get anything for anybody.'

'You think Jag wanted *Lech* to store the guns?'

'And a refusal often offends. I think he just panicked, boss. Get me out of this. He said he was very appreciative of the way he'd been treated. Like a holiday.'

'In Hewell?'

'By the police, everybody.' Vaynor paused. 'He was especially pleased to see me, and he asked me if I'd been sent by the chief.'

'Which chief?'

'Ah...' Another pause. 'Prepare yourself, boss. He'd had a personal visit from a very distinguished man.'

'In Hewell?'

'Very friendly man. Of mature years. Nice suit. Paternal – he actually said that. "Like my father." Not quite tearful, but you get the idea. Lech wasn't sure what this nice man's actual position was at the minute, but he did assure him that in a few months he'd be the big chief. He expressed himself sympathetic to migrants who, through no fault of their own, had fallen foul of British restrictions. He said he was talking to a wide range of people, collecting information about the situation. And then he asked him some other things you'll be quite interested to know about.'

Bliss looked up at an eruption of rain on the window.

'This a joke, DC Vaynor?'

34

Concrete

HUW OWEN HAD always laid it down that you didn't just leave without doing something. Prayer, blessing, *something*. You didn't just walk or drive away saying you'd sleep on it, maybe come back tomorrow, because tomorrow might be too late. Huw would talk about suicides he'd known caused by delays and hesitation and simple scepticism.

Merrily watched Lara Brewer walking slowly away, head bowed, towards the pub and the sporadic lights of the newer Kilpeck.

Call me, she'd said to Lara. Call me anytime. Day or night. I'll come out.

OK, people lied to you sometimes. Although experience told you that mostly they didn't. Occasionally they were deluded but, more often than not, whatever had happened to them would have been far enough out of the box to shock them into complete openness.

Still, what could she have done? This was all second-hand. She needed Lara to persuade Gareth Brewer to make himself available. And it needed thinking about, too, because its origins might lie in the churchyard at Ledwardine.

Lights had come on in the farmhouse, distant lights in the hills beyond the church. Julie Duxbury was unlocking her old Renault Clio.

'Her father was a psychiatrist at the Stonebow unit in Hereford, her mother was a teacher. As was Lara until she had the kids. Her parents' house was near a riding stables and she used to help out there during her summer holidays from college. Gareth Brewer was in and out over the summer months, doing what farriers do, which was how they met.' Julie looked up from the car door. 'Can you take it from here?'

'If I'm allowed to.'

'Is it always this difficult?'

Where did you start? There would always be somebody on the fringe of a situation who would think you yourself were dangerously deluded and shouldn't be allowed near normal people. Partly why, in these litigious times, there was often a deliverance panel and exorcists went out in pairs, like cops at night.

'I'm prepared to help,' Julie said. 'I do realize there's something here that needs resolving, and I'm working on it. But that shouldn't affect you.' She turned, tossing her keys from one hand to the other. 'Don't you get tired, as a woman in the ministry, of being treated like some mumsy figure? Soppy?'

'Male clergy get that, too.'

'I know, I married one. But I'm *not* soppy, you see, and I've been doing this job long enough to know that we're the only people left who can take some things on. In the old days, people used to listen to the parish priest, whatever their social position. Don't any more, but that's no reason for us to keep our noses out.'

'Did *you* know Aidan Lloyd?'

'He didn't live here.'

'What did she mean by the Man of Leaves? And the mask.'

'She meant the green man.'

'Like on the church?'

'I find it all rather juvenile. Nor do I like the black faces.'

'I wonder what Lara thinks about that.'

'Doesn't seem to bother her. Bothers me. Wishy-washy, guilt-ridden liberal.' Julie was half into the driving seat. 'I shall *have* to go. Parish council in just over an hour. Please let me know if this goes any further. I—' She came out of the car again. 'Look, it's difficult. He helps us.'

'Sir Lionel Darvill?'

'With the church. I'm not even sure of the figures involved. The money would normally go through the parish accounts, but it seems to be paid directly to the diocese. A national treasure. I'd rather have a big congregation worshipping in precast concrete, but there we are.'

Merrily looked up at the church, remembering its response to the sunset.

'I should take a look at the corbels before I—'

'*No*. Please don't. Go up in the daytime. It's... not terribly safe.'

'The masonry?'

'Nothing wrong with it. Could've been built yesterday. That's remarkable, isn't it? The castle in ruins, village gone, church as good as new.'

Julie got back into the car.

'You really don't like it, do you?' Merrily said.

A cluster of ancient churches in her care, including Dore Abbey, lofty, rambling and far less well preserved.

'I *did* like it. I ought to like it.'

It was just over eight miles to Hereford. Merrily drove into the lights, up past the Plascarreg estate where the drug dealers hung out, and all the time Lara Brewer's voice kept coming back to her, what she'd said about Aidan Lloyd.

Gareth always said he belonged here.

Kilpeck. She joined the traffic crossing Greyfriars Bridge over the River Wye, the Cathedral on her right, through the traffic lights and into the concrete canyon that Jane called Death Valley. She drove slowly, her mobile phone open on the passenger seat, switched on.

Had they come that night, the Kilpeck Morris, to bring Aidan Lloyd home? In a manner of speaking.

With the heater still gasping, she drove slowly through the security-lit trading estates which not so long ago had been open fields. Thinking about Paul Crowden and his insistence that investigation wasn't part of an exorcist's job. Let God take care of all that and accept your role as his device. Presumably, Crowden would also urge Julie Duxbury not to interfere in the feud between the Kilpeck benefactor, Sir Lionel Darvill, and his *bête noire* Iestyn Lloyd, Ledwardine's biggest farmer whose ground arrowed into the churchyard and who hadn't put a penny into the parish. Iestyn. Last seen on the edge of Aidan's grave, muttering, *Devil took*—

Something occurred to her, with a small mental explosion, just as she cleared the last of the city lights and the mobile barked on the passenger seat.

With its famous disinterest in tourism, Herefordshire Council didn't provide much in the way of lay-bys and picnic places. She had to go off-road to take the call, the Freelander up into the verge, hazard warning lights on, the mobile on speaker.

'Things have moved on,' Lara Brewer said. 'I told him you were ready to come out here. He said that wasn't going to happen. Not in front of the kids.'

'What had you said to him?'

'Asked him what they'd done. Left the kids in front of the TV and took him into the kitchen and asked him what they'd done in Ledwardine. I had the strong impression that you know exactly what they did. You wouldn't've come over here so quickly, otherwise.'

An old Land Rover went rattling past, dangerously close.

Merrily said, 'I admit there are some things I couldn't talk about. Other people were affected.'

'These aspects – would they have made me feel better?'

Lara's brittle laughter was like the snapping of twigs. Merrily sat back, firing up the vape stick.

'What did your husband say when you asked him what they'd done in Ledwardine?'

'He asked me what *you'd* said. I told him everything, but we were still going round in circles. Look, they've been changed, these men. They'll do things for Darvill now, without questioning much. Things that might seem completely crazy to you.'

'Try me.'

'I've said too much already. I'm not from round here, which is pretty obvious to everybody, and if you're not *from* a place, as they say, you keep your nose out, don't you?'

'While keeping your ears open.'

'And your mouth shut. If I were to say I think Darvill's mad, that would be too easy. Look, the reason I'm ringing, I'd had enough, I got angry. As I said, I don't really know what I believe, but it seemed to me that you needed to talk to each other without delay. I told him that if we had another sleepless night I might just start being less discreet. But if it's not convenient I'll call him on his mobile.'

'Sorry?'

'He's coming to you. To Ledwardine.'

'When?'

'He's on his way. Left about five minutes ago. I can call him—'

'No. Don't do that.' She took a hit on the vape stick. 'He knows where it is, the vicarage?'

'He's going to your church. He's been there before.'

'Yes.'

'This is… none of it's normal, is it? I just want it sorted, and better it's dealt with by someone like you than…'

The police?

'Lara…' She stared into the white vapour clouding the cab. 'He's coming alone, presumably?'

'Of course.'

'So nobody else knows…'

'I don't know. I wouldn't like to say. I never thought about that. The KM, I suppose he could've rung any of them from the van.'

'Or Darvill.'

Silence.

'He might've felt obliged to tell Darvill what he was doing?'

'In which case...' Lara sighed. 'While he left the house saying he was going over to Ledwardine, that doesn't mean he'll arrive.'

She rang Jane, told her something had come up that may or may not take over the night.

'Good luck,' Jane said soberly. 'Seriously.'

A couple of miles from home, coming off the bypass, the headlights found a commercial sign for Churchwood Farm. It had a streamer urging passing motorists to buy the best of British meat.

You didn't have to live on the Welsh border very long to know that feuds in these parts were like guerrilla warfare and could go on for generations until the reasons for them had been almost forgotten, leaving only enmity set like concrete. And periodic collateral damage. Usually, they were between neighbouring farmers, but what was twenty miles on the Welsh border?

A snatch of voice came through to her, three more words, the most she'd ever heard from the man in the overcoat, under the blood-blister sun, looking down into an open grave into which he'd thrown no earth.

Devil took him.

Small mental explosion.

This time it came out as *Darvill took him.*

35

Catching murderers

ANNIE HAD BEEN waiting for Bliss at his semi in Marden, curtains drawn, one small table lamp casting morose light and sullen shadows over the sparse sitting-room furnishings.

She'd arranged his mail in a pile on the coffee table, the one with the familiar crest uppermost. She nodded to it.

'Do you want to get that out of the way first?'

'Christmas card come early,' Bliss said.

'It looks like your solicitor.'

'I know. The bastard.'

'*Your* solicitor?'

'They're all bastards.'

He ripped it open to the familiar fold of headed notepaper. Left it folded on the table and sank into an armchair.

'Hadn't you better read it?'

'Whatever it is, it won't be the worst news I've had today.'

He picked it up, a poison-pen letter from Kirsty's lawyer, filtered through his own brief. You never realized, when the end of a marriage left a hole in your life, how much shit was going to fill it. Bliss's chest was already tightening. There'd been a few weeks' silence from the Kirsty camp, which was ominous.

He read it. Quite a long letter, as usual, but the message was simpler than most.

'She wants the house, Annie.'

'Why?'

'Because her lawyer thinks it's worth a punt, I imagine.'

Kirsty's old man's farmhouse had about six bedrooms and

holiday accommodation. But Kirsty was only living there *officially*. Her boyfriend, Sollers Bull, had his own farmhouse.

'After she gets me out, she and the kids'll move in for a while, for the sake of appearances. Then she'll flog it or let it and take up residence with Sollers.'

The Sollers Bull who, in Bliss's informed opinion, had got away with murder, but he was too wound up already to start thinking about that now.

'Surely if she eventually moves in with somebody else,' Annie said, 'and sells your house, then you're entitled to something. I'm not an expert on this kind of law.'

'Nor me.'

'But she wants… all of it?'

'No, she's leaving me the shed.' Bliss threw down the letter. 'Of *course* all of it. She's got kids to accommodate.' He picked up the envelope, stuffed the letter back inside and shoved it at the bottom of the pile below four Christmas catalogues aimed at Kirsty and the kids. 'Now I'll give you the bad news.'

Maybe it was fate, all this happening at the same time. Karma. Although he couldn't see exactly what was coming back at him. Never thought of himself as a friggin' saint, but when seriously bad people like Sollers Bull and Charlie Howe were waving down at him…

'All right, look,' Annie said, 'I'm clutching at the last straw here, but if Lech Jaglowski didn't specifically name Charlie, is it possible he was talking about somebody else? Or that it's not *quite* what it looks like.'

'I don't *know* what it looks like. On which basis, unless you have any objections, I'd like to drive over to Hewell tomorrow, with Vaynor, and talk to the feller meself. Thing is, even if he didn't gerrit done – and I'm still not convinced about that – Lech still looks like the quickest way to Jag's killer.'

'And you get to ask him about Charlie.'

'Would you rather do it?'

'God, no. He scares me. Still. Can you believe that, my own father? Even as a teenager, when my friends were making fun of their parents, at how out-of-touch with everything they were, I never could join in. My dad was a big powerful man, in a glamorous job. He'd caught murderers. He had his picture in the papers. He was on TV for *catching murderers*.'

'One of his phrases. "I'm known for catching murderers, Brother Bliss." He liked saying that. Always murderers.'

'Francis, I know exactly what you're going to say next, and—'

'What?'

'Something to do with murder being one of the few crimes he didn't commit during his period in charge of Hereford CID.'

'As far as we know,' Bliss said.

'Stop it.'

'What's he doing, Annie? What's he friggin' *doing*?'

'All right.' Annie sat down on a hard dining chair on the other side of the coffee table. 'Let's start by establishing what he *isn't* doing. I think it's reasonable to assume that Charlie isn't terribly interested in helping economic migrants who've arrived in this country with insufficient knowledge of the minefield that is British criminal law. What else did he have to say?'

'He wanted to know all about Jag's business. He told Lech that he was horrified generally at the way the Brits treated migrant workers. Exploitation.'

'Continues to make no sense. What's he after?'

'A powerful job. For which even I would acknowledge he'd be more qualified than most of the twats who apply, if he wasn't bent. But in order to get elected, he needs to get himself better known throughout the whole police area. What's his strong points? Thief-taking. Catching murderers. Old-style policing. That's what the people want. Old-style bobbies in smart uniforms and tall hats, one on every corner. And smart detectives to follow their hunches and catch the bad guys. By fair means or foul. He thinks people like that.'

'They like maverick cops,' Annie said, 'because they don't understand what being a maverick actually means.'

Bliss leaned back and looked at Annie, whose face was severe in the bilious light, who could never be a maverick, who'd protected herself against it, like a disease, but had never been admired for that, let alone inspired affection the way Charlie had over the years.

He looked down at the envelope. This wasn't exactly going to turn him into a rough sleeper in search of a hostel, but it was a slippery slope. There wasn't room for him in Annie's dinky flat at Malvern, even if they dared be seen cohabiting – not a career-builder even without the Charlie factor. Another signal to leave Hereford, sooner rather than later. He could contest it, of course. His lawyer against Kirsty's lawyer. His dithering bank balance against Kirsty's dad's millions and Sollers Bull's millions.

And they all had links with Charlie, not least from the days when Provincial Grand Master was a firm stepping stone to Chief Superintendent.

Bliss stood up and went to stand behind Annie's chair.

'You know what I think? I think he wants to solve a crime.'

She looked up at him.

'To be *seen* to solve a crime?'

'Yeh, yeh. A big crime. Solved in the old-fashioned way by an old-fashioned copper.'

'He knows who killed Jaglowski?'

'Possibly. Now, if he's particularly interested in Jag's link to the farmer's death, what's that suggest? An incompetent, unqualified driver in one of Jag's vans. How would the lad's family feel about that?'

'They wouldn't know, would they?'

'They would if Charlie told them.'

'And then, with the actual driver out of the picture, one of them goes and kills Jaglowski? With a gun?'

Bliss thought about it for all of a couple of seconds.

'You're right. That would be beyond insanity. I'm overtired and stressed out and talking bollocks. I've gorra stop obsessing about this.'

36

Man of Leaves

EDGING ALONG THE village square towards the church, under a clear and frigid sky, Merrily sensed new frost forming beneath her boots. As she moved under the lychgate, a diesel engine sounded behind her and she turned to see a green van on the square, reversing into a space beside the oak-pillared market hall.

Only one man got out. She didn't wait for him, hurried through the gate to the porch without even a glance towards the graveyard, pulling the ring of big keys from her bag.

Inside the church, she reached up and switched on the lower lights and waited in the shadows by the font, with the great oak door ajar, until his footsteps stopped outside.

'Come in.'

He slid in through the gap. A thock of the wooden latch as he closed the door behind him, stood there breathing hard and slow, as if steadying himself for an ordeal, each breath borne aloft by the acoustics.

'Thank you,' he said.

'Mr Brewer.'

'Gareth, it is. Garry. Whatever.'

'Erm, as it's not going to be all that warm in here we could go to the vicarage. It'll be quite—'

'No, no, I'd rather not, if you don't mind.'

She didn't recognize him from the funeral. In the muted light, his face was...well, gaunt. The first word that occurred to her, *worn* and *ravaged* not far behind. He would have been good-looking, maybe a week ago. He wore this patched and battered Barbour and didn't take it off but removed his black beanie. His hair was dark and curly, some rolls of grey. Not yet forty and ageing by the minute.

'Don't have to tell anybody about this, do you?'

'One woman at the diocese, that's all. That's as far as it need go.'

She slipped off her coat and draped it over a pew end. The background heating was on, but not so you'd notice. She didn't mind. She felt safe here, spiritually and physically, knew its smells, the sharp musk conditioned by centuries of applewood-burning in the village.

She left the main door unlocked for now. The chances of anyone else coming in on a winter's night were remote. Gareth Brewer stood at the foot of the nave, under the closed eyes of the night-time stained glass windows, his shadow on the wall behind the font.

From an inside pocket, he brought out a mobile phone, its face dark.

'Would you mind?'

'No. Please.'

The phone blinked into life. He looked at it for a few seconds and then held it up.

'Four missed calls. One from my wife. The other three all the same.'

'Darvill?'

He nodded and switched off the phone.

'He en't gonner like this. That's a foregone. Tried to ring him, see. Felt I owed him that much, but it was his answering machine. Left him a message, saying I couldn't stand n'more and I'd been offered some help and I was gonner take it. Then I switched the phone off.' He pocketed the phone. 'I need to ask,' he said. 'How did you know?'

'About Aidan's grave?' Better keep this vague. 'It's a big village, but a village is a village. We heard you'd all stayed the night at the Ox. Most of the night, anyway.'

He shook slightly. She thought his shadow shook.

'My daughter woke me up in the early hours after the funeral to tell me something was happening in the churchyard. Which is next to our house. So we went out there.'

'*You* did? You yourself?'

'Nobody else to do it.'

'We never seen anybody.'

'We didn't hang around for long. Jane had gone over on an ankle, and she was in some pain so we had to get home. I expect you were too... absorbed in what you were doing.'

Despite the cold, she saw sweat on his forehead where the beanie had been.

'He expected more of me than I thought I could give.'

She backed into the aisle.

'Do you want to sit down?'

He didn't move.

'I just... He was a good boy, look, but there comes a stage when you... I can shoe a stallion, no problem, but this was asking for a different kind of strength and I en't got that.'

'And you believe I can help? You're not just here because your wife talked you into it.'

'It was a relief, if I'm honest. Don't augur well for the future, but what can you do? Family and all.'

'All right. Just... hang on there a minute, would you?'

Merrily eased off her boots, slipping into the pair of sandals she kept under the prayer-book rack. Feeling around in her shoulder bag for the old Zippo lighter, she padded up the nave to the foot of the chancel steps where she pulled out two chairs, setting them up under the rood screen, angled towards the altar not quite facing one another.

Went up the steps. The Zippo flared at the fourth attempt, and she lit two candles.

* * *

235

'Tell me about that night. You prepared to do that?'

Gareth Brewer shuffled out a smile.

'En't got much of a choice, do I? Not if I wanner stay married.'

'You said that didn't—'

'Sorry. Bit nervous, I am.' He clasped his hands between his knees. 'Sir Lionel had me book us in at the Ox. Couple of us hung around on the fringe of the burial, so we'd know... what we needed to know. Then we all met up at the pub. Got something to eat. And drink. We're just blokes, look. There's some things you can't do sober.'

'You knew you weren't going to be in any state to drive home, which was why you booked into the Ox?'

'They got a reputation for not asking questions, long as you pay up front, and get through a fair bit of beer. We knew the funeral tea was at the Swan, so we just showed up at the Ox in dark suits. Didn't hide that we were there for the funeral. And we stayed there.'

'Until it was time to dance.'

He let out a breath but didn't reply. Merrily shifted in her chair.

'On Aidan's grave. You danced on Aidan's grave, and then you—'

His hands came up.

'Wasn't *like* that.'

'What *was* it like?'

'It was to put things *right*.' He lowered his head, pushing stiffened fingers through his hair, deciding something. He looked up, swallowed. 'He was a Kilpeck boy. And a Kilpeck Morris man. The rector tell you about the fire?'

'The effigy.'

'That's it. Thought it was a real man at first. You hear about these religious nutters pouring petrol over themselves. Some big public gesture. I'm thinking, oh God, it's somebody Lionel's offended real bad. Sometimes, he don't care what he says.'

'Does he know who phoned him about it?'

236

'Muffled voice. I met him at the church. He was yelling at me to fetch a rug from the truck to smother the flames. I was trying to tell him it was too bloody late. This man, he had to be dead – bound himself to a wooden frame before setting hisself alight? But there was no smell of… you know… we've all been to a pig roast, nothing like that. Then we seen it was just a fencing post stuck into the ground, with a crosspiece for the arms, the rag jacket hung over the crosspiece.'

'A crude effigy. Got up in dancing kit.'

'Aidan's kit. Aidan's actual kit.'

'Ah. What made you think that?'

'We knew. Bells proved it when we seen them after they'd cooled off. Bells made special so they sounds partic'lar notes. We recognized the bells, the maker's marks. They'd stuck the post in the ground where it could be seen a way off and set light to it, like a beacon. Message for Sir Lionel.'

'From?'

'Iestyn Lloyd, sure t'be. We reckoned he found Aidan's kit, going through his stuff. Same time as he found the dope. Well, he din't know, did he? He din't know any of it. Least of all that Aidan was still dancing with the KM.'

The candles on the altar had long flames now, but the more he'd talked about fire, the colder it had felt in here, Merrily wishing she hadn't taken her coat off to look like a real vicar, in the clerical shirt and the dog collar.

'So Iestyn…'

'He'd've felt betrayed, wouldn't he? By his dead son. All these years betraying him. Smoking dope and dancing with…'

'Dancing with the enemy. As the… what did you call it, the green man…? Julie told me.'

He looked at her, candlelight paling one side of his face.

'He was the Man of Leaves. Some sides have a straw man. Or a man with a horse's head. He was the fool. The wild card. Sir Lionel likes to call him the Man of Leaves.'

'Why? I mean, what's his purpose?'

'He's part of the side, but he's out of it, too, mingling with folks watching the dance. In and out. Scaring them. The joker in the pack, only he en't that funny, not really. And in this case, they already know him from the church. Like he's down from the church, out of the ole stone.'

The face in the archway image came to her. The vegetable yawn. They weren't exactly ubiquitous, green men, but they were around, on the walls of churches, mainly rural, and they were all different: hair of stone twigs and leaves, stone stems in their teeth. It would have been odd if, amongst its famous bestiary, its knights and its Sheela-na-gig, Kilpeck hadn't had a green man.

'So he always wore a mask. A foliate face.'

Suddenly, she was collecting moments: flash-images super-imposed, one upon another. Something Jane had vaguely described from the open coffin colliding with something she'd seen herself in the fog and mistaken, in that instant, for a crown of thorns.

'He was different then, look,' Gareth said. 'As the Man of Leaves. A different person. Normally, he's this quiet boy, bit shy. *Christ*, he— Sorry. Sorry for my language. He'd go a bit mad, as the Man. Prancing around, in and out of the dance, rearing up in your face, spouting nonsense. But he was special, for Sir Lionel. He had the instinct.'

'Instinct for...?'

'The *instinct*. You know? Dunno what else you'd call it. All I know is that the whole atmosphere of the dance changed when he was in it. He took you somewhere else. If you were up for that. If you were up for following him.'

It was old, Ledwardine church, and probably built, like most of the churches in the border country, on a sacred site older than Christianity. In the middle of a long-buried henge, according to Jane. Layer upon layer.

But nothing as demonstrative as St Mary and St David at

Kilpeck, whose walls carried the frames in a medieval cartoon that nobody today could follow.

'You said he *came down* from the church,' Merrily said. 'The Green Man… the dancer… the Man of Leaves. What did you mean by that?'

'We all come down at one time or another. All the dancers were out of the church. The dances Lionel taught us, sometimes we'd all take on different characters from the walls. Like in one dance, you'd be the knights from the doorway, and your sticks'd be the swords. But Aidan, he was always the Man of Leaves. Aidan Lloyd didn't exist in Kilpeck, see? Only the Man of Leaves.'

'Like when he came home to Kilpeck he was taking on a different identity?'

'That's it.'

'And when you said he was a natural…'

'It's what Lionel'd say. We didn't ask. *I* didn't ask. I got obligations, but I also got a wife and kids. Don't need complications. The church and the dance… they're part of the same thing.'

'That's why you don't do it anywhere else? Why you don't… dance around?'

'Wouldn't work the same.'

'How does it affect you? Personally. The dance.'

'Well, it… I dunno.'

'Can you try to explain?'

'If I tell you…' He looked uncomfortable, moistened his lips. 'Some nights, I'll put in a day's work, then we'll dance, and I feel I could do *another* day's work… just to work it off.'

'It brings out energy you didn't know you had.'

'That's it. It don't always happen like that.' He looked down at his clasped hands, then looked up. 'If I tell you about Bob Rumsey – part-time college lecturer, a local historian. Studious kind of bloke, lives in a cottage where you can't move for books. Bob got in a fight outside the pub. On the green, with the Trafalgar oak.'

'Sorry?'

'Big tree. Planted to commemorate the victory at Trafalgar. Anyway, this was after the dance. Somebody taking the piss. Bob, he just beat the sh— Hammered the other feller into the ground at the foot of the tree. Nearly got hisself arrested. One-off, never happened again. It just takes you by surprise sometimes. Summat getting into you.'

'When did Aidan get drawn into it? The dance.'

'He was just a boy. His mother, Sarah, she never wanted him to join the dance – 'cos of the asthma, look. Din't want him struggling to keep up with fitter men, not wanting to let the side down, but not finding the breath, you know?'

'Right.'

'But it was the makin' of him. Lionel, he'd known Aidan since he was a little dab and Lionel was in his teens. Aidan'd had this asthma, pretty bad, nearly died couple of times. Not much use on the farm, disappointment to his dad.'

'This was before the rift opened up between Henry Darvill and Iestyn Lloyd?'

'Don't get Sir Henry wrong. He didn't push it too hard with Lloyd. He was learning how to do it, how to run a farm, how to buy and sell stock, manage the mix. A real learner, Sir Henry. Been at this college... a college for folks too old for college, and mabbe that changed how he approached things. What I'm saying is, he didn't come strolling in like the big boss, saying what was what. None of that.'

'You were here then?'

'I was still a boy, I din't really see it. My dad – he was a farrier, too, retired now – he told me all this much later, after Sir Henry was dead. How humble he was. Ready to be a pupil was how my dad put it. And then, once he knew what he was doing, he'd start to make changes, developing his own ideas. He'd have Iestyn Lloyd banging his bloody head against walls, and he'd just be walking away, real casual. Not fazed at all. All the rows, they was started by Lloyd, seeing his power base getting undermined.'

'Power base?'

'It'd been *his* farm, how he saw it. The Lloyds used to be real big landowners both sides of the border, but Iestyn's ole man, he was a big drinker and it all went to shit. It was Sir Peter took Iestyn on board, give him a free hand. Iestyn who built that place up to what it was and now here's Henry Darvill taking it apart.'

It was the most he'd said all night. Much happier talking about situations he hadn't been involved in, situations he couldn't change.

'And during all this,' Merrily said, 'Aidan's asthma…?'

'Lionel'd took the boy under his wing, and the sick kid got better, 'gainst all the odds. But this was around the time of the split, so Iestyn stopped Aidan dancing, or thought he had. And then they moved out and come up by yere.'

He said Iestyn's marriage, never too solid, had finally broken up around the time of the move. Iestyn feeling everyone was against him, reacting with aggression and a determination to see his new farm expand and prosper. And that was when Aidan, aged around fifteen, started quietly coming back to Kilpeck, to dance.

'All that way?'

'Twenny miles or so. His ma used to bring him. He'd be spending more time at the farm now, with the asthma gone, but still living with Sarah in Hereford weeknights, after they got him into the Cathedral School. And *she'd* be bringing him over to Kilpeck – anything to stick one on Iestyn. Then, when he was old enough, he had a motorbike. No problem then.'

'And it was all still kept secret? Behind the leafy mask?'

'That's it.'

'So Iestyn really didn't find out till Aidan was killed.'

She saw Iestyn Lloyd looking down into the grave. Throwing no earth, only his rage.

'So you think he brought the effigy himself?'

'Mabbe had somebody else do it. Lot of employees, now, and

he's not as young as he was. But he was behind it, no argument there. I don't expect you to understand how deep this goes.'

'Doesn't take a degree in psychology, Gareth. He's lost his only son, his only child, which for any farmer is… well, it goes beyond personal grief, doesn't it? And then learning his son's been dancing with Darvill's men. OK, it was a fairly extreme reaction but… you know… nowhere near as extreme as what Darvill did next. Or rather got you to do.'

No reply.

'That's the big puzzle you see, for me. What you did.'

She saw Gareth Brewer biting his upper lip. She looked hard at him, but he was looking at the candles.

'You didn't *just* dance on his grave, did you?'

She saw his hands were squeezed together, white-knuckle tight.

'He follows me.'

'Who?'

'You wouldn't see him come in sometimes. He was always like that. He'd just be there, watching. Never talked much. You always felt much more was going on inside him. He'll be sitting next to me in the van. That four-day stubble still around his mouth. I'll be in the forge and he's there. See him through the sparks.'

'Aidan?'

'And with the horses. I'm out shoeing a horse, and the horse knows. Got kicked twice. Spooked. Funny we always say that, ennit? *Spooked.* I en't making this up, Mrs Watkins. The world we're living in, it's more than we need to understand.'

He was gazing not far over her head. She glanced up at the rood screen with its wooden apples, realized that wasn't it. They were sitting where, just a few days ago, Aidan's coffin had been, on its bier.

'You dug it up,' she said. 'The coffin.'

'We'd… brought the spades earlier, look. Left 'em under a bush. On Iestyn's ground.'

He was sitting very still, and his gaze never shifted. She felt colder than ever before in her own church. She hugged her arms.

'What was he wearing? When you opened the coffin?'

'Suit and tie. But his face, it was, it was gone. All just sewed up. We cut them off him, the clothes, with a Stanley knife. Took them away with us and burned 'em later. In the forge.'

'And you'd brought a rag jacket with you.'

'Who told you that?'

'And a top hat. And bells. And you—'

'How'd you—?' He'd started to shake. 'How'd you *know* that?'

'You dressed him as a dancer. And then you put the mask over his face? Made him into the Man of Leaves again?'

Not Jesus Christ and his crown of thorns, and *oh dear God*, the truth of it seared her, as if she'd grabbed one of the candles and squeezed the hot wax between her fingers.

He brought his gaze down, to face her.

'It's like a bad dream, Merrily, what we done.'

'And turned into one.'

His eyes blurred with candle-glimmer... and guilt, fear, misery, what? Strange new feelings, maybe, for a farrier who always had to be relaxed and steady, to win the trust of the horses and ponies and donkeys he was approaching with a bagful of tools.

He was shaking freely now. The images rolled: the men in top hats with ribbons in the fog, the men like hawks, in pairs, coalescing, then parting to show that they were...

'... dancing with him?' Merrily said. 'With the body? You'd pulled Aidan Lloyd out of his coffin and made him dance again?'

243

37

Engage

NEVER JANE'S FAVOURITE room, the scullery. It was small and didn't lead anywhere, and all its window showed you was the churchyard wall, reminding you that life would one day dump you on the other side of it. Particularly ominous on a moonlit night, like this one, when the phone was ringing.

She'd bought Mum the phone a couple of years ago, a present. The kind of phone you associated with doctors' surgeries and village police stations in old black and white British movies. It had seemed cool at the time; tonight it seemed like the kind of phone the angel of death would use and felt heavy and portentous when she uncradled it.

'Ledwardine Vicarage,' Jane said.

A relieved breath was trapped in the earpiece then a woman's voice.

'Merrily, I'm sorry to ring you at this time of night, but we have a problem.'

'Erm... Sophie, it's Jane.'

'Oh. You sounded just like her.'

Was that supposed to be a compliment?

'She's out,' Jane said. 'I'm not sure when she'll be back. Did you call before?'

'Twice.'

'It's been a complicated night. Apparently.'

'Trust me, Jane, it isn't going to get any easier if I don't speak to your mother soon. Is it possible she can be reached on the phone, wherever she is?'

'Erm…' Jane sat down behind the desk, felt around for the Anglepoise switch. 'I don't think she'd want me to bother her right now. She's in the church.'

A period of, like, restraint at Sophie's end. Jane tilted the cup of the Anglepoise lamp so that it made a tight circle of light on the desktop with its sermon book and stubby pencils. She sank back into deep shadow and felt inexplicably calm.

'You said there was a problem.'

'If you could just ask her to call me…'

'She'll probably be very tired, so if you could tell *me*—'

'… as *soon* as she gets in. In fact, if you can reach her on her mobile…'

'In church?'

'It's not a service, presumably.'

'Depends what you mean by service. Look, I know you think I'm still some irresponsible kid, all clothes and clubbing and stuff, but—'

'I never quite thought that of you, Jane.'

Never *quite* thought that?

'But when I'm here and not injecting heroin into my arm I do try and relieve her of some of the burden. And I don't talk about things to anybody outside the loop. As she thinks of you as *inside* the loop, I can tell you that this is what we like to call a night job?'

'*Damn.* Does it involve someone from Kilpeck?'

'I think it does.'

'In which case I'm probably too late. How long's she been gone?'

'Over an hour. Look—' Jane sprang out of shadow. 'I do know about Innes and what a knife-edge Mum's on. And I actually don't want her to have to leave this place because of that bastard or anyone else, so anything you can tell me…'

'Let me think about this. If I don't hear from Merrily in the next hour I shall have to call you back.'

'Thank you *so* much,' Jane said.

Only Ethel was waiting in the kitchen. She put some Felix out in the cat bowl and went to the dresser to cut herself a slice of fruit cake. She was carrying it back into the scullery when the phone rang again. That hollow, visceral ring that shrilled *emergency, emergency*. Bloody hysterical phone.

She hefted it to an ear.

Ledwardine Vic—'

'Merrily?'

'Bloody hell, Sophie—'

Realizing, before the name was quite out, that this wasn't Sophie.

'That's her daughter, is it? Jane?'

'Yes, I'm sorry, I thought—'

'Jane, this is Julie Duxbury, from Ewyas Harold. Is it possible you can get a message to Merrily, or am I too late?'

'Too late for what?'

Another one?

'Jane, is she in the church?'

Jane hesitated. Julie Duxbury didn't.

'I've been talking to Gareth Brewer's wife, who— I'm trusting you, Jane, because I have to start trusting people, or nothing will ever stop all this. Lara's been getting calls from Sir Lionel Darvill. Angry and frustrated and certainly suspicious of me. I meddle, you see. We have such small congregations, scattered over so many churches now, that we're inclined to feel superficial, and so we meddle. All that's left for us to do, I sometimes fear.'

'Nothing wrong with that.' Jane said. 'Someone has to. OK, yeah, she's in the church.'

'With Gareth?'

'I think so.'

'That's all right then. That's good. Jane, your mother needs to know that Darvill knows she was here this evening – *I* don't know how he knew, he has eyes everywhere. Suffers from an increasing paranoia and he'll damage people without a thought.

Doesn't want her talking to Gareth. Well, that's no surprise, and it shouldn't affect anything, it's her job. I just wanted her to know, but it doesn't matter.'

'Are you at home?'

'Yes, but I may have a visitor later. I'll give you my mobile number just in case but it doesn't matter. Just tell her not to worry, and we'll talk tomorrow.'

Jane took the number down, encouraged at someone treating her like an adult, for whatever reason. Then she called Sophie back.

A tick had formed in Gareth Brewer's lower face, seeming to follow the rhythm of the fluctuating candle flames.

'Wasn't about *making* him dance,' he said. 'It was what he wanted.'

'You thought that?'

'It was what we had to believe.'

'You mean that was what Darvill told you.'

He'd admitted to putting a menthol inhaler up his nostrils to block the smell when they opened the coffin. He'd read police did that at post-mortems.

On his feet now, backing away from the chancel. She'd had to stop him trying to demonstrate how he and another dancer – Jed, the cheesemaker – had shared the dead weight. The two of them lifting the body, carrying it between them, its arms over their shoulders, at one end of the open grave. The grisly customizing of a dance that Lionel Darvill had learned from his father.

'So you *were* bringing him back. Into the fold. Into his Kilpeck persona – the Man of Leaves.'

'That's it. We put the mask on him first. By the time we'd cut the jacket off, got the bells strapped to his calves, it was like, Oh, we gotter get him out to get the rag jacket on proper. So out he comes. One of the boys was sick. Got sent into Iestyn's field to throw up.'

Jane had described the holly and the white-berried mistletoe set in bark, the fissured features that had seemed to alter their expression in the unsteady lamplight.

Gareth Brewer looked up, that vibration in his jaw.

'I s'pose what we'd forgotten was how he'd died. *Instantly*, it said in the *Hereford Times*. Sounds clean, that. I never figured he'd be, you know, mangled. Nobody said his face'd been half ripped off. And the post-mortem and sewn up and that. It was just a blotch. I'm sorry to be telling you all this, I—'

'No, go on...'

'When the lid come off, it was horrible. No blood, like, but that made it worse. This drained thing in the suit and tie. Me, I just turned off. At first. We'd agreed to do it, put the bells on him and the jacket and the mask, to bring him back into the side. We were the Kilpeck Morris. We'd had the benefits of it, and we accepted there was things you gotter do sometimes. Things outside normal experience. Seemed like a good thing to do, sending him *from* here as a dancer. Reverse the damage Iestyn done. We were happy with that idea.'

'Happy?'

'We were up for it. Specially after a few drinks. Making jokes, the way you do. Burke and Hare, all that. We had two good spades, so it didn't take that long to get down to the box. We'd danced first. We didn't need music. It was slow. You could almost find the rhythm by your own heartbeat. We'd bound cloth over the sticks so there wouldn't be much noise. We felt energized. Up for it. Feeling... not good, but capable.'

'How long was all this going on?'

'I dunno. An hour? Hour and a half? An energy starts to come through, look. The energy you put in, it increases the energy you get back. When you first start dancing, you might think you're fit, but you get tired quite soon. Gotter keep on till you break through it. Till you *engage*.'

'Like moving up a gear?'

'That's it. When that happens, you come out... I don't know

where you come out, but it's somewhere else. When you're doing it proper. When you're in the right place at the right time. On the right day… night.'

'Festive days?'

'Aye. Saints' days. And the equinoxes. When you're holding the balance between the seasons. Dancing the summer in. Or, in our case, more often, it's the winter. Summoning what we needs for the hard days to come.'

'And the energies, where do they come from?'

He shrugged.

'Out of the earth. And the air. The rain sometimes. The wind. Ice. Or fog. Even fog. You work with what's around. You goes at it steady till it starts to engage.'

Gareth talked about the euphoria that would often emerge in the whoops and roars of the Border morris men. And the fusion, all of them becoming the same organism. She remembered the grunts and the rhythms of breathing in the churchyard, and the smell of the country fog. No roaring, no whooping. Only what must have been the muted cackling of the bells around a dead man's legs.

'I still can't imagine how you got through it.'

'We just did, Mrs Watkins. We had the energy between us, all of us together.'

'What were you feeling then? Inside.'

'Nothing. It was only afterwards, when we'd gone our separate ways, that it started coming back to me – feeling what I hadn't felt at the time. This cold bony arm bent round my neck. The sheer, bloody horror of that. But while it was happening I never felt like that, see. I was able to do it.'

'How did it end?'

'We put him back. And the soil, the earth.'

Not properly, though, jammed halfway down; they'd wanted out.

'And that was it?'

'We replaced the turfs. Neat as we could. And then we…'

He looked puzzled for a moment, as if something had occurred to him for the first time.

'Jesus, we never done,' he said, 'what we should've done. When you finish the dance – they all do this, all the morris sides, all the ones I seen, anyway – you all walks in a circle. Around the place where you done the dance.'

'Why do you do that?'

Like she couldn't recognize the ritual aspect, the hint of magic: the closing of the circle, making sure that whatever energies they'd awoken would remain inside...

... the grave? Lara's voice came to her. ... *started to breathe through his mouth, in great gulps, as if he'd been underwater, no air... And the cold. And the smell...*

In the cold of the nave, Gareth was sweating freely, his eyes flitting erratically from the dull lustre of the organ pipes, past the pulpit to where the nave escaped the candlelight and shut down into shadow.

'We took him out,' he said, 'and we made him dance, and now the bugger's dancing and he won't go back. *Oh Jesus.*'

Shaking now.

'OK.' Merrily stood up. 'We need to do something about this, Gareth.'

'Just get him away from me. Get him *back.*'

'Yes.'

She was close to trembling, too. Felt a pulse in her gut.

This would not be quickly dealt with. She asked him to excuse her and went down to call home, explain to Jane, but it was engaged.

There was a text, from Julie Duxbury. it said,

whatever anyone else tells you, DO THIS!!!

*

'You need to tell me what she's doing,' Sophie said.

'I don't *know* what she's doing.'

'How long have they been in the church?'

'Most of an hour? She didn't have time to explain much. Except that the guy was in a mess and she needed to organize something quickly. You probably have a better idea than me of what that's likely to be. Now... if you think this is important enough for me to go and bang on the church door with a big stick...'

'No. Don't do that. Let it take its course.'

Sophie's voice sounded surprising. Shocking, even, in its roughness, its... vulnerability? Sophie? Jane stared hard into the circle of lamplight.

'You're going to have to tell me, Sophie. I know that this guy Darvill, for reasons of his own, is doing his best to keep her away from Brewer. I know he's been leaning on Julie Duxbury and... well, obviously, someone's been leaning on you as well. So like who would *that* have been? As if we didn't know.'

Cavernous silence in the old phone before Sophie's voice came cautiously back.

'Your mother's presence in Kilpeck tonight was noted. The person you mentioned assumes he has the Bishop's ear.'

'By virtue of being *Sir* Lionel.'

'And a significant patron of the church. And while the current bishop's ear is far less accessible than the ears of his predecessor, it does tend to... prick... at the mention of certain names. Merrily Watkins being one of them. He didn't actually speak personally to Sir Lionel Darvill, the call was intercepted by Ben. Who passed it on to the Archdeacon. From whom I received a call.'

Siân Callaghan-Clarke. That figured. Jane had met Siân and, in the end, they'd got along OK. But she was a former barrister and ambitious. Becoming Archdeacon of Hereford wouldn't be a career summit for Siân.

'Sounding, I have to say, not her normal self,' Sophie said. 'Insisting that Kilpeck is a purely pastoral matter.'

'What the hell's that mean? It can safely be left to the cows? Sorry—'

'Something for which deliverance is not considered appropriate. The rector will also be receiving a call telling her it can be dealt with by prayer and counselling. I asked the Archdeacon informally if she could tell me what was behind all this. She said Sir Lionel Darvill seems to think that your mother, misguidedly, is interfering in a delicate situation that Julie Duxbury is already trying to resolve. He thinks she may be superfluous. And likely to make unnecessary waves.'

'But... hang on, Sophie, Julie Duxbury told me, not ten minutes ago, that Darvill's accusing her of exactly the same things. She's, like, *meddling*. He's bonkers.'

'Nonetheless, the Archdeacon suggests it might be advisable for your mother to suspend all activity in connection with Kilpeck until further notice.'

'Bloody hell, that's—'

'And I've been asked to keep it off the Deliverance database. And there are other complications. So you see why I thought I needed to speak to Merrily. However—'

'I'll get her to call you as soon as she gets back,' Jane said.

'*No.*'

'Sorry?'

'Don't. Not tonight. It's too late. She'll have done what she thinks is necessary. And whatever she's done, it needs to settle. I'm not a priest, but... it needs silence. She can call me tomorrow. Tell her nothing tonight. It's too late.'

'How can I avoid—?'

'Go to bed or something.'

When she put the phone down, Jane stood by the window, looking up into the awful clarity of the sky, stars gathering like a huge audience over the churchyard wall. Then she called Lol.

38

Each of our dyings

IN THE BRECON Beacons, the ringing stopped, and the machine cut in.

'This is Huw. Tell us what you're after or just leave a number, and if nowt's happened to me I'll get back to you when I can. God bless.'

She said, 'Huw? It's me.'

In the vestry, the phone on speaker on the table beside the rack of Ledwardine picture-postcards. She'd packed the airline bag: wine, chalice. Unhooked her woollen funeral cape to take on the cold.

Nothing. Sometimes he let the machine do its bit to find out the score, then picked up. This time, he really wasn't in.

'Huw, don't call me back. Just stay with me, if you pick this up. Couple of hours? I'm sorry, you know what I'm saying? I'll call you when I—'

Bleep.

Damn.

She thought for a moment and then flicked through the numbers stored in the phone, selecting one and getting through instantly this time.

'You're asking for *my* advice?' Abbie Folley said.

'Second opinion. And, erm, back-up.'

'I've never done anything like this.'

'Well, me neither. That's to say I've done it, but not in these circumstances. Or for this reason. Though that's what a Requiem's about in a deliverance context, isn't it? Ostensibly

253

for the soul of the departed, essentially for the people whose lives he's complicating.'

'You're in the church with him now, Merrily? I mean the bloke who—'

'Both of them, if you like. I'm in the vestry, Gareth's close to the altar. And keeps looking around as if his dead friend might have followed us in.'

'Jesus, you're spooking me out already.'

'This is a man whose funeral was... not as thorough as it might've been. Partly my fault. *Mainly* my fault. But there's someone else who's seriously screwing things up. Who's... playing with the dead to score points. I'm not even going to... mention Darvill's name. Or Iestyn's name. Keep them both out of this. 'If I had more time I'd probably try and summon a few more people, but the way things are, I just can't see... oh God...'

'Something happened?'

'Good *God*, woman, you—'

'What've I said?'

'Not you, Abbie, me. Me. I'm stupid. I keep missing the obvious. It was staring me in the face, but if I hadn't rung you it might not have occurred. Might be possible, might not. I need to call somebody else. Sorry, I'm all over the place...'

'Listen, what time?

'Not planning to start later than nine o'clock. Let's *say* nine. If there's a delay I'll call you back. Would that be OK?'

'Does Huw Owen know about this?'

'He's not answering his phone.'

'Scraping the bottom of the barrel then. No, listen, I'll be there. As it were. Do you want to give me the name?'

'It's Aidan Lloyd.'

She gave Abbie details of his death, told her where she could find a picture on the Net.

'I'll get into fancy dress, then,' Abbie said, 'and go down the church. Give me a call when it's a wrap, if you're not a gibbering wreck.'

* * *

She'd said the Lord's Prayer with Gareth Brewer, advising him to keep on repeating it in his head, slowly, while she was away. A firewall.

When she walked back up the aisle, put down her bags, he was looking up at her, trusting, like a dog, putting himself in her hands as people, even today, tended to. When you were all they had left. Merrily thought of bereavement apparitions reported by friends in the pub, colleagues in the workplace – the ghost at the watercooler. Even children in a classroom when a favourite teacher had died. Usually, they just stopped. But when they didn't…

The wrestler, Paul Crowden, cut in, so many of his words printed on her memory like the government warning on a cigarette packet.

I don't want to get to know it, whatever it is, or find out what it's after, or why it might be unquiet… As we have no means of understanding what's actually happening, we should regard it all as potentially evil…

No.

She brought out her mobile phone, muted against incoming calls, and conjured up the picture of Aidan Lloyd from the *Hereford Times.*

Evidently a blow-up from a group shot at some farmers' gathering. If there'd been time she'd have printed it out, because this was the Aidan she knew, if she knew him at all: face like a weather map, all smudges and shading, dark around the mouth, dark around the eyes.

'Exorcism? Forget it,' she told Gareth Brewer. 'This is a Requiem Mass, or Eucharist, if you prefer. A second funeral service, if you like, the central purpose being to take the pressure off Aidan, wherever he is now. Which, thanks to Sir Lionel, could be anywhere. Reject this if you want, but I think what Sir Lionel had you do, out there in the churchyard, was… not a good idea. To say the least.'

'You think we didn't know that?'

Despite the cold, he'd been sweating, hair glued to his forehead. Molten candle wax was in freeflow on the altar, the flames erratic now. Yes, he'd said, he'd been to Holy Communion many times in his younger days. He was familiar with the procedure. She talked to him, keeping it conversational, as she prepared the altar.

'*I* don't know where Darvill's coming from, and I'm not sure we have time to go into it. But whichever spiritual path you're following – or psychological path, whatever – you have a guy here, a possibly troubled guy, with two personas, whose death came – bang! – in a crash. Unexpectedly. Who gets a duff funeral because his father's angry, embittered, feeling betrayed by the son he's burying. Whose grave is immediately invaded on the instructions of a man who's convinced Aidan would rather be in Kilpeck.'

In full kit now, under the cape, she turned back to the chancel.

'Now tell me there's more to it than that.'

He shook his head, which could mean anything.

'You can still back out, Gareth, I'm not going to twist your arm. Though I do feel obliged to tell you that, even if you walk away now, I'll be going ahead with the Requiem – *hopefully* – because there's someone else on her way.'

He looked up in alarm.

'She won't know about you, you won't know about her. That all right?'

'*Her?*'

She nodded and shed the cape. He stood up and took off his patched jacket, as if, she thought, for the sacred ritual of shoeing a horse.

It began, at its own pace.

We have come here tonight to remember, before God, our brother Aidan and to give thanks for his life.

Keeping it simple, using lines that Gareth might remember

from the Sunday Eucharist.

Dying, you destroyed our death

Rising, you restored our life

Do not let your hearts be troubled, neither let them be afraid.

She'd done this many times, no two Requiems the same except for that sense of tremulous anticipation. The candles flickered occasionally, as if from some spear of draught out of the Bull Chapel behind the organ pipes.

When it came to responses, Gareth remembered. What you dreaded most was a situation where the words wouldn't come, leaving a hollow silence that someone had once told her was apt to fill with a distant malevolent chattering in the back of your head.

Lord, have mercy.

Christ, have mercy.

Lord, have mercy.

Merrily's mobile was propped up against a prayer book on the altar, the picture of Aidan dulled. Jane would approve of the picture. Sympathetic magic. Merrily no longer had qualms; the foundations were universal.

She was aware of her own breathing, amplified, as if the walls were breathing around her. As she'd placed the phone there, inclined her head and then moved away from the altar, Gareth Brewer had spontaneously talked about the worst feelings of all, as he'd fought to awaken in the bedroom. Always been claustrophobic – couldn't work in the van without all the doors wide open. Certain now that he'd had the unbearable sensation of Aidan and him changing places in the smothering dark.

Suffocation. Asthma.

At this point, Rachel Peel had entered silently and Merrily had trotted down and locked the church door with the big key and switched off the lights. Then they'd walked back up the aisle and she'd performed very brief instructions and hands had been shaken. No discussion necessary, no happy-clappy hugs; they didn't know one another, never need meet again.

let us not run from the love which you offer,
but hold us safe from the forces of evil.
On each of our dyings shed your light

As she lifted the chalice, she had one of those devilish panic images: Gareth choking on the wine, the wafer turning to clay in his throat.

She ignored it.

Earlier, she'd said he might feel the need to make a kind of sacrifice. To shed something. *Give up the morris,* he'd said. *I know. And get out of the village.* And lose significant clients – he hadn't said that. She'd told him he might want to give up the morris just for a while. See how he felt.

Merrily let the candles burn and the shadows absorb her, the air carpeted by Rachel's soft sobbing.

Gareth didn't choke.

Rachel's presence... God, how could she have lived with herself if she'd gone through with this without even offering her the opportunity to be here?

The shaded Aidan had vanished from the phone.

After it was over, Gareth walked down the aisle, shaking his head as if he'd given up trying to make sense of it. She was unlocking the door for them, asking if they'd like to come back to the vicarage for a coffee, but she was only half there and glad when they both thanked her and declined.

She threw open the double doors to a sky swimming with starlight, letting it in.

'Have a walk around before you get into the car. And drive carefully.'

Gareth nodded.

'This over?'

'I hope so.'

Rachel was still breathing hard. She put her arms around Merrily. Over her black-coated shoulder the stars were chips of ice in a frozen firmament.

'I'm so glad you rang,' Rachel said.

And that was what mattered, what all this was about, a degree of customer satisfaction.

And nobody mentioned the alien smell that had come down from the rafters and settled in the air around them. After they'd gone, Merrily went back to extinguish the candles, drink the rest of the wine and put everything away, and the smell seemed stronger than ever, forcing her to her knees at the altar as a weight of exhaustion came down.

When she stepped out under the loaded sky, pulling on her waxed coat, Lol was there.

She smiled.

'I thought I told you not to come into this place again in the hours of darkness. Not *ever*.'

'You look shell-shocked.'

'Just a bit dizzy.' She turned to lock the church door. 'It's never what you expect. Which I suppose is how it should be. Otherwise, be routine, wouldn't it?'

So glad it was Lol, that he was here. So grateful, wanting to hold him close, to love without complications.

'Jane told you?'

'She's having an early night.'

'Good.'

As they stepped away from the porch, pocketing the big keys, the ground was noisy in her head, as if some of the stars had drifted down and were getting crunched under her boots. She was grateful for his arm around her. Wanted so much to re-assure him when he asked if this was over.

'I'd like to think so.'

But she didn't. For Gareth maybe and a turning point for Rachel, but it wasn't over.

She glanced briefly towards Aidan's tump as they walked towards the lychgate under the vast, unexpected planetarium of the Ledwardine night.

'From a practical point of view,' she said, 'if Iestyn Lloyd wants to install some immovable granite monolith over his son's grave, with bars all round, there won't be any objections from me.'

She thought one of them might smile, guessed that neither did. The stone archway shielded her from the stars' assault, but she still felt feather-headed and put both hands on the cold stone.

'Haven't missed anything, have I? Nobody called?'

'Nobody important,' Lol said, and she knew he was lying.

The stars were swarming like bleached insects around the church steeple. On the other side of the lychgate, the muted, mullioned lights of the Black Swan were less threatening, but the cold gnawed at Merrily's hands and, for an instant, she was back in the church with its guttering candles and the pervading sweet, somnolent scent of marijuana.

Part Five

The Morris is a religious dance concerned with energies. It is something of a miracle that it survived until modern times, especially when we realise how effective the Church was in eradicating nearly all traces of earlier beliefs.

A.G.E. Blake
Article in *The Enneagram* (1975)

39

Tent over the sundial

NOT THE BEST time of year for this. Bliss, still in his coverall, was hunched under a trellis supporting roses, a couple still in flower. His beanie was pulled down over his ears and the phone. The rest of him was freezing. He was thinking it was about time some bugger invented a thermal Durex suit.

He looked back at the square stone house.

'Car in the drive. Keys found on the edge of the lawn, car keys and house keys on the same ring.'

'So we're looking at a disturbed burglary?' Annie said, from the warmth of Gaol Street.

'What it looks like to me, but early days, obviously. Norra difficult house to burgle – they may've tried to get into another not too far away but buggered off when the alarm went off. In this case, no alarm. Pane of glass at the back smashed for entry, then they just open the front door. And they're still here when the occupant gets home.'

'Why didn't they just leg it?'

'A question I've asked meself, Annie.'

You'd think they might've heard the car pulling in and buggered off the back way, but so many of them nowadays weren't like that. Being disturbed, that was an irritation, an injustice. Well hacked off at not being allowed to get on with their job, and if you insisted on getting in the way, it was your own friggin' fault for being a property owner. That was the way in the cities, all too often. That sense of entitlement. But out here?

Bliss peered through a hole in the trellis at lumpy countryside of small hills and woodland. The sky was unfriendly, clouds like the old, greying knots of wool you found on the barbed wire around a field of sheep. And such a lovely clear sky last night, if cold as hell.

'I think I should come out,' Annie said. 'In fact, I think I should tentatively take this one off your hands. Before it's taken off both of us.'

He was in no position to argue. Should've been on his way to Hewell by now, with Vaynor. Been driving into the city through mean, sleety rain when Terry Stagg had come through on the mobile, telling him Karen Dowell and a posse were already there, and he'd turned the car round immediately, headed south-west.

Karen was coming out of the cottage, from the back entrance. Carefully. Unzipping her suit when she reached the end of the path, raising a hand to Bliss, leaving it raised to convey she needed to talk. The small front lawn had been taped off. There was a tent over the sundial.

'Country cottages?' Bliss said. 'Hardly worth it, surely? Some of them around here are just holiday homes. Nothing of value inside. Not much to be had at all apart from marginally antique furniture, for which you'd need a bloody big van, and where do you put a big van on a lane this narrow?'

'You can't give antiques away any more. What's it look like?'

'A full-time home, but quite modest. A working home. Old computer and a lorra bookshelves. Cupboards and drawers ripped open, dresser pulled over. Routine ransacking.'

'Let's not waste time,' Annie said. 'We need to swamp that area. I'll chuck it upstairs, though local knowledge is going to be paramount. We need to involve the village from the off. I'll get an incident room organized. Shit, Francis, we don't need this right now.'

'We don't need this ever,' Bliss said.

Having seen the victim. The face in ruins from being smashed repeatedly into a concrete sundial. The face framed by bloodied white hair, above the reddened dog collar.

'This is how it looks,' Karen said. 'The car's in the drive, locked – OK? So she's come home, locked the car and she's walking to the house. Not realizing she's left her sidelights on – which is how she was found. Still on just before dawn when this fitness freak from the village comes jogging past—'

'Where's he now?'

'Probably in counselling. We can get him back anytime. So… he sees the car lights just about still on, wonders if he should wake her up before the battery goes flat. Finds the front door slightly ajar.'

'Which also explains the patch of vomit outside the gate?'

'It does.'

'So, to go back to last night, or whenever she's walking to the house…'

'Has the keys in her hand. Drops them when she's hit? Could be she saw some movement inside, and she's backing off, as anyone would, and that's when she's attacked. And it doesn't stop. I mean, this isn't just to disable her so someone can get away, this is someone who really doesn't care.'

'Yeh.'

Karen led him to the low hedge separating the short drive from the lawn. Pointed at the tent over the sundial.

'Concrete, hexagonal, sharp corners. But it looks like she was hit with something first. We're thinking the spade. No blood on that. She goes down. Someone picks her up by the hair and starts slamming her head and face into the sundial. You saw the left eye.'

'Yeh.'

Where the left eye had been.

'That thing that used to stick out of the middle, to throw a shadow. Can't remember what it's called.'

'Something like gnome,' Bliss said. 'That did her eye?'

'All this to be confirmed by Slim Fiddler and Dr Grace, but it was probably broken off in the process. Also a crack in the concrete table-thing. That shows you the sheer force. And then they dragged the body back into the house, shut the door on her.'

'Like you say, they wanted closure. Place like this, they could've got away easy. So it *could* be she saw one of them. If there were lights on in the house.'

'Somebody she knew?'

'I was about to say that. They get around, these vicars, multiple parishes. Somebody's son? What about the neighbour who reported the attempted break-in? That match up?'

'Dunno about a neighbour, boss, it's nearly half a mile away. But, yeah, broken window in the front door, inside a porch.'

'When?'

'Last night. Alarm went out at eleven-fifteen. Occupants were on their way back from the Temple Bar – pub in the village – but saw nothing. Uniform called in on them last night, wasn't much they could do.'

'Didn't check if the neighbours saw anything?'

'They checked with the nearest neighbours but they're on the other side, nearer the village. You can't even see this place from there even in the daytime. Anyway, we're down there now, looking at it again.'

'So they just move on to the next house, and Mrs Duxbury gets in the way?'

'Too coincidental to ignore.'

'Yeh.' Bliss turned away from the garden. 'So where did they come from? Down from the Midlands, up from Newport?'

'Not if she recognized one, boss.'

They'd closed the road at both ends, only two other homes affected by this, and the folks there were probably used to disturbance – the SAS base at Pontrilas was only a few fields away, lot of helicopter traffic. This was the Sass's less public

266

base, where they set up siege-and-rescue situations, where elite soldiers came to learn how to dispose of people with minimum fuss. No access to it from this lane.

'May not be my problem for much longer,' Bliss said. 'Ma'am may be taking over. Calls for rank, this one.'

Karen was nodding.

'A priest? If her head had been cut off, you wouldn't be able to move for anti-terrorist guys.'

'And they'd throw open the gates at the SAS,' Bliss said.

The friggin' sleet was coming back, along with the old numbness over his left eye, residue of a beating in a cellar under the Plascarreg. It wasn't even ten a.m., and they hadn't brought the body out yet.

Karen patted him, with affection, on the arm.

'I know exactly how you must be feeling, boss. Really, really want these bastards for yourself, and you're stuck with Jag.'

40

This side of the Second Coming

A DARK MORNING, but the gatehouse office was unlit. It looked almost derelict, like one of the shut-down shops in the old city awaiting a new charity and another consignment of second-hand clothes.

Merrily stopped on the edge of the green and gazed up in disbelief. All the ominous clarity of last night had been fuzzed by the cloud and the rain and the confusing messages passed on by Jane who, when she'd staggered downstairs, had already been in the kitchen, fully dressed, kettle on, cat fed.

They'd talked for nearly an hour, nothing hidden, but not much of it making sense. She'd rung Abbie Folley to say thanks for last night. No answer; she'd left a message.

Sophie? No, she wouldn't ring Sophie back, she'd see her at the gatehouse. She wanted all this logged. She wanted it official. She'd left the Freelander on the Gaol Street car park, walking rapidly up through the city centre, already crowding-up for Christmas, and following narrow Capuchin Way to the Cathedral.

The door to the gatehouse stairs was locked.

She'd never known this before. She pulled out her mobile and rang Sophie at home, leaning up against the sandstone wall under the office. Across the yard, the Bishop's Palace was dimly lit like a posh department store.

'Jane told me you were coming,' Sophie said.

'But you're not here.'

'Merrily, don't do – or say – anything rash.'

'What?'

'I won't be in the office today, but the Archdeacon's coming to talk to you.'

'About Darvill? Listen, I'd very much like to talk to her about Darvill, but not now. Not till I know what's behind it. Not going in cold. Sophie, I've had it with these people and their back-alley politics and their... sense of privilege.'

Shouting into the phone because she was frightened.

'You'll find Siân is not unsympathetic,' Sophie said. 'She's just stepping carefully around the Bishop. As, indeed, are all of us. Not that, in my case, this will be as difficult as it was.'

'Sophie?'

She heard the gatehouse door opening, turned to see Siân Callaghan-Clarke, standing there with no lights behind her.

'I'm so sorry, Merrily, really don't have long. Apparently the police are coming to talk to me. Don't know what it's about. Very annoying.' Siân admitting Merrily to the main office, then locking the door. 'Wouldn't take off your coat. Economy heating only today, to stop the pipes from freezing.'

The Archdeacon wore a dark woollen suit over a grey shirt. Grey eyes, grey hair cut short. She still made grey look vital.

'Now don't look at me like that.' Palms of her hands coming up as she sat down behind Sophie's desk. 'Sophie works directly for the Bishop's office. Nothing to do with me.'

No signs of Sophie in the office. No spare reading glasses, no packet of tea, no winter cardigan on a hanger. Siân didn't put on any lights.

'Never seen you as naive, and I'm not going to talk down to you. It's a time of upheaval. The diocese – we're hardly going to recover, financially, are we, this side of the Second Coming?'

'I don't understand. You're talking about money?' Merrily sat down in her old chair and loosened her red scarf. 'You'll be all right for a while, though, surely. Just flog off another green-field site for executive housing.'

A sore point in Hereford, the diocese's land deals. Siân's smile was a slit.

'Property transactions are not within my remit either, so I won't take that personally. Now I realize you're upset about Sophie, but—'

'I'm sorry?'

'Oh.'

Siân didn't blink. Before being called to the altar, she'd been called to the bar; useful training for the modern C of E.

'Upset?'

'She hasn't told you yet, then. I'm afraid she only learned yesterday afternoon. Perhaps you've been busy.'

'What hasn't she told me?'

'Sophie's job – and this is said to be entirely an economic decision – has been reduced to a two-day week.'

'*What?*'

'As from today.'

'He can't just—'

Merrily half out of her chair.

'I didn't say who'd taken the decision.'

'You mean it was you?'

'No, of— I'm not Sophie's boss, you know that. Oh, this is one of those weeks when, if I could desert this post... Look. Bernard Dunmore preferred to work closely with his lay secretary, as did his... his predecessor. New bishops don't always adapt.'

'That woman's more important to the Cathedral than *bishops.*'

'Merrily...' Siân's palms were up. 'You don't have to spell anything out to me.'

'Including that the drastic reduction of Sophie's working week may not be entirely unconnected with a winding-down of deliverance?'

'Again, as the deliverance ministry reports directly to the Bishop, it's not my—'

'Now that's a bloody joke, isn't it? I've never spoken in any depth to that bastard since they put him in purple.'

'A degree of paranoia is entirely excusable.'

'Paranoia in the sense of being convinced someone's out to get you? When in fact they have your best interests at heart?'

Dangerous ground; she didn't care. The traffic on Broad Street had its lights on which made the gatehouse office feel like a bomb shelter.

'I'd like to deal with this Kilpeck issue,' the Archdeacon said.

'I hope we're going to come *back* to Sophie.'

Siân's expression said this would be pointless.

'Sir Lionel Darvill and his obsession with Kilpeck Church. I do know about that. He's hardly alone, although he *may* be alone in claiming it was built by his ancestors. For which, as far as I can see, there's not a shred of proof as his family only seems to have been in the area for a couple of hundred years. However—'

'If it ensures regular donations...'

'Regular donors do tend to be humoured, yes. And I think, with his handicap and his refusal to let it limit his activities, he's to be admired. All the same, there are aspects of this that I'm not *over* happy about.'

'Like that he seems to have tried to get in the way of me carrying out a fairly routine deliverance procedure?'

'That's not how he put it, obviously.'

'For the record, Siân, it was textbook. I'd been asked for advice by the parish priest on behalf of one of her parishioners and concluded that what it called for was a comparatively routine Requiem.'

'Which you agreed with the family.'

'Erm...'

'Merrily! *Textbook?*'

'Oh, Siân, come on, when is this job ever straightforward? I had a guy in mental and spiritual turmoil, and I had to make a fast decision. No, I didn't talk to the subject's divorced parents, but it *was* done in the presence of someone closer to him than either of them. As for Darvill, he's no relation at all, so it's not his place to make any demands. Did you talk to him?'

'No.'

'So who did?'

'I believe someone *will* be going to talk to him. If he hasn't already been.'

'Sorry... who are we talking about?'

Silence. Siân looked around the fast-dimming room, appeared to be listening, then shook her head as if trying to clear it. Then she sat up behind folded arms.

'I won't be putting any lights on, Merrily. As we're not here.'

'We're not?'

'This is very difficult for me. Quite a lot has become difficult since—' Siân's gaze had come to rest on Merrily's bag, on the floor next to her chair. 'I'm assuming you don't have an active iPhone in there.'

'What?'

'An iPhone. Switched on.'

Merrily reached down into her bag, brought out her elderly phone and opened it up on the desk. Siân went through the procedure for switching it off.

'Forgive *my* paranoia, but it's a rather formidable device, isn't it? Good at multitasking. Seems to have the facility to record voices in full broadcast quality.'

'So I'm told.'

'Essentially, my job is head of human resources in the parishes. Carried out more efficiently if people trust me. So let me say that, while it's hardly in my interests to fall out with the Bishop, I certainly have no wish to be part of a clandestine campaign to reduce what he likes to call "relics of medievalism" in the diocese.'

Siân folded her arms, the dimness settling around her like smoke.

'I say clandestine...' In the poor light, her grey eyes had become grey patches. '... though it won't be for long, originating, as it does, at a rather more senior level than Craig Innes.'

'I think we all have ideas about who at the top of the Church—'

'And keep those ideas to ourselves.' A glimpse of Siân's teeth. 'Bishop Craig is seen as... as a cleansing agent, if you like. Quietly removing stains.'

'I'm a stain now?'

'It was a metaphor.'

'He thinks I was sleeping with Mick Hunter.'

'Merrily, he probably *doesn't*. He's been assured enough times that you certainly were not. But the very fact that you're followed by rumour, no matter how tenuous, and that you're doing a secretive job for which he nurtures a distaste... Need I go on?'

'Yes.'

'Very well. You should know – bearing in mind that *we are not here* – that this particular— I'm going to have to call it an *inquiry* —has been arranged with the full cooperation of Paul Crowden's Bishop.'

'You *know* about Crowden?'

'Crowden is the nearest you'll get to the public face of deliverance scepticism. He has approval for an independent study of exorcism practices. Nothing to do with the House of Bishops or the Archbishop's Council. Nothing, in other words, to do with Craig Innes. Ostensibly, it's something he feels strongly about, and he feels he represents a body of opinion within the Church.'

'Blimey, anyone who thought ecclesiastical espionage had eased since the years after the Reformation—'

'Now I don't know Crowden at all, but he's certainly all over you, Merrily, and it shouldn't tax your skills too much to be aware of when and where he's poking around.'

'So when Darvill contacted the Bishop, the Bishop alerted Crowden?'

'Let's say *someone* did. Which I know because he was copied into a memo that the Bishop's clerical secretary innocently copied to me. Sophie, less innocently, had also asked me about Crowden, so that trail inevitably led back to you. So, basically, Mrs Watkins, *watch your step*. Jump at shadows. Expect anything which might be regarded as unorthodox to go into Crowden's notebook. Which may, if politically expedient, even become an official report one day.'

'Siân, this is—'

The phone rang, Siân reached for it.

'This is as far as I'm going. And I've told you nothing. *Yes…*' Into the phone. 'All right, thank you.' She replaced the phone, pushed her chair back. 'For some reason, the police are on their way to see me. Please cover yourself on the way out – scarf, hood, anything.'

'You're serious, aren't you?'

'Just a weather warning.' Siân standing up, peering out of the window. 'The sleet's back. And I'm always serious.'

41

In memory of me

SHE DIDN'T GET further than the edge of Cathedral Green before they'd eyeballed her, the very tall young detective she recognized as DC Vaynor and his boss, Annie Howe, who raised a hand. The ice-maiden in her cream trench coat, a retro cop cliché that wouldn't have occurred to her. Merrily raised a hand back and kept on walking until she saw that Howe had stopped and Vaynor was loping towards her through the slanting downpour.

'We've been trying to call you, Ms Watkins. Your mobile appears to be switched off.'

Merrily pulled the scarf away from her mouth but left her hood up.

'Battery must be low. Good morning, Annie. Erm… Darth.'

No smiles. Merrily nodded towards the gatehouse.

'I think the Archdeacon knows you're coming.'

'As we'll need to talk to you as well,' Annie Howe said, 'perhaps you can show us the way.'

'Has something happened?'

Uneasy, inevitably. Talking with Annie Howe always felt like a prelude to arrest, and she wasn't in the mood. One anxious night they'd come close to communicating as human beings. Just that one night.

'*If* you don't mind, Ms Watkins,' Howe said.

And she knew the way, of course she did.

Barry was waiting for them in the gallery. Lol doubted Jane had been in here since Lucy Devenish died. He certainly hadn't.

Now the jungle of colour that had been Ledwardine Lore was long gone, whited-out.

'What do you think?' Barry said.

Lol looked around.

'Looks so much bigger.'

'After its soulectomy,' Jane said.

The building was sixteenth century, possibly earlier. You couldn't take that away. Jane walked to the centre of the room, hands sunk into the side pockets of her parka, inspecting the ceiling beams which now carried spotlights for the remaining few pale paintings, none involving apples.

Lucy had accumulated all things apple: ornaments and mugs, books and greetings cards. A small cider press, an orchard ladder. Lol remembered an old display of reduced-scale replicas of the Original Sin window in the church in which Eve was holding an apple thought to represent Ledwardine's own Pharisees Red. Lucy Devenish had believed Pharisees to be a corruption of *farises*, the old local word for fairies. Little crystal farises had dangled on threads from the beams and the rungs of the orchard ladders.

'We wouldn't be able pay you much, Jane,' Barry said from the doorway. 'But there might be side benefits.'

Jane didn't react to this. It wouldn't matter, Lol thought. Whether she could still feel the spirit of Lucy here, *that* would matter.

This might not be a good day to have brought her here, but he hadn't had a choice. Barry had reached a tentative agreement with the owners and needed an answer before deciding whether to take it further. Lol had called Jane, confessing his doubts as they were walking across the square in a gathering east wind.

'Like I might think I'm too clever to be a shop assistant?' The wind dragging Jane's hair into her eyes and she'd fingered it away. 'What's Mum say?'

'Haven't asked her.'

She'd stopped and turned to look at him.

'You're an adult,' Lol said. 'If you don't like the idea, we just won't mention it again. Not as if she doesn't have enough to deal with right now.'

'She thinks I still have an unhealthy attachment to Lucy.'

We all still have that, Lol had thought.

'Could we call it Ledwardine Lore?' Jane said now.

Barry shrugged.

'Why not. Part of local history. Scatter a few appley things around – it *is* the Village in the Orchard after all. Just don't, you know, overdo it. We all remember Lucy's shop. Leave a bit of space for the booking office and the CDs.'

'She told me there was no way she'd be selling mine,' Lol said. 'Described it as misery from Off.'

He remembered there used to be a long curtain screening off a black-painted wrought iron spiral staircase to the windowless loft where he'd hidden himself away the day he'd first met Jane. The curtain was gone and the spiral was an ethereal white, like a stairway to heaven. He wished he could say he'd changed as much as this shop.

'What's upstairs now, Barry?'

'Ha.' The gleam in Barry's remaining eye emphasized by the patch over the other. 'Proper room now. Torch no longer needed. They put a small dormer in.'

'You have to haggle?'

'Nah, that would've been vulgar. They're not the kind of people who'd want you to know they were ready to snatch your hand off but that was the feeling I got, so I just said the rent might be a bit stiff for us, and they said they'd think about it. This was last night. Half an hour later we had a deal.'

'How long would we have it for?'

'Year. Option on longer if the festival works. They seemed happy with that.'

It occurred to Lol that the people who ran Ledwardine Fine Arts never seemed to be referred to by name. They lived in a big house somewhere in the country beyond the village, and slipped in and out, as minimal as their stock.

'You'll like this,' Barry said. 'Before I left, one of them said, almost in passing, laughing it off, the way they do, Oh, apparently it's haunted. A couple of the people who'd minded the gallery for them had heard bumps and things from upstairs. Nothing ever damaged, I was assured.'

Lol thought Jane looked a little pale, a goose-over-the-grave moment. Then she laughed.

Barry gave her the hard stare.

'Well?'

'Yeah, I'd love to do it. Really.'

'Good girl.' Barry tossed the shop keys from hand to hand. 'We better get out of here before some tourist tries to buy a picture off us.' He smiled wryly, then his face dropped suddenly. 'Bloody awful about that woman vicar, innit? Expect Merrily knew her.'

Lol stared at him.

'Give me just five minutes in a dark room with that kind of scum.' Barry locked the gallery door. 'Nah, make it one minute.'

Merrily saw the Archdeacon's face stiffening to parchment.

'When *was* this?'

The gatehouse seemed overcrowded, like a bus shelter in a sudden storm. Siân and Howe and the high-rise Vaynor and a disclosure that was itself like a dark, winged presence.

'We're not sure,' Howe said. 'She was found early this morning. If Mrs Watkins confirms speaking to her mid-evening, that would narrow it down further.'

'It was my daughter. She spoke to Jane.'

'We'll need to talk to Jane, then.'

'I also had a text from Julie. Later, I think. That might've been her last... last anything.'

Last anything. Merrily's half-whispered words were circling like grey moths in the air. She was aware of Annie Howe peering at her through the gloom and the silence, then Howe was on her feet asking if there was something wrong with the lights in here.

'Put them on, Merrily,' Siân said, 'you know where everything is.'

Merrily went over to the door, threw on all the office lights and when she turned back into the room they were all looking at her: Annie Howe in the window chair with its back to Broad Street, Vaynor standing by the smaller window overlooking the narrow slope of Gwynne Street, Siân still behind Sophie's desk.

Merrily felt suddenly suffocated, wanting to stumble down the stairs and out into the cold and the wet.

'Are you all right, Ms Watkins?'

'Yeah, just…'

'How well did you know the Reverend Duxbury?'

'Not well at all. I mean I only met her yesterday.'

'Unless there's another phone we haven't found,' Annie Howe said, 'her text to you was indeed her last message to anyone. Would you like to tell us what it said?'

As if she didn't know. As if DS Karen Dowell, the IT specialist, hadn't stripped everything from the phone.

'It said…' Merrily's voice giving way. '"Do this".'

'That was it?'

'More or less.'

'Do what?'

'A priest,' Siân said, 'would see it as a reference to the Mass or Eucharist. *Do this in memory of me.*' She looked at Merrily. 'She texted that?'

'I'm not sure she meant it that way. It was just an expression of encouragement.'

She folded her arms. Julie Duxbury hadn't known she was about to conduct a Requiem. Nobody had. Death imposed significance where there was none.

'Are we the *last* to know about this?' Siân said.

'It's been on the radio,' Vaynor said. 'And the Internet, of course. We were forced to put out a press release naming the victim earlier than we might normally have done. Someone getting murdered in a country village, it's not the same as a city or a suburb. Especially the vicar. Everybody knows soon enough.'

'Rector,' Siân said.

'What's the difference?'

'Tends to be a matter of local tradition nowadays. Nothing you need worry about.'

'Canon Clarke,' Howe said, 'we'll need to know everything about the Reverend Duxbury's work schedule, who else she might have met yesterday. That's why we're coming directly to you as her... manager? I'm not sure of the—'

'Manager will do. I'll assist any way I can. Surely you don't think—'

'It looks, on the surface, like a burglary gone wrong, a random attack. But the extreme violence... is inescapable.'

'So you're not thinking of... religious extremism. Terrorism.'

'We have no reason to think along those lines. It's more likely that she knew her assailant or assailants. Therefore not unlikely that the killer is still in the area. So we need to move quickly.'

Merrily gazed past Howe, out along Broad Street with its blur of dipped headlights and its bundles of pedestrians. Imagined Julie Duxbury gliding through the grey weather in her shapeless bomber jacket. Mature, brisk, purposeful. After the shattering news, she caught an unexpected arrow of grief. Julie Duxbury would be walking along every street today, and always walking out of the picture.

Annie Howe was looking at Merrily.

'"Do this". Do what, exactly, Ms Watkins?'

42

Trust

MEDDLED. IN THE living room at Lucy's cottage, the word was rattling in the corners and flapping like a trapped bird in the window.

'That was what she said. Kept saying. She *meddled*.'

Jane had kept it all pent up until they were inside, Lol messing at the laptop, looking for news flashes. He looked up.

'In what?'

He'd had another bad night, his whole body aching when he awoke, as if he was coming down with flu. He'd felt dizzy. And now this.

'She's like, "I'm trusting you, Jane. I have to start trusting people or… or nothing's going to…" Jane shut her eyes for a moment. 'No, what I think she actually said was, "or we're not going to stop this".'

'Stop what?'

'Should've asked, but I didn't think I'd get any answers. I'd been talking to Sophie who, as usual, wasn't interested in telling me anything. Julie Duxbury, I'd never met her, didn't even know what she looked like, and she was trusting me. She had to tell somebody.'

'Did she seem, I don't know… scared… worried?'

'More kind of annoyed. Offended. And impatient. Like she didn't want to waste any more time. She went on about congregations getting smaller, like the job was diminishing, the world making vicars feel superfluous to requirements. The reason she meddled. Because she wanted to do something.

Make a difference. God, I didn't even know the woman, why do I feel like I didn't do something that could have saved her? Why didn't I call her back?'

'Here it is. *Hereford Times* Online. An hour ago.'

Police have not yet formally released a name, but devastated locals in Ewyas Harold say the victim is their rector, Julie Duxbury, who took over only a few months ago. 'Everyone is shattered,' one said. 'Some people are just gathering at the church in silence.'

Lol read it out, then went through to the kitchen where the kettle was boiling, listening to Jane going over those couple of minutes on the phone last night. Over and over, as if she could squeeze more out of them. He came back to find her eyes widening.

'Oh God, she said she might have a visitor. Suppose...'

'You couldn't very well ask who she was expecting, could you? Come on. Sit down. How could you know?'

She went down on the edge of the sofa, hands on her knees.

'The police will want to talk to me. What am I supposed to tell them? What do I say that won't lead them back to...?'

Lol shut the kitchen door, stood with his back to it.

'You just answer the questions. They're not going to be trick questions, they won't be bringing up graves. It'll just be a formality. If they think she disturbed burglars, maybe they're right.'

'Except they're not, are they? Come on, Lol, we know, deep down, that all this can't be unconnected. Random burglars don't kill people.'

'People get killed all the time disturbing petty burglaries. Get killed in the street because someone wants their phone. Or because somebody's done too many drugs, or urgently needs money for more drugs. OK, not usually in places like this.'

'No. It's *connected*. And we're the only ones who know that, and we can't talk about it.'

'If it comes to it,' Lol said, 'I can explain—'

'*No!*' Jane springing up. 'What are you saying? You want Gomer arrested for desecration? An old guy? It would kill him!' Her eyes had filled up. 'And you assisting him? The vicar's boyfriend digging up a corpse? Nobody gets a slap on the wrist for that. You think Mum's job would survive? You think any of us would?'

'Jane—'

'We'd all be out of here before the winter's over. All gone, all the good things – this cottage, the festival, everything. All gone.'

Sitting down at the other end of the sofa, Lol had to physically stop himself from letting his face fall into his hands, through fatigue, physical and emotional.

And because she was right.

Jane wiped her eyes with the back of a hand.

'Do I sound like a little kid?'

'No, you're...'

Making distressing sense. He didn't want to say that.

'We shouldn't've given up,' Jane said. 'We should've found out the whole truth behind what happened in the churchyard. But then you let that bastard Darvill warn you off.'

'And now a woman's dead?'

'Lol, I'm not *saying* that. I don't know what I'm saying, except that there's something here that's just so— I mean, when you think of those guys dancing with a dead man... it's like black comedy but you *imagine* that? How could they do it? What could bring someone to—?'

'We can't talk about that. Not to anyone. She only told us—'

'I know that.'

His head was back on the square, the oak-pillared market hall hard against the wild, starry night. Merrily telling him, quite prosaically, about what had happened that night. He'd seen her like this before, both connected and detached.

Nothing to get excited about, and it was over now, she'd said.

And then it wasn't.

* * *

The one night they'd managed to communicate, Annie Howe had said *I'm an executive, an administrator.* Meaning she was an office creature, didn't often come out to talk to people who weren't in the police. Merrily had thought she preferred it that way, being *not* like her father, Charlie, who was everywhere – a county councillor, a governor of Jane's former school. Perhaps Annie just didn't like to go to places her dad was known, where the rumours about him lingered like an infection.

The Cathedral?

She didn't remember Charlie ever being in the gatehouse.

Do this. She'd explained about the Requiem, determined to hold on to the names. Hard to imagine what would happen if word reached Iestyn Lloyd that she'd conducted a second funeral service for his son without even asking him.

'This was part of your... *exorcism* role?'

Howe throwing down the question like a dead rat. Siân Callaghan-Clarke, formerly chair of the short-lived diocesan deliverance panel, picking it up.

'A Requiem is not an exorcism, it's a service for the dead.'

'But not, I take it, something that Julie Duxbury could have done for herself?'

'She *could* have done it for herself,' Merrily said, 'but it's something I've become more familiar with. And it related to someone who had lived in Ledwardine.'

This was getting perilously close to forbidden ground. All she could hope for was that Annie Howe's atheism would erect its own barriers.

'Let me get this right,' Howe said. 'As a specialist consultant to Mrs Duxbury, you were conducting a service – at night, and with just two people – relating to a deceased resident of Ledwardine. Who was this?'

Merrily flicked a mute plea at Siân, and was grateful when Siân caught it, with her barrister's gloves on.

'Chief Inspector, as you know, the relationship between the diocese and Hereford Police has always been founded on

284

a degree of mutual trust. But I'd ask you to accept that there's also an essential trust between the clergy and the people who approach us with personal problems. When these don't involve law-breaking or any form of serious social malaise, we feel obliged to respect privacy. So, until you can show precisely how this information would assist your investigation of Julie's murder, I would have to ask you to respect that obligation.'

Impressive, especially as Siân had no reason to suspect a connection with Julie's killing. Which, *oh God*, might well exist.

Howe turned to Merrily.

'What time did it finish?'

'Quite late. About ten forty-five.'

'And your... small congregation left immediately?'

'Yes.'

'Did you have any further contact with them that night?'

'No.'

'And you had no further contact at all with Julie Duxbury.'

'No.'

'And what you were doing did not involve Mrs Duxbury in any way.'

'She'd left it in my hands.'

Howe nodded. Julie's phone would have given them a direct link at least to Lara Brewer and perhaps through her to Sir Lionel Darvill. Merrily kept quiet. So much she didn't know. She fielded some questions that were more routine and tried to ask some, but this wasn't Frannie Bliss who saw the advantages of occasional indiscretion, and she learned nothing. Annie Howe turned briefly on the way out.

'Ms Watkins—'

'I know – don't leave town.'

Howe looked almost amused.

'I was actually going to say that if anything occurred to you that might help us, don't hesitate to come through to me directly.'

'Oh.'

When they'd left, the sleet had stopped but the sky was no brighter.

'Well...' Siân Callaghan-Clarke gathered up her briefcase. 'I'm really not sure whether I have time to hear the rest.'

'Let me know when you're ready,' Merrily said.

Siân nodded vaguely.

They didn't talk about the death of Julie Duxbury when Lol and Jane went to the Black Swan for a lunch of soup and sandwiches that he didn't really want, although he felt a little better now. Barry came over and they discussed Lol's signing of Moira Cairns for the festival and his hopes of getting Simon St John over from Knight's Frome, on bass and cello, and – more tenuous – the veteran guitarist Tom Storey. He'd forgotten all about this, and it was hard to concentrate.

'We need to get out a programme early in the new year, printed and online,' Barry said. 'We need more big names.'

'Big names cost big money,' Lol said.

'Unless they're mates. We need to find more big-name mates. Mates of mates, you know how this works. Don't you go lukewarm on this, Laurence.'

'He works for me now,' Jane said. 'I don't do lukewarm.'

Late morning, a detective called Kate, who'd been brought over from Worcester, had called Jane on her mobile and then come to take a statement about the phone call from Julie Duxbury. All very formal. Jane had kept it brief. Lol thought she was trying to come across as not very intelligent. Kate had told her not to worry.

When they left the pub, Lol hoped she'd go home. There was a call he wanted to make that he certainly couldn't make in front of her, but she followed him back to Lucy's Cottage.

'If we don't get back onto it now,' Jane said, as the bitter wind prodded them back across the square, 'it'll only get harder. One day it'll come back on us, big time. We know what they did, we still don't really know why. And that all comes back to Sir Lionel Darvill.'

'He doesn't have to talk to us.'

'He rang you to threaten you. To warn you off. What's that say? He has things to hide. He could be the key to everything, and if you get a solid hint that he's behind all this, that he might even've—'

'He's in a wheelchair.'

'That doesn't mean—'

'Not out here, huh?'

When they were back in the cottage, the woodstove awakened, he saw that the little green light on the phone was blinking. Message. He hoped it would be Merrily, but the female caller had an American accent.

'Mr Robinson, my name is Nora Mills. I've withheld my number, so you can't call me back, but I'll call again at two-thirty precisely. Thank you.'

'You know anybody under the age of ninety called Nora?' Jane picked up her parka. 'If you want to take it in private, I'll leave.'

'It's probably just some management person. Somebody famous who once passed through Ledwardine and—'

The phone rang. Lol picked up on the third ring.

'Lucy's Cottage.'

'Mr Robinson? This is Nora.'

'Hello.'

'I called earlier. I work at Maryfields.'

Lol tried to relax.

You know where that is? Who lives there?'

'Yes.'

'Mr Robinson, I was gonna maybe drive over there, but I have a client at five. Not sure I'd make it back in time. Not and talk. I mean fully. Which we need to.'

'We do?'

'I think so. Don't you?'

'What do you do at Maryfields?'

Lol saw Jane look up sharply.

'I'm a therapist,' Nora Mills said. 'Physio and stuff? I provide treatment for the man here. And other people.'

Jane was crouching close to the phone, head on one side.

'And, um, what exactly do we need to talk about?'

Jane frowned. Lol lifted a hand to cool her off. Mustn't sound too eager to comply.

'Things have happened,' Nora said. 'If you were able to drive over here, I guess we would have more time.'

'Now?'

'Would that work for you?'

Jane started drumming fists on the desk, like *do it, do it, do it.*

'It's possible, I suppose,' Lol said.

43

Favours past

ANNIE ARRIVED IN Ewyas Harold just ahead of the mobile incident room. The TV cameramen shot her and Vaynor getting out of her car, although most of them were national news outlets and wouldn't know who she was anyway.

'Amazing.' Bliss guiding her between the cars and vans by the side of the Memorial Hall to an unoccupied corner of the yard. 'No bugger goes to church any more till they're wheeled in on a trolley, half the country thinks Jesus plays in goal for Brazil, but a vicar gets topped and all hell— what?'

'It's *rector*,' Annie said mildly. 'I don't know the difference either, though apparently it doesn't matter.'

They were putting the incident room here, the only big tarmac space in the village, Annie would be doing the press conference outside the church, picturesque stone job with a timber-frame porch and a conical hat.

'Rich Ford's setting himself up as office manager,' Bliss said. Nobody better, knows the area well – wants to retire to those hills.'

'The Black Mountains?'

'Madness.'

'We don't appear to have anyone with significant form in the area,' Annie said. 'Few weekend pub-fighters, one ABH, all drink-related.'

'It's farming country, Annie. The real psychos have other outlets.'

'I'm not even going to ask what that's supposed to mean.'

'But if you want a real weirdo, check out the squire.'

'Darvill?'

A bunch of uniforms were keeping local people away from their community centre. Annie was on tiptoe, looking over all the heads.

'Dropped in on him before lunch,' Bliss said. 'Thought it should be me, lower-class Scouser. Strangely, he wasn't pompous and he didn't talk down to me.'

'How terribly disappointing for you. What was weird about him?'

'He just is. A throwback. His number was on Julie's phone. He said they'd been talking about some pre-Christmas service they were planning at Kilpeck Church. I had the vague feeling there were things he wasn't saying, but... he didn't do it. And not only because he's in a wheelchair. We all saw *Little Britain*.'

'What?'

'Except for you. He was also making flip remarks. "All the time you spend training your parish priest and then this bloody happens." But you could tell he was gutted. And angry.'

'Angry?'

'Because he's a cripple and he's unlikely to be in a position to kill the bastards. He liked her a lot, and I don't think he's the kind of feller who normally gets on with the clergy. What are you doing, Annie?'

'Probably mistaken...' She came down off tiptoe. '... but, for a moment, I thought I saw that woman from Midlands Today with... my bloody father. Starting to see the bastard every-where. Probably wasn't. Men start to look similar when they reach a certain age. Gone now, anyway.'

'Talking of Charlie...'

'You still want to go to Hewell?'

'Not really, and all this has made that harder to justify. Mr Jag isn't in the same league as the nice lady who pats your kids and visits your granny in the hossie.'

'But you think you need to.'

290

'Yeh.'

'All right, go on. Bugger off. But make it quick.'

'You're all right with this? 'Cos if you're not—'

'You can have Vaynor, just don't take Dowell, I need to talk to her about phones. The rector's daughter here yet?'

'Expected in the next hour with her husband. They had to arrange kiddie-care. You get to talk to them, I'm afraid.'

'Thank you. You know how much I love that part of the job.'

'If you want me to hang on…'

'Just don't take all night. And make it worthwhile. If we can crack Jaglowski, it won't look quite so bad. Least it clears the decks.'

He noticed she didn't mention the other reason for visiting Hewell. Or how good it would be if they also could crack Charlie Howe.

A white sun threw a fan of cold light over Ewyas Harold, Bliss jogging through it. It was a big village, capital of the Golden Valley, a lot going on there, more shops than all the rest of the valley communities put together, but the countryside to the west was rougher, more forested, less golden.

Somebody said the Harold in the name was the last Saxon king, the one who got hammered at Hastings by the invading Normans. The one who got an arrow in his eye, like poor bloody Julie Duxbury got the spike from a sundial that was called something like gnome.

As he reached his car, Amanda Patel from BBC Midlands Today pulled up behind and brought her window down.

'Big story, Mandy,' Bliss said. 'This mean you get to cover it for the ten o'clock news?'

Patel made this hissy sound that meant no chance.

'It's big enough for them to send their own. They generally put someone in who doesn't know anything about this area – and that's just the Brummies when I'm on holiday. The Londoners spell it Hertfordshire.'

'How long you been doing this now, Mandy?'

'Eleven years next March. You can swing retirement at fifty, if you time it right, then come back after a couple of years as a freelance on the radio. BBC's answer to the cold-case squad.' She leaned out of the window to scrape a flake of red soil from his tie. 'How's it going, anyway, Frannie? Anything you could very quietly slip me, in return for favours past? Not that I want to score points or anything.'

Bliss shrugged.

'I'm off the case. Insubordination.'

Mandy smiled.

'I met Julie Duxbury once – not on a story. She married a friend of mine at Abbeydore in the summer. A fairly distant friend, and we only got invited because I was on the telly. So today – guess what? – I had to ring her up, this distant friend, to ask if we could borrow the wedding video for pictures of Julie in happier times.'

'She tell you to piss off?'

'Sadly not. They'll still do anything to be seen on telly. And the minister's a murder victim? Wow. Cool. Aren't people shits?'

'You liked her? Julie?'

'Yeah. Yeah, I did, actually. Women clergy, in general they're either ultra-feminist or a bit too cosy. She was quite earthy and she drank beer. I don't often say this, Frannie, because murders are easy to cover after Day One, but I really hope you get this bastard.'

'We will. Mandy, did I see you with Charlie Howe earlier?'

Mandy Patel looked away, sucked air through her teeth.

'Briefly.'

'What's he doing here?'

'He didn't tell you?'

'What do you think?'

'This is between us, right?'

'As always.'

'It doesn't involve me. One of our elder statesmen wanted some shots of Charlie at a crime scene. No chat, just wallpaper.'

'What – for his obit? Haven't you got footage in the files or is all that in black and white?'

'I doubt it's his obit. *I'll* be dead before him. Might be for when he's elected Commissioner. Or a promotional video on YouTube. The truth is I don't know. Which is annoying, but I don't. It was fixed up between this elder statesman, whose face you'd probably recognize, and the cameraman, who's freelance.'

'Doesn't suppose it's conceivable they're planning an exposé? Charlie Howe, the sordid facts.'

'Quite the reverse. This guy's been there a long, long time. Him and Charlie Howe...'

She held up two fingers, crossed below the varnished nails.

'Even at the BBC?' Bliss took a step back. 'What's going on, Mand?'

'I really don't know. He seems to have old friends every-where. Mainly veterans who got taken under his wing as very young reporters, and now they're elder statesmen. Could be something quite innocent.'

'Charlie doesn't understand the word *innocent*,' Bliss said. 'He thinks it means the same as gullible and naive.'

Or the fit-up failed. Bliss blew Mandy a kiss and got into his Honda.

44

Hatched

THEY WERE LOOKING out for a private sign in a dip in the hills outside Kilpeck. No more than knee-high from the ground, according to Nora. Discreet, easily missed. Not, Jane thought, like Iestyn Lloyd's loud Churchwood Farm placards, promoting local meat at the roadsides.

'There.'

Jane pointing between two sturdy saplings. Apple. In the late summer, passers-by would get to help themselves. Generous. The sign said,

Maryfields

'I've just thought,' Jane said. 'That's the church's dedication. St Mary and St David.'

'Only two saints, a church that special?'

'Nobody ever calls it that. It's just Kilpeck Church. Built by a Norman baron called Hugh de Kilpeck, who threw untold wealth at it. His fast-track to paradise. See, I'm being useful already.'

'I didn't need to know any of that, so it doesn't count,' Lol said wearily.

Evidently still unhappy that she was here, but there'd been no way she wasn't coming. She'd stay in the Animal while he went to suss out the situation, but she wasn't missing an opportunity to check out this place, not after all that research. Felt she knew it already, could probably point out the very field where Peter Darvill had vanished under the last big tractor.

Lol turned the truck in, and the drive dipped suddenly, hedges rising steeply on both sides. Single-track, but there were escape routes leading off it to slip away into old woodland, some of it caging the smudgy shapes of buildings.

'You could easily find someone else,' Jane said.

He slowed right down and turned to look at her.

'For what?'

'The festival shop. Cool job, for Ledwardine. Be a queue of applicants.'

'I doubt it. We'd run up against the national minimum wage. Barry's thinking whoever does it would have to be part of the enterprise.'

'What, like self-employed?'

'To an extent. I'm not sure. He deals with all that.'

'Right.'

Jane went quiet again, absorbing the place. The drive went uphill again, past lines of young trees, hedged fields – no fencing, no barbed wire – with strong wooden gates, crude signs on them with names, hand-painted: *Haresfield, Quarryfield, Job's Meadow.*

'How it used to be, I suppose,' Lol said. 'All the fields known by individual names.'

'Still are in most places round here. You just don't often see them inscribed on the gates.' Jane lowered her side window, breathing deeply into the cold air. 'If this is all Darvill's organic farm it must look amazing in summer, all the wild flowers you get when you're not spraying death everywhere.'

A kind of fairyland. Even in winter, it sang of an older country, the Herefordshire that Thomas Traherne had gazed on. *So lovely did the distant green that fringed the field appear.*

She liked what Darvill was doing. Pity he was such a twat.

The wind had died and the afternoon had brightened, the sun battling to break through before it had to set, making the grey sky shine like foil and turning a row of bare poplars into a barred window on the green hills. Directly ahead, more woodland and then an orchard with some very old apple trees shouldering planets of mistletoe. Squat, massive oaks were hanging out along the drive like overweight but muscular bouncers. Jane imagined Darvill strolling between them in designer green wellies, then she remembered. Also about the men who'd delved in darkness for a dead dancing partner.

Suddenly, she didn't want to think about any of that. She turned from the window.

'So it would be like... my business?'

Lol braked and turned to her.

'Sorry?'

'Ledwardine Lore. I'd be like the proprietor? This what Barry wants? Someone with flair and commitment who won't make demands on his time? Who'll make it pay for itself.'

'I'm not sure.'

'Like Lucy coming back,' Jane said. 'To oversee things.'

'Now you're scaring me.'

Jane laughed. And then went quiet. The truck moved slowly into an avenue of vast and ancient yew trees, a living temple of winter greenery.

She sat up hard.

'Holy *shit*...'

'Quite.'

'This is the real thing, Lol.'

'It's only a house,' Lol said.

'I don't think so.'

The struggling sun had found it first. It was sprawled, sinuous and relaxed, over a rise or a mound. It was long and low with one gable end. Its oak-framed walls were the colour of red Herefordshire mud, age-bleached timbers worming through the fabric, some projecting like old bones from the earth. A private place, some windows so densely paned that their leading looked like twig-mesh.

Except it wasn't leading, it was actually wood. It was like the house had hatched from the mound many centuries ago. An organic house.

'We don't actually go there.' Jane was disappointed but Lol sounded relieved. 'It's the next right.'

296

'What are we looking for?'

'A stable. With a small sign on the door.'

A curving dirt track led to an assembly of big outbuildings, probably cowsheds. There was an open barn, loaded with hay in traditional small bales; Lol stopped the truck in its shadow. He hesitated, Jane sensing his discomfort, knowing he wasn't good with strangers unless there was an orchestra pit between them.

'Lol, just turn the engine off and go and look for your stable. Leave the key. If the truck's in the way, I'll move it. Find a door and knock. Go *on*.'

He nodded and leaned on the door handle.

'Uh-oh,' Jane said. 'Too late.'

A woman was walking round the side of one of the barns, heading directly for the truck. She was tall, taller than Lol anyway, wore a sheepskin jacket over a mauve roll-neck sweater and tight jeans. Her brown hair was tied back.

She was carrying a double-barrelled shotgun under an arm. It wasn't broken. Lol brought his window down.

'Just leave it here, Mr Robinson.'

The woman was… handsome. OK, more than that. In that serenely unconcerned, aristocratic way that fitted in so well with places like this. If not with her accent. Lol raised his eyebrows at Jane, switched off, opened his door and slid down from the cab.

'Not a bad day,' the woman said. 'They keep forecasting snow, but it doesn't happen.' She put out a long, slim hand to Lol. 'Nora.'

'Lol.'

'Arguably the most popular name on social media.' Nora had the kind of accent that would sound, to an American, like cut-glass East-coast-plus. She glanced back at the truck. 'You gonna bring your friend in?'

'That's… Jane.'

'I know who she is. We have you all sussed – Mrs Watkins and what she does, you and your songs. Jane and her interests.'

Nora smiled at the windscreen. 'Social media? All those pagan groups?'

Jane sank into the seat. *Shit...*

'None of us has a private life any more,' Nora said. 'Anyhow, it's not getting any warmer out here. Also...' She hefted the twelve-bore. '... there's a killer on the loose. Never thought I'd be saying that here.'

45

Talking to the help

It was part of what once might have been a full stable block. The door was pine, with a caged lamp over it, and the sign said:

Nora Mills
CLINIC

Inside, a small waiting room with deep pink walls, uplit. Two wooden chairs, a low table with magazines and catalogues. Nora opened another pine door at the far end, and there was a bigger room, beamed with a single square window. There was a sink, a treatment couch, rubber mats. Two exercise benches, one high, one low, and a grey curtain, floor to ceiling, across what looked like a changing area.

Nora put the shotgun down on the couch, Jane eyeing it warily.

'What do you shoot with that thing?'

'Skeet. Clay pigeons. We have a range here. It's about, uh, diversification?' Nora shed her sheepskin coat and sat astride the taller exercise bench. 'You wanna grab some chairs?'

Lol brought in the two seats from the waiting room, and they sat down. In the clinic.

'Consider this neutral ground,' Nora said. 'You can say what you like in here. Ask questions.'

'Here's one,' Lol said. 'Who exactly are you?'

Nora peered at Lol's chest.

'I like your sweatshirt. *Alien*. Area fifty-one? I went there once as a kid. A birthday treat. This was your first album?'

'First solo album. Tells you everything you need to know about me.'

'Well, me too,' Nora said. 'No matter how many years I get to spend here I'm never gonna be a native.' She shrugged. 'But that's OK.'

As if this was a cue, she gave them her CV. It was all pretty glib, like she'd said all this before, many, many times: how she'd come over as a teenager, with her family when her dad was with the US Army. Now a trained nurse, qualified physiotherapist. She treated clients here. Another Maryfields business like Gareth Brewer's farriery and the cheesemaker and the cidermaker whose ciderhouse was just around the block.

'So you don't actually work for Sir Lionel,' Lol said.

'I work *with* him. The reason I live here. I hold him together. Part therapist, part housekeeper. *Lifekeeper*, he likes to say. Absurd flattery. Balanced by occasional abuse, when he's in pain.'

'And that…'

'Is an ongoing situation. He has complex injuries. Essentially, nothing happening below the waist.'

'Um… an old injury?'

'Since he was a young man. He likes to call it a morris injury. Although that's not strictly accurate except he'd been out drinking with other guys in the morris side the night it happened. At the inn here. Walking back in the dark, there was this scaffolding left by guys repairing the church roof? So he climbs it. For no particular reason other than he's young and smashed and it's there. Like you do.'

Lol said nothing. *Not* what he would have done, Jane guessed, even as a kid.

'Not so high, that roof,' Nora said, 'but it wasn't a clean fall. He came down on a tomb, a headstone and this little cart – a wheelbarrow? Full of builders' stuff, jagged masonry. He didn't walk again.'

Lol winced.

'Or dance?' Jane said.

Not looking at Lol, knowing he was tossing her a hard look. Nora turned to face her, swivelling her hips on the bench. She probably rode horses.

'From then on, he needed guys to dance *for* him. That's how it's been, ever since. You see, I'm answering all your questions in full.'

'Except,' Lol said, 'you know... the one that goes, Why are we here?'

'Ah yeah. *That* question.'

'You said we needed to talk.'

'We need to talk. That old cliché.'

'And also...'

'Why are you talking to the help?' Nora flashed him a brilliant smile. 'Because, Lol, I am good at it. I deal with people day to day. And usually they feel they can get along with me. Even when I'm carrying a twelve-gauge. Now *Lionel*, it usually starts with people feeling sympathetic towards him, and he hates that, so he's rude to them. Sometimes he's rude before they even say a word, to repel any sympathy. Sometimes they take great care not to appear to insult him with sympathy...'

'And he hates that worst of all?' Lol said.

'Oh, yeah. Lionel Darvill, in a word, is an asshole. But you knew that. He called you. Nice to hear your opinions confirmed?'

'Still doesn't explain why we're here.'

'No. OK.' Nora came down from the bench, sat on a high stool. 'Things've been happening. Not good things. One of the first was you calling Lara Brewer on some pretext, but it was clear you wanted to know what the Kilpeck Morris had been doing in your village. Which came directly back to Lionel.'

'People asking questions about his morris side,' Lol said. 'People trying to book them for their festivals and fetes. I'm guessing he hates that, too.'

'Yep. The Kilpeck Morris isn't for hire. It's not about entertaining an audience, it's part of the mechanism that runs this place. The motor— No, don't ask that question. If it's the

301

right thing, you'll find out. So Lionel makes a friendly call to you.'

'That was his friendly side?'

'And then who should show up in Kilpeck but your partner – would partner be the right term?'

'I wish.'

'And she's with the minister in charge of the church here. The minister who, just a few hours later, is found killed. In a truly barbaric way which more than justifies a crazy colonial like me walking around with a shotgun. For which, yeah, I do hold a permit. And meantime... meantime your lady is persuading the leader of the Kilpeck Morris that the dance he loves is not a good thing for him to be involved in. Now does this—?'

'No—' Jane was out of her chair before she knew it. 'It wasn't *like* that.'

Nora didn't move.

'Take it easy, Jane. Because that's certainly how it seemed to Lionel when Gareth Brewer showed up this morning, maybe a half-hour after we learned about Julie, and said he was gonna have to quit dancing. Does this sound like a reason for us to be talking yet?'

Lol exchanged glances with Jane. He was thinking that he rather liked Nora Mills but didn't trust her, suspicious of the way she was bad-mouthing Darvill. He felt they were in trouble. They'd come over here without a thought. Knee-jerk. He was never going to learn.

Nora curved a trainer up and over the spindle between the legs of the stool.

'She somehow got along with Lionel. Julie. Took a while. They talked last night about a service we plan to hold at Kilpeck Church. She was to have... what would you say, presided?'

'Something like that.'

'A midwinter service. A solstice service. The solstice is important to the Border morris. The morris is important to Li.

302

The service we were planning – I get to do the organizational stuff – involves the KP. The minister prays for a good year to come. The Man of Leaves leads the dance to the south doorway, where his image is set in stone?'

Nora arose from the stool, walked over to the window. It was going dark.

'The Man of Leaves... he comes knocking on the door. And the minister, the rector, is waiting with a candle to welcome him in.'

Lol saw the slow smile animating a corner of Jane's mouth. Mention of the Man of Leaves. That old atavistic buzz.

'The Man of Leaves would have been Aidan Lloyd,' Nora said. 'And now Aidan's dead. That was, uh, a big death here.'

'Not a good omen,' Jane said. 'And now another one. Only worse?'

Nora turned to her.

'How old are you, Jane?'

'Nineteen.'

'How's your mom view your pagan inclinations?'

Jane looked at Lol. Lol shrugged, unsure where this was going.

'We've had our problems over that,' Jane said. 'Not for a while, though. I'm more open to what *she* does. And like, while she's never going to dance naked in a stone circle, she's come to accept that, living in a place like this you can't be too... rigid in your beliefs. I suppose we meet in the middle, around the space occupied by Thomas Traherne, the poet. And vicar.'

Nora nodded. Lol was thinking there had to be more to the role of *lifekeeper* than physiotherapy. He wondered what she looked like from a wheelchair.

'What will you do now?' Jane said.

'Gareth Brewer was to have succeeded Aidan Lloyd as Man of Leaves – as the soul of the morris. For a while anyway. To get us past the solstice. Early this morning, like I said, Garry came to see Lionel to tell him he was having to step down as the Man.'

'This is about my mother, right?'

'She seems to have convinced him the morris is harmful.'

'I'm not sure that's quite right.'

'The Church has always been that way. Anything it doesn't understand it mistrusts. Like any attempt by ordinary people to develop their higher faculties. You hear that everywhere. Priests who warn kids off Harry Potter – doorway to black magic.'

Lol couldn't let this go by.

'You don't think she was just trying to help him deal with something he couldn't personally handle? That was damaging his sleep, his family life, his… mental health?'

'I guess what Lionel would tell you, if he could bring himself to speak to you, is that she interfered with a process – a rite of passage. A transition. The transference of something from Aidan to Gareth.'

Lol saw Jane kind of vibrate.

'You're talking about the spirit of the Man of Leaves,' Jane said. 'The Green Man.'

Nora nodded.

'If you like. Let's just call it the essence of what Maryfields is about. And has been since Lionel's dad split from Iestyn Lloyd and all he represents. It's no big conundrum.'

'Whatever it was,' Lol insisted, 'Brewer couldn't handle it.'

'Lionel would say you're in no position to know that. That you don't understand that all rites of passage have an element of ordeal. That to achieve the objective you have to go with the suffering.'

'And take your wife and kids along for the ride?'

Nora frowned.

'He called the Bishop, Nora,' Lol said. 'He'd learned that Brewer had gone to Merrily for help and he tried to get her warned off. Using his influence as a patron of Kilpeck Church. He didn't even try to call Merrily, he just went over her head. No worries about the trouble he might be causing for her. Titled guys talk to bishops.'

'Aw, Jeez.' Nora sighing. 'That isn't… this wasn't supposed to be difficult. You're a mild-mannered, soft-spoken, innocent kind of guy. Unsure of yourself. Maybe a little timid.'

'With a history of mental illness.'

Man's voice. The grey curtains concealing what they'd taken to be a changing area parted on their rings. The man glided in his wheelchair into the treatment room, ragged grey hair falling over his eyes.

Jane, in the path of the big rubber wheels, didn't move, regarding him with an expression Lol identified as disdain.

'Asshole,' Jane said, 'doesn't come close.'

46

Forlorn

POCKETING HER MOBILE, Merrily ran through the rain into the Cathedral and directly to the vast Lady Chapel.

Nobody there. She followed the panelled wall to the little Audley Chantry where she sank down before the blazing psychedelia of the Thomas Traherne windows, the fizzing pinks and greens and the whorls of white light. Blasts of transcendence on a filthy day.

After a few minutes, she sighed and stood up. It was only glass. When she came out of the chantry, a woman had arrived and was sitting alone in the Lady Chapel under the quiet gold, the high sculpted walls, all the Marian maternal imagery.

The woman's hair was wound tight, her smile creased and not benign.

Merrily sat in the next chair, wondered if she should take Sophie's hand and squeeze it, or if that would seem patronizing; theirs had never been a tactile relationship.

She drew a slow, nervous breath.

'How long have you known?'

'Just over a day. But it's hardly a surprise, is it? And hardly the worst thing to happen this week.'

'No. I suppose not.' Merrily looked up at the five Gothic panes above the altar. Pale. Serene. 'I don't imagine Innes told you himself.'

Sophie's laugh was arid.

'Well, you know, he did actually, Merrily. He telephoned me.'

'From the Palace? All the way from round the corner?'

'He said... well, he talked about economic constraints and then he said he realized that many good and faithful servants to the Cathedral were often reluctant to admit, even to themselves, when the workload had become too onerous – i.e., for someone their *age* – and that it was sometimes up to people like him to act in these good and faithful servants' best interests.'

'And kick them down the bloody stairs?'

A more liquid laugh this time from Sophie.

'What does your husband say?'

'He's annoyed on my behalf, naturally, but Andrew's an architect. He thinks the Cathedral is a building.'

'What are you going to do?'

'Oh, resign, of course.'

'*What?*'

'What else could I do? Sit there quietly in the gatehouse two days a week while various people wander in to hang their coats on me? No, I shall formally submit my resignation before Christmas. I don't imagine he'll want me here in the New Year, do you?'

The Lady Chapel absorbed it. Merrily couldn't.

'I don't believe you're saying this.'

'I've never been treated like this.'

'Because of *me*.'

'Merrily, don't be *silly*. Innes is trying to reduce his staffing costs, and he doesn't particularly like me anyway.'

'He doesn't *trust* you. Because of me. Did he mention deliverance?'

'Of course not.'

'No, he wouldn't.'

'That's my greatest regret, of course. I've always accepted that unless you were to move on I'd be gone from here long before you, I just didn't think it would happen so quickly. Anyway, as I've been eased out of the inner circle, I'm not going to be much of a loss. *Merrily*' – Sophie, surprisingly took both her hands, shaking them gently up and down, looking directly into her eyes – 'don't look so *forlorn*. You're a much stronger person than you were when we first met.'

'No, I'm not. I just know who my friends are. I think.'

Sophie let go of her hands.

'What happened last night?'

'Oh God, I haven't really had time to think about it.'

'Well, do try. I haven't gone yet.'

'Unlike Julie Duxbury.'

'That...' Sophie whispering now. '... will change everything.'

Talking to Sophie, as usual, brought clarity. They talked about the police visit to the gatehouse. What Merrily had revealed and what she hadn't, why that might be dangerous.

Sophie didn't find it particularly worrying.

'As far as the police are concerned, the deliverance aspect will simply be seen as something best avoided. It doesn't speak their language. Within the Church, however, the appallingly *deliberate* murder of Julie Duxbury will affect everything. Whoever is responsible, it'll reverberate, not only here but nationally. And the fact that the poor woman's last night in this world involved an element of exorcism will be noted. And underlined.'

'Very few people know about it. Nobody's going to tell the media. I hope.'

'Of course not. But it'll filter through within the Church. As these things do.'

'Thanks to Crowden.'

'The Archdeacon...?'

'Told me about him.'

'This man poking around like some sort of private investigator is inconvenient. Even though Julie Duxbury was not directly involved in your Requiem... even if it turns out she was attacked by some deranged prowler, mentally damaged or high on Class A drugs, her death *will be linked*.'

'I'll write you a full report for the database, although certain details will be omitted for obvious reasons. I'd like to tell you, however.'

It took nearly half an hour, of low voices and looking over shoulders. Occasionally there would be footsteps and clips of conversation from the arteries of the Cathedral, but nobody came in.

'Criminal offence,' Sophie said. 'You can't cover up a criminal offence.'

'I already have.'

'These people...'

'Believed it was happening for a quite logical reason.'

'On the instructions of Sir Lionel Darvill.'

'To whom they're in debt. In various ways.'

'He tried to stop you interfering, as he saw it.'

'This is how it gets iffy. I'm ready to accept that there's some kind of semi-pagan ritualistic thing to which the Kilpeck Morris subscribes. I may not be happy with it personally, and I hate to think of it happening in my churchyard, but if it's over I'd be tempted to let it go. However... if this is Darvill using men who owed him favours to even the score in a private feud by doing something illegal, gruesome and deeply distasteful...'

'That's why you went ahead with the Requiem?'

'Because I thought that Gareth Brewer – and Aidan Lloyd, too, if you want to go further down a dark road – deserved to be free of it.'

'In which case, you did the right thing. But why would Darvill put so much at risk? He could be looking at a prison sentence. Pride? Family pride? I do realize this is an area where family feuds are a way of life, but surely...'

'I can't turn away now, Sophie. If Julie's murder is linked to it...

Sophie looked up at the altar.

'You could – however difficult you might find it – turn away from *that*. It's something for the police. I'm sure we could arrange for them to receive pertinent information without it coming back on anyone innocent.'

'Yeah, but I wouldn't be—'

'No… listen.' Sophie's hand on Merrily's arm. 'What you *won't* be able to turn away from is any information coming back to the Bishop from Sir Lionel Darvill via this man Crowden. Which might not happen today – the Bishop would certainly not want to walk into the middle of a *very* high-profile murder inquiry. Would never want to risk being questioned by the police, thus bringing everything into the public domain.'

'Not how he works.'

Merrily was aware of a courtroom echo in the Lady Chapel. And the panelling to the side. She was reminded of her most frequent nightmare, the one set in a dim, panelled room where her risible role as a deliverance consultant was being delicately dissected by some smarmy atheist in a dirty wig.

'But it *will* happen,' Sophie said. 'It will *happen*. Perhaps within days. And then I'm afraid you're in trouble.'

'Yes.'

47

Go figure

FOR A FEW moments, the only movement in the room was a slow, jagged smile opening up Sir Lionel Darvill's narrow face, like when a tin-opener was applied to a can.

His battered wheelchair had thick rubber tyres, as from a mountain bike. He was wearing a grey gilet over a white T-shirt with holes in it. His feet were in trainers, his legs in jeans, both spattered with dried mud. His face had seen-it-all lines, like some rock star who'd lived too hard, too fast, and was old at forty.

Jane had come to her feet, taken off her parka, letting it fall in a heap beside her chair. She wore a bright scarlet top and had her hands in the hip pockets of her jeans, as if to prevent herself from using them. Lol saw that she was actually shocked, realizing Darvill had been there all the time, listening to everything, and that Nora had known that.

'Am I like going to feel guilty later?' Jane's hands came out of her pockets as fists. 'Over hitting a man in a wheelchair? Never done it before. Lol—'

Darvill looked up at Jane, tilting his jaw, as if inviting the first punch. Jane's fists were clenching and unclenching.

'Lol went through like… years of total hell. And misplaced psychiatric treatment. It was all wrong, and all these self-satisfied tossers read about it on the Net and—'

Lol said, 'Jane—'

'—and it just keeps getting dragged up, all the time. Makes me *sick*.'

Darvill's hands had begun slowly to applaud.

'It's very kind of you, Jane,' Lol said, 'and don't let me stop you hitting him. It's just I get the impression he knows this already. All on the Net now. Somewhere.'

'Only idiots believe what they read on the Net.' Darvill was easing his chair away from the curtains, its deep-tread tyres leaving mud flakes on the flagged floor. 'Certainly not self-satisfied tossers. But I shall give you the benefit of the doubt.'

Jane growled. Abruptly, Darvill reversed his chair, spun it round with some flair, like a kid on a skateboard, then looked over his shoulder.

'Not in a hurry to be sick, are you? Come and see my house.'

The grey curtains concealed a short passage, at the bottom of which was a small, modern door, leading into what had evidently been the stable yard. A sensor somewhere brought exterior lights on, one of them a lantern over a Gothic oak door. The sky was grey and purple; unlike last night, there wouldn't be a starshow.

The oak door opened on its own as the chair approached it. Lol felt a nudge from Jane.

'It's *him*.'

Projecting from the shoulder of the doorway arch was a wooden face: bulbous eyes, a fish-mouth spewing fronds. It looked like part of the arch. That old?

They entered a passage that was quietly lit, low and narrow and rounded, like a wormcast. A wheelchair route. Even Lol had to bend his neck. He caught Nora's eye and she smiled faintly. Another Gothic door and then they got to straighten up in a square hallway with walls like an old countryman's skin.

Narrow stone stairs curved away under a fat oak beam. A symbol had been embossed on the middle of the beam: three concentric squares, with lines and dots marking out what seemed like a simple maze. Jane was staring up; she clearly didn't know what it meant either. Darvill saw them looking up at it.

'Hold that in your mind,' he said.

Jane frowned. Nora crossed the hallway to a door of wide oak panels, ridged and dented as if the door had been kicked open by generations of farm boots. The latch was halfway down, and she bent to lift it, and Darvill glided through, Nora holding the door open for Jane and Lol.

On the other side of the doorway, the whole atmosphere changed.

'Sit anywhere,' Nora said. 'But make sure you *do* sit.'

But Jane just stood there, taking in the kind of soft, muffling silence you only experienced deep in the countryside in winter. Like, real winter, with snow drifts outside. She turned to find Nora, but Nora was gone, back through the doorway, leaving a trail of laughter behind her, light as a chiffon scarf.

'Blimey,' Jane said.

There were a few well-worn rugs on the floor but they were sidelined by a flagged alleyway of rosy stone all the way to the fireplace in its cavernous stone inglenook. A log fire was the focus of the room. That and the painting hanging above it, flat to the wall, no frame, illuminated by a downlighter.

'Sit,' Darvill said. 'Don't want a crick in my neck.'

Jane moved to the nearest of two sofas, a sagging, ochre-coloured Chesterfield, side-on to the hearth. Sat with her parka scrunched up on her knees like a security blanket. There were also two armchairs that didn't match and one long, low table with a magazine on it: *Dowsing Today*, journal of the British Society of Dowsers. Jane and Lol ending up either end of the sofa, their backs to the two tightly wooded windows, opposite a wall of floor-to-ceiling bookshelves. Apart from a pole with a brass hook on the end leaning against the shelves and a basket of logs, that was it for furnishings.

Darvill cruised down the flagged alley, stopping with his back to the bookshelves. They were rudimentary, separated by stone blocks and bowed with books. Not stately-home type books, those static matching sets with leather bindings, but *real* books that had been read and read. Some books that Jane had read, familiar spines: *The Secret History of the World, Daimonic Reality, The View over Atlantis, The Book of English Magic.* A library of deep mystery. Jane began to feel a muted excitement. She turned to the fireplace and what was above it.

A huddle of big logs were fusing in ashy pink and orange on the hearth, but the real heat seemed to be coming from the painting.

Unmistakably Kilpeck Church. The view was from the lane below its mound, under the curved apse. Looking up towards the little bell tower, behind which the setting sun had vanished leaving only an amber smear, while a post-sunset deep blue claimed most of the sky.

The church itself was a glowing ember.

'Like it's swallowing the setting sun,' Jane said.

Darvill smiled.

'Reminds me of somebody,' Lol said. 'Famous painter. Victorian, or earlier. Moonlit fields.'

'Who in particular?' A forefinger compressing Darvill's stubbled left cheek. 'Go on, Robinson. Try someone.'

'Can't think of the name. Famous for his harvest moons. Fields full of ripe hay you could almost smell. Intoxicating. Somewhere down in… Kent? Samuel Palmer?'

'Congratulations,' Darvill said.

'Palmer came here?'

'Don't imagine so. Even better. This is a Tom Keating. Legendary faker of old and modern masters who specialized in Palmers. You ever see that old TV documentary of Keating at work – *as* Palmer? When he was getting it right he'd go to pieces, dissolve into breathless sobs. Very moving.'

'I didn't see that.'

'Could've been he was just bloody good at faking emotional responses for the camera. But that was what appealed to my old man who commissioned this a few years before Keating died, in the 1980s. Posted him a stack of photographs to work from.

"Do me a Palmer, Tom. Let the old bugger work his magic on *my* place." He actually meant work *with* the earth magic. And Tom did, God bless him. Remarkable thing was that my old man told him nothing about what sometimes happened to Kilpeck Church at sunset. Which of them got it so right, do you reckon, Keating or Palmer?'

Darvill reached out his hands for heat.

'Keating was as good as most of the painters he faked. So good that he had to plant anachronisms and deliberate mistakes in his pictures to prove they were intentional fakes, avoid fraud charges. And he's come to the right place. Fake.'

Jane glanced at Lol. He was looking all round the room with its bumpy ochre walls. Then he turned to Darvill, eyebrows raised.

'*All* this?'

'My old man didn't like the farmhouse he inherited from his brother. Been rebuilt too many times and horribly modernized. Fortunately, it wasn't listed, so he knocked it down. Started again about fifty yards away, on what the dowsers told us was a Bronze Age tumulus – burial mound. Not on the map, never been excavated. Perfect.'

Jane stared at him.

'This house is *new*?'

'Not *new*, girl, just fake. There's a difference. The old man bought a collapsed barn for the timbers, raided the salvage yards, found a builder who knew what he was doing, and it gradually took shape.'

'Wow. It looks...'

'Looks older than most old houses. It's like Tom Keating – start by faking it and then something takes hold. The spirit enters.'

Jane felt momentarily breathless.

'That's why you were able to have a green man carved into your back doorway.'

'Another practical advantage. Dad didn't want an old house,

315

in government aspic, dependant on some awkward little shit from the council for every minor alteration. New house made from ancient materials, it can be what it ought to be. Yes, quite right, the Man of Leaves – three representations of him around the place. None of *them* in aspic. He's not a historical image at all. He's absolutely contemporary. His time's *now*. Do you understand? No, you don't.'

He wheeled himself further into the firelight, and Jane saw he had a flat wooden box across his knees. He opened it, brought out a folded board, like a chessboard, and when he opened that out, Jane saw the concentric squares from the beam in the hall.

'Ever played Nine Men's Morris, Jane?'

'Sorry?'

'Not many do any more.'

There were holes and black and white pegs inside the squares. The square in the middle was raised up and painted pure white.

'What's it mean?'

'The three squares date back to prehistory. Found in caves, burial chambers, ancient Egyptian monuments. Widely played in medieval days and also by the Romans. A crude labyrinth. The pristine square in the centre is where you want to be.'

'And how would I get there?'

Darvill's eyes found hers. They were brown. Kind of wolf-eyes. Something passed between them that she found slightly disturbing as he talked in his even, educated way.

'The number nine has significance in most parts of the world. Triple-trinity, trinity squared. The symbol is a guide to marking out the boundaries between worlds, temporal and spiritual. These pegs, or counters...' Darvill lifted one out. '... seem to create a dance as they move towards the centre. Or many dances. Many ways to the centre. Could you...?'

He held out the board, and Lol took it from him.

'Academics will tell you the connection with morris dancing has never been proved, but fuck *them*. Put it on the

316

table, Robinson. That's just a modern one, made by George the carpenter – has a workshop here. I admit to never having heard of Nine Men's Morris until, a few years ago – get this – an investigation of the castle mound yielded the remains of a medieval board. Well, stone, actually. An interesting enough find for everyone involved, but I doubt any of them *quite* shared my excitement when I found out what it was. Sit *down*, please, don't like being loomed over.'

'It matters to you...' Lol found his old place in the corner of the Chesterfield sofa. '... that it *is* connected to morris dancing? The symbol.'

'No doubt in my mind that they're from the same source. The concentric squares, like the dance, are found in Sufi tradition. Dervishes would attain trance-states in the innermost square, the most protected area. Did you know that? No, you didn't.'

'So the dancers...'

'Given the right conditions, the dancers are connecting with new energies. The energies enter the limbs through movement. Landscape and history inform this house and bring it alive. The body moves on the earth and fires the mind.'

'Old English esoteric secrets,' Lol said.

Darvill's jaw jerked.

'Nothing to *do* with esoteric secrets. *Are* no secrets any more, except for the ones we hide from ourselves. You think I'm running a fucking *cult* here?'

A log shifted in the hearth sending up a small storm of bright splinters. Darvill slid his chair back. Jane began to smile again. She was really starting to like it here, maybe too much.

'That's what we've come to.' Darvill stared into the window's tight, square panes. 'Anyone who wants to get back to truth and honesty and the natural way of life, pre-chemicals, is a crank. Way things are going, this part of the border will be the last truly fertile area of southern Britain not to be shagged to death. You can see the rapists cruising the lanes with their crop-spraying machinery – too big for these old lanes. Unwieldy, menacing, loaded with tubes. Coiled and bloated like diseased veins. Out in the fields, skeletal metal arms extended to dispense species-genocide.' His fingers tightening on the worn leather chair-arms and then his face split into the vulpine grin. 'Sorry – get carried away.'

Jane caught her breath. He was opening himself out to them. He was a shit, but he was turning out to be her kind of shit.

'Tell me about the dance,' Lol said quickly. 'If there's no secret…'

Darvill leaned back into the worn leather of his chair.

'Cecil Sharpe, the folk song and dance man, was getting hints of it over a century ago, when he attempted to establish rules for morris dancing – no, no, it must be done *this* way. Old boy missed the point. Morris dancers don't learn from books and diagrams. Their own bodies teach them. Eventually.' Darvill settled back, hands in his lap. 'Well…?'

'I get that,' Lol said cautiously. 'I think.'

'I know you do. Otherwise I wouldn't be talking to you now.'

'Never any good at it,' Lol said. 'But some barrier eventually came down. Cotswold Morris, this was. Just the basics.'

'Basics are everything,' Darvill said. 'Start to analyse and it'll go away.'

'Too late, anyway. The side broke up and… other things happened to me.'

'An outsider,' Darvill said softly. 'Like Drake. Dad used to say Drake was pulled between worlds. Like this girl, too, I suspect.'

That feral gaze settling on Jane almost fondly. She felt herself blushing. God knows what he was like when he could walk.

'I suppose' – She started to talk too fast – 'that the discovery of this stone game in the ruins confirmed something for you. That Kilpeck and the morris…'

'I didn't *need* confirmation, Jane. It was more of an affirmation. A sign that we'd been acknowledged.'

'By whom?'

'Go figure. As Nora would say.'

He wheeled himself to the hearth, picked out a fat log, its bark falling away,

'What do you want from us?' Lol said.

Darvill tossed the log with both hands into the fire. Something collapsed in a blizzard of sparks.

'Want your souls,' Darvill said. 'What did you expect?'

48

A line

MERRILY DRANK STRONG black tea and vacuumed the downstairs rooms, going at it hard. It was an old Hoover, and it was loud, but not loud enough to blank out Sophie's voice in her head telling her that it would happen, perhaps within days, and then she'd be in trouble.

Not dressing it up. No reassurance. This was Sophie isolated. Sophie close to screaming, *Do something.*

The Hoover crunched over a bump in the big parlour rug.

The Bishop tells me less and less. Everything on a need-to-know basis.

Sophie on the way out. Un-bloody-thinkable. *Do something.*

Nothing she could do except go for Innes. She began to laugh, all the caffeine in the tea fuelling hopeless rage. If it was difficult for a bishop to remove a vicar, turn that around and you were facing the thirteenth labour of Hercules.

The black tea burned into her head and the Hoover picked up something metallic and screamed, and when she'd unplugged it and was down on her hands and knees on the floor with a hand between the brushes, the phone began ringing.

Take it in the scullery. She picked herself up, tore through the hall and the kitchen and the back hall and snatched the receiver across the desk.

'All right, lass?'

The only Yorkshire accent that lifted you to the South Wales snow-line.

'Huw.'

'Rung a few times, lass, but—'

'No, I should've rung you.' Groping her way round the desk, sinking into the captain's chair. 'Things just got a bit…'

'I've got a course on, see. In and out of the chapel. Didn't get your message till late, anyroad.'

'Sorry. I didn't realize.'

'Not *too* late, mind. I were still there for you. Happen you smelled the beer?'

'*What?*'

She sat down hard in the captain's chair.

'Left the buggers in the pub, arguing about the existence of black-eyed kids. You had any of them little sods?'

'Thankfully, no.'

'Anyroad, I'd had a pint or two but I managed to find the church keys. Now, what exactly did I say?'

'Sorry, I—?'

'Just then. When I said happen you smelled the beer, summat went wrong with your voice.'

'Oh. Well…' *Here we go.* 'I didn't smell beer, Huw, but I did smell marijuana. In the chancel.'

'Nowt do wi' me. Not since I were a lad, anyroad. Me and a mate went to Glastonbury once. Lebanese Red. Well, that's what they said it were. Sorry… go on.'

'Only three of us in there. But the man we were doing the Requiem for, people claimed he was stoned when he died. I imagined that scent, obviously.'

'Did you?'

'Still, I took it as a sign to myself that we were… connecting. You know?'

'And you had a result.'

'I think so.'

'I give up worrying about these details long ago, me. But you're not happy, are you? I know that voice. That's your not-happy voice. Plus, I've just heard on the radio about the lass over at Ewyas Harold. Which might've been what prompted me to ring. You knew her?'

'Yes.'

'Thought you might. Go on.'

'She was the priest who referred the case to me. All a bit coincidental.'

A crisp, Bakelite silence.

'It's a very long story, Huw.'

'Are *you* all right?'

'Yes. Yes, I am.'

'I'd come over but for this course. They don't get easier. Scepticism's one thing but some of these buggers, it's like they've studied under the saintly Dawkins. Half of 'em think God's a brain-chemical and the Virgin Birth were just Mary being a bit coy wi' Joe the joiner. Or would've been if she'd existed. Never mind, not your problem. Who you reckon killed this Julie, then, Merrily?'

'*I* don't know.'

'But you might know why?'

'I think I *should* know why.'

'Gone through the system, what you did last night?'

'Yes, thankfully.'

'What's Sophie say?'

'Sophie. Yes. That's the other thing.'

She told him about Sophie, who no bishop could reduce to a two-day week, only stop paying her for the other five.

'And happen change the locks,' Huw said.

'Yes.'

'That's a bugger, Merrily. That really is a bugger. You need Sophie. She's your eyes and ears at the Big Church. Owt I can do? About Innes.'

'You've done enough. And you couldn't get to him, anyway. We don't see him. He's keeping his head down, but he's not giving up. Working quietly, through others.'

'Don't do owt rash, lass, that's all I'd say.'

'There's somebody at the door, Huw.'

'That just summat you're telling me to avoid a long conversation?'

'You want me to lift the phone up so you can hear the knocker?'

'I'll be back,' Huw said.

Though wearing a suit of muted tweed, Liam Hurst looked uncomfortable in his role as Iestyn Lloyd's representative in the non-agricultural world.

'No, I won't have a cup of tea, thank you.' He stood in the hall by the *Light of the World*. 'In fact, I really don't want to be here, Mrs Watkins so, if you prefer to tell me to push off, have no fear of causing offence.'

'We never tell anybody to push off, Mr Hurst. It's not in the contract.'

He smiled shyly. She could see why he was able to work with farmers. None of the ones she knew in this area responded to pushy people.

'I take it you're here on behalf of Mr Lloyd?'

'And Aidan, I suppose. I'm here to talk about a particular church service. For Aidan.'

Christ.

How much worse could this day get?

'Erm… you'd better come in.'

'Iestyn… hears things.' Liam followed her into the kitchen, bent his wiry frame into a seat at the refectory table. 'He doesn't talk to a great many people, but they tend to be the people who know what's happening.'

God, God, God… How? Nobody knew what had happened in the church last night except Jane, Lol, Huw, Abbie Folley… and Gareth Brewer himself – the only one of them who knew Iestyn personally. The only one she hadn't spoken to since the Requiem. It could only have come from Gareth, but why would he…?

She sat down at the top of the table and looked helplessly into Liam Hurst's thin, freckled face.

'Sometimes you have to make quick decisions.'

'Must've been a difficult day for you,' he said. 'I know it's the other end of the county, but I expect you all know each other.'

'Been a difficult few days.'

'I can imagine. Did you know this... sorry... can't remember her name.'

'Oh... yes. Julie. Duxbury. Yes, I... did know her. A very nice, good-hearted woman. We're all... '

'Horrible,' he said. 'Nobody's safe any more.' Shaking his head, his short ginger hair up in spikes. 'The countryside's not what it was when I was growing up. Even out here. I've been talking to a man who's running for, what is it, Police and Crime...? Charles Howe?'

'Yes, I know him. From when he was a governor at my daughter's former school. And other... events.'

'He sees a worsening situation. He's known Iestyn for some years and came to talk about Aidan. He's talking about migrants without a proper licence, driving like maniacs on country lanes then fleeing the country before they can be brought to court. Not good.'

'He does seem to be using the rise in rural crime to support his campaign. Look, if I can just explain...'

Just get this over. Yes, she could have tried to get through to Iestyn Lloyd about the Requiem for his son, but it would have taken a lot of explanation and he may well have objected. Couldn't tell his stepson that.

'If it's impossible,' Liam said, 'it's impossible. I know Christmas is approaching and it must get difficult to fit these things in. It's just that Iestyn would like to draw a line under it. Especially the drugs. Charlie Howe sees Aidan as a victim of criminal intrusion into the countryside. They're even selling drugs now in the lanes outside some rural schools. From Land Rovers, for heaven's sake. Howe's attitude is, don't cover it up, bring it out in public. And if it's in a church, at a memorial service...'

'I'm sorry...?'

'You could, of course, expect a donation.'

'Oh.'

The room lightened. A memorial service. They wanted a memorial service for Aidan. Nothing to do with a Requiem; they knew nothing about that. Thank you, God. She felt her spine relax.

'Yes,' she said. 'Sure. Of course. I'd be happy to. You're right, it would draw a line.'

'Thank you,' he said. 'If you could let me know what days you have free... an evening, I suppose.'

'And perhaps you could supply me with, erm...'

'Biographical details. Without limitations, this time. Yes. It was a mistake, the funeral. And there'll be eulogies this time.'

'Iestyn?'

He grinned.

'That's unlikely. But I'll step into the breach as... as usual. And there's Charlie Howe, of course. Not that the idea of a memorial service being used as a political platform appeals to me that much, but, as I say... drawing a line. I'm sure you could steer him towards discretion.'

'Yes,' Merrily said. 'I imagine I could... do that.'

The phone rang; she let the machine take it.

When he left, she was shaking. Couldn't go on like this.

49

Made up

BLISS GOT BACK just after nightfall and found Annie in his office chair, her scarf and trench coat tossed across his desk. He'd missed her on the national TV news but heard her on the Radio Four six o'clock, where she got about five seconds asking for people to come forward – witnesses, anyone who'd seen a strange vehicle in country lanes miles from the nearest CCTV.

'That was awful,' Annie said. 'I'd forgotten.'

'Doing telly?'

She peered up at him. She looked tired, a bit raddled which, for some reason, he found sexy as hell. He wanted to take her home. But that wouldn't be happening for some hours yet. Not with what he was bringing back from Hewell.

'Telly was awful?' Bliss said.

'No, the… the nearest and dearest. Had to take them into the cottage. We'd had the worst of it cleaned up after the videos were done and crime scene were satisfied, but obviously we needed the daughter to tell us what might have been taken, so…'

'No FLOs to support them?'

Annie shook her head.

'I didn't think. Family liaison, for me it's always been where kids are involved. There is now, anyway. They're staying at the Three Counties, and I've asked Sandy Gee to see them. We'll talk again tomorrow. Essentially, they thought her mother would just sell the place after her husband died.'

'Did a deal with the diocese, apparently,' Bliss said. 'Maybe they only hired her so they could flog the existing vicarage and stick the next priest in a flat over a shop.'

'The daughter blames the Church.'

'For what?'

'More or less everything. She says having a father who was a vicar was always slightly odd but, when her mother decided that being a vicar's wife was not enough, the marriage was put under a lot of strain that just got worse. Women priests – why the hell so many women want to embrace superstition has always been beyond me. But… they seem to feel they have to prove they can deal with situations that men tend to avoid. Personal issues, family problems.'

Bliss nodding. Fellers with any sense would naturally avoid that stuff.

Annie told him how the Duxburys had ended up with neighbouring parishes in the Gloucester area, and Julie would keep bringing work home. People at the door and ringing up at all hours. Husband couldn't handle it. He was quite a bit older. Died after a heart attack coming down from the pulpit.

'Lot of self-recrimination on Julie's part. Her bishop suggested a new parish might be in order. The daughter says she was horrified when her mother announced she was moving to the parish and their cottage was going to be her rectory. She'd keep laughing it off, saying her neighbours, the SAS, would protect her.'

'You talked to them yourself, the Sass?'

'Quite helpful in the end. A few of their guys knew her – attended her services, even.'

'Religion of all kinds being rife in the special forces,' Bliss said. 'As we know.'

'I was told they would indeed have kept an eye on Mrs Duxbury, had they known.'

'Yeh, but known *what*, Annie? What was there to know?'

'Too much, really. By all accounts, she was back into her old ways, looking for people to help. Somebody with mental problems arrives at her door? We're checking social services. It's a big area – she has about half a dozen churches. Got to be a few screwballs.'

Through the window behind Annie, the early night sky was like coal-dust over the red-brick buildings.

'The place was ransacked,' she said, 'but surprisingly little seems to have been taken, according to Jennifer Welch – that's the daughter. Money probably taken from her purse, but the jewellery box was undisturbed, and it did contain some quite valuable pieces. Could've been they fled when they realized she was dead, but given the ferocity of the attack, how could they not have realized that was a strong possibility?'

'Could be they surprised her and she slipped, keeled over and bashed her head against the sundial. If they were blokes – or even women – who she happened to know or might recognize, then maybe they panicked and... Don't look like that, Annie, it happens. People commit terrible crimes to avoid gerrin nicked for comparatively minor offences. Or were they in there looking for something?'

'Hard to imagine what. We got Mrs Welch to check out everything we – or she – could think of.'

Her face said they weren't going to have this cleared up by the morning, and the media would be all over it: picturesque location, little river bubbling under the bridge. Annie said she was awaiting a call from the ACC, which might result in a cavalry charge from Worcestershire. Two simultaneous murder inquiries in Hereford, a bit much, that.

'Tell the ACC she can send anybody but Twatface Brent,' Bliss said. 'Is it possible somebody actually wanted the vicar dead?'

'Rector. A calculated killing would be the worst case scenario. Not something we could even explore until we'd pulled someone for it. It might look to the press as if we're in some Agatha Christie story where we're looking for the one parishioner who really had it in for the priest, but that... doesn't happen, does it?'

'One day it just might. And no library in which to assemble the suspects 'cos the friggin' council's shut them all down.' Bliss leaned forward. 'Listen, Hewell... Lech Jaglowski...'

'Oh God, yes. What've you got?'

Bliss beamed, rubbing his hands together.

'I'm made up, to be honest, Annie. Nice lad, Lech. And what a source. Yeh, all right, I'm not sure how much of it I believe, but it's enough to bring someone in. Tonight.'

50

Tarot

THE SKY WAS a deep and luminous grey, not fully dark. There was nobody else about. A silent farmhouse, an open barn, no indication of the rambling modern village within easy walking distance, and you couldn't hear the sounds or see the lights of the pub Jane knew was fairly close. The church was in a different place, raised up on its island mound, separate.

Lol parked the truck close to the mound. They took a flashlight up the short, inclining footpath, past the gnarly yew tree.

'They're coming,' Jane said.

Beyond the church, she could see vehicle lights on the now invisible lane winding up from the wooded hills: Darvill and his lifekeeper in the adapted van. He'd wanted Jane and Lol to go with them, but Lol had politely refused, and Jane was glad about that. They needed some time to talk, though they hadn't had time to say much. At Lol's suggestion, she'd called Mum from the truck. No answer. She'd left a short message explaining where they were, how they'd come to be here, then switched off the phone. This was no time for a long-distance argument.

'We can leave anytime,' Lol said. 'And maybe we ought to.'

'He does like to feel in control, doesn't he? Probably a disabled thing. Or just a titled country gent thing.' Jane stamped her feet to get some feeling into them. 'I just need to know what he *wants*.'

They were outside the great oak door, the colour of old, tanned hide. She let the flashlight follow the curve of the arch where images were arranged like forgotten signs of the zodiac.

Below all this, aligned with the top of the door, the pop-eyed Green Man, the Man of Leaves, glared out, fat strands curling from his gaping mouth like the loops of a belt.

'The doorman,' Jane said. 'The guardian. Observes everyone coming in, everyone going out.'

High in the arch she saw what she thought at first was a second green man, but what curled from this one's mouth were a couple of snakes facing one another over his head, open-mouthed like they were going for a French kiss. The strangeness continued in a stone chain along the top of the wall, under the eaves.

'Just don't tell me all this means nothing, Lol. Don't tell me it's just decoration. And don't tell me it's Christian. It's like… half secular and half sacrilegious. And why here? A tiny little church in the middle of nowhere, with a cathedral doorway.'

The images drew you in. Mesmerized, she led Lol around the outside of the building. It didn't take long, but it could take years or a lifetime or more to understand the corbels, these little blocks of stone, each one enclosing an image. Some were scary – devilish faces, deformed faces – some friendly like the cartoon dog and rabbit. Some possibly erotic, even homo-erotic, although the guidebook called them wrestlers.

She was drawn to one that looked like someone about to cut a mournful creature's throat with a carving knife, but it wasn't. She looked at Lol. The mournful creature was actually some medieval instrument that looked not unlike the Boswell guitar, and the knife was a bow. The musician's face was round and had only two prominent features: its circular eyes with drilled out black pupils. Jane thought about the sweatshirt Lol was wearing under his fleece, with the Roswell humanoid. *Alien.* If he got the connection, he wasn't saying anything.

'It's like some kind of stone tarot,' Jane said.

Too loud. She took a step back, half afraid of finding her whole life, past, present and future, in stone images on a medieval church wall.

'Perceptive of you, Jane. More enigmatic than the Sphinx, this church.'

Darvill had come sailing out of the darkness like some will-o'-the-wisp, one of those head torches on a band below this Russian-looking furry hat.

'What about her?'

Jane shone her torch up to find the famous Sheela-na-gig all goggle-eyed and shameless, wearing a vacant smile which, in a different light, might look cunning but right now suggested a disturbed innocence. As if she'd been set up for this. Doomed to display for all eternity that enormous fanny.

She'd read somewhere that maidens in the Caucasus would embroider Sheelas to promote easy childbirth. She thought any woman with one that size could drop triplets without even noticing.

'I'm still not sure what to make of her.'

'You make of her what you will,' Darvill said quietly. 'And she'll make of you whatever she wants. She scares you?'

Talking to Lol, now, who took a while before replying, as the torch beam moved to the next corbel, a comical cat.

'Not quite the word I'd use. Is it just me, or is there an element of irony here? You can't help wondering why she's, um, next to a pussy.'

There was a sharp, metallic creak from the wheelchair, as if something had snapped, and then Darvill's voice was slicing the night air.

'Take that back, Robinson.'

'Sorry?'

'Take it fucking *back*.'

Jane stepped away, nearly dropping the flashlight, catching a parting glimpse of the Sheela still wrenching herself open but now looking confused. Lol and a gravestone were bathed in white by Darvill's head torch.

'I'm sorry,' Lol said. 'Stupid remark.'

'Thank you,' Darvill said. We can go on now.'

They moved around the church, anticlockwise. Was this good? Jane wondered, remembering churches and monuments where you were supposed to be able to summon the devil this way. It didn't seem to bother Darvill, who was talking about the church like he was trying to sell it, pointing out its uniquenesses: *not* oriented exactly east–west, as were most Christian churches, to face Christ on the cross, but to follow the path of an underground stream. Eternal flowing water underneath. One reason it was so alive, Darvill said. So *current*.

Round the back, it was bitter, open to the fields, farmhouse lights here and there. Maryfields was down there somewhere, sunk into the woods.

'You'll notice the anachronisms,' Darvill said. 'Like the dog and the rabbit, or the hare and hound as some people prefer. The Disney corbel as it's known. Look at the dog's face sometime. You see dogs in medieval tapestries, they're all greyhound-types, pointed noses. This is a *pet* dog. A *modern* pet dog.'

In medieval times,' Jane said, 'you'd think the dog would be tearing the hare to bits.'

'Especially here. It was hunting ground. King John came at least twice, to hunt.'

'Bastard.'

Jane followed Darvill's chair around the curving apse, shining the flashlight along the path in front of them, Lol following closely behind her, as if he thought she might disappear, absorbed into the masonry until all that was left of her was a Jane corbel.

There were places where the church had been repaired with bricks, and the corbels were more widely spaced, as if some were missing. She was thinking of the Victorian lady who'd been shocked by some of the images but missed the obvious. When Darvill stopped, she swung the light away to where the mounded churchyard faded into bumpy fields.

'Is that where the original village was?'

'And across the lane,' Darvill said. 'Under the barn.'

Jane shone the torch back up at the chain of corbels, heard Lol gasp and then stifle it. She spun.

'You OK?'

'Just tripped.'

He hadn't, though, had he? He'd seen the end corbel near the more modern guttering, which showed a man's stone face. What was left of it. Just the mouth; the rest had been sliced off, as if he'd been in a road accident. Or something.

She switched off the torch. Didn't want to see that again, either.

A stone drain made the path too narrow for the chair, and Darvill had to steer a bumpy course across the grass between graves, and then they were back at the bell tower end with its high window, Darvill ordering Jane to shine her torch up at it.

'See them?'

'I think so. Just about.'

Two more green men in the high window's stonework.

'The Man of Leaves isn't the most talked about image here, but he's the dominant one.'

'See you in and he sees you out.'

'That's the one on the door. These two see you coming from afar. What is he, Jane?'

'Nobody knows.'

'Don't they?'

'I've read loads of books on him. He wasn't even known as the Green Man until 1939, I think it was. Lady Raglan – not that far from here when you think about it. She got fascinated by the foliate face. The first to call him the Green Man. Is that right?'

'She saw him as a pagan woodland god, like Pan.'

'Was she wrong?'

'Might've been.'

Darvill sat looking up, the beam of his head-torch linking him to the wall. Was it here that he'd fallen from the scaffolding? A longer fall because of the bell tower. Every time he came here he'd feel the impact and the agony. She thought, *If I'd fallen off this church I'd hate it for ever, even if it was my fault.*

Nora had appeared at Darvill's shoulder, the collar of her sheepskin coat pulled half over her face. Darvill's Russian hat had slipped back as he looked up at the window and she straightened it carefully. Jane feeling in that moment how Nora must feel about Lionel Darvill, and perhaps an inkling of his feelings towards her. No sensation below the waist but what might be happening in his head?

'Does that mean you think you know what he is?' Jane said. 'The Man of Leaves?'

'I do know.'

'*How* do you know?'

'He told me.'

'Like… how?'

'Through his incarnation.'

She hardly liked to say it.

'Aidan?'

No reply.

'You going to tell us what he is?'

'No.'

Darvill reversed the chair and steered it back to the track and round to the great south door and its doorman. Jane thought, *He comes knocking on the door. And the minister, the rector, is waiting with a candle to welcome him in.*

'Poor Julie,' she said. 'Or maybe she didn't really want to.'

He looked up at her. He must be feeling really resentful. Couldn't order people to sit down out here.

'Stand here with a candle,' Jane said. 'Waiting for a man in a mask.'

'I'm gonna tell them this,' Nora said. 'Julie was a down-the-line, no shit Christian. When we asked her to conduct the solstice service, welcome the dancers into church, she's like, no *way*, because… well, even I can see there's a lot of pre-Christian stuff here. Guy in a green mask, the others with black faces. Julie was never gonna be too comfortable with black faces painted on.'

Jane said, 'But she—'

'Yeah, I know. She'd already decided it was her task, as spiritual mother of this place, to heal the feud between the Darvills and the Lloyds. So Julie goes over to see Iestyn, who, like, *doesn't* see people. Only other farmers, and not many of them. But she's a determined lady. She was gonna sit outside his door, or park outside his gate or whatever, till he came out.'

'When was this?'

'Day she died? Or the day before, depending what hour she was killed.'

'Did Iestyn meet her?'

'We don't know. All she said – this was on the phone to Li – was she was expecting a reply to what she was suggesting. Now whether she got it…'

'You know *what* she was suggesting?'

'She was gonna make the solstice festival a memorial service for Aidan Lloyd. Attended by both Li and Iestyn. Get them into the church together. Let God take care of the rest.'

'Right.'

'His spiritual home. Iestyn gets to keep his physical remains, in Ledwardine, while Kilpeck… I don't wanna talk about his soul, but you get the idea. Biggest night in the Border morris calendar, the Man of Leaves brings his predecessor home. With a promise of peace? But now… it's like someone… something… doesn't want this. No priest. And no Man of Leaves.'

'It's not like you don't have a full morris side,' Lol said. 'Surely one of them would do it.'

'None of them are exactly eager,' Darvill murmured. 'Jinxed now, Robinson. Aidan was the Man, he was killed. Brewer took it on and he was… well, you know about that. And only eight men now. I had a friend, in London, who'd've made up the nine. He's made an excuse. And then Julie Duxbury, who was to have welcomed the Man into church…'

'Murdered.'

'Superstitious people, morris men. If they weren't, what use would they be?'

Jane switched off her torch. Shadows rose and faces vanished. Jane spoke into Darvill's lamp.

'You want my mother, don't you?'

'She'd be suitable,' Darvill said neutrally.

God…

'But you… you complained about her to the Bishop. You put the knife in for her with a man who wants to get rid of her.'

'I don't know anything about that.'

'Would it have mattered, long as you got what you wanted?'

'I had a message that a man would come to talk to me about it. Phoned this morning. I said I'd call him back. I haven't. Yet.'

'I see,' Lol said. 'You want me to go back and tell Merrily that she can either do your service or you'll tell this guy everything you know.'

'He isn't saying that,' Nora said quickly.

'It wouldn't matter anyway. It's all official now. She's filed a report.'

But Mum would still feel she had to do it, Jane thought. She'd do it in memory of Julie, who had the temerity to meddle. She'd do it out of some misplaced sense of guilt at still being alive.

'And the Man of Leaves?' Lol said.

Darvill was silent for just a moment.

'The Man of Leaves is a curious fellow. An outsider who dances according to his own discipline. He arrives when he's needed. Aidan didn't take on the role until he was living somewhere else. Ledwardine, as it happened.'

'*Oh* no,' Lol said.

'The solstice is pretty close, but there's time for the Man to learn his steps.'

'Two weeks?'

'Wrong solstice, Robinson. The calendar changed in the sixteenth century or whenever it was. The medieval solstice – possibly erroneously or for reasons unknown to us – was the thirteenth. Julie was glad about that. Didn't want it too near Christmas. The thirteenth is a saint's day, I think.'

'St Lucy,' Nora said. 'Next Monday is St Lucy's night. John Donne, the Elizabethan poet, called it *the year's midnight*.'

Jane stepped away breathing hard. Darvill's light flared over the south doorway.

51

Anybody but God

THEY BROUGHT DANNI James back into the interview room. Or at least as far as the doorway, where Bliss came out to meet her, with Karen Dowell.

It could look quite sinister down here after dark when the atmosphere of despondency was always denser, when you might catch some felon in cuffs being accommodated for the night, or one of those offensive man-pongs that were so hard to get rid of.

Bit early yet for that, but Danni's fizz was gone. Bliss surveyed her professionally, head to toe: puffy black jacket and biker's boots, hair cut shorter, the amethyst stud gone. Sympathy was not the way in. He beamed.

'Hello, Danni. Welcome back. We've not met before, but I think you know Karen, AKA Ms Nice. DC Vaynor – occasionally described, to his sorrow, as Young Mr Nasty – is otherwise engaged. So I'm standing in. I'm his boss, DI Bliss. Known the length the breadth of Gaol Street and beyond as...' Bliss tilted his head to engage her eyes. '... Mr Total Bastard.'

He watched Danni waiting for him to smile. He didn't. The time for treating her as a bereaved girlfriend had started to ebb away, for Bliss, when he'd first become aware that she was quite enjoying her new status as murder victim's moll. Scary times, these.

'The subtext is, Danielle... you're not being charged with anything yet, but you piss me about at your extreme peril.'

'You can't talk to me like that.'

'Like what?' Bliss peered at Dowell. 'You hear me say anything offensive, Karen?'

'Charm and consideration itself, boss.'

'Thank you, Karen.'

Around the table – no drinks, no bickies – he told Danni what Lech had said about how he'd never been drunk when he'd turned up at Jag's. In fact, he'd been sober and polite, except for the time he'd broken down, told Danni how much he loved her and pleaded with her to go away with him on the grounds that Jag was not, on any level, good news.

'And let's be honest, he's a nice lad, young Lech. Never wanted to be a criminal. All he wanted was a good job and to settle down with a nice girl at least a hundred miles away from his brother. Danni, we believe he didn't threaten Jag, although Jag, probably out of your hearing, certainly threatened Lech.'

Danni slammed her hands over her ears.

'You ever think it's time you grew up?' Karen raised her voice. 'You found Jag exciting. Hard to imagine you getting off on second-hand cars, mind.'

Danni's hands dropped.

'He was good-looking and he was generous.'

'Was it the other things he was up to that you found exciting?'

'I don't know what you're talking about.'

Bliss said, 'Do you remember when Lech pleaded with you to leave Jag?'

'He never did that.'

'He never suggested that if you stayed with Jag you'd wind up one day in a sordid little grey room like this, possibly the first of many?'

'I don't know where you're getting this rubbish from.'

'Well, from Lech,' Bliss said. 'Who else?'

'My dad's got his solicitor on standby,' Danni said.

'Fine.' Bliss opening his hands. 'If you want to move on to the next stage, we'll be happy to arrest you.'

'I don't know what you *want*.'

'You ever go out with Jag on any of his extra jobs?'

'No. That's—'

'I'll ask you again, Danni, and this time I'll be more specific. On a certain night around the beginning of this month, did you go with Wictor Jaglowski to a village down the border—'

'*No.*'

'Did he ask you to keep an eye open while he was pouring petrol over a man's body?'

'*What?*'

'Did you watch him set light to the body?'

'No— *No*... No way!'

'Were you gonna say "no comment" then, Danni? That's what people often start saying at this stage, when they realize we know about things they didn't think we'd know.'

'Leave me alone!'

She looked at Karen.

Karen shrugged.

'Do you know what happened to the body,' Bliss said, 'after the two of you set it on fire?'

'You've got it all—'

'Wrong? I don't think so, Danni.'

Bliss sat back, running over in his mind what Lech had told them about a prison visit he'd had from Jag. Having a laugh with him about the really crazy, but really lucrative jobs he was doing for this new mate of his. Telling Lech – in Polish, of course – about this particularly weird one he'd been set up for the following week involving a can of petrol and a body. How he'd been asked to do this one on his own but he was thinking of inviting Danni along to watch his back.

Pretty clear to Lech why Jag was telling him.

'Rubbing it in, Danni,' Bliss said. 'You and him an item in the fullest sense. Partners in crime. After all Lech's attempts to warn you off. Burning a body – that's not kid stuff, Danni.'

Whose body? And where? Just a village down the border –

there were dozens, either side. Would be better if they had the actual body, charred bits, whatever, but how likely was that?

'This is wrong. You're twisting everything!'

'I don't think so, Danni. I don't think Lech was either. His brother's dead, what's to lose?'

Danni was trying to compose herself and failing. Panting, now, on the verge of hyperventilating, eyes everywhere. Be good video, this.

Bliss was prepared to wait, but she didn't keep them long.

'There was *no body*. All right?'

Bliss didn't respond.

'What do you think I am?' Danni said. 'It was a joke.'

'Lech wasn't laughing.'

'Jag was like... he was probably just winding him up. It was just a dummy? With old clothes on and a top hat? And bells.'

'Bells? We talking about the same thing here, Danni? Where was this?'

'Kilpeck. Near the old castle. We brought it in the van. And the post with a crosspiece nailed on. And a spade.'

'And it had bells, this dummy?'

'Round the post that was holding everything together.'

'He tell you what it was all about?'

'He said it was a joke. He was like, "You English, you make joke out of everything."'

'So it wasn't *his* joke.'

'No.'

'Whose joke was it?'

'He was doing a favour for a mate.'

'And what was his name, this mate?'

'He didn't say. But it wasn't— I mean, it was an English mate. Actually, I'm calling him a mate, but he wasn't.'

'What was he, then?'

'I think Jag was scared of him. Or he'd've said no.'

'How's that?'

''Cos he didn't like doing it.'

342

'Why not?'

''Cos it was a church. He was a big Catholic. He was supposed to do it near the church, round the back of the church, near the graves. But he got like cold feet? I was like, you know, it's only a Church of England church, but he said it was a Catholic church at one time, and he read what it said on one of those public information things, about how important it used to be.'

'And then?'

'He walked around for a bit and then he stood in front of the church and crossed himself? Then he took down the number for the vicar off the noticeboard and he put it into his mobile. Only he couldn't get a signal. So we went across the grass and through this gate and up this hill until he got a signal, and he rang the vicar and told him there was a fire at the church.'

Bliss tried not to react. *Mother of God.* He just hoped Annie was getting this, upstairs.

'You're sure it was the vicar he rang?'

'He got the number off the board.'

'And it was a man, was it, the vicar? Or what?'

'*I* don't know. *He* made the call. I didn't even listen. I thought it was getting stupid. It wasn't fun any more. I just wanted to get the thing burned and go home.'

'And then?'

'Then we dragged the dummy up across the grass towards the castle and he dug a bit of a hole for the post—'

'With what?'

'He had a spade. And then he poured the petrol all over it and set fire to it. Up near the castle. He was like, "We're doing it here. I'm not doing it at the church." It looked… really weird? You could've thought it was alive. But it wasn't. Honest to God, it was just a dummy. It was a *joke*.'

'Wasn't, though, was it? You said he wouldn't do it near the church.'

'That's the kind of bloke he was. I didn't understand it.'

'God-fearing? Rang the vicar thinking he was setting himself up for some kind of absolution?'

'He wasn't afraid of anybody but God,' Danni said, then thought about it. 'And this bloke.'

Bliss's pulse went tick-tick.

'You said you thought he was a *bit* frightened of him.'

'Maybe it was more than that. He made me swear never to say anything about this to anybody. Any of it. Especially him phoning the vicar. He didn't want that getting back.'

'How would it get back?'

'Don't know.'

'You know who this bloke is, don't you?'

'No!'

'But he was English.'

'Yeah. He liked that… He said they'd done favours for each other. Business.'

'Second-hand cars?'

'Don't know.'

'Come on, Danni. You do.'

'I don't.'

'You can't get him in trouble now, can you? Only yourself. So if you help us…'

'He… we stopped off at the garage one time, and he was showing me how he was thinking of setting up a little show-room at the back for second-hand farm stuff – chainsaws and things he'd done up.'

'Quad bikes?'

'That sort of stuff. He said he had a good friend who'd tell him where items were… available.'

'Available. That was his word?'

'He liked that word. It was a new word for him. He laughed.'

'Did he mean stolen, Danni?'

'I never asked.'

'And this was the same man for whom he was returning a favour, setting light to the dummy?'

'He only talked about one man.'

'Who he was more than a bit afraid of. He say why that was?'

Dannie shaking her head.

'What other favours did he do for this feller?'

'Dunno.'

'See, we're probably talking here about the man who shot him. That's what Lech thinks. And he's out there. Maybe not far away.'

'I don't know anything about that. I swear to God.'

Bliss stood up.

'Thank you, Danni. You realize we have to check all this. So I'd like you to go through it all again with Karen. Dates, times, exact locations, anything you might've forgotten. Every tiny little detail, yeh?'

Danni wet her lips.

'Am I going to be charged with anything?'

'There could be quite a few interesting offences in there, Danni. But let's see how cooperative you can be.'

Annie met him in the doorway of the CID room, dragged him into his office, slammed the door.

'Did I get that right? Jaglowski rang *Julie Duxbury* on his mobile?'

'Let's not too excited till we've checked it. But the thing is, if it's true then Duxbury also kept quiet about it. Why? Why didn't she call us or the fire brigade? She didn't know Jaglowski. She gets this really weird call at night telling her about a fire near the church. Did she go and investigate or what?'

'Perhaps she also thought it was a joke.'

'I don't think so, do you? She'd be up there in a flash, or at least ringing somebody she could trust.'

'You believe her that it wasn't a body?'

'Top hat? Bells? That's gorra be true. I don't know what it means – a clown? But only an idiot would make that up. She's norra genius, but she's not insane. Can you imagine what state

Danni'd be in after burning an actual body, all the fats and the smells?'

'No, you're probably right.'

'You wouldn't do it in a place like that, anyway. Too messy, too public. Let's get crime scene organized for tomorrow. First light.'

Bliss found he was smiling in a kind of wonderment. How often did this happen? Well, yeh, more often than you'd think; it was a small county; sometimes crime was almost... what was the word... holistic?

'Come on, Francis.' Annie was in Bliss's chair, looking around for paper; she still liked things inscribed on stationery. 'Let's spell this out before we put it into the system. We're looking at a connection.'

'We could be looking at one case, Annie. One killer.'

'Unlikely, but let's keep that in mind. Cast around for any more links.'

'There's another one already,' Bliss said.

Looking down at her, waiting for the penny to drop. Wondering, not for the eighteenth time, where she'd be today if not for her dad. Most likely not in the police. Maybe she'd've continued with her legal studies, be on the way to becoming a High Court judge: Ms Justice Howe, severely straight daughter of a fabled bent copper turned corrupt councillor.

Someone knocked at Bliss's door.

'In conference,' he called out. 'Give us ten.'

Annie was hunched over the desk, fists tight, the penny in downward motion.

'Meant to tell you,' Bliss said. 'You were right. It *was* him with Mandy Patel. He was only there, according to Patel, for her cameraman to do some shots of him at a crime scene. Old cowboy still in the saddle.'

'What is he *doing*?'

'He's up for sheriff.'

'And who let him inside Hewell?'

346

'You want to know what else Charlie was asking Lech?'

'I don't *want* to know any of this, Francis, I don't want it to be happening.'

'Well... he was asking about Jag's delivery business, his courier contracts. Seems Lech filled in sometimes, as a driver, if Jag was gerrin more work than his Lithuanian crew could handle. And talking of Lithuania... Lukas Babekis?'

'This is the van driver who...'

'Who went home to his mam, leaving a farmer called Aidan Lloyd on the slab. I've had another chat with Rich Ford about Babekis. Dry road, windy day, hard to calculate his speed with any accuracy, so he got the benefit of the doubt.'

'You'd better explain the full significance of that. I've never actually worked in Traffic.'

'Let's say we're talking about the difference between driving a white van fast enough to accidentally cause serious injury and driving fast enough to guarantee death. Difference between causing death by dangerous driving and manslaughter. Or worse.'

'*Worse?* For God's sake, Francis, this is beyond stupid. If you're suggesting that Babekis deliberately killed Lloyd with his van... how would he know Lloyd was going to come out of that field at that particular time?'

'I don't know. I'm just telling you what Charlie was asking Lech. Jag and Babekis, what their working arrangement was. If Charlie was still a policeman you might think he was trying to emphasize to Lech what a serious offence this might yet turn out to be, so if he had any information relating to it, it would be unwise to hold back.'

'So the traffic boffins are unsure, there are no witnesses, Babekis has gone to ground, and it's not even *our* ground.'

'And if he was people-smuggled in, his name's not even Babekis. But if you're Charlie, and one of the props of your campaign for PCC is that insufficient attention's being paid to rural crime – lax policing in the sticks – then, might it not be to your advantage to show that the present system lets possible murderers just walk away under its nose?'

'*Murderers?* You're saying it *again!*'

'Annie... I don't know. I'm just trying to see it through Charlie's slitty eyes. I don't know where he *got* it from.'

'And it would be *my* nose it's under.'

'If he wants it to look that way, yeh.'

'He's my *dad*,' Annie said.

Bliss said nothing. Still haunting him, that night in Charlie's home office. *You know what it's like when you learn something that disgusts you.* Taking out his file of snatched pictures of Bliss and Annie together. *Go on, Brother Bliss, open it... Sheer disbelief when I first saw these, sheer disbelief...*

Still...

'Could be time we made finding out what Charlie's up to more of a priority.'

'You want to put *that* into the system?'

'I most certainly do not. I'm thinking a private chat might be in order?'

'With Charlie? You've tried that before. He hates you.'

'Annie, that'll be right at the top of me application form for a place in heaven. But what I was thinking—'

'And he has a record of taking you apart.'

'I was thinking not just me.'

'Oh no.' She was out of his chair. 'No, no, no...'

'You're only putting it off.'

'In the middle of all this?'

'I'm thinking out of working hours?'

'Forget it,' Annie said. 'Don't mention it again.'

52

Turning over the death card

THEY GOT INTO the cab of the Animal, and Lol switched on the engine and the headlamps, which part-floodlit the church. It looked compact, sealed off, separate, like a landed spacecraft.

Or a time capsule. Jane had pulled out her phone.

'Don't go yet. We need to ring Mum.'

'Just don't tell her what Darvill wants.'

Jane looked up.

'Why not?'

'I mean not yet. We can't just tell her like that. I know you think it's a nice idea.'

'I think it's a beautiful idea. Like a meeting of old ways. And Lucy's night. *Lucy's* night. Jesus Christ, Lol…'

'*Saint* Lucy's night.'

Jane still talked as if the spirit of Lucy Devenish was embedded in the landscape. In some ways, Lucy dead was more of an influence than she'd been alive. Jane could turn dead Lucy into anything she wanted.

She powered up the phone.

'Well, she's Saint Lucy to *me*. Anyway, it's not my decision. How about I just say we're on our way and we'll explain when we get home?'

'Fine.'

The phone cheeped and glowed. He noticed she'd had a text and wondered what had happened with Dr Samantha Burnage. Jane ignored the text and called home.

'Engaged.'

'We'd better just get back.' Lol started the engine, backed the truck towards the church wall. 'I'll go slowly so you can try again in a few minutes.'

'Lol...'

'Mmm?'

He turned the car back into the lane. He'd be glad to get home.

'You haven't said anything about the Man of Leaves. The Green Man.'

'Yeah, well, that was...' He drove off. '... unexpected.'

'You were still thinking about that corbel, round the back of the church. The man with his face scraped off.'

'Possibly.'

'Must've been like turning over the death card in the tarot.'

'It was the only thing tonight that wasn't set up. The rest of it was all so... theatrical. Choreographed. Nora setting it up for Darvill, letting him check us out, then he's taking us on his little quasi-pagan pilgrimage. We started as the audience and now we're part of the play.'

'It has immaculate symmetry.'

'What does *that* mean?'

'You and Mum.'

'Standing in for *two dead people*, Jane. Talk about turning over the death card...'

Jane sank back into the headrest.

'I didn't think of that.'

'What is he? What's he about? Why can't he just get on with his organic farming?'

'Because, for him, it's all connected. Organic. The land, the church, the morris, the green man... He's inspired. And... he's inspiring. I love the idea that Kilpeck Church is a picture book, a tarot, an oracle. That it can speak to anybody, at any time. I love what Darvill said about the hound and the rabbit – eight hundred years old and they're Disney, they're *now*. I like the

350

corbel with the two gay guys. I like the musician who looks not unlike a Roswell alien—'

'Maybe I'll just be him instead,' Lol said.

'He doesn't need a musician. He needs a Man of Leaves.'

'A name Darvill also invented. Or his dad did.'

'*All* the names are invented! It wasn't even known as the Green Man till 1939.'

'So becoming the Man of Leaves is a step into the unknown.'

'Are you OK, Lol?'

'Been a bit tired, that's all. Not sleeping too well since… what we did.'

'You did what you had to do. You couldn't really have got out of it. And it's over now.'

Jane looked back at the church as if one of its windows might offer a flicker of illumination. But the only light was in her phone.

'Oh my God,' she said.

Lara Brewer said, 'After the police had left, I just went out and walked. Up past the castle, around the footpaths. Felt like I was walking on another planet. I just didn't want to believe it. Still don't. Don't want to believe we're in some way responsible. That it's something we did. That it's all part of the same horror.'

Her voice was getting higher and faster. It had taken Merrily four attempts to get her on the phone.

'Burglary?' Lara said. 'I'm just not buying that. Something's happening here.'

'You said that to the police?'

'No. No, of course not. And I didn't mention you. Or Gareth. Certainly nothing about last night.'

'I'm afraid I had to,' Merrily said, 'or it would've looked suspicious. They were interviewing me with the Archdeacon there. They didn't get any names, but they know roughly what I was doing in the church, and they know it was at Julie's behest.'

'Are we all part of this?' Lara said. 'Are any of us safe?'

'If you'd feel safer if we told them more...'

'No!' Then she calmed down. 'No. I'm being silly. When you have young kids...'

'What did the police ask you?'

They asked why Julie rang me, I said she often rang. I said we were friends. Were we? I don't know. She was the rector. Everybody's friend. Clearly *not* everybody's.'

'How is Gareth? Really.'

'Bit disconnected. Merrily, look... this... I really would be glad if you could keep it to yourself. If it's brought Gareth some sleep, then I'm relieved. I just don't want to have to—' A sharp, snatched silence. 'Shit, what am I saying? It's your job.'

'You think I don't sometimes wonder if it's bollocks? We're only human. Crises of faith? I think my record is five in one day. And if you include the nights...'

'Oh, look, stop. I really did *not* mean to start this.'

'You tell yourself moments of doubt are important. Moments when you wonder if it isn't all psychological. Do ancient rituals in an old church make us feel spiritually secure for reasons entirely unconnected with religion? Or does that explain religion for the twenty-first century?'

'That's what you think?'

'No, that's stupid. If you ever reach the stage where you think you know what you're doing, you're probably on the cusp of screwing up. You have to feel – *know* – that you're not in control but you still have to give everything to it. That's faith, I suppose. Something like that.' Merrily sighed, head aching. 'See how eloquent I am?'

'You sound knackered.'

'Listen... I'm sorry if I seem to be suggesting that things don't happen. They do. You just stop questioning it after a while. Something happened to me in the church. Or I thought it did. Either way, I think I need to ask you about Aidan and cannabis. The guy you said you'd never seen with a spliff. How much dope was there really in his life?'

'Lol.' Jane's silhouette shook. 'I seem to have received a text.' She gazed at the lit screen for some time then snapped the phone shut. 'Eirion.'

'Really?'

'He's coming over to Hereford at the weekend. To see an old mate he was at the Cathedral School with. Do I want to meet for a drink at the Swan. Sunday.'

'Do you?'

She turned to Lol.

'Just assure me this is nothing to do with you. You haven't been talking to him?'

'No.'

He hadn't. If he was sounding defensive it was because he'd meant to call Eirion, suggest he get in touch with Jane. But he hadn't. He drove towards the sporadic lights of the modern village, Jane clutching his arm.

'What do I do?'

'You meet him. Don't you?'

'Not in the Swan. Too many people know me. A few of them even know *him*. You know what they're like. Some guys'll be like, *wooooooh*. I couldn't stand that.'

'So go somewhere else.'

'What if he brings his girlfriend?'

'Oh, *Jane...*'

'It's not exactly a love letter. Look...'

She reopened the phone, held up the lit screen. He sighed and pulled the truck into the side of the lane opposite the pub and read it.

No, it wasn't exactly a love letter.

'Jane, what do you expect? He's uncertain. He's sounding you out.'

He'd been her first. That was the problem, perhaps for both

of them. They'd been kids. What if there was so much more they'd never know if they stayed together?

'It's not what I need right now.'

'Might be exactly what you need.'

'You don't really think that,' Jane said.

53

Tingle

THEY DIDN'T MAKE it to the Swan. Clive's pies and mixed salad at the vicarage, in the end. Afterwards, left alone in the kitchen to wash the dishes – she usually found it relaxing – Merrily ended up searching the dresser drawers for the last packet of Silk Cut, dragging one out and lighting it.

Think...

Try to.

If you learned one thing from the night job, it was that spotting signposts, omens, portents – was rarely rewarding. There'd be times when everything appeared to be converging, when you could throw up your hands, say OK, *this* is what's required of me. This is *meant*.

And then you were proved wrong. Time and again, circumstance lied. Occasionally there would be genuinely startling coincidences, but what were they beyond tantalizing hints of some grand design that, if it existed at all, was grandly designed to be ineffable?

Maybe only blank atheism didn't give you sleepless nights.

She leaned back against the dresser, considered the options.

Two suggestions that she should lead a memorial service for Aidan Lloyd, coming almost simultaneously from two villages claiming parts of him. One was relatively straightforward, the other more complicated. One was about closure, the other...

She looked down at the smoking cigarette. It was Jane who'd once pointed out that experts reckoned cigarette addiction was harder to break than heroin. Trying to make her feel like a junkie.

Well, maybe. She took two puffs and then stubbed it out in disgust. She needed help. She picked up the vape stick and went back to the front parlour, where Lol was building a fire in the dog-grate. He'd brought in a basket of fuel from the log shelter: softwood kindling, small apple logs and a slab of oak for later. Taking his time, grounding himself. Lol didn't smoke, he built log fires.

He put a match to the newspaper bed in the grate and stood up, looking at Merrily then at Jane, down on the hearthrug with her laptop and Ethel. When Jane looked up, her eyes were sparkly.

'Got it.'

'Really?'

'It's so obvious when you know. Listen to this, Mum...' She took a long breath. *'Tetra...hydro... cannabinol.* Did I get that right?'

'I wouldn't know.'

Merrily came into the room and shut the door. Switched off the lamps so the only light was from the new flames in the hearth and sat down in the middle of the sofa.

'THC, right?' Jane said. 'One of the principal constituents of marijuana. THC has some of the same properties as the chemicals used in inhalers. Asthma causes airways to narrow, sometimes with fatal consequences. Cannabis contains THC which is known to *open up* the airways.'

'Even smoking it?'

'May not work for everybody, and doctors are reluctant to publicize it because of the obvious side effects – *and* the fact that it tends to involve smoking. Sooner or later it's going to have to be widely available on prescription.'

I know he's dead, Lara had said eventually, *but we were all asked to say nothing and none of us has. But if you think medicinal, it's all on the Net.*

'You're saying cannabis cured Aidan's asthma?'

'Maybe he'd've grown out of it anyway, but it does look like dope came at the right time.'

'And he was introduced to it by...?'

'Darvill,' Lol said. 'Darvill and weed make perfect sense, before and after his accident. Pain relief? And his dad, of course. Henry, who was at school with Nick Drake, sharing a spliff under the big stones at Avebury.'

Merrily lay back into the cushions and closed her eyes. Thought of Gareth Brewer walking out of Ledwardine Church into the star-spattery night. Out of the choking grave and into starlight, out of asthma into...

'So much makes sense,' Jane said. 'Aidan Lloyd was never a big user. Even an *ex*-asthmatic wouldn't push his luck. But cannabis *was* important in his life. Cannabis and Darvill. Darvill, the weed and the morris. And Kilpeck Church. And the Man of Leaves. It's making me tingle.'

More likely the source of the tingle was the text from Eirion, the nervous tension that would go on building until Sunday night. Please God, not an anticlimax.

Merrily opened her eyes.

'Why were so many people in the village saying he was a serious dopehead?'

'It's like somebody put that round,' Jane said. 'Why?'

'Aidan Lloyd. The ghost still hovering over us all. Can we think about this? This vague, undemonstrative guy, such a big presence now. So important that two families want church services held in his honour. What do they *really* want? Iestyn Lloyd wanted a quiet funeral and got one. What's changed?'

'Julie Duxbury,' Lol said, 'looks like the catalyst.'

'I'm ashamed. Julie took the trouble to pursue Iestyn. Did she get him? Did she invite him to Kilpeck? Would he want to go? No.'

Lol nodded.

'So with Julie gone he sees his chance to turn that around.

Sends his long-suffering stepson to set up a service in Ledwardine. Draw a line under it. *His* line.'

'Yes. That would fit. I didn't make any waves last time, did I? And Charlie Howe, perhaps soon to be the face of law and order in these parts, wants to do a eulogy, probably suggesting poor Aidan was a victim of inadequate policing in the sticks – you saw his campaigning stuff in the *Hereford Times*?'

'Maybe he won't want to come to Kilpeck,' Jane said, 'so that lets you off.'

'Oh, I think he will – if we *do* Kilpeck. And as you bring that up...' Merrily hunched forward, hands held out to the fire. 'Darvill. What's *that* about?'

'It's also about Julie Duxbury,' Lol said. 'She'd taken on the task of dealing with a long-standing situation which she felt was harmful. Get Lionel and Iestyn into a church together, let God take care of the rest.'

'But what does *Darvill* want?'

'He wants his Old Solstice ritual,' Jane said. 'In the magic church. It's important to him. The turning point of the year. And it's not been a good year. He lost his Man of Leaves. The guy whose asthma he seems to have cured. Aidan was important to him. Lol heard what he said at the church. Aidan told him what the Man of Leaves was.'

'And what *was* the Man of Leaves?'

'He wouldn't say. Yeah, I know... But it's clear that Aidan was very important to Darvill.'

'Is he pagan?'

'I think it's bigger than that,' Jane said. 'Kilpeck church is bigger than that. Am I wrong?'

'He's disabled,' Lol said. 'Half of him doesn't work. He doesn't have the same... distractions. Everything he cares about is there, and it's become – understandably – an obsession. I don't think it's about any particular religion, Jane's right about that. But there's a kind of spirituality at the core of it. And I think that comes out of whatever his dad was into. And the outward aspect of that is the morris.'

Jane said, 'I suppose...'

Merrily sighed.

'... doing the service at Kilpeck would also be a memorial for Julie,' Jane said. 'Wouldn't it? Finishing something she started.'

'And died for? Sorry.' Merrily shook her head. 'I'm tired. I'll be better tomorrow.'

54

Small favours

So THEY WERE back at the start. Rich Ford coming into Bliss's office telling him about these iffy quad bikes noticed at Jag's Motors. Bliss had done a lot of overnight thinking about this, trying out ideas on Annie. Could use another word with Rich but he was out at Ewyas Harold, office-managing for the Julie inquiry.

Bliss rang him anyway, soon as he was behind his desk at Gaol Street, Thursday morning.

'Always a lot of farm thefts,' Rich said. 'And the kit rarely gets recovered. As you know, all the ID on those quad bikes in the garage…'

'Seemed to have worn off, yeh.'

'I'm not sure what you're after here, Francis.'

'I'm looking for Jag's rural contact. A criminal. I'm not really thinking travellers, they've got their own networks. I'm thinking a thief who actually lives in the sticks. Maybe somebody doing contract work – felling trees, cutting hedges, mowing hay. Jobs that take him round the area.'

'Right. Got you. Somebody who knows where the nickable stuff is. Where the sheds get left open. Which farmers never miss a market day even when they're not doing business.'

'Where all you've gorra do is load your van.'

'How would one of them've got to know Jaglowski?'

'Wondered if you might have some ideas. And we're talking about a heavy-duty nasty person here – which Jag might not've realized at first. I realize office manager's not the best job for gerrin thinking time.'

'People are making wind-it-up gestures to me right now, Francis.'

'Tell 'em to piss off a minute. This might be relevant. I'm assuming you now know from Ma'am about the burning clown and the late-night call to Julie, from Jag.'

'Couldn't make it up, could you?'

'Somebody's been up there, I hope.'

'Oh, aye. It'll all be coming through any minute, I'll copy you in. But basically, yes, burn marks and a hole in the ground below Kilpeck Castle.'

'And that's the lot?'

'As it's unlikely everything was burnt to a crisp, it begins to look as if somebody quietly cleaned it all up. Even the burn marks weren't obvious at first. If they hadn't known what they were looking for they might well not've noticed. Which I find interesting.'

'I see.'

'Anyway, I really will have to go, Francis. Anything occurs to me, I'll come back to you.'

Bliss got Terry Stagg in. Been working with a terp in the Polish community for the past couple of days and not coming up with much.

'Can we have another go at Jag's mechanics, Tel?'

Staggie frowned; for some reason, he disliked being called Tel.

'They never came out of the garage, boss. He worked them hard, and he didn't tell them much.'

'Maybe not, but they were probably there when some of the farm kit was arriving. They'd know who brought it in, and then we follow it back.'

With an eye to the gun angle, they'd been soft-pedalling on the theft and fencing side. Rarely good to have people feeling threatened when you were after information about something more serious.

'All right,' Staggie said wearily – terp work could get wearing. 'What are we looking for in particular?'

Bliss told him about the man who'd done favours for Jaglowski.

'I know it seems unlikely, Jag having a strong contact in the sticks. Be interesting to know how that came about. See what you can get, anyway. Bearing in mind that Jag appears to've been shit-scared of this feller.'

'You talked to Karen? Good rural stock.'

'Yeh, that's why she's been sent out to Ewyas Harold again. Good point, though. Nobody knows more nasty countryfolk than Karen.'

'Even been out with a few,' Stagg said. 'So I'm told.'

It was the afternoon before he managed a decent chat with Karen, who at least picked up where he was coming from.

'Most of the links between migrant workers and farmers come through fruit picking, as you know, boss. The pickers, in general, tend to be loyal to particular farmers, go back year after year. They don't abuse the situation. I don't think Jag was ever a picker. He's urban.'

'Exactly. Urban criminals aren't comfortable in the country. Either that or they're a bit contemptuous of the hicks. What I'm thinking, Karen, after what we learned from Danni, is it starts with this feller tipping Jag off on where he can pick up bits of kit without too much difficulty. Jag thinks it's easy money and he's happy to repay small favours. Then the favours get bigger. Takes him a while to realize what kind of bloke he's dealing with – this is all pure conjecture, me flying friggin' kites again.'

'Sure.'

'I'll continue, however. By then Jag's in too deep. Then he gets invited to take somebody out.'

'Aidan Lloyd? Why?'

'No idea. But he subcontracts the job to Lukas Babekis who – conjecture again – is known to have done this kind of thing

362

before. Either under his real name or another alias, this lad's wanted for something nasty. Either in his own country or another country.'

'Babekis is an international contract-killer? Boss, this is getting a bit—'

'That's far too glamorous terminology. I prefer to think of him as a little toe rag known to be up for anything at the right price. Still a bit of a performer, mind. "Oh God, I'm so sorry, I'm just an ignorant foreigner who doesn't know the roads. Never gonna be able to live with meself for this."'

He heard Karen sigh.

'This is really not going to be easy to stand up, boss. It largely depends on spending money and manpower to track down a foreigner who was likely to have got off a charge of – what? – causing death by dangerous driving, at the most? For more than that we'd have to explain exactly how he calculated when to lie in wait for Lloyd to knock him over as he came out of a particular gate. Did he always come out of the same gate?'

'Apparently, he *did*, but it may not be as calculated as you're suggesting. If Babekis was hired to dispose of Lloyd, in whatever way he sees fit, knowing that Jag's going to deny all knowledge of it if he screws up, he might just've seen his target coming out of the field from quite a long distance... and then, instead of just gently slowing to give the lad a chance to get across, he decides it's his birthday and it's foot-down. I don't *know*. We may *never* know. Right now, that doesn't matter.'

'All right. I'll try and find somebody reliable who knows the Lloyd family, if that's what you're after.'

'And bear in mind – while working your little socks off on what's now become a far more significant murder – the burning incident. What Julie might've done when she came out that night to get her killed.'

'Days later? Could be we're getting a bit too excited, boss. Might just be another one of those small-county situations.'

'It might.'

Bliss's brain was starting to hurt. He wished he was out there hunting the killer of somebody he could care about instead of bloody Jag.

But, then, it wasn't just about Jag.

He was going to have to talk to Annie again tonight.

Seriously.

55

Awakening

THE SITE WAS called ANNALS OF THE DANCE, its home page decorated with line drawings of men in tights with feathers in their hats. One had a side drum, another played a flute. Merrie England type men, and women frolicking behind them in a circle.

All the fun was in the illustrations. Otherwise, it was all dense, tightly printed webpages which Merrily had landed on purely by Googling

SIR HENRY DARVILL, MORRIS DANCING

Sooner rather than later, she'd have to talk to somebody, probably the police, but she'd need to know exactly what she was talking about.

So little time, now. *Yes*, the Archdeacon had said firmly on the phone. *Yes, if it gets this eccentric man off your back, please do it. We'll be having a Julie-tribute at the Cathedral but not yet. Something local, meanwhile, would be not inappropriate, and I'm not aware that the Church has ever persecuted morris dancers.*

No, it didn't seem to have. Even in times when elderly herbalists and their black cats had been treated with ferocious barbarism, morris men had danced unchallenged.

Thursday morning. The weather forecasts had mentioned the possibility of snow. She'd taken a paracetamol for the headache and sat down here in the scullery with a pot of tea. Willing the phone to stay out of it, she'd written down on the sermon pad everything she could remember of what

Gareth Brewer had told her in the church the night before last. Writing things down, by hand, with an old fountain pen, took time but it positioned your thoughts, allowing the memories to fall through.

Sir Henry Darvill and his *severe depressions. On medication – against his religion, we thought, all that stuff.*

What *was* his religion? What had he bequeathed to his son?

Sir Henry was on this specialist site purely because of his role in the development of morris dancing which, it seemed, he'd given tutorials on rather than written about. There was a picture of him sitting on a wall. Shoulder-length hair and a droopy moustache.

Darvill's interest in the morris was first awakened at the College for Perpetual Learning, near Pershore in Worcestershire, an institution at which he studied for two years while also supporting it financially. The college had adopted a morris tradition which had begun in the 1970s at the former Academy for Continuous Education at Sherborne, Dorset, as a relaxing sideline to its major work on realizing human potential.

Intriguing connections had been found between the morris and dervish dances – part of the Sufi traditions studied at both these centres. This was around the time when the idea of the word 'morris' deriving from *Moorish* (referring to the medieval Islamic inhabitants of North Africa) had begun to be discredited. Henry Darvill, however, found the Moorish connection not only acceptable but necessary as a doorway for anyone wishing to penetrate the secrets of the dance as he was beginning to understand them.

Merrily Googled the College for Perpetual Learning, Pershore, and found very little of use. But the Academy for Continuous Education, Sherborne, was more illuminating. There was a photograph of some huge mansion with the suggestion that whatever had taken place there had ceased in 1974.

Continuous Education – it didn't sound very sexy. It didn't sound like a cult, but when she went into the pages of photographs she found men and women dressed in white judo-type kit engaged in what looked like formation dances, described only as *movements*. She saw people with their arms outstretched as if in praise, a man with one hand placed on his chest, the other arm making a right angle.

There were mentions of the study of the teachings of Gurdjieff. You didn't go through even theological college these days without picking up odd references to the Armenian spiritual teacher – bald head, big moustache – who set up study groups in western Europe over the first half of the twentieth century. Like most twentieth-century mystics, he'd explored the wisdom of the ancient worlds, in his case mainly Sufism, the esoteric side of Islam.

Gurdjieff's main premise: we exist in a state of sleep. Awakening was far from easy and required a lot of diligent work and some 'conscious suffering'.

Awakening meant existing on a higher level of consciousness than our normal somnambulistic state.

If only…

The *movements*? She looked up dervishes, *whirling* themselves into ecstatic trance-states to find illumination, reach God. No obvious whirling in morris. Perhaps it was linked more to the earth.

She'd heard there was a Gurdjieff group in Hereford, but making meaningful contact with these people could take time, and she didn't have that.

But she did know a Sufi.

Oh God…

Above the churchyard wall the sun was already giving up its token resistance to the tightening day. She had to keep going. Nobody else would investigate this. Nobody would see anything here worth investigating.

The shadows spread. Ethel appeared in the darkening

doorway, just sat there and mewed. This would be about food, rather than a reminder of the Sufi fondness for cats.

Oh well...

Merrily picked up the phone. Raji Khan's secretary said he was in a meeting and took a message. What kind of meetings did nightclub owners and suspected drug dealers attend in the middle of the morning? Never mind, move on.

She rang Churchwood Farm to talk about the need to switch the venue for Aidan's memorial service, to include Julie, and got a woman who said that Mr Lloyd was unavailable. She pushed.

'Is Mr Lloyd unwell?'

'Absolutely not,' the woman said sharply. 'Someone will get back to you.'

'It doesn't matter.'

Wasn't as if they'd agreed a date for an Aidan service. She'd try an approach from the other side.

The clouds glowered, then an irritable rain spattered the scullery window. She pulled open the bottom desk drawer, uncovering a stack of funeral leaflets. Aidan Lloyd's Order of Service was on the top. Brief details inside: parents Iestyn Lloyd and Sarah... *Baxter.* She pulled out the local phone book, working her way through the Baxters. *Is Sarah there? Could I speak to Sarah?* And then...

'Is that Sarah?'

'Yes, it is. Who's that?'

'Sarah... formerly Sarah Lloyd?'

'Who *is* that?'

'Erm, my name's Merrily Watkins. I conducted Aidan's funeral. At Ledwardine.'

'Yes. You did.'

Despite what they said, there actually was such a thing as a cold, clipped Hereford accent.

'Wasn't proud of it, Mrs Baxter.'

'I shouldn't have imagined pride comes into it for a minister conducting a funeral.'

'Well… I thought it was a bit perfunctory and didn't do what a funeral is supposed to do. Which is why—'

'It got him buried.'

And that was *enough*? What kind of family *was* this?

Ex-family, now. She remembered Sarah in church, bare-headed, severe, on the opposite side of the aisle to Iestyn Lloyd.

'Your son… Liam… on behalf of your ex-husband… has asked me to hold a memorial service to perhaps say some of the things that… perhaps ought to have been said at the funeral.'

'And did he say *what* things?'

'Liam didn't tell you about this?'

'I haven't seen him this week. Anyway, you've told me now, and I won't be coming. I've seen enough of Ledwardine.'

'Erm… It now looks like it may not be held at Ledwardine. We're thinking Kilpeck.'

A pause.

'Iestyn wants you to do it *there*?'

'Well, it *was* to have been conducted by the rector of Ewyas Harold who… died yesterday. Kilpeck was one of her churches and I believe it was her idea. Not sure if she spoke to you about it, but I believe she did try to see Aidan's father.'

'And he agreed to that?'

'I don't know, Mrs Baxter, I haven't been able to speak to him.'

'I very much doubt he did, Mrs Watkins.'

'I did try to speak to him, and I'll continue to try. I'd like this to be a proper tribute to Aidan.'

'I've changed my mind,' Mrs Baxter said. 'If it's at Kilpeck, I may well be there.'

'Oh.'

'When will it be?'

'Probably on Monday.'

'So soon?'

'If it's to be done before Christmas. As you probably know, a memorial service is more than a funeral, so I'll be expected to say quite a lot about Aidan. Various people have told me different things.'

'I'm sure they have.'

'Don't want to put my foot in it. Easily done.'

'Yes, and if you want to know the truth about my boy, then I'll tell you. But not over the phone.'

According to the phone book, she lived in suburban Kingsacre, out on the road pointing at Wales. And Ledwardine, for that matter.

'I can be there in under half an hour. If the traffic's kind.'

'No... come tomorrow,' Mrs Baxter said. 'I'll call you. I need time to control my anger.'

Blimey.

With the black Bakelite phone back at rest, Merrily sat looking across the room through the window at the glistening lichened wall between the vicarage and the churchyard where Aidan Lloyd lay when he wasn't being exhumed. She shuddered, picking up the phone to call Lol and ask him to turn his computer on so she could send him ANNALS OF THE DANCE, and almost cried out when the shudder seemed to transfer itself to the phone and she found she was connected before it could ring.

'Mrs Watkins.'

'Mr Khan.' She found her breath. 'Erm... some things I wanted to consult you about, if you had time.'

'I'm quite busy today,' Raji Khan said, 'but it's always delightful to talk to you and I could call you back later. Perhaps you could convey in a few words the nature of your enquiry..?'

'I'll try. Sufism... Gurdjieff... morris-dancing...'

'Interesting.'

'And the Darvills of Kilpeck.'

'I can be with you in approximately thirty-five minutes,' Mr Khan said.

56

Intentional suffering

OF ALL THE seriously iffy characters she'd encountered in Hereford, he remained, strangely, the most civilized. Barely twenty-five minutes had passed before he was at the front door, in his grey, faux-Edwardian overcoat with the vicuna collar. She hung it carefully in the hall, wondering if he realized that, in winter at least, he resembled everyone's idea of an old-fashioned drug baron.

'When the radio news headlines included something about the murder of a woman parish priest in Herefordshire,' he said, 'my heart almost stopped. So you see you already were very much in my thoughts today.'

The kettle was already nearing the boil. She made a pot of Earl Grey, sat it on the refectory table between them.

'But to address your original questions...' Raji Khan stretching his elegant feline frame into the cane chair. 'Yes, I have indeed heard of Sir Henry Darvill and the College for Perpetual Learning. Indeed, if I'd known of it while it still existed, I might even have been amongst its alumni. Where, after all, are any of us if we lose touch with education?'

'The college,' Merrily said. 'I mean, it wasn't woodwork lessons, was it?'

'Nothing so intellectually stimulating.' Mr Khan, Cambridge educated, looked amused. 'At Gurdjieff's schools, the wealthy, the famous and the high-born might be instructed to clean the toilets, dig trenches, saw logs, whatever... and *do it consciously.* "Stop!" the dear old fellow would roar, and the pupils would freeze in mid-task and... *remember themselves*. Moments of consciousness.'

'Before the age of the bandsaw, then.'

'Oh, I doubt the odd severed thumb would have altered his methodology.' Mr Khan beamed. 'Gurdjieff was virtually unique in his translation of various Eastern and Middle-Eastern methods of self-development into a language accessible to the Western world... to those willing to work hard and make personal sacrifices. A path to higher levels of *being* in the context of everyday, seemingly mundane life, through conscious labour and intentional suffering. No one said it was going to be fun.'

'And this kind of thing went on at Pershore?'

'For some years. A spin-off from the former Academy for Continuous Education founded by Gurdjieff's disciple, the late J.G. Bennett, in Sherborne. Where morris dancing was first adopted as a kind of recreational light relief – until a few people realized they'd stumbled on something quite significant.'

The Pershore college, it seemed, had closed within two years of Sir Henry's departure. The costs of maintaining the building alone must have been prohibitive. He'd invested in it a good proportion of the money left to him by his father – the first son had the farm, the second a lump sum. But then, to his sorrow, Sir Henry had wound up getting the farm after all and was forced to leave his beloved college.

'And, erm... you know all this how? Do you mind me asking?'

'Through his son. Lionel.'

'You get around, don't you, Mr Khan?'

'Lionel spent his early years in Pershore,' Mr Khan said, 'and was therefore exposed to his parents'... diversions.'

'Both parents? His mother was involved in all this, too?'

'Until she ran off with one of the other students. All part of college life, Mrs Watkins. When one experiences true aware-ness of self, it can be extremely powerful and effect all kinds of personal changes. There are... casualties.'

'So Henry and his son came back to Kilpeck on their own.'

'I'm told that when Henry took over the estate after his brother's death he went into it with an air of Gurdjieffian *intentional suffering*. Changing the estate into something perhaps less profitable but more spiritually rewarding. But he himself... was not destined to get much of a reward.'

Merrily wondered how Mr Khan had come to know Sir Lionel, who must be at least a decade older. He watched her firing up the vape stick.

'When you asked me about Sufism, I wondered if you were interested for personal reasons?'

'A convert? Me?'

'It's not so absurd. I've met several Christians who've studied Sufism in a practical sense without necessarily abandoning their faith. It's about working on yourself. There's much to be learned.'

'It's Islamic.'

'Older, actually, but we did come together, for protection, so it's now considered a part of Islam. Even if the Sunnis and the Shias tend to hate us with an equal passion, but let's not dwell on that.'

As she understood it, Sufism was the only aspect of Islam which regarded music as sacred rather than abhorrent and might therefore tolerate Mr Khan's nightclubs. As for his less public earner... well who knew for sure, or would, until such time as Frannie Bliss fulfilled his career-long ambition of putting him before a Crown Court.

Raji Khan sipped his tea.

'There comes a time when even the most committed student stops regarding suffering as an incentive. We are all human, Mrs Watkins. The conversion to organic farming was time consuming and costly. Sir Henry had been forced to sell off property to avoid a potentially even more costly industrial tribunal – which might have gone against him even though it was his land to do with as he pleased.'

'Why didn't he contest it?'

'I think he was simply tired. He'd reached the point where he was no longer able to see it all as a spiritual exercise. His will was broken, his wife was not coming back – perhaps she also wanted money from him. His mental collapse... was it suicide...?'

'Oh my God.'

'... or an accidental overdose of antidepressants? Did it matter. Lionel was nineteen years old, a student at Magdalen College, Oxford. Not a very distinguished student, he says now, but still rather hoping that his father would have married again and had another son to take over the estate and allow him to get away. But then... no father.'

'He could've sold the estate, I suppose.'

'After centuries? A man of Norman ancestry finding himself the recipient of a title and all it represented? Couldn't very well walk away from that. Knew he'd have to face it sometime – although there *was* a period of what you might call drink-sodden procrastination. With unfortunate consequences.'

Mr Khan accepted more Earl Grey, in no hurry.

'He was young. He'd barely lived. He'd watched his father following obsessions that backfired on him. Long hours in the pub, I'm afraid. Pursuit of women. Until his accident. Have you met Lionel?'

'No.'

Mr Khan drew in air through his small, white teeth, let it out thinly.

'Let me try to explain. I've known him for some years – my only titled friend – and most of what he does is admirable. A man directing a large, diverse organic farming enterprise from a wheelchair. A handful of faithful employees and co-workers, including what one might call a Girl Friday, who I like to see as perhaps more than that. On the practical side, he keeps a selection of extraordinary all-terrain wheelchairs and adapted vehicles with hand controls. And receives a good deal of assistance from his morris... team?'

'Side. So the morris...?'

'Is a largely vicarious pastime. I believe he occasionally allows himself to be brought into the dance, physically supported by the others, which I suppose— Are you all right, Mrs Watkins?'

'Somebody walking over my grave. Can we deal with this? Can you tell me what you think is different about the Kilpeck Morris and how this relates to what happened at the college? We're talking about dancing which is... a path to something else?' She saw him hesitate. 'You need to know why I'm asking you about all this.'

Mr Khan smiled.

'All dancing is a path to something else. Ballroom dancing was a courtship ritual. As for the frenetic, narcotic movements experienced at the raves I organized in my youth, I doubt you'll need that explained.'

'On the Net, I found some pictures of white-clad people clearly involved in some kind of circle dance.'

'The movements.'

'Something dervish-linked?'

'Only to an extent. Gurdjieff's movements were about disconnecting what you might call our normal circuits, so that – for example – one's arms and legs would perform different actions simultaneously. This requires considerable practice. Its benefits are not mere physical fitness.'

'And they corresponded to aspects of the morris.'

'To an extent. There were traces of it. Suggestions that the original morris dancers – and we're talking many centuries ago, if not millennia – were, shall we say, a priestly, even monastic order. That the morris was indeed a *sacred* dance. Shamanic, perhaps, in that the dancers might receive... I don't know... messages from other realms. I do know that what began at the Sherborne Academy as a diversion turned, at the College for Perpetual Learning, into a serious study. When Henry Darvill left and the college closed, he invited some of his fellow students to come to his home, Maryfields, and continue the work. And thus a new tradition was born. Most of those chaps have since moved on.'

'But Lionel...'

'Henry tried to bring his son into it, yes. Lionel... he'll tell you he was too young. Didn't realize how important it was to his father that he should continue the tradition. He'll tell you now that his disinterest could only have contributed to Henry's decline into depression. By the time Henry died, the Kilpeck Morris had disintegrated into little more than a boozy pub ensemble. It was only *after* his accident that Lionel became committed to his father's values. Obsessively so.'

'And the church?'

Mr Khan smiled his cat's smile.

'I know,' Merrily said, 'that he fell from the church roof.'

'Yes.'

'He seems to have seen a connection,' Merrily said, 'between images on the church... and the morris. The Kilpeck Morris, anyway.'

'Perhaps he's made those connection himself. I don't know. I suspect there was a time when he almost hated the church. As if it represented something that was dragging the male members of his family back to the village to – if I may be excused an element of melodrama here – their doom.'

'You can understand that. Almost like a curse.'

'Mrs Watkins, let me say something... apart from being my only titled friend, he's a decent man. But I'm not sure he knows what he's doing. He isn't following Gurdjieff's system, Sufism or any other teaching. He seems to be following his own instincts, and that... that may not necessarily be a good thing. I would not go so far as to suggest he has a death wish, but... I think he could use some advice.'

'He doesn't strike me as a man who'd be easy to advise.'

'It would be a challenge, certainly.'

'You're looking at me?'

'You telephoned me, I responded.'

'I only rang you for some background information because I couldn't think of anyone else. I didn't expect you to *know* Darvill personally.'

'Small county, Mrs Watkins.'

She nodded, automatically pouring him more tea.

'His fall…'

'I doubt it was simply a fall.'

'He's told you—?'

'He hasn't told me anything. And I'm a friend and also a spiritual sympathizer. And he still hasn't told me.' Raji Khan spread his hands in sorrow. 'Intentional suffering, Mrs Watkins. Intentional suffering.'

57

The fool

LATE AFTERNOON. LOL ran across the forecourt through the last light and the half-frozen rain, to the half-open front door. Nora Mills, waiting for him under the great beam, wore a clinical white coat and a sombre expression that seemed to be saying she hoped he knew what he was doing.

At least she wasn't carrying a shotgun.

'You're early.'

'Is that bad?'

He'd awoken early again, feeling dizzy when he was out of bed, the winter song rumbling in his head; he didn't like it now, wished he'd never started it. No time to go to the doc's, even if he could get an appointment. He'd just sat down at the desk and scribbled a couple of new lines: *the wind is prowling in the east, to raise the devil, scorn the priest.*

The scuffed interior door swung open before him to the ashy logs in the hearth and Kilpeck Church, in Tom Keating's painting, blossoming like a clump of bright poppies. Nora didn't follow him in. Sir Lionel Darvill looked up over reading glasses.

'You're early.'

'I'll go for a walk and come back if you like.'

'You're on your own?'

'People were beginning to talk.'

'Not the girl, Robinson.' Testily. 'Her mother.'

'She'll be here on Monday. She needs to square it with the Archdeacon. And it's a very busy time of year for a vicar.'

'And she thinks I'll interfere with her service.'

'You mean you don't have form for that?'

Darvill snorted.

'It's not her church.'

Wasn't his either, except in his head. The church, the remains of the castle, the disappeared village: all part of the extended Maryfields, the Maryfields of his mind.

'You didn't arrive early by accident,' he said. 'What do you want to know? And *sit down*.'

'Thank you.'

Enclosed in the Chesterfield, knowing he had to get this right, Lol struggled to collect his thoughts. He'd spent most of the morning dredging what he could about the green man from the Net and Jane's bookshelves. He'd read about the fool who danced with the morris men and sometimes *against* them. In the morris world, the Man of Leaves was the fool, who thought he was the king and could, for a moment in the dance, *be* the king. He'd get to that, but first...

'Aidan Lloyd. You had him exhumed.'

Unloaded. He leaned back.

Darvill didn't react at all.

'You put the Border morris kit on his body,' Lol said, 'and the green mask over his face.'

Darvill's eyelids lowered for a moment, tightened. Then he relaxed.

'Of course. Brewer told Merrily Watkins that nonsense. In the so-called sanctity of his deliverance.'

'I don't know. I wasn't there. He didn't need to, anyway. She and Jane saw something happening in the churchyard, and the next day it was obvious someone had tampered with the grave. So we – that's me and a very trustworthy friend – we dug it up again. At night.'

Darvill's upper body lengthened in the chair, his head rising.

'*Did* you now?'

'I'm afraid we did.'

'Not being deliberately insulting here, Robinson, but I wouldn't have thought you were capable of that.'

Lol shrugged.

'Can't say you're a real man till you've stared death in the face. By lamplight. With a shovel in your hand.'

Darvill leaned forward.

'Prove it to me.'

'How?'

'Tell me what you found.'

'Yes. OK.' Lol's hands were clasped, shaking. 'It looked like they couldn't get him back into the coffin... with the bells around his legs. So they put the bells on top, loose. The bells... rattled... jingled, when we took the lid off. The mask... that was also loose. It had holly and mistletoe. From your orchard? And yew, I think. Yew from Kilpeck churchyard?'

'Yew for immortality.'

'Of course.'

'All right,' Darvill said. 'I believe you.' He looked suddenly happy. 'How did you feel?'

'Sick. It was awful. The worst thing I've ever done.'

'The final taboo.'

'Probably.'

'The darkest part of a rite of passage.'

'Don't...' Lol pulled back into the leather sofa. 'Don't tell me that, Lionel.'

'You said it yourself. "Can't say you're a real man..."'

'That was a joke. That was me trying to make light of it.'

'Make *light*.' Darvill's eyes sparkling. 'Yes. I bet you did. I bet you can remember every moment of it. Vividly.'

'More or less. Going to haunt me for a long time.'

'Shocked into consciousness.'

'I have dreams I can't remember, and I don't feel good when I wake up.'

'It isn't easy.'

'Oh, for—'

'No wonder it didn't work for poor Brewer.' Darvill was excited. 'No wonder he was fucked up and had to be unfucked. Wasn't meant for *him*. Such a balanced man. Admirable guy, grounded, normal – wife, kids, steady income from doing something always going to be needed in the countryside. No need of a wooden mask. Not enough of—'

'No. Do *not*—'

'What?'

'Don't say it. Not enough of a misfit. Insufficiently deranged. Like Aidan Lloyd.'

'The Man of Leaves is an archetype. He was the making of Aidan.'

'No.' Lol gripped the deep arm of the Chesterfield, his last attempt to reach for reality. '*You* were the making of Aidan. You cured his asthma. You introduced him to cannabis. You broke him through to something. The Man of Leaves was just—'

'Enough. Don't dare try to talk yourself out of this.' Darvill spun his chair round, rolled towards the door which opened for him. 'It's time.'

He never seemed to change. The short, stiff white hair, the suntan that lasted all winter, the face that was creased but always smiley. Like a poster-boy American GI from the 1950s, but his accent wasn't that far west of Hereford.

'Now, Merrily, if I'm intruding on something, you just tell me, girl. Kick me off the premises. It's just I was passing, and I thought, I surely oughta talk to Merrily about this, it'd be only polite, look, but if this en't convenient—'

'No, it— Come in, Charlie. Kettle's on.'

But he was already in. Behind him, night had fallen. He'd arrived within a few minutes of Raji Khan driving away, as if he'd been waiting. Thank God he hadn't recognized the car with its personalized registration, SUF 1. If he didn't already know, he wouldn't have picked up on that anyway.

'Coffee for me, Merrily. Splash of milk, two sugars. Gotta

keep the energy levels up, else folks'll be thinking the ole boy's on the slide.'

'Not me, Charlie.'

He followed her from the hall into the kitchen, holding the door open over her shoulder. The only thing about Charlie Howe that creaked was his latest cream leather jacket. His current girlfriend was rumoured to be similar in age to his daughter, Annie, in whom he'd always declared a fierce pride: youngest head of CID in the history of Hereford policing.

Merrily heard a door closing at the bottom of the kitchen: Jane slipping away into the inner hall and up the back stairs to her apartment. Jane had a low bullshit threshold these days.

'About this poor boy, Aidan Lloyd, it is, Merrily.'

'Wondered if it might be.'

'Excellent idea of yours, to hold a memorial service.'

'Erm...'

'These things slip by, look. That's the way of it in the country. Don't make waves. Country folks tend to accept fate like a slap in the face, turn the other cheek.'

'But they don't forget.'

'True. But what they didn't know in the first place they en't had a chance to forget. And in the country there's always things as don't get known about.'

'Well, yes...'

'I was a copper nigh on forty years, and it never ceased to... to *interest* me... how really quite serious crimes happened in quiet places and nobody knew – or, if they did, they let them go by, on account of it wasn't neighbourly to make waves.'

'So I'm told.'

Seemed a little disingenuous this, coming from Charlie, rumoured to have turned his head away from one or two quite sickening crimes. She plugged in the percolator.

'Charlie, is there by any chance something I don't know about Aidan's death and you do?'

'Well now, Merrily...' He lounged in the cane chair, hands

behind his head, relaxed, more than a little smug. 'A few people do have ideas about how that boy died.'

'Like riding a quad bike under the influence of drugs? I've heard that. But I'm coming to the conclusion that it's probably not true. He used cannabis, but words like *stoner* could be a serious exaggeration. Gossip, eh?'

'Gossip's a useful tool,' Charlie said, 'to some folks.'

'You plant the same idea in different places and then two people who've heard it from different sources meet, and suddenly it's fact?'

'Exactly. Thank you, Merrily, I wondered what you might think of that. Likely we're on the same side, then.'

'I'm not sure which side you're talking about. What I'm just a *bit* worried about is you using Aidan's memorial service as a platform for your… I don't like to say political ambitions because I realize you've always aspired to nothing more than having the people of West Mercia sleeping safely in their beds, but…'

She registered that Charlie Howe was no longer smiling and stopped.

'Things as didn't get known about,' he said, 'well, that was normal. Country folk took care of their own problems. What you didn't know about, you didn't worry about. But when it all gets polluted from outside…'

'I'm also a bit worried about what you might want to say about migrants, like the guy who hit Aidan?'

'An illegal. Paid to get hisself smuggled in. Deeply repentant. Don't get me wrong, Merrily, I'm all for migrant workers. They're hard working, cheerful and cheap, and how else would we get the fruit picked? No, there won't be any racist remarks from me. Not in my *political* interests, is it?'

'I suppose not. Did you know Aidan?'

'I know the family. In fact I've just today been talking to his mother. Her second husband serves with me on the council. Archie Baxter. Wrong party, mind, but I wouldn't hold that against him.'

She was guessing that the official line would be the vicar of Ledwardine inviting County Councillor Howe to deliver his eulogy as a friend of the family. A low annoyance began muttering inside her like an idling motor. But, like an idling motor, it wouldn't be taking her anywhere tonight.

'So this eulogy, Charlie...'

'A eulogy for all the victims of poor policing in rural areas. A promise of better.'

'If you're elected.'

'When I'm elected, yes.'

They were on him as soon as he was in there. No introductions, no preamble, no examples. Within a couple of minutes, he was in the black and white rag jacket, the line of bells buckled onto his calves and his face was wet with what smelled like sharp cider before the burnt cork was applied, and they gave him a stick, thick as a broom handle, shorter than a baseball bat – *Sally, this is – willow. Don't hold back* – as the musicians started up and they were dancing and he was dancing.

He felt a small pulse of fear, expanding into awe, when he took in the vastness of the barn, a cathedral barn, hard earth floor with scatters of straw and huge timbers lofted into shadows beyond the hanging lights, the whole place resounding with squeeze box, fiddle and drum played by two men and a woman, so that he could dance with the men who'd danced with the dead.

He was aware of Darvill directing the dance from his chair under the glassed-in barn bay, his voice raw border now.

'*Back-step, swing-step, heel-and-toe...*'

Nothing complicated. Two rows of four, an alley of dancers. For today, he was part of the side. He didn't recognize the dance, only the tune, from somewhere in his past, but it got under your feet fast enough and the dance seemed slower than the music. He was getting it all wrong but it didn't seem to matter; he was moving, his legs were moving the way they had all those years ago, only it didn't seem like years, it seemed like he'd never stopped. *Basics are everything,* Darvill had said. *Start to analyse and it'll go away.*

After a while – this was disconcerting – it felt like his natural state was to be in the air and his feet had to find the ground,

'... *and turn... two taps... strike!*'

At the first clash of sticks, he was shocked by the violence of the impact, vibration up both arms as he took in a black face, the gash of a grin.

'You'll be all right, mate. We'll see you don't get any fingers smashed.'

His name was Alec. He was a racehorse trainer. There was also George the carpenter and Jed the cheesemaker. There was a cider maker and Darvill's farm manager and a shepherd and Bob Rumsey, the academic who'd got into a morris-fuelled fight outside the pub. Bob had a grey beard of the size you only found on veteran imams and members of ZZ Top.

They were having a break. There was cider you didn't have to put on your face for the burnt cork. Eight men with black faces and top hats.

'You better have a hat,' Bob Rumsey said, 'though you won't need one on the night. Just the mask, and you don't get that till you're ready.'

And then he was pushed behind a bale-wall and out through a small door into darkness, the smell of hay and manure and the sounds of shifting cattle.

'Looks like we couldn't find a hat after all,' Bob Rumsey said.

Then there was another voice, kept low.

'Garry Brewer, this is, Lol.'

'Oh, right. So you're not...'

'Not dancing. I'll be back in the side, I will, when they put the mask on you. Just felt I oughter have a word, see, after what Mrs Watkins done.'

'Right.'

'Don't take this as a warning, more a cautionary word, and

386

don't you say nothing out there. Thing is, Lionel, his heart's in the right place, but he's busking it, you know what I'm saying? His dad, it come out of knowledge and experience. Li, it's out of a chair and a sense of time running short and mabbe some guilt and regret.'

'Over what?'

'If I really knew, boy, I'd tell you. I'm just saying don't see him as any kind of guru, that's all. And remember that when they puts the mask on you – and they won't do that till the night – it can be a bit of shock to the system.'

'In what way?'

'Look... I grew up, like most of the village boys, rejecting all this. It was offensive. Superstition. Like we were yokels. All the customs that gets brought back, it's always some buggers from Off, thinks they knows more about it than you do.'

'Darvill's not from Off.'

Sound of a breath expelled.

'Lol, I... I dunno how to put this, but fellers like Lionel, they're allus gonner be from Off. Listen, you better go back in, else he'll be after you. Go on. You en't got that much to worry about.' Brewer patted him on the shoulder. 'At least you din't dig nobody up.'

58

The man he was

'I HAD A male child already,' Sarah Baxter said on Friday after-noon. 'Job done.'

A severely modern fitted kitchen, with all the works hidden behind white wood, only dials visible. White tiles underfoot, white light from the walls and white-haired Sarah Baxter – Sarah Lloyd as was and Sarah Hurst before that – wraith-like at a white worktop.

Not a farmhouse kitchen, essentially.

'He'd been grooming Liam for the farm from a ridiculously early age. Had him shooting crows by the age of eight, which I didn't approve of. And I was pregnant. Unexpectedly. And had refused to do away with it.'

'Iestyn wanted you to?'

'He already had a boy. Most people, they marry someone with a child, they have to have another of their own. Iestyn, he'd acquired a good strong boy without all the nappies and the teething. And I was there already, handling the office work. That was how he saw it.'

'A practical man.'

'I'm not sure that's the word for it. When Aidan turned out to be a sickly child, with the asthma, you'd've thought it was all my fault.'

'And when he got rid of the asthma...?'

'Oh, yes, altogether different then. He suddenly remembered which of them was his son. I was glad for Liam at least. He liked the countryside but he never much liked the idea of being manacled to a farm and being Iestyn's unpaid skivvy. It amuses me that Liam works for DEFRA now, good, well-paid job with a pension. Inspecting farms, making judgements on Single Payments, and Iestyn Lloyd has to be polite to him.'

'I talked to Liam,' Merrily said. 'He wasn't optimistic about a future for farming. Also saw it as a destroyer of lives.'

Sarah brought two coffees in long china cups to the white-wood table, sat down opposite Merrily. She wore a jersey top and jogging pants. Must be approaching seventy, and very spry and fit and contented in her clinical kitchen.

'What would you expect? He knew what Iestyn was like – you're not doing *this* right, you oughter be doing *that*. No, he never wanted that. He likes the country life, but he likes his freedom, too, and his foreign holidays. Goes abroad a lot – to Africa and places like that. He has an interest in wildlife. Not many farmers get holidays of any kind. A few because they love farm-life too much, Iestyn because he wouldn't trust anyone else to manage it. A slave driver, and he was driving himself just as hard. It's what broke us up in the end.'

'All work, no free time?'

'That's how it was. Even on the farm, Liam'd always rather be out shooting rabbits than raising sheep. So Iestyn was stuck with two boys, one too sick for years to work on the farm, the other healthy enough, but didn't want to do it. Quite funny, really. I'm so glad to be out of all that.'

Her new husband ran a reclamation business: architectural salvage, the sort of rubbish Sarah said she wouldn't have in her house but, thankfully, some people did. Archie was at a meeting with colleagues on It's Our County, the local party set up by people who didn't like the way the council's ruling Conservatives were failing to conserve.

'Iestyn… I suppose I was flattered at first. Good job, a good income. And a good-looking man. He'd always had girlfriends and not always one at a time. And I was part of the business – a small part but important at the time.'

'You did all the paperwork.'

'Still do, only for other farmers. There'll always be some as don't want to know about VAT and form-filling. And so much better when you don't have to live with one.' Oddly, in this blanched environment her voice was warmer, more flexible than it had sounded on the phone. 'Now. Why isn't my son being left to lie in peace?'

Pale blue eyes unmoving. Eyes that looked all-cried-out. Merrily momentarily jolted.

He wasn't *normal*, Sarah always knew that. Liam had been normal – played football, did his share of underage drinking, one of the boys – whereas Aidan was awkward, didn't even try to fit in, and the asthma didn't help. In and out of the doctor's surgery for that. And all those funny phobias, and making up stories.

'I'll be honest with you, Mrs Watkins. There were times I felt almost painfully close to him and times when I wondered if he was really mine.'

'Phobias?'

Here was a word nobody had mentioned before in connection with Aidan Lloyd.

'World of his own, that boy. He'd go off – from an early age, he'd wander off and I'd be worried sick, and they'd find him on his own in some little wood or a dingle, quite happy. Playing with his friends, he'd say – well, he didn't have any friends.'

'Imaginary friends?'

'And always some places he wouldn't go near. I would've had him to a psychiatrist. Iestyn wouldn't. Not the sort of son he wanted, see, a mental case. Iestyn's tragedy, again – never quite got the son he wanted. I'm telling you this 'cause there's people down in Kilpeck who know all the background. It'd be foolish to cover things up that are known about in Kilpeck. Like his fear of the church.'

'Kilpeck Church?'

'Wouldn't go in. Wouldn't go in through that big doorway with the arch. He'd start to cry till you took him away.'

'Was he like that with all churches?'

'I was afraid he would be, but when we had to go to weddings in other places it didn't bother him, so I don't know. It's a strange church, isn't it, Kilpeck? Maybe they frightened him, all those the faces on the walls. I don't know. There are things I wouldn't talk about in his lifetime and maybe it'd've been better if I had.'

'The phobias – was this just when he was a child, or did they persist?'

'Well they – you know, I only thought about this for the first time the other day – but it all changed, like a lot of things, about the time the asthma cleared up.'

'How old would he have been then?'

'In his teens.'

'And when you say it all changed…'

'He was calmer. More… outgoing. Still quiet, he'd always been quiet, but more… more relaxed within himself. Are you sure this is the sort of thing you're looking for?'

'Well… phobias are perhaps not too appropriate for a memorial service. Did you, by any chance, talk to Julie Duxbury? The rector?'

'Oh my God.' Sarah drawing an appalled breath. 'I had a phone call from Mrs Duxbury, and she was to have come to see me yesterday. When it was on the television, what happened to her, I just went as cold as ice.' She shivered in the warmth of the kitchen that looked so cold. 'Anyway, you haven't come to talk about that. What is it you want me to tell you? The asthma, that was quite a miracle. But then there was too much to think about – too many bad things over a period of about three years. Sir Peter dying in an accident, then the title going to his brother who was… a bit mental, I always thought. Unstable. Scatterbrained at the very least, with all his stupid ideas. I expect you know what happened there?'

'Most of it, I think.'

'Iestyn always said you couldn't use a working farm to experiment with stupid ideas, so it ended badly. Except for Aidan's asthma. Miracle. Like, I said, it seemed like a miracle.'

But it was said in a sharp and final way. Sarah's face had become a mask. She probably knew what might lie behind the miracle. But, even now, with a new husband and Aidan dead...

'If I were you, Mrs Watkins, I'd simply say he was at last able to become the farmer his father had always wanted him to be. At a time when he was needed the most.'

'So the new farm, at Ledwardine...'

'Went from strength to strength. Became what you'd call an agricultural factory. It was time for me to do what I'd been putting off for years and so I did. I doubt he even noticed me leave.'

'But you continued to see Aidan...'

'Aidan lived with me for a time during the week, going to the farm at weekends. This was till he left the Cathedral School and went to agricultural college and I'd met Archie. There'd been what you might call a widening chasm between Iestyn and me that Iestyn did absolutely nothing to heal. When Aidan left college he went full time with his father and I was seeing very little of him. I rang Iestyn once and asked him quite civilly if he wasn't working the boy too hard. His reaction... well, if I tell you that was the last time we spoke...'

'What did he say – do you mind me asking?'

'I told you you'd get the truth from me. He claimed Aidan had as much time off as he wanted and if he didn't choose to visit me then perhaps he just didn't want to hear any more of my lies.'

The mask was dissolving now, Sarah on the edge of breaking down with grief or rage, hard to tell which. She drank some coffee.

'They weren't lies.'

'I'm sure they weren't.'

'What's sickened me... do you know what they're saying in Ledwardine?'

'Possibly.'

'About Aidan taking drugs?'

'Erm, cannabis. I've heard cannabis. It's just mindless gossip. Who told you about it?'

'I hate that place with its posh little shops and everyone from Off.'

'Was it Charlie Howe?'

'My husband says I shouldn't trust him, but why would he make up a story like that? If it's in any way true, all I can say is that working with Iestyn must've driven Aidan to it, but I don't believe it's true. They seemed to be getting on a lot better.'

'Really?'

'Aidan told me that a few months ago. He had his own ideas about the future of farming, and he thought his father was listening to him more. 'Specially after they won a contract to supply meat to Waitrose. I have to say he was happier than I'd seen him in a long time.'

'Because they'd got a Waitrose contract? Erm...'

Had she known about Rachel? Probably not. Don't go there.

'Who'll take over the farm now, Mrs Baxter? Liam seemed worried that now Aidan was... gone, that there'd be pressure on him to give up his job and get ready to take over from Iestyn... eventually.'

'He doesn't want it, and he knows I don't want him to have it. Though I expect Iestyn will try to persuade him to take it on at some point. He's seventy-five now, but he has his own manager, and a good housekeeper and about a dozen people on the payroll. It'll tick over, with Liam's help some evenings and at weekends, and when he consents to retire, he could sell it as a going concern. But he won't want that.'

'I, erm...'

Merrily didn't know what to say, having been aware for some minutes of something snaking poisonously between her thoughts, perhaps her own prejudices coming through? She started again.

'I've tried several times to get through to Iestyn on the phone. He doesn't seem to want to speak to me.'

'Or anyone, it seems. When I saw him at the funeral, he didn't even acknowledge me. Not that we parted as friends, but we were on speaking terms. And stayed in touch. There are things you need to discuss sometimes. But he looked at me as if he didn't even know me. Perhaps I've changed.'

Sarah drained her coffee, stood up with the cup. At the gleaming sink, she turned round and her smile was almost malicious.

'Or perhaps he's not the man he was. Do you know what I mean?'

59

Hereford's finest

It wasn't the bright lights, Leominster. You didn't drive into the town centre, you burrowed in through side streets. Strangers needed a guide.

Bliss quite liked that about it. Lot of things he liked about Leominster. One thing in particular he didn't.

'All right.' Annie was suddenly straining against her seat belt. 'Stop. Let's stop this now.'

'Annie—'

'No, just… stop here.'

'Yeh.'

Bliss pulled into a bay marked loading only, left his engine running, his lights on. His Honda was the only car on a short street where the shops were all closed for the night and the pavements were dully gleaming, about to freeze over.

'Bad idea,' Annie said. 'At least, without thinking it out.'

'It was *your* idea.'

'No, it was yours, and I gave in. What was I thinking of? He's cleverer than me. Always was. We have to do better than this.'

'Annie, he's not clever, he's just—'

'And a bloody sight smarter than you, too, if that's what you think.'

Might even be true. Charlie didn't break rules, he created what he thought were better ones. How, if not a wise and decent man, could he remain so popular with both the great and the good and the small and the needy?

The old bastard.

Annie had unclipped her seat belt, was huddled in her trenchcoat, hands gloved, her back to the door. She had her mobile in her lap, probably willing it to summon her back to Gaol Street. All the windows were silver with condensation.

Bliss switched off the engine. His own mobile was on the dash. It was after hours for both of them, but with two murder inquiries on the go you were never really off the leash. They'd had another go at Danni, another go at Lech, and also the feller on remand, awaiting trial in connection with the caravan site used as a halfway house for smuggled East Europeans. How many had subsequently been employed – if that was the right word – by Jag?

Annie said, 'Charlie allegedly told Lech Jaglowski about giving migrant workers a better knowledge of the British legal system and how not to fall foul of it – had he acquainted Headquarters with what he's researching?'

Bliss sighed.

'Thought he might have,' Annie said. 'Like I said, not stupid.'

'But how many other convicted felons has he spoken to, apart from Lech? As far as I can find out, none. He's only interested in Jag. Who may've sent an employee – if that's the word – to kill a farmer and make it look like an accident.'

'But we don't know why Jaglowski's dangerous friend wants Lloyd dead.'

'I bet Charlie does. And when he's gorrall his ducks in a row he'll present it to someone far more senior than us and collect all the credit at the end of the court case.'

'Just in time for the election.'

'We've gorrit all to lose if the bugger comes out of this a public hero. And he will. He's gorra go on climbing, never looking back at the rising pool of shite below his shoes. I reckon he was *glad* to find out about us. Never a big family man. They just gerrin the way, families. He wants me out 'cos I know too much about him, and you were just a slight problem before, but now…'

It went quiet. An old lady, in a beanie like his own, tugged a shopping trolley brimming with kindling across the street. How Dickensian Leominster could look sometimes, despite its drug problems.

'I remember when I was a kid,' Annie said, 'Charlie becoming very distant, you know? Never at home and, when he was, it was like I wasn't there. Same with Mum. He was... I don't know, maybe a detective sergeant.'

'Long time ago.'

'I was eleven or twelve. Mum saying, you'll have to excuse your dad, he's in line for promotion. If he gets it he might remember we exist again. And I began to notice – the higher he went, the more distant he'd become. Approaching super-intendent, it was not only like we didn't exist, it was like we'd never existed. Clear we weren't part of the future any more, the grand plan. My mother left him not long after that – I was at university. Did he care? I don't think so. He didn't see her as a detective superintendent's wife. That was all that mattered, you know?'

'Is the lovely Sasha a crime commissioner's girlfriend?'

'Crime commissioners don't have flashy girlfriends, I hope she realizes that.'

Bliss reached for Annie's hand, couldn't find it in the dark. He wasn't sure if she'd ever actually told him that she'd only joined the police in some vain attempt to gain the respect of her old man. If Charlie had been straight, it might even have worked.

Annie prised herself away from the door and fastened her seat belt.

'On the other hand, this is cowardice.'

Bliss didn't move.

'Go on.' As if the memories had hardened her. 'The only other option is the transfer list.'

'We can come back over the weekend.'

'Francis, start the damn car.'

397

Bliss nodded. He started the Honda and prodded it back into the roadway, taking a right into the town-centre car park and out the other side to pick up the zigzag one-way system that took them out of town towards the thinning streetlights. Of course, Charlie might not even be in. Busy man.

The tall terraced house was on the left before the Morrisons' supermarket. Bliss spotted a space four cars past the house.

This time he switched off the engine as soon as they were parked. They'd both clocked lights in the downstairs rooms. Charlie wasn't not in.

He came to the door with a whisky glass in his hand. Letting them in without argument. Without a word, in fact.

Not into his office, where some secrets might be stored, but his high-ceilinged sitting room, newly redecorated as if for glittering receptions to come: magnolia walls under trembling light from an expensive-looking electric chandelier, an old-fashioned drinks cabinet opened to mirrors, crystal glasses and a bottle of Chivas Regal. Whisky fumes scenting the room. A log-effect gas fire putting out cold, curling flames.

Charlie was dark-suited, still bronzed from some late-autumn break or an out-of-town tanning parlour owned by a mate. Looking like he was ready either to go out for the evening or welcome significant guests.

Not these guests, obviously. Still, Bliss thought he didn't look sufficiently displeased to see them.

'Well, now.' Raising the glass to his leathery face. 'If it en't Hereford's finest.'

The three of them standing there under bright lights, empty chairs around the walls. Charlie didn't invite them to sit down.

'Won't offer you a drink, folks, seeing as how you got some hefty crimes on your plates. And yet still time to spare for a senior citizen. Aren't our modern police wonderful?'

'We…' Annie coughed, awkward. 'We were in the area. And it seemed ridiculous to go on like we have been. Pretending.'

Charlie sipped whisky, looking into her eyes over the glass.

'You know what, Anne? In all seriousness, I'm half wishing you'd gone on pretending. Just kept quiet. Let the ole man go on deluding hisself that his only daughter wasn't as thick as the evidence suggested. Let this desperate fling play itself out.'

Half wishing? What did the other half want? Bliss's morale was already sinking like the sediment in a river. The way it always was, in the end, with Charlie. He'd thought Annie's presence might change that, put the old bastard on the back foot, but Charlie didn't have a back foot.

'And I…' Annie trying again. 'I was actually thinking that, for once, you could do the same for me.'

'What you on about, Anne?'

'Stop pretending. Level with us… me?'

'In what way?'

'You could be up front about why you're poking around the edges of one of our inquiries. About what you're trying to do. And to whom.'

Charlie grinned – surely more teeth than he used to have. Bliss looked at Annie, white-blonde hair tucked into the collar of her trench coat, skin pale as milk. Tried to see a family resemblance, but it wasn't obvious. Not for the first time, he nursed the appealing thought that maybe she wasn't Charlie's daughter after all.

'The word is, Charlie, that you've been prison visiting,' Bliss said.

Charlie didn't react. His back was straight, his crew-cut stiff and white as a new toothbrush.

'Lech Jaglowski,' Bliss said. 'Ciggy smuggler. You talked to him about an RTI involving a van owned by his late brother, Wictor. Two cases here. One's uniform, but one's obviously ours.'

'That's what the boy told you, is it? No mention of my inquiry into the treatment of migrants by the justice system in West Mercia?'

Bliss squashed a laugh, recalling a story from the 1980s about Charlie Howe and a waiter in an Indian restaurant who'd kept on denying knifing the chef.

'You think not enough of them are getting their heads trapped in cell doors these days, then, Charlie?'

Avoiding Annie's eyes, wishing he hadn't said that. It was possible she didn't know about it.

Charlie frowned.

'Brother Bliss, I feel we're approaching, even quicker than usual, the point at which I invite you to leave the premises.'

'And take your daughter with me?'

'You've already taken my daughter.'

Charlie's eyes were cold.

'I do resent the idea,' Annie said, 'that I'm someone who can be *taken* anywhere, by anyone.'

'Especially by him, eh?' Charlie said.

All the sediment was gathering in Bliss's gut with the realization that this was the first time in nearly a year that he and Annie had appeared together in front of anyone apart from an audience of coppers in an incident room.

Still, he pushed on.

'Charlie, you've been suggesting to the media that there's a connection between the murder of Wictor Jaglowski and the death of a farmer in a white-van accident.'

'Oh really?' Charlie's head on an inquisitive tilt. 'A shooting and a road accident? I suggested that? To the *media*?'

'If you know something you think we don't,' Annie said, 'why not come to us? How did you know we weren't deliberately holding that connection back?'

'And how could I, Anne, as a member of the general public, be expected to know how much – or how little – the police have in their back pockets?'

'I often wonder that, too,' Bliss said.

'You know, Brother Bliss, it's always been hard for me to take you seriously. If I was still running CID you'd still be in uniform, arresting drunks for pissing in High Town.'

Annie said, 'Withholding information—'

'Time you left, Anne.'

'You're—?'

'I'm asking you to vacate my premises. I got people to see. You want to come and talk to me on your own sometime, we can arrange that, if you promise not to bring the rubbish in.'

'You—'

'Annie,' Bliss said, 'I hate to say he's not worth it, like somebody off *EastEnders*, but he thinks he can walk all over me now. And you. Knows how easy it would be to have certain pictures appear on the walls in Gaol Street. Or, better still, turn up on dozens of computers.'

'I'll likely wait till I got one of you naked.' Charlie drained his glass, dumped it on the cocktail cabinet. 'With your tiny dick.'

He sniggered.

'Funny,' Annie said. 'I'd heard you could be like this, but I'd never seen it. Now I have, it makes me think everything else is true as well. That is frightening. Everything I've been in denial about all these years.'

'*Denial*. I'll tell you something you can't deny.' Charlie's forefinger came out, rigid. 'Now you've done the job for a few years, and seen how increasingly hard it is to get results... is that Charlie Howe was *a bloody good copper*. And the best... the *best* is yet to come.'

He went across to the drinks cabinet, poured himself another inch of Chivas.

'And the *wairst* of it is, Annie,' Bliss said, 'he believes that.'

Worst of all, on paper it was true. On paper, if you ever looked at his record of arrests, he'd been an uncommonly good copper, nothing on file about the suppression of evidence linking a prominent landowner and freemason to a murder, back in the day. A good bent copper. Back in the day, a *good* bent copper never got found out.

When he turned back to face them, there was a twitch of a smile on Charlie's face, swiftly removed. In the past, Bliss had seen Charlie's eyes agleam with malice and triumph. None of that tonight. The eyes were slits, like the light on the rim of freezer drawers. A line. A line had been drawn.

'It's different now, Charlie,' Bliss said. 'You can't just come back. Not the way you're seeing it. It's all different, now.'

'Aye. Different.' Charlie nodding. 'True enough. But not in a way people like. Not in a way that makes them feel secure like it used to be. My day, they knew me, see. Knew who I was.' Pointing at Annie. 'Frightening. Aye, like Anne just said, to the scum, detectives like me were frightening. Now you're all just part of some grey machine. Shiny-arsed computer-clickers. Public don't trust you any more to defend what's important. Way they see it, if they're attacked in the street by some kid with a machete, cops'll go into risk-assessment before they intervene. En't *that* true?'

'And with the PCC system, all that'll change, will it? Most of the commissioners... they're not even coppers, just public entertainers who know how to collect votes.'

'Not me, boy, that's the point. I been there, done it all. Still in its infancy, the idea of an elected police chief. Means you can mould it into whatever works. You put a real cop in the job – a man who can *lead* – then you'll see the difference. And the fact that he's elected... by the people... long as the people want him, he's...'

'Untouchable?'

Bliss glanced at Annie, saw the horror in her eyes. Saw that Charlie had seen it, too. He took a long breath that he hoped didn't show.

'Course, all this is academic, Charlie, if you don't get elected. Which even with your loveable personality and all your contacts, is no... no cast-iron *cairtainty.*'

'En't it? You wait and see, Brother Bliss. You wait and see. Or, better still, don't wait and you won't have to see. Get yourself out of West Mercia while the going's good. Both of you. Piss off out of Hereford, before my city shows you the door.'

'Perhaps we'll just quietly let ourselves out and forget we came. Lost cause, Annie.'

'No.' She didn't move, except to tighten the belt of her coat. 'Not going anywhere. I'm a DCI, and I've worked bloody hard for it. I didn't want to get into a political argument, all I wanted was for him to tell us why he was so interested in the Jaglowskis – gangsters. I'm not having anything rebounding on us because he thinks we can't touch him. I'd rather be completely open about this relationship and, yes, if necessary, get out of West Mercia. Because this is…' Annie backing off, hands wiping the air between her and Charlie. '… this is a bad, *bad* joke.'

She stopped talking, nearer to angry tears than Bliss had ever seen her. Charlie looked at her with the kind of compassion he'd perfected. Then he had a pensive sip of whisky, and that smile came and went like a fast train in the night, and Bliss knew Annie was in trouble, heard it coming, heard it in the tone of voice.

'Women, eh?' Charlie said. 'In the old days, look, when we were thief-taking with abandon, we didn't have women detectives, not in any real sense. We weren't up for senior woman cops of any kind – not in charge of men, anyway.' Charlie left a pause. 'Not that we didn't *like* the WPCs. We liked them a lot.'

'Let's go, Annie,' Bliss said.

'And they liked us. Back then, there were wives and sweethearts. And there were policewomen.'

'Annie,' Bliss said. 'Remember this man is only nominally your dad.'

'But they were ambitious,' Charlie said. 'Even then. Still, they had their principles. And I never knew one… not *one*…'

Bliss looking hard at Annie. Don't. *Don't.*

403

'I never knew one,' Charlie said sorrowfully 'who spread her legs for a lower rank. Let alone one with mixed parentage, out of a Liverpool gutter.'

He stopped when Annie moved. When her left hand pulled the glove from her right hand. Charlie stood still as a monument, chin lifted, that glaze of hard ice on his eyes.

Really, really wanting her to cross the line.

60

Things that move

IN THE FIRELIT parlour, with the rain coming at the windows in contemptuous spurts, Lol became aware of Merrily's restlessness. She kept edging forwards on the sofa, pushing her hair back, focusing her gaze on something that wasn't there.

They'd made not love but toast, over the fire and afterwards opened a bottle of English whisky someone had generously left in the church for the vicar last Christmas. Anything to establish a sense of normality, Merrily had said.

Ethel had settled on the rug under the hearth. But normality wouldn't come in. Merrily stared at her glass, aglow on the coffee table. She'd said she hadn't drunk alcohol, apart from communion wine and the occasional half of cider, in months and it had gone straight to her head, like a hot wire.

Jane had gone to bed complaining of a vague sore throat.

'Fifteen drops of echinacea,' Merrily said, 'and possibly prayers that it isn't going to be a cold and she'll have to cancel the meeting with Eirion on Sunday night.'

'He'll come back, if necessary.'

'You think?'

'Unless he's changed into someone entirely different. He's had time to get to know lots of other girls.'

'Yes.' She picked up the glass and put it down again. 'What did you learn from Darvill today?'

'I learned... the rudiments of the Nine Man Morris. It's the one dance they always finish with, whatever the occasion. Not as difficult as it looks. At first. It's the one that ends with the

Man of Leaves dancing a kind of counterpoint until the others turn on him with their sticks and he contrives to meet each one with his own stick and then escapes. We didn't get that far. It was my first time as the Man of Leaves, but no mask yet.'

'Are you finding you can do it?'

'The Man? Well… yes. It's just about getting into a state of mind. A bit like paranoia.'

'How's that?'

'Don't know. It's just how I felt.'

He hadn't told her what Gareth Brewer had said to him in the darkened cowshed. Just as he hadn't told her about waking up with aching limbs and having dizzy spells that wore off during the day. On one level it was frightening, on another terrifying. He was scared of going to see superfit Kent Asprey at the Ledwardine surgery and ending up going down the brain-scan road, and scared of what else it might mean. He hoped it was psychological, although he didn't know what he could do about that either.

Merrily slid the glass across the table.

'Do you want to finish my whisky?'

He picked up her glass, but he didn't really want it. He pretended to take a sip and put it down again.

'Are you still OK about Lucy's Night?'

'Sure. In fact that… that's become the least of it.'

Lol felt his chest tighten.

'What's wrong?'

'I have a problem,' Merrily said.

She was right. It was one of those problems that made all other problems seem banal and trivial.

Lol picked up the glass.

'Had you met him before? I mean before the funeral?'

She shook her head.

'He doesn't go to church, he's never been dangerously ill and in need of someone to visit him. Or got married, or anything

406

like that. You don't see him staggering down the steps at the Swan. You don't hear him booing and jeering at parish meetings. He isn't one of those vaguely sinister guys of whom people say – when they'd digging up his garden – that he kept himself to himself. He doesn't. He keeps himself all over the place.'

'Have I seen him anywhere? What's he look like?'

'There you go. He's nondescript. Like most ginger-haired people, he has freckles. Which we always think of as friendly. What I'm asking myself is would I be thinking like this if I hadn't talked to Charlie Howe for the first time in a while, and then Sarah Baxter, who I didn't know.'

'What was the first thing that… struck you?'

'Just… warning bells. The kind that most people wouldn't notice. You can't live in an area like this and automatically suspect everybody who hunts or shoots. Although you know you'd never do it yourself, you come to accept that some of them are pleasant, generous people who just love horses and riding. And, and… shooting at things that move. When you hear about someone who's been shooting wildlife since the age of ten and thinks that's the best thing about living on a farm… that's a bit… you know… disturbing, but not particularly shocking. And when you hear this person likes to take holidays in Africa because of an interest in wildlife…'

'Ah.'

'Is that a huge leap? He might just enjoy taking photographs.'

'Doesn't *necessarily* mean he goes after lions and elephants.'

'Even if it's antelope, it doesn't make me exactly warm to him. But then I'm just a soppy woman. And he seems like a decent guy. Helping his stepfather, after the death of his half-brother. Helping him with the farm he insists he never wants to take over because farming can ruin your life.'

'It can. It's no rural myth that a lot of farmers end up hanging from a cross beam in the barn.'

'No. It isn't, Lol, it's just… is he protesting too much, supported and encouraged by his mother? *This is Liam, the guy who on no account ever wants to inherit his stepfather's multi-million pound farm.* Sorry, I'm being... it all comes down to nothing, doesn't it?'

'I wouldn't say it's *nothing*... Tell me the Charlie Howe bit again.'

Inevitably recalling the one time he'd taken on Charlie Howe, when Charlie's daughter, Annie, had been giving Merrily a hard time over the Frome Valley hop-kiln case. This was before they were any kind of item. *But you live in hope,* Charlie had said, not long before they'd parted, amicably enough. And then, less amicably, *Don't think this a victory for you, brother.* Charlie liked to apply the term *brother* to men he wanted to feel threatened.

'Smug,' Merrily said. 'Full of it, like "Look what I've got." Then snatching it away, like kids do. Sometimes I've come close to liking Charlie. But – you know – not *that* close. I've no illusions about him. He was going on about crimes that go unnoticed in the sticks. How people don't make waves because it isn't neighbourly. Perhaps because they're more isolated, don't have many neighbours. Bottom line: he's as good as saying Aidan Lloyd's death was not an accident.'

'How can *he* say that?'

'I said he was *as good as* saying it. I don't know what he knows that nobody else knows, and I was really trying not to speculate. It just... things come together in your head like... like a tune you really don't like but can't get rid of. *I* don't want it to be true. I don't want *any* of it to be true. I do want Aidan Lloyd's death to have been an accident.'

'Well, yeah, but...'

'Charlie Howe's an ex-copper. They don't start to see things differently when they're retired. I'm not a copper.'

'Pretend you are. Just for a minute. Who else might want Aidan dead?'

'Not his dad. They were getting on well for perhaps the first time, according to his mother. A lucrative deal with Waitrose, apparently more down to Aidan than Iestyn.'

'Bit of an enigma, though, Iestyn Lloyd.'

'Good farmer, good businessman. Proud of what he's done. What he's got. Always played his cards close to his chest. Not much of a mixer. And – oh yeah, there's this. His ex-wife is convinced it's dementia. The reason he's become even less of a mixer.'

'Oh.'

'I'm in no position to know. At the funeral, I heard him say just three words, looking into his son's grave. He certainly didn't say anything much to me. When I went to say how sorry I was, he just shook my hand and nodded. I took that to mean he just wanted it all done and dusted, didn't want gossip. I tried again to ring him – today – but he was *in a meeting*, as they say. In the end I left a message with his farm manager to say the service for Aidan would now be held at Kilpeck, in memory also of Julie Duxbury, and if he wanted to talk about it, et cetera, et cetera. Had a brief call from Liam Hurst to say he wasn't sure if his stepfather would be there or not, under the circumstances.'

'He'd know, of course. If Iestyn was...'

'Of course he'd know. If you want to talk to Iestyn, you wind up talking to Liam. Who fixed up the quiet funeral? Liam. Who didn't tell me much to say about Aidan? Who was better placed, in his travels from farm to farm, to put it around that Aidan spent most of his time behind a spliff?'

'You could definitely be right about that.'

'Sure, when you put all this together, it still doesn't amount to much. Aidan Lloyd was still killed by a foreign van driver who skipped bail or whatever. Nobody has suggested otherwise.'

'You know what I'd do?'

'Tell Frannie Bliss.'

'Wouldn't be the first time. And he's no friend of Charlie. Or Charlie's daughter.'

'He's got Julie's murder on his hands. And that garage guy on the Rotherwas. He doesn't need half-arsed theories dumped on him. Besides...'

'No… please… don't start thinking this is going to wind up with me and Gomer nicked for illegal exhumation. It's gone a long way beyond that now.'

'I'll think about it. Wouldn't have much chance tomorrow anyway. Wedding.' She looked at him. 'You look knackered.'

'Border morris… it's supposed to be looser, more free-wheeling than Cotswold. Actually more like a contact sport. I keep asking myself how I got into all this.'

It was already all a mist. Like asking himself how he came to dig up a grave. Like torturing himself with the insane thought that, because the Kilpeck Morris had not done their traditional walking circle around that same grave after their last dance with Aidan, the remains of his corrupted energy had entered the unremembered dreams of the last morris man to open his coffin.

61

Hassma

ALL NIGHT JANE had kept returning to the same overgrown part of the churchyard, where there'd been bones in the grass.

Old bones, scattered, discarded. She'd kicked something that turned out to be an ancient brown skull which had moved quite slowly and then fastened its jaws around her boot at the ankle, bringing her down, and she'd awoken. And then, later, there was the open grave that she didn't want to look into, kept turning away from, but whichever way she turned the open grave kept appearing in front of her. Until at last she did look and there, sitting in the stagnant water in the bottom of the grave, was Sam Burnage, naked, and that was the last time Jane awoke, to bare trees through wet windows

But at least she didn't seem to have a cold, and her throat wasn't sore any more, which was something.

She scrabbled around on the floor for her phone.

Nothing new.

Lying on her back, she held up the phone and flipped through the old messages, the cursory exchange with Eirion.

Yeah, all right. The Ox? 8.00pm?

What's wrong with the Swan?

You KNOW what's wrong with the Swan.

Maybe she should've been more polite. They never had been polite to one another – what kind of relationship would that have been – but it wasn't as if she'd emailed or texted him in many weeks. Couldn't bear to. No way had she wanted to discover he was living with some nice Cardiff girl who had shown him how easy love could be with a sane person. Well into his second year at university now. Another year, then a post-grad year at some journalism college, and then he'd be springing into the world, a player. If she went to uni next year, as planned, she'd be two years behind him. By the time she was out of the education system, he and the nice Cardiff girl or her successor could be, like, parents.

The semi-sob caught her by surprise. Life moved like the wind when your third decade was in sight. Usually an ill wind that blew you away and then dropped you somewhere you didn't want to be. For so long, she'd thought she wanted to be here, Ledwardine, capital of the new sodding Cotswolds, but perhaps she just wanted to belong somewhere.

Somewhere she could feel she was making a difference, and if it wasn't going to be here then wasn't it best to get the hell out ASAP?

Third decade!

No sooner had Mum buggered off to her wedding – another smiley for the album or the video, how could she keep that up? – than the phone rang.

Sophie.

Oh.

'Sophie listen, I'm really sor—'

'I'm not *dying*, Jane. Could you get her to call me when she gets home? On the mobile.'

'It's not more bad news, is it?'

'It's information she might be able to use. *Will* be able to use. Or, if she doesn't, I shall.'

'You don't want me to—? No… OK.'

The next call was from Fred Potter of the Three Counties news service, the freelance agency serving newspapers, radio and

TV. Wanting details of the Monday night memorial service at Kilpeck.

'Why?'

He laughed.

'No, really, why? What've you heard?'

She put the scullery computer to sleep. The phone had started ringing while she was Googling *St Lucy*, immediately getting sidetrack by the brilliant poem from John Donne. *The year's midnight* – how wonderful was that, from round about half a millennium ago?

'All right, I'll tell you,' Fred Potter said. 'A memo's gone round that a person of interest might be saying something newsworthy as part of a tribute to the late Aidan Lloyd. I've been asked to see if I can find out some background in advance to judge whether it's going to be worth people actually turning up.'

'What, TV crews?'

'Regional TV. They do think twice about paying people to come out at night.'

'I'll tell her you rang,' Jane said. 'I'm sure if she can think of anything likely to discourage them from turning out, she'll get back to you.'

'Actually, I don't think they'll need that much discouragement,' Fred Potter said. 'Snow's forecast.'

'Doesn't mean a thing. Snow's been forecast every day this week.'

It didn't come that night. It hadn't come by Sunday morning. It was probably too cold for snow. On awakening, Jane checked her emails and there was nothing from Eirion. Well, that was good. Wasn't it?

When she came downstairs, Mum had left for Holy Communion. She made herself some tea and toast and honey, then pulled down her parka and walked down Church Street to Gomer Parry's bungalow.

'Can't stop thinkin' about it, Janey,' he said in his kitchen, puffing on his vape stick. 'Why'd they do it?'

He deserved to know. She didn't think Mum or Lol would object. She didn't even ask him to sit on it because she knew he wouldn't say a word.

'He was actually a member of the Kilpeck Morris. He kept going back to dance. His father didn't know that.'

'Ar,' Gomer said.

He didn't question these things.

'After he was dead, someone at Churchwood evidently found his morris kit and they took it to Kilpeck the night before his funeral and put it on like a scarecrow frame? And poured petrol over it and set light to it.'

'Buggers can't leave nothin' alone.'

'It didn't go down well in Kilpeck, so the morris side came back the next night. With a full kit for him. And a spade.'

'And made a bloody mess of it.' He took a puff of his vape stick. Jane had got him the flavour that seemed most like roll-up. He didn't wince at the taste, anyway. 'Boys could've assed *me*.'

She stared at him.

'You'd've dug him up for them?'

'Oh hell, aye. Never seemed right, Janey. All too bloody quick, that burial. Just get him in the ground. Never even throwed the soil on his box. Iestyn Lloyd, he got part of him missin'. Part as says there's more to life than turnin' a few bob. Or a few million. *Don't tell the ole feller.*'

'What?'

'What the boy said when he found where we oughter sink the borehole. Mabbe not *exaccly* them words, but that was the sense of it. Well, now, if Iestyn got a bit missin', that boy got an extra bit.'

'You reckon?'

'Only he din't know it, see. Not till he was growed up. Couldn't do it as a kid.'

'Dowse?'

'Or nothin'.'

'Who told you that?'

'*He* did. When we sunk the hole, I says, how long you been doin' that, boy? Year or so, he says. An' don't tell the ole feller. I reckon he couldn't do it till he got rid o' the *hassma*, see. The hassma stopped it. Feels it comin' through, the ole whatdyou-callit, his breath just closes up. Must've been frit to buggery, poor kid.'

'It was like a nervous reaction? A block?'

'Sure t'be.'

'And it wasn't just dowsing. What he did?'

'I en't no hexpert, Janey. But I've met a few folks like him, over the years. En't allus hassma. Could be bad headaches. Anything as stops 'em bein' what they could be. Mabbe there's a word for it. Mabbe you knows it, what that word is.'

'No,' Jane said. 'I'm not sure I do. But I think I know what you mean.'

'And young Darvill, he'd know,' Gomer said.

Jane blinked.

'Lionel Darvill? You *know* him?'

'Done his ditches a time or two.'

'Why didn't you *say*?'

Gomer looked affronted.

'No bugger assed me.'

62

Fairy tales

MERRILY LEFT AT twenty to seven to prepare the church for the Sunday evening meditation, having waited until the last minute for Jane to come downstairs. She'd spent what must have been a couple of hours upstairs in her apartment, presumably deciding what to wear to meet Eirion, though you wouldn't have thought it when she eventually came down wearing perhaps her third best white hoodie, cursory make-up and a sad, defiant smile.

'That's what you're wearing?'

'Aren't you going to be late, Mum?'

'I thought Eirion was picking you up to go somewhere.'

'No. I'm meeting him here.'

'In the Swan?'

'The Ox. Less public. Unless Dean Wall is there, but I expect I can deal with him.'

'Right. Flower...'

'Mmm?'

'I was going to say, it'll be fine, and good luck and... all that.'

'Thank you.'

She flung on her parka and slumped out into the icy night. What would Eirion see after all this time, at the end of a fractious period during which Jane appeared to have embraced adulthood but not with any conspicuous joy or relief?

What a strange kid she was.

Kid: no apology. Merrily didn't recall going out on anything approaching a date without striving to look her best. That was *part of it*. Eirion, she recalled, had been doing work experi-

416

ence at the South Wales Echo, mixing a lot with journalists. The adult world, the city. Jane could well be back home before the pubs closed, with Eirion consigned to the flat file marked *friends*. Was that what she wanted?

Had to put it out of her mind. Off to the church and *The Cloud of Unknowing*. She'd left them in darkness last week but, at this time of year, the Middle Ages would have been ready to light solstice lamps. St Lucy's Night was a festival of light, celebrated these days more in Scandinavian countries – Denmark, Sweden, with their long, long winters. In the third century, Lucy had brought food to Christians hiding in the catacombs, wearing a wreath of candles around her head to light her way, leaving her arms free to carry more goodies. Reminded Merrily, slightly uncomfortably, of the crown of lights worn by women in certain witchcraft ceremonies.

At least there wasn't much else here for Jane. Having died at the age of twenty-five, all St Lucy shared with the seventy-something Lucy Devenish was a kind of demonstrative courage: when they tried to burn her she wouldn't stop talking even when a Roman soldier stuck a spear into her throat.

They never ended well, these stories, but a good St Lucy's night, well celebrated, would ensure sufficient light for the long dark months to come.

The wind was down, the street deserted, the night air quiet, and something landed like a cold moth on Jane's face.

Snowflake. First of the year?

She was walking slowly down Church Street in the direction of the river, hands deep in the pockets of her parka. More lights across the river now, with the expansion of what Gomer called the hestate. Jane scowled. According to the *Hereford Times*, over ten per cent of dwellings in Ledwardine were now second homes, used just a few weeks a year by rich Londoners who brought their fancy food with them and would never drink in the Ox. Result: need for more local housing, erosion of the countryside.

She looked up. Three of them this time, one in her eye, almost certainly snowflakes. She just wanted to stay out in it, let it come, but a door on the left of the street was hanging open to mustard walls and sallow light and the whizz and clink of gaming machines.

Some incomers apparently wondered why nobody bought the Ox and turned it into a swish bar with tables spilling into the street.

Only a matter of time. Jane walked in and wasn't sure whether to feel good that nobody looked up from the pool table. She gazed around, under the sagging beams, past the sagging beer guts, the beer-stained sporting posters and the jukebox loaded with country and western classics, and he wasn't there.

Wasn't there.

Oh well...

There were other people she recognized, including Ledwardine's iffy councillor Lyndon Pierce, accountant and crony of builders committed to turning Ledwardine into a pink-brick hell twice its current size. What was Pierce doing deserting the Black Swan for this dive? He glanced at her and pretended not to recognize the woman who'd once publicly called him a bent bastard. And who was—?

'Jesus!' Jane said.

Someone rearing up in front of her, a hand reaching out and then hesitantly drawing back.

'Damn. I'd always hoped you'd never discover my middle name.'

Jane collapsed into a wild grin. She genuinely hadn't recognized him. A bunch of gigantic teenage males standing around the bar had concealed the table he was saving in the corner. Time was he wouldn't even have fitted in that corner.

'You been ill?'

Well, it broke the ice.

'I just lost weight, OK?' Eirion raising his eyes, addressing the ceiling. 'You'd prefer it if I got diabetes or wound up taking statins for rampant cholesterol?'

'It's just… not Welsh, Irene.'

Jane started to laugh and smothered it, but he was smiling and his eyes hadn't changed, and – bugger – she'd called him Irene.

He was inspecting her.

'Still sweet cider, is it?'

'No, I'll have a Manhattan, please. With extra tequila.'

'Jane, there's no tequila in a Manhattan.'

'I knew that,' Jane said.

She sat down at the wobbly table, damp with cider and beer, Eirion's beanie on the driest corner.

He said he'd driven over to see a guy he'd been at the Cathedral School with, just out of hospital after being badly hurt in a car accident. Could've been killed. It had, he said, made him think. The guy had just got engaged in hospital. Didn't want to wait any longer because he'd realized you just didn't know what might happen tomorrow.

Jane pushed her chair back, alarmed. Eirion got it at once, rose up.

'Oh no… look, I didn't mean—'

'I know you didn't, I was just—'

'On the other hand, I didn't *not* mean… Oh, shit.'

'I, erm…' She was suddenly serious. 'I'm not saying I never want to get married or live with somebody, just that I don't want any kids.'

'You always used to say that.'

'Nothing's changed. Not for the better anyway, and it isn't going to on a horribly overcrowded planet where everything gets built on, layer after layer, and anyway I want to *do* something, I want to find something, I need to *stop* things—'

This was ridiculous. She was just talking, faster and faster – *lecturing* him, for God's sake – creating distance between them and dragging the conversation, as rapidly as possible, to the point of no return.

She looked across at Councillor Lyndon Pierce, who'd been joined by an older man in a leather jacket who she recognized from somewhere but couldn't immediately put a name to.

'… like *him*. And the rest of his disgusting council? They just want to pile more and more people into Hereford – more council-tax payers. He's still got plans for a supermarket and a big estate where the Ledwardine henge is. Well, where I think the henge is.'

'You getting any further with that?' Eirion asked.

'Erm… there's… there's…' Oh God, she'd done it, put herself slap in the centre of the target area. '… there's this archaeologist I met in Pembrokeshire, at the dig, who thinks maybe she can interest one of the universities in sponsoring an exploratory excavation.'

'Excellent,' Eirion said.

'Yeah, it's, er… it's pretty good.'

The sounds of the Ox – clink, whizz, raucous laughter, pool-clink and beerpump-gasp – exploded in Jane's ears then faded.

'If I tell you something… something personal.'

'I was hoping you might get around to that.'

'To what?'

'Something personal.'

'Yeah. Right. Well, I can think of two possible reactions to what I'm going to say. One's you putting your glass down and quietly walking out.'

Jane looked for his eyes, but his face was distorted behind his cider glass. She thought, ludicrously, that his old face wouldn't have fitted behind a cider glass.

She moistened her lips.

'And the other's all sleazy jokes and like, can I watch next time? Only there isn't going to be a next time, and I'm not sure there was a last time, due to me being very pissed.'

Eirion said nothing.

'And grateful,' Jane said, avoiding his eyes. 'That she was on my side. My wavelength.'

'Wavelength. How very pre-digital of you, Jane.'

'You—' A surge of interior heat drove her chair back hard into the corner. 'You bloody hate me already, don't you? She's a good archaeologist and a nice woman. Who happened to believe in the same fairy tales as me. Ley lines, earth energies, dowsing.'

'Unless you've changed a lot, Jane,' Eirion said, 'you don't think they're fairy tales.'

'Only I'm not sure if she actually did – does – believe in them. And I'm not sure if I did anything else. Other than actually sleep with her.'

She looked frantically around to see if anyone else had heard.

No sign of it. She looked across the sticky table at Eirion and then away. Through the glaze of desperate tears, she looked back at Eirion, but he was already on his feet.

'Time to go, I think,' he said.

63

Lamping

LOL STAYED BEHIND after the meditation, helping her put the chairs back. Then they stood together in the porch doorway, hand in hand.

'It *was* snowing,' Merrily said.

'Been trying to all day. So he wasn't there, then? Crowden.'

'No. No, he wasn't. I didn't really expect him to be. Not a second time. He'd know I'd have to approach him, and what was he going to say?' She pulled her scarf tighter. 'Might have saved time if he *had* been here.'

'I'm still finding it hard to believe that the C of E goes in for this kind of clumsy espionage.'

'This is nothing. And it's going to get worse. I thought Huw Owen was exaggerating when he told me, years ago, that the clergy fight like rats in a sack, for position and influence. And now it's about survival, so much more vicious. Anyway… I had a message to ring Sophie, and she's been talking to people about Crowden.'

'Women? Boys? Cocaine?'

'I'm not going to say, "I wish", because that would sound… awful. No, he's happily married, a family man. Drugs? Unlikely.'

'You can't win.'

'It's not about winning.' She leaned into him. 'I mean, he's not *popular*. Sanctimonious sod. Laughs a lot, but no sense of humour. However, listen, if Darvill hasn't spoken to him yet, perhaps you could ask him to do me a favour. Next time he talks to Crowden, perhaps he could arrange to meet him.'

She turned and pulled the porch doors together.

'I'm scared to go home, Lol, in case Jane's back. It might seem trivial and domestic, but I just want something to go right for her.'

'She'll be OK.'

'I think there's more wrong than she's telling me. It's like she wants him to walk away.'

'I *think* she'll be OK,' Lol said.

'Well,' Jane said. 'I have to say I really wasn't expecting this tonight.'

Eirion's car was parked in near-total darkness in what might one day be a building site but was still a small wood at the edge of Virgingate Lane. Ironically, not far from where Lyndon Pierce lived, right on the eastern periphery of Jane's imagined henge. There really weren't many places left around Ledwardine where you could find seclusion with your engine running, for the heater, and nobody likely to pull in along-side. Seeing Lyndon Pierce in the Ox had reminded her of this place.

She thought she could hear the light patter of snow on the rear window, which was wonderful, although...

'I think I'm actually starting to feel a bit cold now, Irene.'

'Hang on...'

Eirion pulled the travelling rug up over her bare shoulders.

'You, erm, never used to keep one of these in your car,' Jane said, 'as I recall.'

Pathetic. Shut up.

'Once again, Jane, I swear to God,' Eirion said, 'that you're the first woman to lie under it.'

'Sorry. Sorry, sorry, sorry. Seriously, I'm sorry. What right have I—?'

'There really isn't anyone else. Not even another bloke.' He kissed her lightly. 'So what did you say?'

'When?'

'When the gay lady in the bookshop asked you whether your teddy was a boy or a girl?'

Bugger. Why the *hell* had she told him about that?

'You presumably remember,' Eirion said. 'Not going to forget something like that.'

'Gus said hers was always a girl.'

'Well, that would figure, but…'

'All right. I said teddies were, like, beyond all that. Without gender. That was the whole point.'

'Teddies go both ways?'

'But then I had a woolly dog, and he was called Ron, and I was still sleeping with him when I was twelve, if you must know, so…'

'OK, that's fairly conclusive,' Eirion said crisply. 'You can get dressed now, Ms Watkins.'

'Look, I just needed some sound advice, all right? In the old days, when women were expected to fight against it—' Jane was leaning up into the cold, feeling along the back shelf for her bra, when it came to her. 'Oh God, of course – Charlie Howe!'

'Sorry?'

'It was Charlie Howe with Lyndon Pierce in the Ox. He was the chairman of our school governors. Very iffy. Nearly as iffy as Councillor Pierce. Who'll have a slice of the action if his mates get planning permission for this field and Coleman's Meadow and God knows where else. You do remember?'

'Of course I remember.' Eirion was generously helping her on with her bra. 'News story in that yet?'

'Wouldn't give it to you if I knew. You're a mere student.'

'Could be a working journalist in a couple of years, Jane.'

No doubts, no uncertainty. She reached up and ruffled his hair.

'You know exactly where you want to be, don't you?'

'I know what I want to *do*. And no time to waste any more, the speed newspapers are closing down. The way unbiased journalism's getting replaced by semi-literate, opinionated, fantasist bloggers on the Net.'

'You sound quite bitter.'

'It's scary, Jane. Nobody knows where to find the truth any more. Anyway, I don't want to ruin the best night since I don't know when. *You* decided yet? Like which uni?'

She was quiet. Hadn't wanted to get into a discussion on this either. Didn't want to get into another bloody lecture.

'Jane?'

'I don't know. I'm not sure.'

'Not sure of what?'

'Whether it's the way. Digging up building sites before the concrete goes in. And anyway, there are too many universities now. Shows the education system up for what it's become – just a business. A degree's worth shit. There are guys who can't spell poncing around with PhDs in subjects you don't need to be qualified for. Just another self-perpetuating industry in a country run by people I hate. Whoever's in power.'

It went very quiet. If the pattering on the window had been snow, it was no longer snowing. She felt Eirion sitting up beside her.

'I love you, Jane,' he said. 'How sad is that?'

Merrily stopped on the square, snow falling lightly again, and she didn't care at all.

'You didn't!'

'She's never going to know, OK?' Lol said. 'Not from me.'

'Ever?'

'If you say so.'

'What happened, when his text arrived, she asked if it was me who'd put him up to it and I hadn't – hadn't spoken to him in weeks. So it seemed OK, now they were back in contact, to ring him. And put him in the picture about... what I just told you about. And I never told you that, either, or Jane and me will be over.'

'I can't believe she couldn't tell me. Well, actually, I can. What I can't believe is that she told *you*.'

'I think, in some strange way not unconnected with your job, that she thought you might feel compromised. Don't ask me how. Also she probably owed me a secret.'

'*What?*'

'Never mind.'

'You bugger.' She felt dangerously light. 'What did he say? Eirion.'

'He didn't laugh. Well, not at first. Then he did. I suspect he wasn't sure what he ought to think.'

'What would you have said if he'd been horrified?'

'Tried to talk him round. Or if he couldn't be talked round, suggested he just didn't meet Jane.'

'How did you know she was going to tell him? How do you know she... has?'

'Can you imagine Jane *not* telling him? Also, I didn't want him coming out with, "Woo, can I watch?" I didn't think he would, but if it came as a surprise...'

'You're a good person, Lol.'

'Please,' Lol said. 'It's been embarrassing enough—'

And then they were kissing publicly. Or would have been if the weather hadn't cleared the square.

Eirion started to laugh. It had made him, he said, not want to be a student any more, get university behind him. Get some working years in before journalism became history. Literally.

'Something will happen,' Jane said. 'The Internet as we know it will become unfashionable. Passé. I mean, what else is there to do with it? Facebook's already a refuge for old people – sheltered networking. Shit, that's another car gone past. Is everybody going home because of the weather? People are afraid of everything these days. Every trip to the pub's a risk-assessment situation.'

She told him about the job she'd be starting after Christmas, minding the shop for the Ledwardine Festival. How she planned to make it into a proper business, almost a little tourist centre for Ledwardine.

'For as long as it's worth visiting.'

'You know,' Eirion said. 'We really have to make the effort to become more optimistic about things.'

'I feel optimistic about *some* things tonight. What was— You hear that? If it's those bastards lamping hares again. Or foxes.'

'Jane...'

'Oh!' She thought at first it was the banging of her heart. Someone up against the misted windscreen, peering in, making faces. 'Sod off!' Pulling on her hoodie, struggling to zip it up as Eirion scrambled up between the front seats. 'No! Don't put the lights on!'

'I wanted to see who this pervert is. I— *Oh God.*'

The boles of trees had come up all white in the headlights, and also the man's face, up close, squashed for a moment against the windscreen then sliding away.

'It's him,' Jane said numbly. 'Charlie Howe. What does he—?'

She saw Charlie Howe turn abruptly away, as if he was disgusted at what he'd seen in the car. Then she thought she saw a pinkish lump come jumping out of the side of his head and he slid silently away down the car bonnet, and the thin layer of snow on it was slicked red and pink and there was a crack in the air.

Part Six

'Tis the yeares midnight, and it is the dayes,
Lucies, who scarce seaven houres herself unmaskes,
The Sunne is spent, and now his flaskes
Send forth light squibs, no constant rayes;
The worlds whole sap is sunke:
The generall balme th'hydroptique earth hath drunk,
Whither, as to the beds-feet, like is shrunke,
Dead and enterr'd; yet all these seem to laugh,
Compar'd with mee, who am their Epitaph.

John Donne (1572–1631)
'A Nocturnall upon St. Lucies Day'
Being the shortest day

64

The best is yet to come

A WINTER'S DAWN. A *real* winter's dawn with mauve-veined sky and scraps of snow littering the car park.

Not the police car park, the adjacent public park on Bath Street, where Annie had left her Skoda Yeti. Bliss had never been in that car, and he didn't get in now. They stood on the car park and shivered, and the sparse flakes floated down like cold ash.

The snow was coming in from Wales. All over the Black Mountains in the west, sprinkling the Malverns in the east.

Annie's trench coat was hanging masochistically open.

'You don't call me,' she said. 'Not on the landline or the mobile. You don't email.'

Like he'd even think of it. He was still in a cold sweat over how close they'd come to spending last night at his place in Marden instead of going their separate ways.

They were standing between the Yeti and a florist's van. Annie's face made him think of one of the marble effigies he'd seen on tombs somewhere. She'd be treated like a suspect now – she'd *be* a suspect – her flat *visited*, her phone stripped down to the last chip. Sympathy would be restrained and formal. This was what happened when a senior cop was close to a big killing, especially a man like Charlie. She had few friends in the building behind them, and until she was proved to have had nothing to do with it, she'd be in solitary.

Just before four a.m., Jack Kenny from Warwickshire and an FLO she didn't know had taken her to identify the body. Yeh, even Annie qualified for family liaison. Her only advantage was that at least she knew the FLOs had a dual role.

'Both of them watching me looking at him. Wondering if I'd do something out of character.'

Like sob?

Jack Kenny had been whizzed over from Warwickshire to head up the inquiry. No time wasted there, they must've dragged him out of bed within minutes of having the mind-boggling name. Car and a maniac driver outside Kenny's door, then foot down all the way to Hereford by way of Ledwardine. The MIR for this one would be sealed off like a quarantine ward.

'He's straight, apparently,' Bliss said. 'Hard bastard but straight.'

'Of course he's straight. You think they'd send anyone to investigate Charlie's murder who'd even had a parking ticket cancelled?'

'Who's taking over on Julie?'

'Brent.'

'Shit.'

'You get to keep Jag for the time being, but Kenny's going to be on your back now it's looking like the same gun. Listen, I need to get back, they're virtually accompanying me to the toilet.'

He hadn't asked how she was feeling and he wasn't going to. She probably hadn't even worked it out yet. Could be weeks, months before she managed to separate some distant, smiling, soft-hearted daddy from way, way back from the hard-eyed, suntanned psycho who used to like WPCs *a lot*.

'When they put me under the lights,' Annie said, 'I'm not going to be able to lie.'

'At all?'

'Are you?'

'I'm gonna tell them everything I'd put in a report. Beginning with Darth at Hewell. I'll admit to deciding not to feed that into the system until I'd checked Charlie's story. I'll tell them quite openly that I didn't trust him. I'll say I believed there were senior fellers here who might still be too close to him. I'll give them chapter and friggin' *vairse*, if necessary. I could even tell them the whole truth right up to...'

'Friday night?'

'Yeh. Up to then. That's where the screw tightens. They're gonna ask you when you last saw him. They're gonna ask his neighbours if they've seen anybody visiting him or watching him or walking slowly past his friggin door or—'

'You think I don't *know* everything they're going to ask? You think I don't know that sooner or later they're going to find out about us? Finishing both of us for this division and putting us bang in the frame for anything anyone wants to hang on us?'

'No. I don't think that.'

No way at all around this one. Clear enough to everybody here that, in the normal way of things, the last person Bliss would go to with suspicions about Charlie would be Charlie's daughter. With whom he'd been seen outside Charlie's front door. Or was it some other bloke in a beanie driving an old Honda CRV?

Funny, really, in the darkest possible way. You never imagined there could be anything worse than Charlie getting elected to the big one. But Charlie dead... Charlie dead would be ticking all the way to the crem.

There was, for a start, the matter of historic corruption. Old coppers who'd been shit-scared of Charlie would start finding their voices any day now. However much or how little came out, Annie would be under pressure to leave the division, or even – if the brass were feeling generous – the service itself, for some well-paid if anonymous ancillary office job. Meanwhile...

'Compassionate leave, is it?'

'When they've finished their... their strip search.' Annie blinked a snowflake away. 'And if I don't take compassionate leave, how would that look? What are they going to find for me to do?'

He'd heard they were trying to stop Sacha talking to the media. Misguided, in Bliss's view. They'd be better letting her pay her tearful tribute because, bearing in mind what might come out within days, no copper would be wanting to stand in front of a camera and rabbit on about Charlie's exemplary record as a thief-taker of the old school.

Win-win, for Sasha, if she only knew. He would've dumped her within days of cracking the election.

They stood looking at one another, him and Annie, for a few silent seconds. Between the Yeti and the florist's van, the tips of their cold fingers touched once and parted.

'Charlie was right,' Bliss said bitterly. 'The best *is* yet to come.'

At this stage, there was very little black humour in Gaol Street, but give it time.

He managed a more relaxed chat with Vaynor, not long back from Ledwardine, while Jack Kenny and his inner cabinet were setting up their MIR. He'd been invited to Kenny's first big production, but not with a speaking part. Waiting to be summoned, he'd beckoned Darth into his office for a quick coffee.

'The boyfriend,' Vaynor said, 'has journalistic ambitions. I leaned on him as hard as I could, given the circumstances, and I think he'll sit on it, but I thought you ought to know.'

'I'd be more afraid of the girl,' Bliss said. 'Knowing her as I do, through her mam.'

'The girl was actually quite shattered, boss. Even though she didn't seem over-fond of Councillor Pierce.'

'Why's that?'

'Thinks he was bent.'

'And, in spite of that, a mate of Charlie's?'

He'd had to fill in a form detailing his various points of contact with the victim before he could even be admitted to the MIR. He'd kept it tight but expected a personal summons at some point, to be grilled in depth by Jack Kenny, who he didn't know very well, with someone he didn't know at all sitting in.

'It was all a bit coincidental,' Vaynor said, 'but it's a village, with nothing very far from anywhere else. Jane Watkins and... how do you pronounce this boy's name?'

'Like Irene, only a bit longer. I've met him once. His dad runs Wales Gas, or some such.'

'Jane and Irene were in that same pub, and Pierce and Howe were still there when they left to... have a private conversation that wouldn't wait. Jane says that seeing Pierce there reminded her of a secluded parking spot just off the lane where he lived. So that's where they went.'

'That *is* coincidental.' Bliss rubbed his bristly jaw. 'But that's the way Jane Watkins thinks. Kid has a perverse streak.'

'Another coincidence,' Vaynor said, 'is that Jane Watkins also fielded a call for her mother from the Reverend Julie, the night she was killed.'

'I do know that. And, yeh, you can have one too many small-county situations. Perhaps I should get word to the MIR that, given her mother's sideline, this is no time for overreaction.'

'It's fairly clear it *was* purely a coincidence, boss. I listened to the recording of her 999 call. They didn't know about Pierce, and she seemed to think he might've done it because they were together in the pub. They were back in the car with the doors locked. Irene said he didn't want to move and dislodge part of Charlie from the bumper.'

Bliss had happened to see some of the video: Pierce's body hanging half out of the passenger seat of Charlie's car outside his house. Two in the head, a bit like Jag.

A lot like Jag.

'What was Pierce doing in Charlie's car?'

'The Ox isn't too far from Pierce's place and he'd walked down, but when they came out it was snowing, according to witnesses at the pub, so it looks like Charlie offered him a lift home.'

'They'll need a list of everybody in that pub last night.'

'They're getting one.'

'And anyone who might normally have been in and wasn't.'

Vaynor nodded.

'What's your feeling boss?'

'Now the Makarov's confirmed? I think there's so much information now that if it's not cracked by Wednesday we'll be looking like muppets.'

'I meant Charlie.'

Bliss leaned his chair back against the window recess.

'Still doesn't feel real, Darth. All the times *I've* wanted to do him.'

'Had your moments, boss, you and Charlie.'

'Not last night. Only kid in our street who didn't want an airgun. Not even to shoot bent councillors.'

'*Independent* councillors. Allegedly. Both of them.'

'Norra hit squad from It's Our County, then. They'd go for the official Tories.' Bliss brought his chair legs down. 'Somebody waiting for them. Somebody who'd seen them in the pub. If it's not whoever did Jag, then somebody's been flogging Maks for longer than we know. Pierce got it first?'

'That's the most likely sequence. Pierce first, just as Charlie was letting him out at the entrance to his drive. Charlie having reversed in, to turn round and get on the bypass.'

'So the passenger door's open, Pierce get popped and he's either hanging out or pulled out of the way to leave the shooter a clear shot at Charlie in the driving seat. Which is when Charlie makes a run for it. I think there are some cottages in that lane, but not too close to the Pierce house, so he makes for the wood. Lorra trees to hide behind.'

'Is it possible the shooter was *only* after Pierce?'

'And ended up doing Charlie as well?'

'Couldn't've known Pierce would be in Charlie's car, boss. And if Charlie hadn't been dropping Pierce off...'

'It's a point that I'm sure Jack Kenny's team will've worked out hours ago. So… in the wood Charlie spots a car. No lights, windows all steamed up. Could be he didn't see the car till he virtually walked into it.'

'And then he's shot from behind. Jane Watkins – fortunately, or unfortunately for her – actually saw him taking the bullet. Which would've been the second bullet? He already had one in the back.'

You know what this looks like?' Bliss said. 'Looks like only one shooter. If there'd been two of them, the other would've gone round to the driver, make sure Charlie didn't get out.'

'Your phone, boss.'

'Sorry?'

'Your mobile's flashing.'

'Oh yeh.' He'd muted it. Picked it up from the desk, checked out the number and took the call. 'I'd've rung you later, Merrily. We could probably use a chat, but not right now, and definitely not in Ledwardine.'

65

Evening work

MAYBE SHE WASN'T telling it too well.

He'd rung her from his car, on the mobile. She was in the scullery with Lol. She'd sent Jane and Eirion to the Crown in Dilwyn, a few miles away. The police had offered them counselling. They didn't need counselling, in Merrily's view, they needed one another. Only not in the Swan. Not today. Maybe not for the rest of the week.

She was still confused, upset, so maybe she wasn't telling it too well.

'It *could* be interesting, Merrily,' Bliss said. 'However, it's my duty to refer you to the SIO, Detective Chief Superintendent Jack Kenny. Which means one of his team. And they *will* want to talk to you, but... it won't be quick.'

'Because they don't know me. They don't know me from some psychotic sensation-seeking—'

'It won't be that bad.'

'And I've an important service to do tonight.'

Bliss sighed.

'Merrily, no church service not involving the reigning monarch can ever be described as remotely important during a murder inquiry. And murder inquiries rarely get bigger than this one.'

'Sure. I do understand that as a former senior copper—'

'You *don't* understand. Charlie's lurid past could start to surface at any moment. Alive, he's always been bulletproof. Dead, it's open season, and the brass are shitting breeze blocks. And I didn't say *any* of that.'

'Oh.'

'Yeh.'

'OK, well... forget I called. I'll talk to somebody tomorrow, when I've got time.'

Silence. She could hear him thinking.

'I'll call you back. You at home?'

'Frannie, nobody can get out of Ledwardine today without having to bribe the police.'

They watched the one o'clock TV news. An assistant chief constable of West Mercia, a severe-looking woman who had to be close to retirement, said that Charles Howe had led several major inquiries and was known for getting remarkable results. Restrained.

'I remember the first time I met him,' Merrily said, 'it was with Morrell, Jane's headmaster, a fairly aggressive atheist. Charlie was vice-chairman of the county education committee at the time. We were discussing the seances some of the kids were holding in the lunch hour, and Morrell was being typically scornful. But Charlie supported me all the way. Talking about the murderers he'd known who believed they'd been instructed to kill by voices – he'd worked on the hunt for the Yorkshire Ripper. I remember him saying I had a thankless job.'

'He knew how to make friends,' Lol said.

'When I subsequently found out what he'd done, what he'd covered up, I was quite sad.'

'It didn't stop him, though, did it, people knowing what he'd done. And if you happened to get in his way...'

'I don't think he – this is going to sound awful – but if you'd told him he was going to die with Lyndon Pierce, who... Oh God, shut me up, I'll probably have to do Lyndon's funeral. Say good things about him.'

'Lyndon have a wife, partner? Can't remember.'

'He split with his wife. His partner, fortunately for her, perhaps, was at a leaving party in Hereford. Jim Prosser told me that. She works for social services. He also has a business partner, in Hereford, who I'd guess will now be under pressure to suggest what Lyndon and Charlie might've been meeting about. In the Ox, rather than the Swan.'

'It won't come out.'

'Or not for years.' She sniffed. 'I'm becoming a cynical bitch.'

'Go on like this, you'll be bishop material. Listen...' His hand on her arm. '... it wouldn't've made any difference. If you'd rung Bliss on Friday night.'

'You know everything I'm thinking.'

'No evidence, not even circumstantial.'

'It was you who suggested I should tell him.'

'For your own peace of mind. Not because I thought he'd be able to do anything about it. Not quickly, anyway. And it wouldn't have saved Charlie. He wouldn't have gone out of his way to help Bliss.'

'But worse still... what if Jane and Eirion...?'

'Merrily, stop it, please, you can't keep—'

The phone rang.

The Three Horseshoes was just off the Abergavenny road, ten minutes or so from Kilpeck. It had just started snowing again when the CRV pulled in and Bliss climbed into the Freelander, his navy-blue beanie glittering with flecks of snow.

'How come *you're* doing this service for Mrs Duxbury?'

'Who told you about that?'

'We know everything Julie-linked. As for Julie *and* Charlie-linked... Charlie wanting an audience. What might he have said?'

'I'd have to think about that.'

'All right, never mind. Tell me about Lyndon Pierce. Aside from the fact that Pierce represented Ledwardine on the Herefordshire Council and little Jane hates him, nobody at the nick knows as much about him as I'd thought they might.'

'Probably because you've never had him in custody.'

'We missed out there?'

'Pierce is… *was*… an accountant and prominent member of the county planning committee. Believed to provide extra services for clients who happen to be builders. For a consideration. It's said.'

'Said?'

'Even I've said it. There are tentative plans for a much bigger Ledwardine – high-density housing, supermarket complex, all sugared with a fancy leisure centre. Jane's furious because it would be all over what remains of the original orchard – Ledwardine, the Village in the Orchard?'

'Yeh, yeh.'

'She's convinced – well, she hopes – that the roughly circular orchard actually marks the site of a Bronze Age henge, which would be the biggest prehistoric site in the county. She might be wrong, but…'

'Lorra money for a few lucky people, if this development goes through, you reckon?'

'Including a substantial wad under the table for Lyndon Pierce for escorting it through the planning process. I didn't say that. Oh hell, I did. I *said it*. I said everything.'

'Who are the builders?'

'I'm not sure, but there are a couple of firms famous for this sort of thing, as I'm sure you know. Nothing out of the ordinary, goes on all the time.'

'Could Charlie've been involved?'

'I can't really see how, and I couldn't see him getting involved in anything iffy while campaigning to be in charge of West Mercia policing, can you?'

'Could he have been just socializing with Pierce?'

'In the Ox?'

'OK. Liam Hurst. Would Pierce know *him*?'

'Possibly. Or his stepfather. Pierce handled a lot of farmers' accounts. It's conceivable that Iestyn Lloyd was his client. I expect you could find that out easily enough.'

'In a murder investigation, Merrily, we can find out anything.

Would this proposed expansion of Ledwardine intrude on Iestyn's spread?'

She nodded.

'He recently bought quite a large field connecting his farm to the churchyard – which would be almost surrounded if the plan goes ahead. But Iestyn wouldn't be open to a deal. Farmer through and through. He acquires land, he doesn't sell it. Against his fundamental principles. He makes it work, in the old sense.'

'Everybody's gorra price.'

'No, you don't understand. It's a matter of pride. The only money Iestyn Lloyd's interested in is profit from actual farming. It's what he does. What he wants to be known for.'

'And this lad Hurst, would he share that viewpoint?'

'Now you mention it, probably not. Never particularly interested in farming, as such, as much as other things you could do in the countryside.'

'All right, just give us a few minutes.'

Bliss got out of the car and went back to his Honda.

Merrily watched the snow. It didn't seem to be trying very hard, but the Black Mountains were just a few miles away, and they hadn't been black for days. Blizzards could make roads round here impassable within a couple of hours. She smiled, a bit desperately. There was a local saying: as rare as a Herefordshire Council gritter on a winter road. It was only funny until you were trying to get from A to B on a winter's night.

The passenger door was wrenched open, a sandwich of snow dislodged as Bliss climbed back in.

'I'm gonna tell you this, though it amounts to bugger all except as a character reference. When we first talked on the phone, couple of hours ago, I had my intellectual mate DC Vaynor run a few swift checks on Liam Hurst.'

'Blimey.'

'Hurst is forty-three, civil servant, as you know with DEFRA, the Min of Ag as was. Spends a lorra time around the farms which is... interesting. Valued by the department as he gets on extremely well with farmers – countryman to the core, and not afraid to get his hands dirty – or bloody, for that matter – in time of national need. During the last Foot and Mouth crisis when hundreds of thousands of farm animals were being slaughtered...'

'Holocaust.'

'What?'

'Jane's word for... that kind of thing.'

'Yeh. Well the young Liam was out there with whatever kind of rifle they were using to dispose of stock quick.'

'Massacre – Jane again. Sorry, go on.'

'And then – much more recently – here he is again, butchering badgers for the government, to stop the spread of TB to cattle.'

'Instead of vaccinating them, as in parts of Wales.'

'Where's the fun in that? Didn't interfere with his job. Evening work. Went out with a team of shooters in south Gloucestershire.'

'I see what you meant by character reference.'

'Positively public-spirited, Merrily.'

'May have been less so in Africa.'

'Who's watching out there? They don't call it the dark continent for nothing. Let's put that one on ice. I've not quite finished, however. Hurst also belonged, for a couple of years, to a club safely based at the army base in Brecon. Pistol range. Professional targets, real ammo. All absolutely legit. Even our senior CSI, Slim Fiddler does it. Does he know Mr Hurst? He's out on manoeuvres presently but will be snatched by Darth on his return to barracks.' Bliss beat his fist on the dash. 'Friggin' *hell*.'

'You're moderately excited now, aren't you?' Merrily said cautiously.

'It'll take a shitload more than this, Merrily. And it won't be my decision to go after him. Right. When Hurst first came to see you, to ask you to conduct the service for Aidan, would he've known Charlie was likely to be there?'

'He was first to tell me Charlie wanted to speak at Aidan's service, which they wanted to be in Ledwardine. He seemed pleased. Charlie had told him he was going to use the occasion to highlight the problem of unqualified foreign drivers on rural roads.'

'Course he did. Easy to forget how persuasive Charlie could be. Sadly, the old bugger'll be there only in spirit tonight, so nobody'll ever find out what he was gonna say.'

'They might.'

'But *he'll* be there? *Hairst.*'

'With or without Iestyn. I'm guessing without.'

Bliss scrubbed at the vapoured windscreen.

'Doesn't leave much time. You think it might be better to gerrit called off because of the weather?'

'You wouldn't persuade Sir Lionel Darvill to do that if the whole valley was snowed in. There's only one St Lucy's night. But the less you know about that the more convincing you're going to sound to… whatever his name was.'

'Kenny. If I'm granted an audience. You going over there now?'

'Might be safest. Overnight bag in the back, with all my kit. You can go home and not come out for a week.'

'Might be safest, Merrily, if all the lanes got blocked. Right, I'm gonna ask yer about one more thing, on the off chance. Norra word about this, all right? Kilpeck. An incident involving the burning of a dummy in fancy dress, too late for Guy Fawkes Night, up by the cas— What you looking at me like that for?'

66

Complicating the ministry

STRANGELY, IT HADN'T even started to snow yet in Kilpeck. You could get that anomaly in the border country, stray pockets of protection under the wall of the Black Mountains. But it rarely lasted, and the countryside this late-afternoon was greyly tense, water half-frozen in the ditches and the sound of birds moving inside the hedges like broken biscuits in a shaken tin.

Merrily stepped out of the Freelander on the edge of the grass apron. Last time she'd been here, there had been Julie Duxbury, brisk and fearless in the bomber jacket. Now, under an anxious sky, there was just the church that Julie had felt she ought to like but didn't, the church that had *a cold glow sometimes.*

No glow at all tonight. No sun to set. The church of St Mary and St David on her mound.

Her mound? Why did she think that? Was it the rounded apse, jutting like a pregnancy?

Merrily stood by the car, cold inside the too-thin waxed jacket, the overnight bag at her feet, black like the exorcist's bag in the film posters. She didn't feel like an exorcist, never really had. Julie Duxbury had looked more out of that mould. But there was no sense of her here. She was not the kind who came back.

'Mrs Watkins? Merrily?'

A woman calling from across the parking area wore a sloppy sheepskin coat and baggy wellies and she was out of breath.

'I'm so sorry, I shoulda been here to meet you, but I didn't think you'd be so early. I, uh, snuck off to the inn for a Scotch.

445

Doesn't really warm you at all, you just fool yourself.' A hand came out of her coat. 'Nora.'

'Of course.' They shook gloves. 'As there doesn't seem to be anything happening maybe we should both go to the pub.'

'Hell, no, he'd kill me. I'm supposed to show you around. You been in there before?'

'Not for very long.'

'Gonna seem a little disappointing. The Victorians got at it. They didn't take anything away, they just brought in new stuff and polished it.'

Merrily followed her past the tangly yew tree, its evergreen branches clogged with dusk.

'How many people are we expecting tonight?'

'A lot. It's a magnet, this place. People show up who aren't even local.'

'On a night like this?'

'Makes no difference. Bad weather adds to, uh, the otherness, is that the word?'

'One of my daughter's favourite words. Not necessarily mine.'

Nora laughed, approached the south door, reaching for the iron ring handle.

Not much light left now. Merrily had called Lol after Bliss had left. He had instructions to meet the morris side at the inn, would be leaving Ledwardine soon. Bringing Jane and Eirion. The cops still had Eirion's car because Charlie Howe had died on it. Oh God, like she needed two more to worry about.

They went in under the face of the green man whose eyes looked horror-struck at the foliage issuing from his mouth, as if he was gagging on it.

'What's that?' Merrily pointed up at the tympanum, over the door, the ornate shrub at its centre, with fronds like the one protruding from the green man's mouth. 'That connected to the, erm, Man of Leaves? His larder?'

'That's usually called the Tree of Life,' Nora said. 'Or the

446

Tree of the Knowledge of Good and Evil out of Genesis? All about good and evil, this church. Half the images are kind of demonic. There isn't much Christianity here. What could be an angel in the doorway, only with like monsters' faces all around? Snakes and dragons. And the Sheela-na-gig. She's no angel.'

'The medieval way. Good and evil. Not many grey areas.'

'Oh.' Nora wrapped a gloved hand around the ring handle. 'The guy you wanted to meet?'

'Sorry?'

'Lol called Li about the guy who—'

'Oh hell, I forgot.' Clapping a hand to her head. 'So much has happened since—'

'Only, he's in there,' Nora said. 'He thinks he's meeting Sir Lionel. We agreed six, as you suggested, but he came early because of the weather.'

'Oh God, am I really up for this now? Sorry. Yes. My fault. I have to do this. OK. Do you want to go back to the pub or something?'

She took over the ring handle, turned it before she could change her mind and run.

The halogen lights were on at the bottom of the nave, but the pews were empty. There were candles in the brackets projecting from the pulpit. Many more candles around the church, dozens of them, fat candles in holders, thin candles in trays on every horizontal surface, benches and narrow tables, prayer-book racks and pew-ends.

All unlit.

Nobody in the nave, nobody in the chancel, but she knew she was being watched, turned slowly. Paul Crowden was up in the gallery, looking down.

Big day for Slim Fiddler, head of crime scene, so it was a while before he showed up in Bliss's room, looking, as usual, like he was wearing three Kevlar vests under his pullover.

Worth the wait, mind.

447

'You don't think a lot about it, Francis. Most of us go through that phase when we see the coffin-shaped targets at the end of the alley, and we get a very sharp warning about SAS fantasies. No, no, no, this is not a man, this is a *target*. But, come on, handguns... what else are they for?'

He was right. Nobody, as far as Bliss knew, had ever gone grouse-shooting with a Glock.

'And you knew him, Slim. *Hairst.*'

'I knew a lot of shooters. We'd sometimes go for a drink in Brecon afterwards. Not before, obviously. The point is, he was never one of *them*. Not one of the blokes who really wanted to be dashing into a room then going into a crouch with the gun in both hands, screaming, *clear, clear*, till he spots a movement and gets five off without blinking.'

'That's you, is it, Slim?'

'Not for a long time. I don't do crouches these days. No, Hurst, I'd even say he was more in the instructor mode. Didn't say much, didn't smile, didn't congratulate anybody on nice shooting. But, you know, friendly enough.'

'*He* go to the pub with you afterwards?'

'No, he didn't. I don't think he was doing it for the social side, but, equally, not the kind of guy you feel ought to be watched. Just an ordinary bloke. More ordinary than most of us.'

'Was he good?'

'With a pistol? Shit-hot. Kind of bloke who could drill a neat circle shooting through his legs. Except he wouldn't do that. Far too professional. You'd've thought he was regiment if you didn't know him. What's he done, Francis? Not...?'

'Shurrup, Slim, eh?' Bliss said. 'Norra word about this. Not yet, anyway, or I'll be down the road. Norra *waird.*'

He needed coffee. Black. Lots.

Crowden was sandwiched between the front pew in the gallery and the darkwood rail. He was wearing a heavy herringbone overcoat and a retro trilby-type hat.

'We shouldn't keep meeting like this, Mrs Watkins.'

'We've never met like this.'

He didn't move along the pew until she began to squeeze into the space next to him.

'It's no warmer up here, is it, Paul?'

She shivered, the sleeves of her waxed jacket pulled down over her clasped woollen-gloved hands.

'I was here to speak to Sir Lionel Darvill, Crowden said.'

'As that seems to have been about me, I thought perhaps we could cut out the middle man. Odd that you should be waiting for him up here. Unless I've missed the lift...'

'I do know about his disability and I would, of course, have come down when he arrived.'

'Good observation point, meanwhile. Did they send you on an espionage course, or is that classified information?'

'I really don't know what you're talking about.'

'I've been hearing about your survey... report... whatever. On exorcism in the Church. For which you had to go undercover.'

'That's nonsense.'

'You haven't publicized it. Would you like to tell me who commissioned it?'

'No. And it's not only about exorcism, it's an examination of all the fringe activities within the C of E. You'd be surprised what... eccentricities still go on.'

'All of which cost money.'

'At a time when we're obliged to cut back to conserve the core. I don't want to get into an argument with you, Mrs Watkins. If the evidence shows that some deliverance *consultants* are complicating their ministry and extending it into areas in which it might be thought the church should not be operating... well, that needs to be known about. But it's not *my* judgement call. There are far more senior people who have views on this and are in position to do something about it, whether it's at synod level—'

'Or something less public. Come on, Paul, you can tell *me*...'

He said nothing and didn't look at her.

You're a friend of Craig Innes, I believe.'

'I do know Bishop Craig, yes.'

'*He's* making economies. Just reduced his long-serving lay secretary to two days a week.'

'Doesn't that show he's accepting *his* share of cutbacks?'

'I don't think so. She also coordinates deliverance activity. Runs the office. *Extremely* efficiently. And works assiduously for the Cathedral. This is more a demonstration of the Bishop's views on the importance of exorcism.'

'What am I supposed to say? He's entitled to those views.'

Merrily let this hang.

'Of course, your own economic situation must be fairly tight now.'

'Mrs Watkins—'

'With recently getting married and everything. This your first time?'

'As you probably know, I had a partner. We split up last year.'

'And you wound up with the two kids.'

'I got custody.'

'I'm sure your three new stepchildren think you're wonderful, too.'

'I see no reason to discuss my personal situation with you.' He shifted on the pew. 'In fact I seem to have been the victim of what might be called a set-up. So I shall be leaving now. I was going to stay for tonight's service, as a mark of respect for the Reverend Duxbury, who I knew slightly, but the weather's looking quite threatening and I have a long drive, so if you don't mind...'

'Wouldn't be *such* a problem – the long drive – if you were only coming from Ledwardine.'

'Excuse me.'

Crowden rose, picked up his briefcase from the pew.

'Must be quite crowded in your current vicarage, Paul.'

'This is quite preposterous behaviour,' Crowden said quietly. 'And more than a little juvenile.'

'And with another on the way... six kids. Six! Wow. Problem is, won't find many vicarages these days with that level of accommodation. Used to be the norm, of course – the vicar with a healthy bunch of kids – which is why the Church had so many huge old properties to flog.'

'*Do* excuse me.'

Merrily didn't move.

'But... there's Ledwardine. Almost unique in this area. Personally, I've always felt a bit embarrassed about having all that space, with just me and Jane in there. Especially as the head churchwarden's my uncle. A retired solicitor, as you might know, who's determined that the parish should hold on to this valuable listed building and seems to be able to swing that, somehow, with the diocese. There must be a good economic reason for this, but I don't know much about it, and he doesn't like me asking. He doesn't like deliverance, either, so you should get on with him pretty well if you and Innes get me out.'

'That is absolutely...'

'Ridiculous, yes. If it wasn't so bloody cold I'd be laughing now. It's quite cold in Ledwardine vicarage, too. Only a few rooms we can afford to heat. And just across the road my... best friend... boyfriend... has a far cosier dwelling, and I've been feeling so tired and fed up lately that I've been on the verge of saying, *sod it*.'

'Your level of commitment to the ministry impresses me.'

'But then... finding out how small and squalid all this is, the idea that it might all come down to getting a much bigger house—'

'It's nonsense.'

'Anyway, I've decided to fight back. And I won't be alone.'

'May I come past, please?'

'Certainly.'

Merrily stood up and stepped out of the pew and into the one behind.

At the top of the stairs, Crowden turned to face her.

'My perception is that you're becoming an embarrassment. You've become almost drunk on your own perceived success… your relationship with the police, your ghost-hunting, your liberal attitude to your daughter's paganism… and your relationship with former Bishop Hunter.'

'You believe that?'

'No smoke…'

'Really.'

'I don't believe you have anything you can use against me, and if I were you I'd think very carefully about your future. We don't want any *unpleasantness*, do we? Merrily.'

Silence.

He smiled and buttoned his overcoat.

'Thank you, Paul,' Merrily said. 'That's a start.'

She unclasped her gloved hands, and the iPhone slid from the right-hand sleeve of her coat into her palm. She looked at it to make sure the recording needle was still in motion.

It wasn't. It wasn't even visible, and the screen was dark.

'Gosh,' she said cheerfully. 'Holds its charge really well for an old phone.'

When she turned back towards the wooden stairs, he was gone and she found she was trembling.

67

Harbinger

NOT LONG AFTER ten p.m., it began like a few grey feathers blown from an old nest. Soon it was filling the cracks in the walls and gleaming like epaulets on the sagging shoulders of the graves in the churchyard.

On the edge of the pathway between the church and the castle mound, Darvill looked up from under his Russian hat.

'This is good. Cleansing. Do you want to go and light a few candles in there, Nora?'

'I'll help,' Merrily said.

She was wearing her heaviest funeral cape over the meditation outfit of black cashmere and dark jeans. In some conditions, the cassock and surplice just didn't cut it.

'No need,' Darvill said, as Nora walked around to the south door. 'We begin at eleven with a dozen candles. Then snuff them one by one. We only light them all at midnight.'

They'd talked in the big kitchen at Maryfields, over soup, about the structure of the service and the ritual at its centre. It *would* be a ritual, and not a fully Christian one, and she was glad Crowden wouldn't be there to see it.

The church had felt lighter after he'd gone. She'd felt surer-footed on the wooden steps down to the nave and a certain gratitude to the building itself. It put her in mind of the Celtic chapel where she'd found sanctuary after Sean's betrayal and death. A church that she felt you could know even if you didn't understand it.

And it did, of course, know you.

There was at least a possibility that she'd seen the last of Crowden, though she wouldn't be taking bets. She'd thanked Darvill for organizing their meeting, and it seemed to please him that he'd been part of some clerical sting, even if it could have been more successful.

Now they were alone for the first time.

'Julie didn't want to do this,' he said. 'I wanted to make sure you knew that.'

'I think she was entirely sure of what she wanted it to achieve. But maybe a bit suspicious of the church itself. The castle in ruins, the original village gone but the church as good as new. As if it was leeching off the community.'

'You feel that?'

'Not really. It has an air of independence. And mystery, of course. I get increasingly fond of mystery – this kind, anyway.'

'All that matters to me now,' Darvill said, 'is appeasing the mystery.'

She wasn't sure what he meant. He wasn't what she'd imagined. Under that sheen of arrogance, she was aware of a sadness and an apprehension.

The snow had stopped again and she lowered her hood.

'He won't come, you know,' Darvill said.

'Iestyn? He might.'

'It's strange,' he said, 'I hardly knew him. We've never quarrelled. Never had the opportunity to. And then he sets fire to...'

He looked up at her.

'Looks like he found out a lot he hadn't known about Aidan, and all very quickly. And not exactly at a good time.'

'How can you be sure he did that?'

'Don't think he did it in person. He'd've got Hurst to do it.'

'You think?'

'Iestyn's halfway demented.'

'You know that?'

'Doesn't live much in the present, and the past, for him, is a noxious place, full of an old hatred. He thinks I'm my father. He thinks Henry Darvill's still here and out to destroy him.'

'Who told you that?'

'Aidan.'

'When?'

'He's always told me everything. This was a couple of months before his death. I'm telling you, to clear the air. I want this finished.'

'The feud? How can that happen if he's not here?'

'We're bringing Aidan home tonight.'

'I don't understand. You took the extraordinary decision to dig up his body, clothe him as a dancer... and dance with him before putting him back.'

'You think that was an awful thing to do, don't you?'

'I do, actually, yeah.'

He shrugged.

'And then you – they – put his body back.'

'But the dance goes on,' he said.

'But—'

'The less you know, the less you'll have to worry about.'

'I tend to think that's up to me to decide, don't you?'

'Please.' Darvill's chair began to roll along the path to the corner of the church. 'Call me an old mystic – and people do, and not in a good way – but it's all I have to hold on to. You're right about this church. It's like a yew tree, it has immortality. It's its own powerhouse. The white square on the Nine Men's Morris stone. You can't reach it through the Bible, or the Koran or the witches' Book of fucking Shadows. It transcends the lot. Can't be interpreted, only felt. What I'm trying to say is that round yere we don't put things into words.'

'This is morris talk again.'

'The morris is the oldest sacred dance in these islands. Spiritual energy transmitted directly from the earth. And *this* earth, by God... the red earth of the border country...

when it hasn't been turned to dust by pesticides for short-term profit.'

'I have to put things into words. It's what we do.'

'Not what this church does. It transmits wisdom through images. Like him.'

He stopped the chair at the south door. Merrily looked up to the right-hand corner.

'The Man of Leaves. As you call him. What's he want with us, then? What's he telling us?'

He looked up at her.

'Really getting your pound of flesh tonight, aren't you, Watkins?'

'I'm practically a veggie these days, Lionel, what would I want with a pound of flesh?'

He laughed.

'All right. For that, I'll tell you about the Man of Leaves.'

They gave Lol a can of cider.

'Weston's,' Tim said. 'Nothing but the best. Now wet your face with it and then apply the burnt cork yourself. All over. Don't want to see any pink bits. Neck, too. Go on, I'll tell you when you're all done.'

Tim was a small man, a Londoner perhaps in his sixties, fit-looking, not much hair and an up-curving scar at the end of his left eyebrow that made him look a touch devilish. He said he'd been in the army, and everybody knew what that meant in Hereford.

Lol said, 'But if I'll be wearing the mask...'

'Even with the mask, you got to have the whole face blacked. Then the hands. You got to *feel* different.'

They were in a small room behind the kitchens at the Kilpeck Inn. They'd leave, when the time came, without going through the pub.

When they were all blacked up, Tim looked at Lol, got him to turn side-on.

'You'll do. A blacked-up face always reminds me of the old days.'

'Somebody called us that once,' Chris, the farm manager said. 'The SAS of morris. We're perfectionists and we don't give up.'

'I'd've done the Man of Leaves,' Tim said. 'I didn't want to, but I would have. But he wouldn't have me. You're a good dancer, mate, he goes, but that's not what it's about.'

'Lionel?'

Lol felt his left cheek.

'He wanted you, son. Soon as he heard from you, he was on your case. He gets feelings about people. He'll do, he won't. He finds you when you're not sure who you are. Me, I was out of the regiment, no money problems, two kids, nice wife, nice house. Another year of that I'd've topped meself, know what I mean?'

'I think so.'

'Morris dancing saved me. You wouldn't think it, would you? Anyway, congratulations, Lol, you're a bigger basket-case than me.' Tim peered over Lol's shoulder. 'Here's your proof.'

Gareth Brewer was carrying something the size of a small grave-wreath: twigs, holly, eyeholes.

The imminent darkness played with the green man in the arch. The stems curving from either side of his mouth seemed like lengths of a belt with notches.

Darvill strapped on his head lamp.

'No one knows what he means, and, do you know, I don't believe they ever did. Not even the stone carvers who put him into churches. Why churches? Most likely because they're the only buildings in the countryside that would survive. Some more perfectly than others. Look at him. Think he was finished last week, wouldn't you?'

He must hate it, Merrily thought, that the green man is so far above him, while tall men can look him in his goggle eyes.

'They didn't know,' Darvill said. 'Knew what he looked like, didn't know what he was for. He probably came out of a vision. Or a host of visions, who can say? Don't have those now, most of us. God, what I wouldn't give for a vision...'

'By all accounts you have a lot of vision.'

'Not what I mean. We've shrunk, Watkins. The human race has shrunk. Only have to look at the appalling dregs of humanity posing as politicians. But there's a reason, you see, why those Norman sculptors – and the Saxons and Celts before them – didn't know what they'd created. Because it wasn't *for* them. It's true. Meant nothing to them in their green paradise, heavy with all those intoxicating scents and colours. This chap was a harbinger of the distant future.'

'In what way?'

'Taking a message to their spiritually stunted descendants living in an unthinkable future. Where the colours and the smells are dying back, year by year, as the countryside gets poisoned by chemicals and suffocated under concrete. For *us*.'

'*Yes...*'

Merrily spun round.

'Jane. I didn't hear you coming.'

'Soft snow,' Jane said. 'Absorbs sound.'

A young man she didn't recognize came up from the path.

'Hello, Mrs Watkins.'

'Blimey.'

He'd lost weight and actually seemed to have grown. At twenty?

'I didn't recognize him either,' Jane said. 'This is Eirion. That's Sir Lionel Darvill, Irene. He's a prophet. OK, introductions over. Back to the crucial stuff. Message for the future? God, Lionel, are you the first to say that?'

She looked quite unsteady, as if rocked by a surge of unexpected empathy.

'Didn't want an audience, Jane,' Darvill said. 'And no. I'm probably not the first.'

'Well, I have several books on green men, and none of them gets that far.'

'I think you mentioned Lady Raglan, Jane, who came up with that term. It hadn't really started then, or perhaps it had. Interesting that she was from round here. This could be the last area of southern Britain that had it all – lovely soil, meadows, wildlife, a manageable population. Every year now, they're building the equivalent of a new English city. Soon it'll be two. As for the countryside… East Anglia's gone, hedges ripped out for chemical prairies. My old man saw it coming, though. The Man of Leaves knocking on his door, teeth bared. My dad invited him in. What else could he do?'

Merrily was looking around through the thickening snow. She saw slow cars and people coming down from the direction of the pub, a few carrying lanterns. Not long now.

'Where's Lol?'

'He's with the morris side,' Jane said. 'I don't know where. You don't get to see them until they're changed. Rules of the dance. I think Sir Lionel's trying to avoid telling us how he came to what sounds to me like the truth about the green man. If not through a vision, that is.'

'Not my vision, Jane. Had it from the Man of Leaves himself.'

Merrily thought about it.

'Your Man of Leaves. Aidan?'

'Gomer,' Jane said, half turning, her face shining in the beam of Darvill's lamp. '*Gomer* knew what Aidan was.'

Darvill looked up.

'Not the old plant-hire man?'

'Ow're you, boy?'

'Parry! Bloody hell!'

Darvill's head lamp reflected in Gomer's bottle glasses.

'Couldn't not persuade him to come,' Jane said.

Gomer peered not at Darvill but his chair.

'Big tyres. Power steering?'

'This dreadful man doesn't have to come into the church, does he?' Darvill said.

Merrily smiled and turned the ring handle, opening the door into quivering light.

But she didn't feel as good as she'd hoped.

68

Foliate face

A RAG JACKET was for show not protection. Lol was shaking, ankle-deep in snow, as they laboured up the rise to the old earthen castle ramparts. The remains of the medieval keep were already swollen to the shape of a plump bird, some stone projection, coated in grey snow, creating a beak – or maybe that was just his eyes, his glasses having been abandoned to fit the mask.

Tim, veteran of many a winter exercise, said that to avoid broken limbs they'd be better taking a long, circuitous route down from the mound. They would descend in procession, sticks over their shoulders. Wives and partners would carry hurricane lamps, a chain of white light.

Nobody would speak. The music would follow them.

Bob Rumsey had the clock on his phone lit up. At around eleven-twenty p.m., he nodded to the young guy with the side drum. A muscular bellow from the squeeze box, and they were on the move, in single file, sticks over their shoulders, doing the slow Border step, one hop, two hops, snow flaking around their boots and lamplight dancing in their rag jackets.

Lol smelled the sharpness of evergreen and tasted wood. His views of the night and the falling snow were restricted by wired coils of yew. The slender branch between his teeth was holly. It pulled the wooden mask into his cheeks.

He didn't mind it after a while. Despite the cold, a calmness stole over him. He found the muscles in his gut becoming relaxed and there was a soft vibration like the distant sea in his ears. He kept getting images of the symbol on the big beam in the hall: a square inside a square inside a square, and then he thought of Merrily waiting in the church. His best memory, replayed so often that the colours were fading and the soundtrack reduced to hiss and crackle, was of the granary at Knight's Frome on a summer night: the thunderstorm, the lightning in their bodies, the euphoria of *beginning*.

He prayed that Liam Hurst, whether or not he'd killed people, would not be in there tonight.

There would be prayer, but no hymns. Just a little too early for Christmas carols and it was no occasion for any of those trite Victorian hymns, the iron girders of evensong.

Merrily had slipped out of the cape, put on the pectoral cross, freed her hair.

She was freezing.

From the pulpit between two lit candles in extending holders, she talked about the woman who was to have conducted the service. The woman who had *meddled*. She talked about meddling. How perhaps too few people were doing that nowadays, perhaps because they were afraid of the consequences. Julie Duxbury hadn't been afraid. The inference was that if more people had meddled she might be here tonight, conducting this service on Lucy's Night.

There was silence and prayers.

Somehow, over fifty people had appeared in the church, mostly downstairs. Crowden was not amongst them. Nor, thank God, were Iestyn Lloyd or Liam Hurst but she saw Sarah Baxter, perhaps with her husband. And Rachel Peel, down by the great stone font.

Darvill had wheeled himself to the top of the nave, before the chancel arch, its uprights guarded by stone monastic figures, one of them St Peter with a huge key over a shoulder, like a dancer's stick.

You didn't need a microphone in Kilpeck Church.

'I don't recognize half of you,' Darvill said. 'You're from Off.

Well, that's fair enough. You're probably here because you've wandered down from the pub after a big meal. Or because, although you didn't know Julie Duxbury and certainly not Aidan Lloyd, you've seen the pictures on the news and you want to demonstrate some sort of sympathy. Fine. If she'd lived, you might even have come to her service tonight because it is, after all, at Kilpeck Church – romantic, mysterious. And there'll be morris dancing. And it's St Lucy's night – who celebrates that any more? But, hey… John Donne.'

Nora had appeared at his shoulder. She was wearing a long skirt and a black stole. She held a hardback book, the size of a prayer book.

> 'Tis the yeares midnight, and it is the dayes,
> Lucies, *who scarce seaven houres herself unmaskes…*

Merrily thought some of the congregation were about to applaud.

There was actually twenty minutes to go before Nora would throw the book in the air and yell, *It IS the yeares midnight!* and Merrily would carry a candle to the south door and throw it open to welcome her Man of Leaves.

Jane and Eirion were with the crowd outside, waiting for the morris. Mainly younger people, a few with bottles of alcohol. It was snowing hard now. It was the place to be.

In front of the church, the lamps were doused.

It was coming up to the darkest time.

Jane, holding hands with Eirion, was thinking about Lucy Devenish whose shop she'd be reopening after Christmas. How cool was that? The truth was that most women her age would not think it was all that cool. They'd be thinking about university at the end of the summer. Jane was thinking that, by the end of the summer, there could be an excavation to find the Ledwardine henge, and no way was she missing that. She'd have all the good months to turn Ledwardine Lore into a serious going concern that it really would be crazy to leave...

There was a whoop from the crowd. The lights were bobbing down from the ramparts of Kilpeck Castle.

*

> *The old year's hanging on a rusting hinge*
> *Kids in the city on a drinking binge*
> *And no one hears the ancient engines*
> *Grinding underground*

It had started spontaneously in Lol's snowy head when the church had come into view through the near-blizzard, and it was picked up and carried along by the squeeze box and the fiddle and the drum. He was watching through the face of the Man of Leaves as the Kilpeck Morris, layers of snow on their black top hats, formed two lines of four and the chorus, only skeletal until now, came alive in his head.

> *And it takes all of a winter's night*
> *To change the chords and put things right*
> *And it takes all of a winter's night*
> *To dance the darkness down*

God, he loved that. *To dance the darkness down.* His legs were aching in anticipation of song and dance for the darkest night. Sticks clacking in the frantic air. Dancing on the old solstice, dancing on the cusp. The time when you felt the hollow earth under your feet, and the earth and the sky were all one, joined by snow, and you were in a different space from where you'd be if you weren't in movement. In flow with the drum and the squeeze box and the fiddle.

He bit on the wood, stood poised, feeling the strange weight of snow, and ran into the dance.

Weaving between the lines, narrowly dodging the clashing

464

sticks, then bouncing up and instinctively intercepting with his own stick. Then around the musicians – an accordion belch, a rip of fiddle – and dancing back up, out the other end and then, one hop, two hops, back into the dance, clack, clack, the sounds softened by the snow on the sticks, the music thickened by the sound of an engine, a big throaty engine, like the engine grinding underground.

And then, with angry cries, the morris men turned on him, the way they'd said they would, sticks cracking over his head, then the dance broke apart in the darkness, all torches doused, the dancers barely silhouettes, rag jackets alive like crow-wings, and Lol, with no glasses, struggling to follow the lines when a stick smashed into his shoulder.

He went down. Becoming aware that the air all around him was vibrating with a sudden feral joy and the song had darkened in his head.

> *The wind is prowling in the east*
> *To raise the devil, scorn the priest...*

Like being inside a street fight, except this was orchestrated, purposeful, a pitiless, rhythmic rage, and there was no stopping a rhythm, and when he found his feet his limbs were moving in response and the night was inside him.

He rose. He swung the willow stick and felt it connect as a bright crack opened up in his head and, amidst the rag jackets he saw an alley of light and, with a joyful yell, ran for it, and a third line blossomed around him.

> *Let's light the lamps for Lucy's feast*
> *And...*

Running across the snow to the yew tree and the path up the mound to the south door, just as it came fully open

> *And dance the darkness down!*

A fidgety hush in the church. He looked for Merrily with her candle but saw only Darvill in his wheelchair, coming at him very fast, too fast.

'... the fuck's going on out there, Robinson?'

Darvill snarling into the blizzard, Lol leaping to one side, spinning round short of the doorway, to engine-roar and yellow lights and great, shining, rigid arms outstretched, and then the snow was choked with a coarse industrial fog in which screams were smothered, and as Lol ran out towards it, there was a vicious, spitting mist in his foliate face.

69

What we are

IN THE END, Bliss just had to call Annie.

They'd have gone through the ridiculous, but necessary procedure of checking her alibi and concluding that whoever had shot Charlie Howe, it wasn't his daughter. They'd have finished with her mobile by now but, if it still wasn't safe to call her, Bliss didn't care. He was tired; he wanted a long, warm back to stretch out against until it was light.

So when his car wouldn't start outside the country pub he'd gone to for an evening meal simply because he'd never been there before, didn't know anyone, he didn't call the AA, he called Annie on her mobile. Finding she was staying at the motel near the Plascarreg, in case she was needed in Hereford. Double room, he was hoping, but he didn't care.

She came out into the Hereford tundra and picked him up in her little Yeti, and he told her about Darth Vaynor's meeting with one of Jack Kenny's bagmen. Vaynor following Bliss's script because of Bliss's need to keep his head below the counter.

'Seems Kenny didn't actually throw it out,' he said as they abandoned his Honda, in the pub car park. 'In fact he put it into the system. For the morning.'

'Only *you* would think the morning might be too late, Francis.'

'The sooner somebody goes down for Charlie, case closed, the more likely it is that we walk out from under this. The longer it takes to get a result, the more likely it is that they come back to you. And Friday night at Charlie's place. When somebody will have seen us.'

She started back towards town, very slowly, on some very nasty roads.

'I keep wondering,' she said after a while, 'if it's best to simply tell them about Friday. Let them take us apart, find there's nothing there. Come to an arrangement, leave Hereford. Maybe one of us keeps a job. I don't mind if it's you.'

'That what you want, Annie? It's *part* of us, being coppers. I mean us as an item. Part of what we are.'

'It's a pretty sorry reason to stay together. Sounds like convenience.'

It was friggin' *in*convenience. And not only because the police wouldn't have senior officers in the same bed, even though they knew it happened. If it could be turned into a good reason for killing Charlie, even if they couldn't make it stand up they wouldn't let it simply fade into Gaol Street folklore.

'If it does turn out to be Hurst,' Annie said, 'you'd need to stay well out of it and let Jack Kenny walk away with all the credit. If your ego can stand that.'

There was, he had to admit, sense in this. He leaned back. They'd passed a couple of abandoned cars and even the Yeti, good for its size, was struggling.

'I cried,' Annie said after a silence, pushing on towards the main road at Belmont. 'I actually cried. For a long time. Don't know what I was crying *for*. Maybe for the dad I used to have a long time ago. On which basis, perhaps it was the kind of crying I should've done years ago. Doesn't matter. It's done now.'

'I've never seen you cry,' Bliss said.

'It's not pretty. I was battering the headboard and telling him what a bastard he was, and if he thought I was going to his state funeral he could fuck off.'

Suspecting she was crying now, he answered his mobile.

'Bliss,' she heard.

Over the wheezing and the sobbing, the rumble of the engine, the poisonous hiss, and the sound of stumbling feet around a snowbed already unmade, brown and slushy and soured.

He won't come, you know, Darvill had said.

Iestyn? He might.

Oh, he came. He was there. You couldn't see the driver, but Gomer Parry had recognized the machine.

'*That's Iestyn Lloyd's fancy American sprayer!*'

'Frannie…' Merrily panting into the phone, weaving between the gravestones, looking frantically all around. 'Please… get us some help. You need to get some people here. I mean fast. All kinds of people.'

In the ill-lit night, through the falling sky, it looked like one of those busy Bruegel snow scenes. But Bruegel, to her knowledge, had never done panic and pain, confusion. His people did not have hands over their faces, moaning and sobbing and calling out for one another, asking why.

'You're still at Kilpeck, right?' Bliss said.

'Yes. Still at Kilpeck.'

Where the smell was sweet. Like caramel. The smell that was part of the falling snow.

'Let me stop you there, Merrily. Have other people called the police? If not, get them to do it.'

'They're doing it now. Phones everywhere.'

What people did now; they reached for their phones.

To video it. Some of them, amongst the ones who weren't burned or fighting for breath, were bloody *filming it.*

'Right then,' Bliss said. 'Calm down. Tell me.'

'It's pesticide.' She'd reached the edge of the wall, looking down. Where were they? Jane, Lol, Eirion. *Please. Any of them.* 'It's a pesticide sprayer, like…' When she'd first seen its extending arms splayed out, she'd thought of the Kilpeck pylon, split down the middle and collapsed. '… like a big tractor with wings and nozzles. It's got Iestyn Lloyd inside it, and he's spraying this filth everywhere.'

'Then where's—'

Her face was stinging with snow.

Hands gripping her arms, now, pulling her back from the edge of the wall round the church's mound.

'Come back, Merrily,' Rachel Peel insisted. 'Now.'

Snow didn't sting. She knew that. Snow didn't hurt your eyes.

'I can't see them.' Her eyes filling with tears, or something. 'I can't see them anywhere.'

'Let's just get you back,' Rachel said.

Outside Clehonger village, normally just a few minutes away from the main road into Hereford, a breakdown crew was disentangling a people carrier from a bus shelter. And there was Big Patti Calder from Traffic, old mate of Bliss, running the show. Annie spotted her too and was already reversing, sliding all over the road, and pulling in under some trees out of sight, to wait this out, wait until anybody who might know them had cleared off.

They might get back to Hereford by dawn. They wouldn't have made it to Kilpeck.

He had Vaynor back on the phone. Vaynor said the incident was known about, but nobody was there yet.

'I'm looking at a sprayer now on the computer, boss. Half-tractor, half-microlight. They're bad enough in a field, slaughtering wildlife. But this doesn't bear thinking about. You're sure he's spraying *people*?'

'That's what I've been told.'

'Do we know what with?'

Annie had been on her own phone, examining the possibilities. Most of them were long words you didn't want to read twice.

'Probably something that deals very efficiently with wild flowers in potato fields,' Bliss said, 'and evidently also causes skin burns and respiratory problems to human beings. Let me know when you find something out. My contact's vanished.'

'Listen, boss, what I wanted to tell you, they brought me in on an interview as local knowledge man. Guy called Adrian Ripley, who is Lyndon Pierce's partner in accountancy. He was very, very scared.'

'I'll bet.'

'I won't say all of it came out, but it's certainly enough to keep the Charlie team going for most of tomorrow.'

'This is Pierce's link with Charlie?'

'That was taken for granted. This is better. This is Pierce and Liam Hurst. Yes, Pierce does indeed handle Iestyn Lloyd's accounts, which is one big earner to start with, but they're never satisfied, are they? It's fact that Iestyn's been losing it up top for a while. Hurst's been... helping him out, shall we say?'

'Fingers in the pie.'

'More like a whole arm. There's a deal on the table, involving Pierce, Hurst and a building firm whose name you'll know immediately, to make available all the land needed for what would amount to something like Ledwardine New Town.'

'That'd be big.'

'Massive, boss. The fly in the ointment was Aidan Lloyd, who was pushing him towards a different kind of farming. They last thing he'd go for would be selling lovely farmland for Ledwardine New Town. Hurst's saying to Pierce, Well, let's not worry about Aidan at this stage, shall we? *He'll* come round. Few weeks later, *bang*. And then Hurst's saying Let's not worry about Iestyn, *he'll* come round.'

'He was gonna do Iestyn too?'

'Maybe just let him vanish into the sunset. Why rush things? But they do, don't they, once they've started. For Pierce, there was very big money in this, but even he was thinking, Oh shit, what have I got myself into? Pierce was greedy, ruthless, all of that, as Ripley's only too glad to confirm, but removing human obstacles is a different league, isn't it? Pierce realizes he might be in bed with a monster, but what can he do? Shares his fears with Ripley – after all, nothing illegal's happened yet involving

Pierce. Should he go to the police and risk them looking into his previous iffy deals? And then it comes to him – why not talk to his respected colleague, Councillor Howe, a man who'd know the best way to take it to the police, by the front door or the back.'

'And Charlie, of course,' Bliss said, 'sees a much more satisfying way of using this information and launches his private investigation with a trip to Hewell. This is nice, Darth. We may never find out how Hurst gorra hint that Pierce was presenting Charlie with his scalp, but let's try and harden this up. Go and talk to Kenny's bagman again, claim all the deductive credit and gerrit over to them that they need to get a warrant to raid his place. Tonight.'

'What are they looking for?'

'You need to go in with them. You'll know.'

From the road ahead, there was this sickening, rending screech as the people carrier was parted from the bus-shelter under the white spotlights and the blues and twos.

In the grey snowlight, phone off, Bliss looked at Annie.

'You gorra charger for the mobile? Could be on this all night.'

He watched her fumbling around in a side pocket. There was a funny side to this: directing a major inquiry, secretly, from the sidelines, through a third party, over a mobile phone. So funny he was close to tears.

He thought about Hurst. Wasn't the big thing it used to be, killing. He thought about the famous Joanna Dennehy, who'd knifed three men to death on the other side of England then, just for the fun of it, went on a stabbing spree in Hereford where she was caught. The whole world now knew that picture of Joanna brandishing a huge, serrated blade like an executioner.

Hurst wasn't like that.

'Some fellers live for it,' Bliss said. 'A *hell* of a lorra fellers live for it. *Bang* – something flying up out of the grass, the bigger the better. Foxes, badgers, they can justify it – stock gerrin slaughtered, lambs, chickens, cattle contracting TB. They still gerra lorra fun out of it, but…'

'The justification almost makes a virtue out of it,' Annie said.

'Exactly. Some of these fellers – never admit to it in a million years – dream of killing a human being. Even good old Slim Fiddler came close to it. They'd like to be in the SAS. Obviously not the bit where you've gorra jog twenty-five miles with a fifty-pound pack on your back, but the endgame, where it's kill or be killed. Preferably without the being-killed bit.'

'Why didn't we have Hurst in the frame earlier?'

'Because we're not looking for fellers like him right now. We never have. We're all looking for Islamic terrorists and creepy blokes with computers full of kiddie-porn. And because killers are invisible in the countryside. And because—' Bliss choked back the dark laughter. 'Because he's a civil *sairvant*.'

'Linked to a bureaucracy geared to making more and more farmland available for development,' Annie said. 'Run by politicians financed by builders. He's killing for the economy. Or this could all be madness. No clear explanation.' She sank back behind the wheel. 'What the hell am I saying? This is not how I talk.'

70

Out of it

A MAN HAD died, a retired university lecturer and a Kilpeck Church fan of many years. He'd been brought up from Abergavenny by his daughter and son-in-law. Heart attack, Rachel had decided, brought on by the effects of inhaling whatever it was that smelled of creamy fudge. His daughter had said he'd had a heart attack earlier in the year and was on medication. They took him into the church and covered him up with the altar cloth.

'That's not him,' Iestyn Lloyd said, watching from the nave. 'Where is he? Did I get him?'

Merrily heard this from the nave, his voice querulous, with the sense of something justified, something owed. But his head was in a different place. This would all be drifting past him like a dream.

the past, for him, is a noxious place, full of an old hatred. He thinks I'm my father. He thinks Henry Darvill's still here and out to destroy him.

Iestyn, this blank-eyed man in a long coat, had been helped down from the sprayer by Gareth Brewer, perhaps the only person here, apart from Gomer Parry and Sarah Baxter, who knew him. It was about keeping him well away from friends and relatives of the people with burned skin, temporary blindness and problems with their breathing.

'He'll be no trouble,' Gareth said sadly. 'He's had his moment.'

Merrily saw Sarah Baxter watching for a while with her husband, big man in a flat cap, and then Sarah shuddered, turned her back and pulled him away.

* * *

There must be sixty people out there now, perhaps a dozen of them in need of treatment of some kind. She'd watched some stumbling blindly around, groping for untainted snow to rub into eyes and skin, the rest having fled, perhaps shocked into a primeval fear by the surreal malevolence of a shiny crablike entity spitting chemical venom.

Among the damaged, oh dear God, was Eirion. He'd swallowed some of the chemical. If you were in the wrong place, all you had to do was breathe through your mouth. In between coughing fits, he kept saying he was OK, but what did he know? What did any of them know? *Yes, flower, he'll be fine, it's just a precaution,* Merrily had said to a white-faced Jane. Just a precaution. What did *she* know, except that this had become an almost mythic horror?

Rachel thought the stuff might be… something complicated ending in *acid*. Said she'd dealt with just one case involving pesticide, a farmer attending to a blocked nozzle on a sprayer with a canister he'd been wearing on his back, and the nozzle had suddenly become unblocked.

'Only I thought the really noxious pesticides had been banned,' Rachel said.

Gomer Parry sniffed and drew Merrily away. He'd been up into the sprayer almost before Iestyn was out of it, making sure it was disabled. He brought out his vape stick.

'Don't like to say this, vicar, but it could be any ole muck in that bloody tank. Some farmers, they don't get rid of it. Allus got stuff in their sheds as is years old. All gets mixed in. Waste not, want not, see.'

'Oh hell…'

'Boy's still on his feet, mind, so that en't too bad.'

'Could you tell the paramedics?'

Gomer nodded.

'You all right, vicar?'

'Feel slightly dizzy. Bit of a headache. It's nothing. I'll be fine.'

'Lol?'

'I saw him a minute ago. He's...'

She was thinking about what Lol and Jane had said about Aidan's face in the coffin, what Lol's face would have been like if he hadn't been wearing the green man mask when he ran out after Darvill.

A snowplough, an actual snowplough, had arrived, to make a track for ambulances.

'I'm going with Irene,' Jane said.

'The ambulance will probably come off the road into a ditch,' Eirion said. 'I'd completely forgotten how exciting life could be with you, Jane.'

And laughed himself into a coughing fit, Jane clutching his hand.

Rachel was trying to explain to desperate people why there was very little they could do not involving cold water. Don't apply ointments. Don't remove anything sticking to a skin burn. Nothing much for Merrily to do. There were times for prayer and times when it sounded like a trite and pointless reminder of what God could allow to happen in front of a church.

'How could he do this?' she said to Gomer. 'You know him.'

'Iestyn? Don't know him n'more, vicar. En't much left. He don't know how he got yere, but summat in him seemed to know where it was.'

She was thinking what a lousy vicar she was. Should have known about Iestyn's condition, gone to visit him. But then, it had been concealed, hadn't it?

And yet Julie had got through.

Or had she only talked – fatally – to his stepson?

summat in him. A conveniently flammable feud, an old resentment kept smouldering. Tempting to see a small apocalypse outside the door of the Darvills' unknowable holy of holies. She hugged her arms under the cape. The low moans were muffled now. White and blue lights flitted over the stone, finding faces.

'Tell you one thing, vicar,' Gomer said. 'Dunno where that thing's been the last day, but a self-propelled sprayer, bit of a handful, he is.'

'Could Iestyn actually have driven it over here on his own?'

'Hard to see how it come all the way from Ledwardine tonight, but he's still got friends round yere, ole roots. Mabbe had it rented out, borrowed it back. Or somebody did, daft devil. But Iestyn, you wouldn't trust him with a shoppin' trolley now.'

'But he'd still...'

'Dream? Oh hell, aye. His pride and joy, that American thing.'

A shining symbol of Iestyn's control over nature, Merrily thought. Killing what he believed needed to be killed, what he saw as weeds. Deciding what lived and what died. Sacrificing both the past and the future for present gain. *We've shrunk, Watkins*, Darvill had said. *The human race has shrunk.*

'Oh aye,' Gomer said. 'He'd dream of bein' back on that bugger, all right.'

Sitting on the side of the bed in Annie's hotel room, Bliss caught the mobile on its first cheep.

Vaynor. Calling from Hurst's house in Breinton, within sight of the city but on the edge of the countryside. Often said to be the perfect place to take one end of the long-awaited Hereford bypass, except too many influential people lived there. Hurst wouldn't have been perceived as one of them; his place was a bungalow, modern but run-down, quite sparsely furnished like he didn't spend much time there.

At the bottom of the airing cupboard, where nothing was airing, they'd found a metal box lined with oily cloth, containing two target rifles and two Makarov pistols.

'Made me wonder if they weren't all his, boss, originally?

I mean the ones Karen found in Jag's inspection pit. Noted marksman. Loves pistols.'

'Yeh.'

'What if he planted some in Jag's garage after he shot him. Make him look more of an underworld figure than he actually was?'

Theory upon theory. But they'd have to get him first.

'They're going out in force,' Vaynor said. 'War-footing.'

'Chances are they won't find him in Kilpeck, Darth. If he was in that sprayer with the old feller, he'll've had his escape route worked out. All the confusion, nobody would notice. Probably gorra Land Rover waiting for him somewhere. Mad, but not stupid.'

'Why?' Vaynor said. 'Why this?'

'Dunno. Unless he chooses to tell us, we might never know. Maybe thought something was gonna come out in that service. Thing is, if they're not mad when they start killing... slippery slope, Darth. At some stage they know there's no way to put the brakes on.'

The worst of this, he kept thinking when he'd let Vaynor go, was Julie Duxbury. Murdered because a quick killing had become the most expedient answer. That pretend break-in at the neighbouring house to make it look like burglars, that had been halfway clever. But an element of madness in all of that. And evil. Amplified now at Kilpeck.

He turned to tell Annie about it, but she'd fallen, fully dressed, into a exhausted sleep, her face weirdly relaxed.

Bliss looked at her in wonderment. She was free from Charlie, probably hadn't processed the significance of this. Not consciously, anyway.

'Lost my stick somewhere,' Lol said to the dancers congregated around the yew tree.

'You won't find it,' Tim said. 'You won't find any of the sticks. It wasn't a stick dance. You won't forget that, will you, son?'

'We won't get away with that,' Bob Rumsey said. 'Somebody'll remember.'

'Why would they? That won't be how he died.'

'Who?' Lol said.

'Him.'

The dancers divided, exposing the hollow in the ancient yew, turned into a grotto by the snow in its sinews.

'*Oh* God.'

Lol jumped back.

The yew had the body in a rigid embrace, like a trophy. Tongue jutting from a twisted mouth. Congealed blood rambling down the neck of a black North Face jacket. Lol took in the hair, red, but less red than the face, with its vivid, chemical death-blush.

'Where... where did he come from?'

'Came from out of the sprayer, originally, I believe,' Tim said. 'But that was a while back. Before he... became part of the dance. But you wouldn't remember that, would you, Lol? You were up there in green man land.'

'Did we...?'

'Who knows what the dance does? What would I know, an old soldier?'

His rag jacket had been replaced by a tweed jacket, but his face was still blackened.

'We were all a bit out of it, weren't we?' Tim said. 'Could've hit his head on anything. Bit stunned, goes crawling out in the darkness, gets a faceful, throatful. Too fuddled to escape. Horrible stuff that.'

Lol stared at him. He was thinking that an old SAS man was never entirely out of it. Had they known? Had they known who he was, what he'd done?

Tim's black face split into a huge smile.

'Nice service, I hear.'

He patted Lol on the shoulder, went jingling away as the air was seared by sirens.

71

Oaf

LOL LAID HIS foliate face carefully in the snow on the tomb next to Darvill's chair, up against the church wall, under the Sheela-na-gig and the comical cat. He'd waited until Gareth Brewer had brought Iestyn Lloyd out, to go down to the ambulance and the two police Land Rovers which had pulled in tight to the mound.

Darvill had a blanket over his useless legs. His head light lit up the holly, the strands of yew, the mistletoe and the small eyeholes in the mask.

'Leave him there, Robinson. Done his job, I'd say.'

'Yes. I suppose he has.'

'I'd be blind. Legless and blind.' He laughed. 'Just when you think it's safe to come out of the spinal ward. Just when you think you've paid the price.'

'Price?'

Darvill reached up and switched off his head lamp.

'Did you even know what was happening when you ran in front of me?'

'To be honest, no. No, I didn't.'

He didn't remember getting to the church door. All he remembered were the words of the song, and then the irony of it, no darkness danced down.

'I remember it on the mask, like a power washer. And the smell. Still smelling it.'

'Looks after his own, the Man of Leaves. Saved us both.'

'Didn't save Aidan.'

'Sometimes,' Darvill said, 'we need to be shown evil, or we won't know the difference. There's evil in these walls. Necessary good, necessary evil.'

Darvill's hands had burned skin which he said Nora, the life-keeper, would attend to later.

'Might ask her something later, too. Good night for it, do you think? Death, destruction and possible matrimony.'

'Why not?'

'Two would-be Lady Darvills dumped me because I told them I didn't want kids. Time this dynasty ended, Robinson. We're not getting any luckier.'

'No.'

'When I go, all these wannabes will be coming out of the woodwork trying to claim the title. What use is a title except for when you're on the pull? Aidan was to have had Maryfields. The Man of Leaves. Would've had two organic farms eventually. End of a feud that should never have been. And perhaps a Ledwardine Morris? The morris sides used to be a kind of priesthood, did you know that? No you didn't, and neither do I, but I believe that's how it was. A band of brothers connected to a place not by dogma but by the dance and what the dance passes on from the earth. It's not whimsy, you know. I don't think it's whimsy. I think it works. I know it works.'

'You never thought of telling Iestyn – about Aidan and Maryfields?'

'No, I didn't. Would you have? He'd think it was a scam. The way his brain worked. Or didn't.'

'You tell Aidan?'

'Well, of course. This was how it worked: the land at Ledwardine had been put in trust for Aidan, possibly to avoid death duties, soon as Iestyn knew he was on the blink. Unknown to Iestyn, we had an agreement, Aidan and I. Whichever of us died first – wouldn't be him, I assumed – would get the other's land.'

'That was a legal agreement?'

'Oh yes. I'm not stupid. Solicitors, witnesses, all that.'

'Could Iestyn and Hurst have only just found out? That what-ever happened, Hurst was going to be on the outside? Without a penny? And all that pretence about him never wanting the farm would be closer to the truth than he could've imagined.'

'If they've seen Aidan's will, undoubtedly,' Darvill said. 'Could lead to years of legal wrangling, at the end of which Hurst still winds up with nothing. That *would* have pushed him over the edge, wouldn't it? Fucking hell. Tectonic plates have shifted under less.'

He was shaking his head, chuckling bleakly.

'Don't panic, Robinson, I wouldn't try to hang anything on you. There'll be a more suitable Man of Leaves – not that you haven't done rather well, one way or another.'

'Got me back in the dance.'

Lol looked up at the Sheela-na-gig.

'Lionel, can I ask...? You came down on me pretty hard when I made a stupid joke about her and... and the cat.'

The Sheela grinned. Darvill blew a soft sigh down his nose.

'Going to have to tell you, now, aren't I? After you saved my face.'

'I was pretty pissed off,' he said, 'when my old man brought us back here. Didn't know anybody, didn't want to. Got myself a motorbike – the one I later sold to Aidan for peanuts – and shot off to Hereford most nights. Hanging out with guys who very much were not farmers. Drank copiously and smoked a lot of dope – which I still home-produce, by the way. Flog the surplus to a chap in Hereford.'

'Ah,' Lol said.

'Quite. Anyway, it wasn't that, it was the dance that saved me from going mad.'

'A lot of people say that.'

'It's true. Even if you ignore the mystical stuff, it brings a strange kind of unruly order to your life. Naturally, as my old man had started the Kilpeck side, I wanted nothing to do with it, and he didn't even try to persuade me. He was clever that way, my father. He never encouraged me to follow whatever he was into, which sometimes made me desperately want to. I watched and studied, while feigning complete disinterest. Practised on my own. Read his weird books secretly. And then, when one of the morris side couldn't make the winter solstice, I offered to step in. Not as good as I thought I'd be at first, but then it just... clicked.'

'It does, doesn't it?'

'We danced to the south doorway. I felt a tremendous heat. I was aware of all the extremities of my body, complete control and mastery, an enormous excitement at the pit of my stomach, the solar plexus. Still didn't get it, mind. Still resented this bloody church and the influence it had. Still behaved like an oaf. Still behaved...'

He glanced up at the Sheela-na-gig and shook his head.

'Some of my mates came down from Hereford and we'd spent all night in the pub in Kilpeck. Short walk from the church. I started talking about my, er, girlfriend – famous, after all, the world over – and we all went over to the church to have a gander at her. Unfortunately, you couldn't actually see her very clearly because of the scaffolding. They had scaffolding up for minor repairs to the roof. Gave me an idea after they'd gone.'

'Oh dear,' Lol said.

'People used to say she was a warning of the dangers of lust. Are you *kidding*? You seen the way she smiles? And when you're, you know, very pissed, she can start to look like a challenge.'

The snow had stopped and he wheeled his chair away from the wall.

'The scaffolding, that was easy. Well, looked easy from the ground. If you were pissed. Unzipped my jeans, hung them over a bar, but they slipped and fell to the path. No going back now. Starlit night and her face had altered. Hell, Robinson, if you think *you've* ever been horny...'

'You must've been *very* pissed,' Lol said sadly.

'Keep *telling* you that. The stone... the roof stone projects over her, I had to lean back to... you know? I'm lying on this fucking plank at the very top of the scaffolding...'

'I'm not sure I want to know any more,' Lol said.

'It was...' Darvill began to choke with laughter. 'All you could ever wish to...'

'Don't,' Lol said. 'Even she can be embarrassed.'

'Bitch. Anyway, that's when I fell. At the moment of ecstasy. Not that far when you look at it now, but I fell crookedly, into the space between the scaffolding and the wall, and there was a big wheelbarrow at the bottom, full of stone. I was laughing through the pain. Until I realized something was wrong. Turned out my back was broken.'

'What did you do?'

'Lay there. Lost consciousness. Dreamed about her. Regained consciousness and looked up and she was laughing. May not have woken up. She may not have laughed. Morning came. People came. People who didn't talk, fortunately. Churchwarden. Nice chap. Awoke in hospital. Was transferred to another hospital. Eventually was told I wouldn't be walking again. Except in dreams. In dreams...' Under his head lamp, his eyes had filled up. 'In dreams I still dance.'

Merrily was waiting for Lol by the south door.

She brought out a hand from inside her cape. It held a candle. She lit it with her old Zippo and presented it to him.

'Better late than never.'

She looked up at the carvings, the green man and the animals.

'It's all here, did you know that? Everything. *Ask now the beasts and they shall teach thee.*'

'Who said that?'

'Book of Job. It's quoted in the church guidebook. It goes on, *Speak to the earth and it shall teach thee.* And then the guidebook recommends reading the rest of the chapter. So I did. Just now. Trying to calm down. Job, chapter twelve. Goes on to say *He discovereth deep things out of darkness.* And – ominously – *he taketh away the understanding of the aged* and *he leadeth counsellers away spoiled.* OK, so the spelling's different.' She took his arm. 'Let's get out of here before we both go insane.'

Credits and background

The morris is, of course, still a part of Welsh border life. The Border morris lay low for a while and was given a new impetus in the 1970s by musicians and dancers led by John Kirkpatrick. On the recording side, check out the *Morris On* albums sequence and (for Border morris, especially) Ashley Hutchings' *Rattlebone and Ploughjack*.

Phill Lister, formerly Green Man of the Breinton Morris, was the first to suggest, some years ago, that there might be a novel in the mysteries of the morris and has been really helpful. It took some time, and other ingredients, for certain ideas to ferment, with the assistance of Ruth and Paul Ferret and the Foxwell Morris, and Mark Roberts, Oxfordshire Border morris.

The Nine Men's Morris stone was indeed discovered in the earthworks at Kilpeck Castle in 2013.

Thanks to James Bailey, Pete Bibby, Jason Bray, Anne Brichto, Richard Coates, Ashley Evans, Anne Holt, Terry Hopwood-Jackson, Mike Inglis, Liz Jump, Ced Jackson, Peter Mahoney, Nick Mole, Gary Nottingham, Mairead Reidy, Terry Smith, Tracy Thursfield, Les Watkins, Allan Watson and Tom Young.

Thanks again to Sara O'Keeffe, editorial director at Corvus, and my brilliant wife, Carol, who spent three weeks finding flaws, masterminding solutions and sharing two gruelling twenty-hour working days at the end.

An early source for the esoteric history of the morris – and an inspiration – was a fascinating pair of articles written in the 1970s for *The Enneagram*, by A.G.E. Blake, one of the most significant studies of the morris tradition, combined with informed speculation that rings true. Tracy Boyd's essay, 'The daunce of Nine-Men's-Morris and the boundaries between worlds' (2004) completed the picture along with two articles in *Dowsing Today*, by John Moss, of the British Society of Dowsers, who led a survey of Kilpeck Church and its environs.

If you want a good idea of where Lionel Darvill is coming from, you should read the profoundly resonant *Meadowland, The Private Life of an English Field*, by John Lewis-Stempel, and its sequel *The Running Hare*. I doubt any books have better caught the threatened magic of the Herefordshire border countryside.

Gurdjieff's teachings are, of course, still circulating widely. Occasionally given the fuel of publicity when someone famous, like Kate Bush, embraces them. And before her, other experimental musicians like Robert Fripp and of course Arthur Brown, the God of Hellfire.

It's also a century since four morris men, members of the demonstration team of the English Folk Dance and Song Society, founded five years earlier by Cecil Sharp, died at the Somme.